BRIGHTSHADE

BRIGHTSHADE

TALES OF AETHER AND SOUL - BOOK ONE

Miriam R. Dumitra

BRIGHTSHADE

Copyright © 2019 Miriam R. Dumitra.

This is a work of fiction. Names, characters, places, and incidents are either the products of the author's imagination or are used fictitiously. Any resemblance to actual persons, living or dead, businesses, companies, events, or locales is entirely coincidental.

Get free chapters and more content at:
http://miriamrdumitra.com

Written and illustrated by Miriam R. Dumitra.
Edited by James Boutin-Crawford and Emma Dumitra.
Cover art by Amalia Chitulescu Digital Art.
Author photo by Annie Konstantinova Photography.
This book was published thanks to support from Friesenpress.

ISBN 978-1-9995536-0-9 (Paperback)

storm crow press
by Miriam R. Dumitra
Langley, BC
Canada

TABLE OF CONTENTS

FELLIN CITY-STATES
Sea-of-Holes
Fort Aquifer
ELESZAN
The IDEON NATION
Theold's Cloak
■ = Captial City
● = Major City
Heron
Neminia
Commiste
Silas' Hill
Cain
Kyra's Hold
Brane
Meara
Indcity
The SAINT BRAZEN REPUBLIC
Salisben
Fisher's Hook
The CAMORRI ISLES
Es
The Camorin Continent

To my mom.

You never read a single page of this book, but
you're still with me every step
of the way.

And to you who, like me,
escape into fantasy—
because that is where you glimpse
your sense of
place.

Vertical Eye, insignia of the Service
blue iris
Pisces hand
half-healed burns
Small Brotherhood tattoo

PROLOGUE

"For a hundred years, we've toiled. For a hundred years, we've slain and been slain. For a hundred years, we've gathered our stories and retold them countless times. We've told Tales of war and conflict, of magic and spirit creatures, of a great nation torn in two by conflicting ideologies. Over the course of these many tellings, it has become apparent that errors have crept into our great oral tradition. At last, it is time to begin writing our Tales down, ensuring the wisdom of the past is not lost to our children."

- From the introduction to *The Complete First Anthology of Ideian Tales*, by Gira Talescribe and Arah vinn Livered

"The discovery of magic was the primary cause of the First War, which culminated in the fragmentation of our once-united land. Those who possessed magic were understandably partial to it. Their partiality blinded them. They took to the west, forming what is now known as the Ideon Nation. The rest of us recognized that true strength must come through unity. Only by sharpening our minds and expanding the work of our hands may we rise above the baser instincts of magic and individualism.

The Service arose out of this split with a twofold mission: to keep the peace, and to see our two countries united once more."

- From the introduction to *A Historical Guide to the Service*, by Sephmet Haze

Sixteen Months Ago
Meara, in Westlake, Saint Brazen

Step Four: secure the fuse around the oldest timbers. Make sure it does not drag or pinch. Beware of stupid instructions.

Grinding the short butt of a homemade cigarette between his teeth, Imp worked quickly on the twisting fuse, winding it around the warehouse's rafters and dropping it to the stone floor below, his step-by-step checklist echoing in his head. He'd added a few points to it himself to make it more interesting.

The fire he was setting reminded him of his first fire, back in Wrovetown. It had been a cold day then, as cold as it was hot now. He'd set the fire in a half-finished timber home instead of a warehouse, but he'd used the same type of fuse, and he'd smoked a cigarette then too. He always smoked when he lit fires.

Step Four-and-a-Half: take a look.

Inspecting his work, Imp smiled, pale eyes glinting, the cigarette clamped between his teeth.

Step Five: ignition. Beware of sparks, smoke, and other hazards. And don't forget about the cigarette.

He jumped from the rafters to a stack of wooden crates and then to the floor. Inhaling one last puff of the fragrant smoke, he dug a small metal file out from the worn leather wallet containing his tools. Imp poked a hole through the smouldering tube and slipped the dangling end of the fuse into it. Dropping the contraption, he strolled out the front door, whistling to himself.

Step Six: disengage from target. Be casual about it.

It was a good day to be alive. The air, humid and thick with heat, bothered Imp, but the city of Meara lay by a lake, so there was almost always a pleasant breeze. According to the locals, this summer had been the hottest in a while.

Step Seven: return to headquarters. Nothing more to do this time.

Imp wished he had somewhere else to go, something more to do. Back when he'd been younger, he'd often spent his time with Old Man Bento, the surrogate uncle who had taken him in. *Now I have no one,* he thought. *Just the Service.* It was something to go back to, but it wasn't all that. *If only...* he started, then chased the thought from his head. Fantasy didn't get you places. Reality did.

Imp headed back to the alley that would take him to headquarters. He was on a schedule, in a way. If he wanted to see the fire go up, he'd have to be back in ten minutes or so. He checked his slick black coat for sawdust, brushing off straws from the warehouse's thatched roof and doing the buttons up to the top. He hoped his sweat wouldn't stain through the shirt. The Gaunt would be angry if he caught him coming back disheveled.

It wasn't always this way. Used to be different. Not better, though, he added. *Just different. Now what? I can set a fire and not get caught. I've got friends and a shiny uniform and all the cigarettes I could ever want. A boy could kill for that. Many of 'em have.*

Somehow it just wasn't the same.

Imp made sure no one was looking; then, abandoning his confident saunter, he ducked sideways into the alley. Wincing at the mud that slopped onto his shiny boots, he ran down the abandoned lane until he reached an intersection. One road led back to headquarters. The other, just a small path, led down to the left, further into the Harbour District, to the docks. He was small for a boy of fourteen, easily missed. He could risk it, he could take a step and disappear and never go back. He indulged the fantasy for a few blissful moments. *Who am I kidding. They've made me a deal I can't run from. I'll always come back to my fires. It's who I am.*

He turned right, reached the main street, and set a brisk pace. People got out of his way, seeing the smart uniform: a split-backed coat with polished brass buttons and the vertical eye insignia embroidered in blue over his heart. Neat trousers tucked into once-shiny black boots, now splattered with mud.

"G'day," a man said, nodding. A woman in a green dress curtsied nervously. A child ducked into a doorway, reaching for its mother's arms.

He reached the tall, red brick facade of the Service's headquarters, an imposing yet beautiful building with finely-wrought iron gates and brass accents on the dark bricks. A few pipes stuck out of the slanted roof, belching steam, and glass sparkled from most of the windows—a luxury, even in the city. A Serviceman stood at the door in full decorative dress, a showy indobalt longsword hanging at his waist. Another one of the Service's reminders.

Ignoring the man, Imp strolled in through the main doors, hung left and reached the reporting room. He knocked on the door and let himself in.

"Peter, reporting back, sir. Done the job."

Two men sat inside the room, one behind a desk, the other on a well-upholstered seat by the window.

"Good lad," Mr. Jergson said from behind his desk. "I'll expect a full report within the hour, as always."

"Yessir."

Jergson turned back to the other man, the one known as the Gaunt, as if Imp had ceased to exist.

"Sir," Imp said. "The usual?"

Jergson looked up, scrunching bushy white eyebrows. "Oh yes, of course. Here. A pass to the observatory." He scribbled a note on a piece of delicate, lacy paper, handing it to the boy.

Imp turned to slip out the door.

"Master Berahsson," a cultured razor-blade of a voice said. "Your boots are muddy."

Imp turned back. "Yes, sir."

"Clean them. Right away."

"Yes, sir."

"Go along now."

Imp left as quickly as he dared. The Gaunt was not known for his patience. Or his tolerance. Or his easygoing nature for that matter.

Three flights of stairs and two hallways later, Imp reached his room. Dumping his muddy boots on the floor, he tore off the shiny, brass-buttoned coat and halfway undid the ties on his sweat-stained white shirt, revealing pale skin underneath, much lighter than his sun-bronzed face and hands. It was one of the few reminders he had of the fact that he was a northerner, by birth at least. The strips of cloth wound around his stockings went onto the floor as well, followed by the stockings themselves. In his bare feet, he slipped back out the door, locking it with an ornate brass key, and headed up three more flights to the observatory, a little turret sticking out of the Service headquarters' roof. A guard was at the door.

"Set another one today, Imp?"

"A beauty, Herald." He grinned. "Redwood rafters and a straw roof that'll catch like a dream." Imp went to open the door but was blocked by the young man's arm.

"Sorry Imp. I've got to see the note."

"Right. 'Course. Silly of me to forget." Imp showed him the scrap of paper.

"Silly? You do it every time, Imp. You just want to see if I'll let you in without."

Imp just smirked, swung the heavy wooden door open, and entered the turret's upper room. He dropped the smirk as soon as his back was turned. "Maybe I do," he muttered.

Hurrying to the north-eastern window, he felt Herald come up behind him to see. A thick column of smoke rose in the distance. Gloriously red and yellow flames peeked out over the roof, catching on the dirty thatch and heating the building's timber frame. Anxious murmurs ran through the crowds in the city streets; the news of another fire was spreading.

"I wonder who pissed the Service off this time," Imp mused.

"Who knows. But whoever did, and whoever it'll be next, we'll deal with them. We always do." Herald clapped a friendly hand on Imp's shoulder. "You're lucky, you know. You get to go out there and show the world what we do with them who stand in our way."

Six Months Ago
Somewhere across the lake, in House Kyra–Bendekan, Ideon

Rise rowed like the shades themselves were after him, driving the shallow dory through the rolling waves and towards a foggy shore. Rain stung his skin, burning where it soaked into the scratches on his arms. His bandaged hands were sore and blistered from the monotonous touch of wood, and his aching eyes were bloodshot, staring out, fixated on the narrow strip of land that marked the beginning of Elmsmount Island.

Though the swell's winds tried to press him further into the open expanse of the lake, current and tide were on his side and helped him inch his way towards a small pebbled beach.

"Oof." With a final push he bumped the dory's nose into the wet sand, staggered up and out of the boat, and collapsed on a heap of stones, vomiting up water and the remainders of what had been stale bread.

"I never—want—another shades-forsaken drink of water in my life," he moaned, coughing.

After a few minutes well-spent feeling sorry for himself, he mustered the strength to rise to his cramped legs. He staggered through the torrent and towards the twinkling lights that denoted a lakeside town.

There. A tavern. The sign depicted a monstrous fish, advertising the establishment as The Lord of the Lake.

Heads turned as Rise stumbled through the entryway and to the bar.

"Look what the lake dragged in, boys…"

"…mud from your boots… just cleaned the floor…"

"—bloody outsiders… barging—on th' hour…"

The voices all muddled together inside his head.

"What'll it be?" The last voice was the tavern keeper's.

"A drink if you please, sir. Make it a strong one. Arak or rum."

"Aye, Master Fishguts." A laugh rang through the hall.

Rise tried to glare down from his normally imposing height, but the large distance between himself and the tavern keeper's impeccably round, pinkly flushed face made him feel nauseous, and he sat down smartly on a stool, drawing another bemused chuckle from the tavern's patrons. At least he hadn't fallen over. *Maybe I should get properly drunk,* he thought. *It might stop the room spinning so much.*

A mug was pressed into his hand, and a good sip of the fiery drink cleared his shaken mind.

"Off to a seat, laddy," the tavern keeper said. "Don't you be fouling up my prime counter space. Drink's on the house. Looks like you could use it."

Rise dragged himself to a corner and sank down onto a bench. He dropped his head into his hands, feeling sick and tired, and aching from several hours' worth of rowing. The crossing had been difficult.

Cloth rustled. The table squeaked. Someone sat down in front of him. He looked up to see a young woman, her head wrapped in a thin scarf. She glanced at his face, then his bloody arm. She made as if to speak.

"Not right now, dearie," he said, then muttered a curse. "Lemme drink some first."

She glared at his rudeness, as forward as any city girl, then slipped the mug from his hand just as he was about to take a sip.

"Hey, I paid for this rum. Go get your own, miss. I'm in no mood for company, so leave well enough alone." He tried to yank the cup back but tipped it out of her hands, sending the liquid spilling across his scratched arms.

"Aieeeeeh," he howled. "Shades, miss, now look at what you've done."

"I didn't mean—you shouldn't have yanked it back," she retorted. "Here, your arm—" She pulled out a linen handkerchief, dabbing at his hand, and he winced, the alcohol stinging his cuts.

"How did you do that? You look like you've been out in that swell. Those scratches are deep."

"Never you mind. Now, what d'you want?"

"No need to be brash. I'm the ta'rn keeper's niece. You looked like you needed a bed for the night, maybe a meal. I just came to ask."

"Then you could've just asked."

"I did. I—you look like you could use a healer for those cuts."

"A bed, you said. Would that offer include you, or is it strictly sheets and mattress?"

"Well I never!" she squeaked, glaring again. "Now you listen here, sir, my uncle won't stand for your nonsense, a'right? Leave be!"

"Hey, hey, I'm sorry. I didn't mean it. Just a joke, miss." *Good.* It had made her drop the healer nonsense. "A meal and bed would be nice. But I carn't pay, see."

"Oh. Well, if you don't have anything, I'm sure my uncle could work something out with you."

"I've naught but the clothes on my back. And they're not much to look at either, I imagine."

She grimaced at the state of his filthy shirt and pants. "That they aren't. Though the rest of you's a pretty enough sight." Her gaze travelled slowly upward, finally resting on his face. "Come to think of it, I haven't seen the style before. Have you come a long way?"

Shadows, an observant one. "Not particularly, miss. Now if you'd kindly go see…?"

The keeper shouted from behind the counter. "Ella? Get a move, girl, there's more to be served."

Good timing old man, Rise thought.

"I'm coming!" she called back. Then to Rise, "I'll see about that meal for you. Maybe a room as well, depending." She turned to leave.

"—wait, miss?"

"Yes?"

"Has another stranger come here, sometime the last week? A man called Daniel?"

"Well, there's been one other visitor. He called himself Daen, not Daniel. Tall like you, dark hair, light skin? Had a strange coat with brass buttons on it. Never seen the like."

"That's him. Where can I find him?"

"Oh, he's gone. Left the same day he came, took the road."

"Gone?" Rise half-rose from his bench before dizziness forced him down again. *He said he'd wait for me. The bastard said he'd meet me here.*

"What road did he take?"

She looked at him as if it was the dumbest question she'd ever heard. "We're a lakeside town. Water on three sides. We only *have* one road. Heads northeast."

"Oh."

"Say, what is your name?" she said. "I almost forgot."

"It's, uh, it's Rise. Forgot what?"

"Rise." Her lilt made the name sound exotic. "He left a letter for Rise Rezah, the stranger did. I'll get it when I bring your meal." And off she went.

Sipping at the few swallows still left in his cup, Rise watched the other patrons from his corner. The girl—Elsa?—came back with the promised letter, a bowl, and another mug, and he ate his fill. The tavern keeper came by to offer him a bed in exchange for a day's work. Rise accepted.

When the tavern's evening bustle slowed down again and Rise's body, giddy from drink, stopped aching as much, he took the letter out from the pocket where he'd kept it: plain white paper, covered in an edgy, block-like script.

Dear Rise,

I hope this letter finds you well—although, I regret it must find you at all since I cannot be here in its stead. I don't have much time. I think I'm being followed. Some Serviceman or other I would imagine, one of your former friends perhaps. Not that I'm blaming you.

I'll go on ahead and lose him before we meet up. No need for both of us to take on any further risk. Follow my letters north and east, and try to blend in. Shouldn't be any trouble with your particular skills. If anyone asks, say you're a traveller from Eleszan. You can 'borrow' one of those wrap-around cloaks to blend in, and shadows send they get Eleszanin here as often as we do, and it'll keep you from having to answer too many unwanted questions.

Be safe and see you soon,
Daniel

Rise growled in frustration. *Noble idiot. I don't need him to do me any favors. I don't need his protection.*

The table jolted, startling him from his thoughts. An elderly man sat down across from him, white haired and dark-skinned.

"Heard you washed up from the lake, laddy," he said. "Name's Avier. Thought you could use this." He pushed a leather pack across the table.

Rise eyed him with suspicion, put the letter down, and eased open the pack. A water skin. A clean undershirt and an oiled cloak. Paper-wrapped packages that looked like food.

"What heaven have I landed in that a ta'rn keeper gives me a meal and an unknown farmer hands me a pack of supplies?" he asked, imitating the locals' accent he had heard from the girl.

"Not much of a heaven, I reckon. Just a small village. We're used to takin' care of our own. Heard you didn't have anything, so I went to my cottage, collected some spare things."

"Well. Thank you, sir."

The man tipped his broad farmer's hat, got up, and walked away.

What kind of land is this? Rise mused. *Not at all like home. And yet, so much like one already.*

Folding the letter and returning it to his tattered breeches pocket, he rummaged through the pack, more thoroughly this time. He was looking for something, though he didn't quite know what. A sewing kit. A leather strop. A small belt knife. Stockings. There. A crisp white roll of linen bandages. He picked it out, smiling.

Look at that. Just what I need.

In the morning, Rise awoke to the sound of waves lapping a rocky shore. Head pounding and feet unsteady, he got up and left the tavern, heading for the beach where he'd landed.

The dory was gone, probably swept out by the tide. Leaves, sticks, and freshwater shells littered the beach, having been washed up by the stormy waves, but the shallow water seemed remarkably clear in the early morning sunshine.

Rise immersed himself in the icy lake, scrubbing dirt and blood from his skin and clothes. A strip of canvas did for a washcloth, and the walk back let most of the excess water drip off him. He begged a towel from Elsa once he returned to the inn.

Back in his room, he put on his new clothing, mouth curling as he replaced his once-fine brass-buttoned coat with the oiled cloak. The fabric went into a waste bin, but he kept the buttons, tucking them into his pack. They'd belonged to his grandfather. He finished off by wrapping the linen bandages around his calves like sandal straps, the way he'd done as a kid. A few pieces were saved for his hands.

Taking off the old cloth he'd wrapped around his wrists revealed blisters on his right palm, reminders of his exhausting experience the day before. His left hand was worse, milky white beneath the make-shift bandages, and red where a puffy scar and half-healed burn mark stretched across his whole hand, fingers to wrist, knuckles to palm. It hurt to move. He inspected the tattoo underneath the wound: a triangle with a curl coming out of its right point and a brand like a stylized eye drawn inside it, with the iris coloured blue.

Rise grimaced, weaving the fresh white cloth overtop his hands, debating whether to visit an apothecary. It would be dangerous, showing that mark around. *But I don't much care for my hand rotting off either.*

The next few hours were spent in the tavern keeper's small stable, mucking out the two stalls and mending some horse tack. His debt paid for, Rise gathered the pack he'd been given, tried to say farewell to Elsa (as it turned out her name was Ella, and she told him in no uncertain terms what he could do to make up for the blunder), and headed out, following the road northeast. The people of the village had been kind to him. He'd steal a horse in the next town.

⸻⸺≋⸺⸻

Two Months Ago
Kaeville, in Arahill, Saint Brazen

An hour or so before dawn, Adriane gathered her pack and exited the metal hut through the deerskin flap that covered the entrance. She looked at the beaten paths, the huts built from discarded sections of pipe and metal sheeting, and the whitewashed town hall—the only building to boast a shingled roof. The mill creaked in the distance, but the threshing machines, for once, were silent. It wasn't much, but Kaeville was still home.

Now that she was leaving, all the meaningless details seemed inescapably important. She gazed at the scattered buildings, trying to memorize the familiar landscape. A worn axe stuck in a stump where Master Adner had sunk it. A lone sheep peeked out from a pen puzzled together from discarded machine parts. Her hunting traps were set out by the butcher's hut, all but the two she carried in her pack.

Had she never noticed how the slanted roof of the forge lined up with the mountain slope behind it? Had she never noticed that the smell of dust and sheep mixed in perfect synchrony? Had she never noticed that a perfectly green pebble sat in the dirt before her hut like a sultry gem? She stooped to pick up the stone, placing it into her coat pocket.

"I worry about her." Hannah, her twin, spoke softly enough that Adriane knew she didn't mean her to hear. "She hasn't been the same since Pa died."

"It's for the best." Max's voice was quiet, reassuring. "You know Graeme Headson saw her. She can't hide if it just tears out of her whenever she's angry."

Adriane turned, better to hear the conversation drifting out of the hut.

"That's exactly why I'm worried. She's angry too often. Sad, too."

Max chuckled. "Not sad. She wouldn't let something like that get to her."

"Maybe you don't know her as well as you think," Hannah retorted, a touch of heat in her voice.

"I know she was there when they died. Like you say, she was never the same afterwards. I can't help but think that's when it must have started. Maybe… she did something."

Adriane jerked away, fighting a memory that tried to worm its way to the surface. Ma and Pa, on the ground, unmoving. A silhouette standing before them, knife in hand. Adriane herself, turning to run, to escape. The emotions had been overwhelming. *That was the first time I lost control—*

A rustle behind her pulled her from her thoughts. Hannah stepped out beside her.

"All set?" she asked, slipping her hand into Adriane's.

Adriane squeezed her fingers. "I'll be fine."

She glanced at her sister, drinking in the sight of her one last time. Hannah's fair skin and dark hair gave her a ghostly appearance in the early morning fog, and her eyes shone like pale emeralds. Her mouth, usually curved in a gentle smile, was set. She wore a soft white nightgown with a grey scarf around her neck and plain wool stockings that peeked out from underneath her boots. A blanket wrapped around her shoulders warded off the chill.

Looking down at her own attire, Adriane felt the differences between them loom all the larger. She'd dressed in her trapping things, a thick brown skirt, wool leggings, boots, and dark coat with iron buttons. Stitched butterfly wings on the shoulders provided the only ornamentation; it had been her mother's coat. Her leather pack was made to be functional and little else, as was the overlarge, partially serrated hunting knife somewhat visible underneath her skirt, sheathed in a thin boot liner.

"They'll see you're a country girl a mile off," Hannah said, noticing Adriane's gaze. "You know, we never meant for it to go this far. I don't want you to—" she broke off, unable to fill the empty space, to make everything better with mere words. "I'll miss you."

"I know." Adriane tucked the blanket more securely around her sister's shoulders. "Don't worry. You won't lose me." She looked Hannah straight in the eye. "You'll never lose me."

Another rustle, and Max came out of the hut. His muscular shoulders framed the top of Hannah's head, making her look fragile. *He'll protect her*, Adriane thought. *If he can.* Max was strong because he worked in the grain fields, not because he'd been born that way. Their arguments aside, he'd do what he could, but Adriane knew he wasn't a fighter. Not like her. She'd always been the strong one.

"—for the city," Max was saying. "You could lose anybody in that maze. And if you need to, you can try to get through the land border. I hear Ideians actually train in—in magic. You know. Not that I hope you'll have to take it that far."

Adriane flinched, then nodded. They'd talked through the options before. "I'll be fine. Once I've learned to control it, I won't have to hide. We'll see each other again." She hugged them for an instant, then turned and walked into the still-dark morning, seeing them in her mind's eye. Max raising a hand and Hannah hugging him from the side.

Adriane fought for control of her emotions with every step she took away from home. A single tear escaped her iron grasp and wandered down her neck, as if exulting in its freedom. She refused to look back.

A now-familiar cold enveloped her, and a sensation like waking from a nightmare, like being doused in icy water rushed through her. Suddenly, she stood a hundred paces away, further down the path, almost to the tree line. Wisps of shadow rolled off her skin. Her magic had had its way with her again.

This is why I need control. Brings to mind the old saying—magic to chaos, chaos to destruction.

Her skin tingled with the magic's energy, and details stood out in the landscape around her. The trees began on her right, growing thicker up ahead. A lone squirrel moved in the bracken. Back at the hut, Hannah gripped Max's hand, having seen her disappear, dissolving into shadows. Adriane's magic seemed to echo through the air behind her as Hannah turned, burying her face in her brother's shirt.

A soft whisper reached Adriane's ears. Max's voice.

"She'll come back," he whispered. "She'll come back to us."

Adriane feared she never would.

PART I

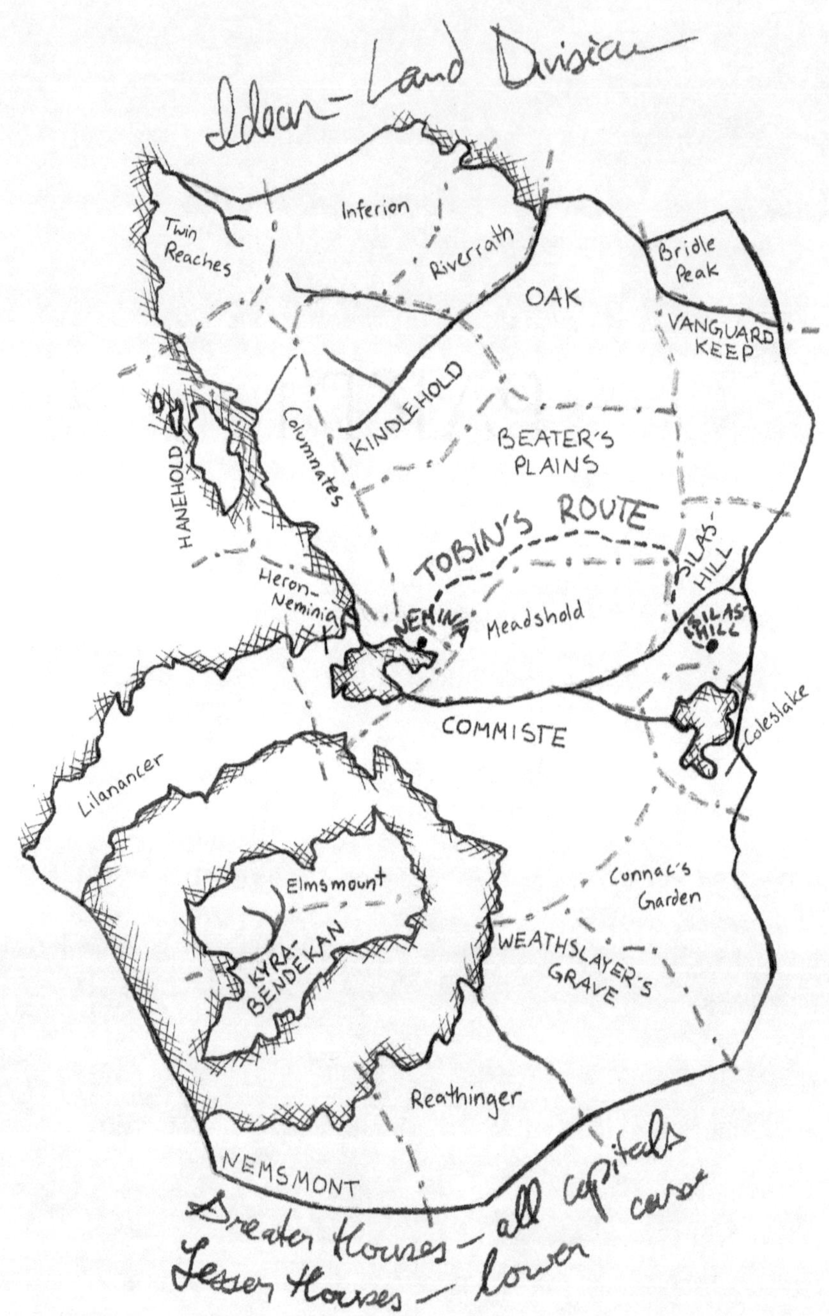
Idean - Land Division
Twin Reaches
Inferion
Riverrath
OAK
Bridle Peak
VANGUARD KEEP
KINDLEHOLD
Columnates
BEATER'S PLAINS
TOBIN'S ROUTE
SILAS-HILL
HANEHOLD
OM
Heron-Neminia
NEMINA
Meadshold
SILAS-HILL
COMMISTE
Coleslake
Lilanancer
Connac's Garden
Elmsmount
KYRA-BENDEKAN
WEATHSLAYER'S GRAVE
Reathinger
NEMSMONT
Greater Houses - all capitals
Lesser Houses - lower case

I

THE SEARCH FOR A SOURCE

Eight Years Ago
Outside Wrovetown, in Arahill, Saint Brazen

Imp stared into the darkness.

"The moon is asleep tonight," Mama whispered. "Close your eyes, my little Imp."

He obeyed. There was a sound. *Pffittzzt.* A match being struck.

"Now open them."

Light, soft and friendly and yellow. Fire. He chuckled in delight, reaching out towards the flames to feel the heat kiss his fingertips.

She grabbed him from behind, laughing along.

"Now you try."

The fire was gone, and she held the match up to him. He grabbed it in his deft little fingers and let her help him strike it. Together they lit the red candle.

"See that?"

He did. Something moved in the fire. Dancing. A flickering figure with wispy skin and a grin full of flames.

"Fire Imp!" he squeaked, delighted.

She kissed his head, navigating the wild tufts of hair with her fingers. "What else?"

He wanted to say there wasn't anything else, but he caught another movement out of the corner of his eye. A different light formed in the flame, then drifted towards his head. It was white, but he could somehow distinguish movements and sounds coming from it.

A sad voice rang out from the light. "Neri's sick again," a man said.

"There's nothing you can do." A second man was speaking. Imp could see both of them within the little light now, moving back and forth, pacing.

"But maybe they were on to something." Desperation replaced the sadness. "The well could make me powerful enough to—"

"You can't. The well must remain sealed."

The images and sounds flickered faster and changed, but the sad man stayed there through it all. Now he was angry. "There's nothing! Nothing here!" he bellowed.

"What have you done?" the second man said.

A woman appeared in the light, her belly round and bulging. She screamed in pain, and Imp tried to duck away from the image. He was scared. He didn't like this story.

"Mama!" he screamed, and the white light flickered out. Feet crunched on stones, and dark-coated silhouettes rushed to surround them. Someone had found their clearing.

"Oh no," Mama breathed. "Please, no."

"Shades take them!" a cloaked man yelled, seeing the fire imp scamper away. It jumped out of the little flame, puffing to smoke.

"Take the boy." There were more of them.

"No, don't touch him!" Mama was scared. She was never scared.

Imp turned towards her, crying, but his hands sank right through her skin. She wasn't concentrating enough for him to touch her.

Gasps went up from the strangers around them, the people he couldn't see because the candlelight was still so bright in his eyes.

"It's not what you think—" Mama concentrated and turned solid again, so she could scoop him up in her arms.

"It's always what we think." Imp could see the man now, the light reflecting off his shiny coat and boots. "Sorceress."

Mama screamed once, and the world exploded into red.

⁂

Present Day
Renforth, in House Silas' Hill, Ideon

Jenna sorted through the stacks of books that littered her desk, setting the ones she didn't need on the floor. *It has to be here somewhere.* She glanced at the growing pile beneath her, then added *Shadows: Beasts of Spirit* to it, followed by *The Eldest Tales: A Treatise on the Lore of the Peace Legend.* She huffed in frustration.

"Can't see the trees for the forest?"

She jerked, then realized who it was and turned to greet Castor with a quick kiss. "I know I put it here somewhere. *A History of Elemental Magics*. I need the passage on the origin of soul and aether."

He rested his chin, rough with stubble, on her head, interrupting her search. Grumbling a half-hearted complaint, she leaned her head back until it lay on his chest. She loved how strong and solid he felt. His shoulders were broad and his hairy arms, resting on her waist, were toned from working as a bell and bronze caster in Renforth's foundry. His build, tall and stocky, was quite unlike hers, but his dark complexion and curly black hair matched hers exactly. Jenna closed her eyes, relaxing against him. It was useless trying to work around him, but he knew how to ease her frustration.

Castor leaned over and plucked up a thick tome that had been hidden under a pile of scrolls. "This it?"

Jenna smiled and reached for the book. "Came in here to save the day, did you?"

"Well that, and to announce that dinner has been growing cold for the past hour."

"Is it that time already?"

Castor's bold face softened as he looked at her, his human features melding perfectly with the canine ears, pointed teeth, and forward sloping nose. His Kane heritage was obvious and made him look all the more handsome. "You should try taking care of yourself more."

"Isn't that what I have you for?" she teased, before realizing his expression was serious. Jenna grimaced, fingering the wooden crutches at her side. "You know why this is so important to me."

"I know, and I am taking care of you. It's just… you can't stay cooped up here until you figure this out."

"I know, love. I know," she said softly.

Jenna stiffened as a sudden burst of energy hit her and her vision tinted purple.

"Jenna."

She focused furiously, trying to keep the energy under control, the room blinking out around her. Power surged through her veins, and the pressure built as the energy clamored for release. *It's getting worse.* The thought distracted her, and the energy manifested itself as her magic. A spark of purple flame shot from her palm, pulverizing the corner of a book on her desk.

"Are you okay?"

She shook herself out of it, letting Castor fold her up in his arms. "I'm fine. I'm okay."

Castor let her go and jerked his chin towards the room's far corner, which was half-hidden by towering bookshelves. "I saw the cat pouncing right before it hit you. Must've killed a mouse or something."

Despite the circumstances, Jenna had to smile. After two years of living in Renforth, two years of her working at the Kalaaman Tower Library, he still refused to call the cat by its name.

"Tabitha's eyes, I'm glad it wasn't more. If anything bigger had died, I might've set the desk on fire. And the cat has a name, Castor. It's Speckles."

"Whatever. At any rate, it wasn't big enough for anyone to see, so we can forget it for the moment. No, I don't mean forget it entirely," he added, correctly interpreting her frown. "But you haven't eaten yet. We should go grab some dinner."

Jenna cast a reluctant look at the books on her desk before turning back to him. "Okay."

Castor stretched with a yawn, then offered Jenna his arm, a mischievous smile on his lips. "Shall we walk to dinner, milady wife, or would you prefer I carry you?"

Batting away his gently clawed hand, she slipped her arms into her crutches and got up, wincing as she stretched her legs. "You'll only trip on the stairs and spill us both."

Resting most of her weight on her arms, Jenna stepped forward, hobbling out of her study and into the library proper. Castor followed, shortening his lengthy stride to walk beside her.

⊷∞⊶

Present Day
Silas' Hill, in House Silas' Hill, Ideon

Tobin's tonfa hit his opponent's sword with a hard crack, the hardwood holding its own, even against unsharpened steel. A quick rotation, his wrist snapping forward, and Tobin's second tonfa went for Timothy's side. The older boy deflected with a last-minute flourish, then backed off, panting.

"Done so soon?" Tobin taunted, advancing.

Timothy growled, baring sharp teeth. He rushed forward. A flurry of exchanged blows, and then Tobin landed a strike into the stomach, doubling his opponent over. Timothy tried to recover, but Tobin kept pressing his advantage. He lashed out at his opponent's arms and legs, feinting every now and then; it was all Timothy could do to defend.

He leaves his side exposed whenever I feint to the left. Analyzing Timothy's movement, Tobin parried a haphazard strike, tonfa whirling from his elbow and out like an extension of his arm. He flicked it forward in a feint to the left—Timothy's sword rushed to meet it—then brought his right tonfa down on his opponent's shoulder. Wood split bone with a terrible crunch.

Tobin dropped his weapons as Timothy sank to the ground with a gasp. "Bendekan! Are you alright, Timothy?"

Timothy groaned. "Don't tell me you didn't mean to do that."

"I didn't! Honest." Tobin bent over his friend, inspecting the injury. He didn't see any blood, although the bone was broken, bulging out underneath Timothy's skin.

"And that's the match," a dry voice intoned from the side.

Tobin looked over at Elder Iram, who was leaning against the practice yard's rails, his staff by his side. "I didn't mean to hit all that hard."

Elder Iram raised his bushy white eyebrows. "Then you had better mean it next time. You are training for combat, after all."

"Well, yeah. But it's just practice."

"Then you can practice intent."

Tobin lowered his head, recognizing the reprimand. "Yessir."

The elder's face softened. "You'd better send him to the healers, Tobin."

"Of course." Tobin helped Timothy up, then called Yemena and Rico over to take him to the infirmary.

The remaining six members of his squad stood at attention, awaiting dismissal. Felias' stance was still awkward—he'd joined Ideon's combat groups a mere month ago, having just turned fifteen. The others, though only a year or two older, stood with a practiced calm picked up from observing the veterans.

"That's practice," he told them. "We've got a free slot before dinner, so the time is yours."

"A word, if you will, Tobin," Elder Iram said as Squad Fourteen broke up, some of the fighters heading into town, others no doubt back to the barracks for a nap.

"Of course. What is it?" Tobin tried to keep his voice as neutral as possible, but his face flushed with excitement. *I knew there was a reason Elder Iram was overseeing us today.* Elder Iram seldom still taught something as menial as inter-squad duelling.

Elder Iram grinned. "It looks to me like you already know what I'm about to tell you."

"Yes! A mission? Is it really a mission?"

"Indeed, I have a mission for you and your squad of miscreants."

Tobin knew the elder meant the name as a joke, but he couldn't help but wince. Bendekan knew, they really were a bunch of miscreants. The greenest squad in the least-respected combat group. But they had finally scored a mission, and Tobin didn't care what it was.

"I have to warn you, it's not exactly a prime assignment. None of the other squads wanted it, so it got handed down to you."

"I don't care," Tobin said. "We're ready, whatever it is."

"I'll keep that in mind the next time I need a squad to take on the latrines."

"It isn't that, is it?" Tobin doubted it, but still, sometimes dung-heap assignments could unfortunately be quite literal. He'd found that one out his first year.

Elder Iram gave him a look that seemed to say, *Would I do that to you?* before turning back to the path that led up to the city. "It's a security detail for a group of minor diplomats."

Tobin's heart managed to both rise and fall simultaneously. Not a dung-heap assignment exactly, but not an exciting one either. "We'll do it, sir." He turned to follow Elder Iram, heading towards Silas' Hill's low outer wall.

"Good. I'll expect you in my study at seven, to go over the details. You may tell your squad now."

Tobin broke into a grin. "Alright."

"And Tobin?"

"Yessir?"

"I know it's short notice, but you'll be leaving in two days' time."

"Yessir." Tobin forced the grin off his face and saluted crisply, before turning to sprint the remaining distance to the gate. *We finally have a mission.* The grin returned, and this time he didn't stop it.

Tobin told his squad the news as soon as he made it back to their barracks, which lay on the more easterly of the two hills that formed Silas' Hill—the city, not the House. Once their free slot ended, he scarfed down his dinner before heading back to the compound to change into a fresh summer uniform: dark grey breeches and a white shirt sporting his combat group's insignia, a broken dagger entwined by a worm. A thin brass band around his left upper arm marked his rank as squadleader.

Cleaned up and ready, he headed north to the low stone bridge that served as a connection between the two hills. It was still light out, and he could see the city spread out beneath him, blocks of buildings and shops ringed by cobbled streets and small gardens, as well as fenced practice yards and stables near the low stone wall. The two terraced hills framed the landscape against the clear sky. Compounds and barracks—all with a narrow flag marking the combat group—ringed the terraces, all but the highest reaches of the northern hill, the taller of the two, which held headquarters.

Tobin crossed the bridge and made his way up, towards the wood-and-stone complex that held the administration buildings, the elders' hall, the councilmen's chambers, and more. Barely out of breath from the climb, he entered the first of the buildings, a low stone bungalow, via a side door and took the few steps to Iram's study. The door was open.

"Come in, Squadleader Tobin, come in." Elder Iram motioned from his desk.

Tobin always liked it when the elder he so respected used his title. Truth be told, not everyone—himself included—had thought he was ready to lead anything, even a squad of ten.

"Excited?" Iram had a glint in his eye that belied his age.

Tobin nodded. "Nervous too, to be honest."

"Everyone is, their first time. Now, I've got your maps here, as well as letters of introduction (which are never needed, really) and your stipend and supply lists." He pushed a thick sheaf of papers towards Tobin, who started leafing through them. "You may visit one of the supply masters tomorrow to draw what you'll need for the journey, and of course, everyone is responsible for their own gear."

Tobin glanced at one of the maps. "Heading to Neminia?"

Elder Iram nodded. "The diplomats will arrive here tomorrow and will wait for you at Caleb's Gate the following morning. You'll head through House Beater's Plains and then down to House Heron–Neminia. Quite straightforward. There shouldn't be any trouble if your squad stays nice and visible."

"Is safety a serious concern?"

"Hard to say. We haven't had an incident in years, but when the peace was first negotiated, we Ideians were none too happy to have

Republicans traversing the country."

They went over the supply list, as well as the diplomats' chain of command. One couldn't be too careful with foreign dignitaries, especially Republican ones. Tobin had taken instruction on matters like this, so none of it was new to him, but Iram always liked to be thorough. "Especially since it's your first time," he said.

Finally, Tobin headed back to his barracks, where the rest of the squad was already in bed.

"How'd it go?" Timothy whispered, even though no chatter was allowed after lights out.

"Good." Tobin pulled off his uniform and changed into loose breeches and a shirt. "Setting out at first light in two days' time."

He could hear the smile in Timothy's voice when he replied. "We'll make it count, Tobin. This is it, hey?"

"Yeah. This is it."

⁂

Jenna leaned on her crutches to knock on the heavy oak door, trying not to show her nervousness. Elder Kieran's summons hadn't exactly been unexpected, but she had hoped it wouldn't come to this. She didn't know for certain why he'd summoned her, of course, but she could guess. The Kalaaman Tower University had turned a blind eye to the mishaps with her magic for several weeks, but if they'd found out about the aether blast she'd created before dinner... *It could be bad.*

A voice called from beyond the door, and Jenna entered, navigating the room's clutter with the help of her crutches; she'd had years of practice, after all. Her stomach gave a brief lurch as she sat in one of the lacquered chairs facing Elder Kieran's lacquered desk. She prayed she wouldn't discharge her dinner all over the fine furniture before deciding the Patrons probably had more important things to watch over than the queasy stomach of one nervous theorist.

"Good evening, Jenna. Are you well?" Elder Kieran's voice was scratchy with age, but he all but perched on the edge of his large chair, childlike and energetic.

"I am fine as can be, Elder Kieran."

"No doubt you are wishing we were meeting under better circumstances," the elder said, fiddling with a reed pen, "as am I. I'm sure you've guessed why I summoned you here this evening."

"My magic," Jenna ventured. "It still hasn't settled." Her magic had been fine up until the month of Niemen. Weak, perhaps, but not unusually so. Then it had grown stronger.

"To be precise, I don't know if 'settling' would be the correct term, since most magic settles by the time its wielder reaches the age of sixteen." Elder Kieran's eyes took on a scholarly glint. "Of course, it could be a second settling, which would still warrant the name, but I do think—"

"Elder Kieran?" She admired him as a researcher and a scholar, but the man could tangent for hours if given the opportunity.

"Right, of course. Back to the point. Your magic. Have you made any progress in determining the source of its outbursts or determining how to control them?"

Jenna hesitated, wishing she were willing to lie. *But no,* she thought. *I've pledged myself to knowledge.* Lying felt too much like a betrayal of that. "I have not," she answered, hoping her pause hadn't been too long. "I can control it when the energy comes from destruction. But when death fuels the magic…" she shrugged. "It bursts out of control."

"I thought as much."

Jenna's heart jumped into her throat at the tone of his voice.

"I didn't want it to come to this, but if things continue as they are, you may have to take leave for a while, until your magic settles."

Jenna pressed her lips together, trying to keep from frowning. *I can reason with him.* She didn't admit to herself how desperate the thought sounded. Elder Kieran liked her, she knew, but her magic and her House made him and the other elders wary of her.

Jenna sighed. "It's an unprecedented case, my magic settling this late. I know that. There's no telling how long it might take—"

"Which is precisely why I have to recommend you remove yourself from the tower for the present time. Let me be frank." Elder Kieran put down the pen and picked up a glass paperweight instead. "Your magic will presumably only grow in strength until it—well, I suppose the term would be *re*-settles—and if that is the case, the university is unwilling to risk the accidents that might ensue."

"I understand, but—"

"It is non-negotiable," he cut in. "I'm sorry. I know what this means to you. Your historical research has already proven invaluable, and I hope you will be able to continue your studies in the future. But to risk the safety of our entire store of knowledge, not to mention that of the other theorists… Your work is important to us, but it does not reckon above everyone's safety—including your own."

Jenna fought to keep from shaking with emotion. *So this is it. They're kicking me out, for who knows how long.*

"You may stay until the end of the week," Elder Kieran said gently. "And, of course, we will be thrilled to welcome you back once your magic is fully under your control once more."

"I understand."

Jenna muddled through the perfunctory farewells, then picked up her crutches and left, her legs limp and awkward, even more so than usual.

They're kicking me out.

She managed to make it out of the tower and onto the streets. It felt as though it took her ages to walk the single block from the tower's base to the weathered apartment building where she and Castor lived. When she finally made it up the staircase and through the door, it was all she could do not to collapse onto the floor.

Castor was waiting for her. "How did it—oh. Darling." He caught her before she fell and held her tight as the tears she hadn't realized she was fighting began to stream from her eyes.

"They're kicking me out," she sobbed into his shirt. "He said—until I can control it—as if I'm somehow endangering all of them by—just by being there." She sniffed. "They wouldn't have said that if I'd—if I were from a *reputable* House."

"Shhh, it's alright. I know it isn't fair."

"Yoel's heart, but it isn't," Jenna swore. "It isn't."

Most people would have looked at her askance for that oath—it didn't do to mention Yoel or Weathslayer's Grave, his disgraced House, *her* House—but Castor just held her. She loved that about him—he wouldn't judge her, no matter what. *I suppose that comes easy, what with being half Kane.*

He waited until the tears stopped flowing, then helped her to the bed, picking up her crutches, which she'd dropped upon entering the apartment. They were beautifully worked, carved in the shape of a hoof at the bottom, with bull's horns at the top, where they fit under her arms.

"Why don't we go riding in the morning, so you have time to clear your mind some?"

Jenna shook her head. "I want to spend as much time at the tower as I can. Elder Kieran gave me until the end of the week—four days. I have to find a lead in that time. I have to figure out how I can—how I can solve this."

She leaned against her husband, still blinking away tears. *I have to find something,* she thought. *There has to be a solution. A way to get my magic back to normal.*

It wasn't for the sake of her job, really. Castor could support both of them for a while if need be. But her magic… Ever since she'd lost the full use of her legs, her magic had been the thing that made her feel capable. It wasn't even the fact that it gave her power. It was the feeling of magic, feeling the energy flow through her, feeling so *alive*—that had made everything worth it. Now that feeling was gone, replaced by something violent and scary, completely unlike her.

Tabitha send, I'll find a way. The thought stayed with her until she drifted off to sleep.

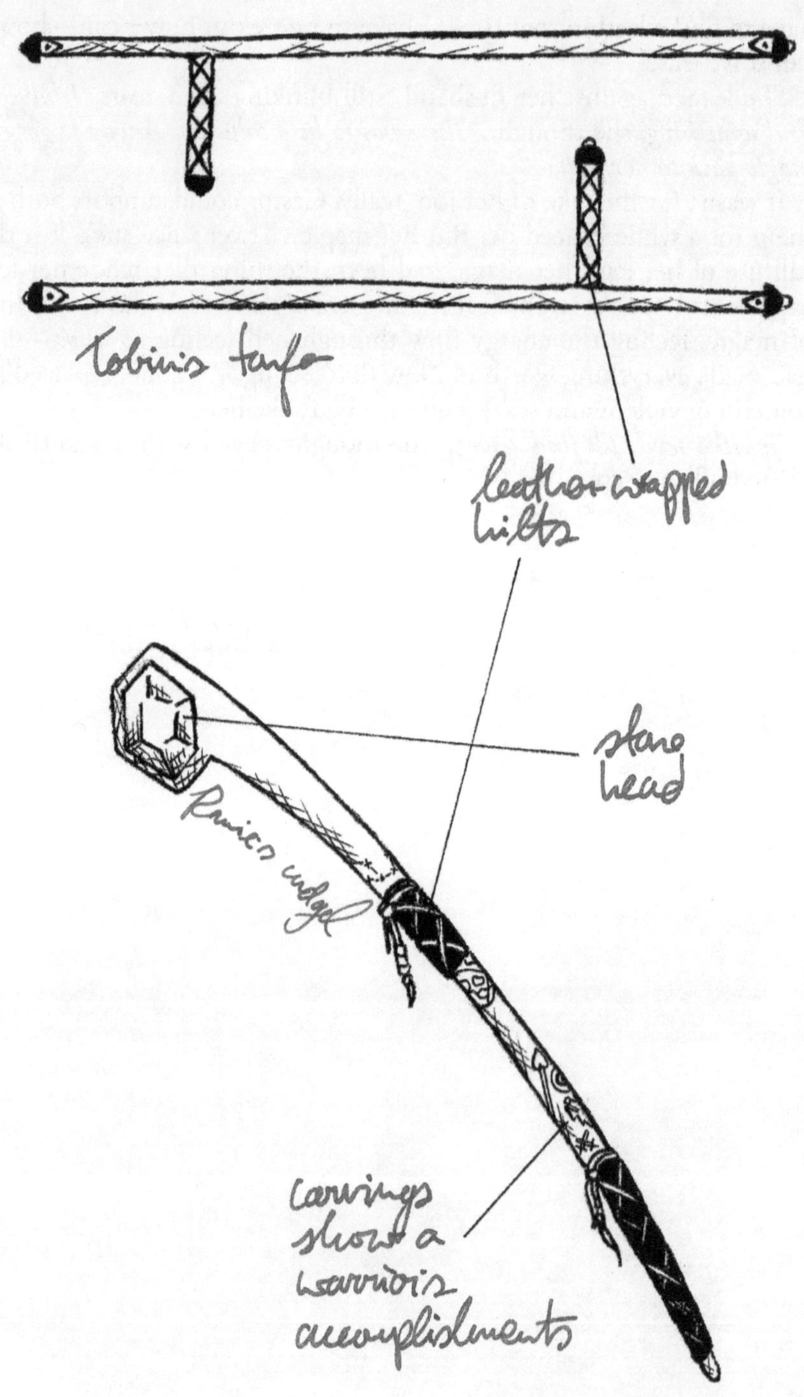

tobin's tanfa
leather-wrapped hilts
stone head
carvings show a warrior's accomplishments

2

TALES' NIGHT

Six Years Ago
Cain, in Arahill, Saint Brazen

Rise laughed as he ran, evading his pursuer with ease.

"That it?" he yelled over his shoulder before sliding to the left, clearing a short fence and then dashing to the rickety ladder that would get him to the intricate maze of city rooftops. Cain was a chaotic city, which was all the better for him.

Rise took the ladder three rungs at a time. He leaped onto the first roof he came across, ran to its edge, and jumped over onto a second, lower roof. He checked his jacket's hidden pocket before moving on to a wobbly flight of stairs. *It's still there. Good.*

His pursuer was somewhere behind him, but Rise could tell he was losing the trail. Not that he wasn't good. *These shades-forsaken Service-men are a sight better than the Standard Force guards.* Still. They didn't know the city like Rise did.

He darted across the next roof, then paused before taking a running start and leaping across a gap in the rooftops. Nothingness yawned underneath him as he jumped, but he made it across easily. Clearing the roofs felt more like flying than falling.

He hit the shingles hard and tumbled into a roll, coming up still running. The sounds of pursuit had stopped. He'd lost the man. Satisfied, Rise smirked to himself. He was about to turn towards a trapdoor set into the roof when something hit him from behind, hard. Rise went down, skidding across the roof, his coat buttons snagging on the gaps between shingles. Someone grabbed him from behind, pinning him down.

"Lemme go," he yelled. "Get off me."

A soft voice spoke right into his ear. "Better stay still if you know what's good for you."

"Who'n the shades are you?"

Deft fingers looped a leather cord between his wrists, tying them together and then flipped him over so he lay on his back. He stared at his captor in confusion. Muscular shoulders and arms were at odds with a slight build and a pale, freckled face adorned with a delicate nose and full lips. "You're a girl."

She jabbed his stomach with a short wooden baton, and he curled up in pain. "I'm a Servicewoman, that's what."

Rise looked closer, noticing the badge. "Shadows, curse you are."

"Tell me where it is, and I'll go easy on you." The girl began riffling through his pockets.

"Pretty thing for the Service to be lurkin' after," Rise spat. "Go find it yourself."

She jabbed him again, and he flopped down groaning, impressed by her strength. *Curse the Service train their people well*, he thought.

Her fingers found the hidden pocket in his coat, and she pulled the ring out with a satisfied sniff. "Don't even know what this is, do you?"

"It's a ring, idiot."

"And why'd you steal the thing?"

Rise shrugged. "What do you care? Pa's not doin' so well with the farm. Any carn'll help. Bunch of the scroll guys said I steal this, I'm in. I'll get to eat."

The girl eyed Rise with an appraising sort of look. She couldn't have been more than a few years older than he was, but when she spoke she sounded in charge. "If it's pay you're after, I can offer you much better than a meal for a ring."

Rise squinted up at her, noting her features—delicate face, wide eyes, strong build—with a new appreciation. *Pretty thing for a Servicewoman.* "Like what?"

The girl reached to her belt, unhooking a small purse. "Like ten plaits is what."

Rise stared hungrily at the purse, then turned his eyes back to her. "What's the price I gotta pay?" Nothing came for free. Especially from the Service.

The girl smirked. "Just a bit of information. You keep your mouth running on what the Scroll Brotherhood is sending out to steal, and I'll pay for whatever that's worth."

Rise licked his lips. Ten plaits would pay for food and more. And she really was pretty. He nodded, making up his mind. "Sure thing."

"Thought you might say that." The girl tossed the purse down beside him. "Now listen here. What's your name?"

"Rise Rezah."

"Rise. You do as I ask now, or there'll be more than plaits to pay. The first of next month you come swing by Flames' Road to visit me. Enter in opposite headquarters and ask for Lena."

Rise nodded again. "Sure. I will."

The girl, Lena, drew a short dagger from her boot. "And if you stand me up, I'll find you and take care of you." Her tone told him exactly what she meant. "You're making a promise to the Service. Don't you forget it."

"I won't. I'll do it."

With a flick of her dagger, the girl nicked his cheek, before sheathing the blade and undoing the leather ties that bound his wrists together.

"I believe you."

Present Day
Cain, in Arahill, Saint Brazen

Adriane breathed deeply, focusing on the air rushing in and out of her lungs. She'd spent almost two months in the city now, and the fresh air seemed almost too good, too real after the smog and grit covering Cain.

She'd have to go back soon—it was too exposed out here, even among the scattered buildings of the outer city—but for the moment all she wanted was to forget. Forget the homesickness. Forget the fact that she was still hunted.

The Service would have guessed that she'd fled to Cain; it was the only place to go, other than the woods. *I need to find a place to lie low,* she thought. *It's either that or wait for the Service to recognize me.* Her magic remained too volatile for her to risk staying out in the open.

She'd taken her time scoping out the local thieves' guilds, learning which could be reasoned with and which were best avoided. Their arrangements with the Service meant they might be the best way for her to disappear.

She almost barked a laugh before stopping herself. *A year ago I was *still roaming the woods, trapping for food and pelts, or helping Max in the field. Discovering mouse droppings while cleaning the grain stores was just about my biggest worry.* She hadn't even believed in magic, not really. Sure, there'd been stories, tales especially of Ideon, where magic reigned free, setting people apart, dividing society itself. *But I never dreamed it would come to me.*

"It's for their own good we're rounding 'em up. Magic makes some better than they should be," she'd heard a Serviceman say. That was back when they'd been searching Kaeville after rumors of a mage had surfaced. Those had been frightening days. She'd hid in a low cellar, praying to the shadows to hide both her and her magic. She wasn't sure if they'd heard. "It makes them think they're above the law, above the rest. It's not right."

The funny thing was she agreed. *Except for the fact that* I'm *the mage.*

Adriane focused on her emotions, calming herself and driving the anxiety down until she could barely feel it. She'd learned early on that emotions set off her magic like nothing else. They'd betray her if she didn't control them. *At least that's something I've become good at.*

Turning back to the gates, Adriane let a grimace pass over her face before smoothing her features and approaching the grey masonry walls. Steam pipes ran their length on the inside, operating the mechanism that allowed the gates to open or close without manpower. She stared ahead, hardly seeing, and listened, letting the now-familiar buzz of the city wash over her—a thousand voices beating to a single mechanized heartbeat.

A farmer with a cart passed her from behind without a second look.

A boy with a wheelbarrow left the city, kicking up dirt with his feet.

Two giggling children raced towards her in pursuit of a piglet, coming so close she felt the air move as they passed her.

This was the advantage of hiding in the city: Here, she was invisible.

Adriane re-entered the city proper and was absorbed into the dim smog that shrouded everything. Buildings, people, wares—all were grey, courtesy of the coal dust that had blown into the city from the mines. Though the houses and storefronts, lumped together in rough blocks, generally faced southeast and away from the mines, both indobalt and coal, the wind still managed to coat them in grit day after day.

She walked along Main Street, observing. A tailor hawked his services from a window. A wine seller pushed a cart through the street. A silversmith rang his hammer on his anvil, pounding his cares away. She balked at the taste of the air, still unfamiliar. *Calm. Stay calm. The city's just a machine, all the people mere cogs, fitted together perfectly.* A pair of merchants began a screaming match, and she flinched. *Very loud, annoying cogs.*

The people of Cain were polite but aloof. Their gazes slipped away when they saw her, which suited Adriane just fine. City folk were above a simple peasant girl, coming to gawk at the wonders of civilization, and Adriane went along with that assumption. She faded easily into the background of people. She preferred it that way.

Adriane turned onto High Street and jerked back against a dirty wall, dodging a windowless carriage steered by a man in the shiny black coat of a Servicemember. Relieved he hadn't noticed her—she was unsure how detailed a description the Service had of her—she ducked past a blacksmith working hot metal at a steam-powered auto hammer and hurried on, afraid her pounding heart might be heard even over the clang of hammer pounding steel.

She headed towards Henderson's shop, dodging another Serviceman as well as two Standard Force guards in plain gear. Though they and the city's more upright citizens ignored her, she could feel the eyes of the gutter rats, the city's shadier residents watching her as she walked.

The nightfolk, as they were called, were different from the rest. They were the crooks of the city, the poor beggars, the petty thieves, the mercenaries, and the scum. It was their trade to see the invisible people, to know who was dangerous and why, and to know where people came from and where they were going. They were the reason she was here. They were the only ones who might keep her from the Service.

From what Adriane had discovered, the city's nightfolk were organized into a rough hierarchy, banding together to stay alive and ply their trade. Street urchins and beggars were at the bottom, thieves' guilds formed the middle, and at the top reigned a thief king of sorts, a chief organizer of the crime in the city. Their strength lay in numbers and the simple fact that the Service cared little for the city's shadier residents—provided they got a cut of the nightfolk's ill-begotten wealth.

Adriane imagined she could sense the dark eyes watching her from alleyways and street corners, noting her slight walk, the way she kept to the side and out of the way, seeing the outline of the big hunting knife strapped to her calf underneath her skirt. She was sure they noticed, but they didn't approach. *Likely waiting to see what I'll do before they make a move.*

Adriane made her way through the beginnings of Cain's Poors Quarter, keeping a wary eye out for pickpockets. They weren't likely to try her, shabbily dressed and hard-eyed as she was, but this part of the city was dangerous, both despite and because of fewer Service and Standard Force patrols.

The Poors Quarter was aptly named, featuring an irrational collection of taverns, workhouses, alleys, storied homes, and shop fronts, all bunched together in layers of colourfully disorganized chaos bordered by steam pipes, heavy industry, and, of course, the walls. Dirty gutters flanked the street corners, and the gurgling of the sewer was a constant backdrop to the bustle of the streets.

Adriane made her way to Henderson's small butcher's shop, squashed in between a chicken butcher and a knife smith. The street's smell was appalling, rank garbage mixed with the metallic scent of blood and the rot of old meat scraps. Adriane entered the establishment through a heavy door without batting an eye.

"Henderson?" she called.

A large, grubby man entered from the shop's back, his ample girth covered by an apron splashed with bright blood, a gory knife in his hand.

"Back already? You can finish off this sheep while I start closing." The man's expression never deviated from a tight frown, but his face seemed to soften when he saw her.

Henderson had been her parents' friend. Back before they'd been killed. Adriane shook her head, expelling the thought. *Don't think about it.*

She followed Henderson to the back, where a plump, half-dissected sheep's carcass hung from the ceiling on metal hooks. Donning an apron and grabbing the large cleaver from the knife block, Adriane went to work while Henderson traded his knife for a stack of lamb chops and thick paper. A bell rang from the front, and he left to help the customer, still holding the slabs of unpackaged meat.

Henderson was a good man, but he wasn't the brightest or the most organized. What he lacked in intelligence and appearance, however, he made up for in charm and generosity. He was a slab of a man, built like one of those bear-humans the legends mentioned, but kind-hearted and gentle. Ever since his wife had died, he'd acquired a hard sort of sadness, a slightly lost look in his eyes that made his easygoing manner all the more heartwarming. He had no one to help him around his shop anymore, and he had welcomed both Adriane's service and her company, poor as it was. He also kept to himself, which would prevent anyone from finding out about her before it was too late, and she was gone.

Adriane fell into an easy rhythm of work, comfortable from all her years spent trapping and skinning, first under her father's tutelage, then alone. Finishing the flanks, she began cutting the ribs to size using a bone saw. She was used to foxes, badgers, and the occasional deer, but sheep weren't so different.

It's all too easy, she thought, *to get caught up in my own head. Nothing but the present moment, nothing but knives and hooks, water, meat, and blood. Maybe I can forget everything.*

The shop provided steady work, between butchering and cutting, selling the meat, and constant cleaning. The place already looked much better than it had when she'd arrived. She'd swept the dust from the corners, updated the sales ledgers, reorganized the meat cellar, and even hung up colourful curtains made from a ripped sheet. She'd miss the place once she was gone.

Once I'm hiding under the nightfolk, I'll be a thief, a criminal—I'll do whatever it takes to stay safe.

She wasn't hiding for her own sake. Without Hannah and Max, she would have turned herself in, maybe. *Hannah never looked at me the same after she found out,* Adriane thought. It had happened soon after their parents' deaths. Hannah had wanted to know how they'd died, and Adriane wouldn't tell her. She'd been trying to protect Hannah, but Hannah hadn't understood that, and they'd fought. The anger, ice cold and terrifying, had rushed through Adriane. She'd blinked to find herself several paces from where she'd previously stood, with wisps of black fog dissipating around her. With those wisps came echoes—she could see the landscape in her mind, could hear her sister gasp. Her own fear hadn't mattered in that moment. The look on Hannah's face changed everything.

Adriane shook her head. *I'll never make her fear like that again. Better to hide. To disappear.* The Service missive had been clear—they were desperate to capture not only mages, but their families as well. After all, the stories said magic was passed on through blood.

Adriane swore aloud, an unusual thing for her. The oath sounded thick and clumsy on her lips. "I won't let it happen. Never." She fingered the butcher's knife still in her hands. "I'll kill before I let them take Hannah—or Max."

"What's that?" Henderson called from the front.

"Nothing."

Saying it aloud didn't make a difference. The threat sounded empty.

She knew she would have to become stronger if she wanted to be able to protect her family—to return home instead of running.

The bell over the door rang as someone entered the shop.

"Help the customer, will you?" Henderson called.

Adriane sighed and wiped her hands clean of blood. She passed Henderson on her way to the shop's front, noting how quickly he retreated to the back. *Something's not right.* She rounded the corner and came face-to-face with a Serviceman.

Her breath caught, and it took all her concentration to keep calm, smothering her emotions.

"What can I get you?"

He smiled, lazily eyeing the display of fresh and dried meats, the sausages hanging from the ceiling amidst curing hams. "Information," he said.

Adriane's heart beat faster. "I'm afraid I don't understand."

"No? Well, I'm sure you see all sorts come into your shop. The Service is paying five plaits for information on a runaway girl. About your height, actually. Black hair. Pale skin."

"Could be anyone." Adriane felt an icy shock of relief. If that was the best description they had of her, then perhaps she was safe after all.

"Right. Except that she's a mage."

"M-mage?" The word stuck in her throat.

"Shadow magic. She's dangerous a'right. Just keep your eyes open, and let a Servicemember know if you see anything suspicious. It'll be safer out once she's locked away."

"Of course." Adriane's fingers twitched as her fear built. *Keep it together,* she thought, clenching her teeth. *Don't let it out.* The icy sensation of her magic activating descended just as the Serviceman turned back towards the door. Shadows flickered around her for a second before she quelled the emotion.

The Serviceman whirled to face her.

She gulped. "Did you want to buy something after all?"

He hesitated. "No, I just thought I saw… Never mind. I think I've had a long day, that's all."

When the door closed behind him, she raced to it and bolted it shut. Shivering, she sank to the floor. *I wonder what the Service'll do if they catch me? Kill me right off? Use me? Take my magic away somehow?* That last would be a blessing, though she doubted even the Service possessed that kind of technology.

But what if I use it? Adriane stumbled to her feet, trying to stop the shivers. What if she could get out of this by using her magic, by becoming truly powerful? An advantage, any advantage, would be welcome, even if it was one she despised—and feared.

She shook herself back to reality. *Magic's the cause. Magic won't solve this. It's at the heart of all the trouble.* The only way she'd be free was to learn control, to surround herself with protective walls, keep her emotions in check so they wouldn't set off her magic.

That was too close, she thought. Henderson didn't like Servicemembers himself—she suspected they'd played a part in his wife's death. She'd have to find a better place to hide, as soon as possible. She decided to set out that very night.

———— ❧ ————

The fire flickered brightly, contrasting the night which was black with shadows and fears. This was Tobin's favorite part of Tales' Night—the beautiful anticipation, as if the entire world was holding its breath, waiting for the teller to begin. Tobin liked to think the ghosts and heroes of old were out there too, listening from just beyond the light's reach.

"You tell it, Tobin," Timothy said. The rest of the squad murmured agreement.

They tried to take turns, really, but Tobin ended up acting as teller more often than the others. He was good at it, they said. It was one of the few things that felt natural to him.

"Alright," Tobin said, "which one?" They had finished off *The Cycle of the Tribes* at the previous Tales' Night with a rather unorthodox rendition of 'The Last of the Seers,' as told by Rico.

"Why don't you tell 'Kyra's Battle,'" Miels, one of the squad's four swordfighters, suggested. Wars between Ideon and the Republic had sparked hundreds of Tales, and 'Kyra's Battle' remained a constant favorite.

"You just like whatever Tale has a good fight in it," Yemena complained. She was a half-Fellin staff and spear wielder, and as one of Tobin's officers—the other being Timothy—her words carried weight with their other squadmates. She swished her cat-like tail in Miels' direction, pointed ears twitching. The irregular patches of soft hair that covered her skin made her look all the more intimidating in the soft firelight.

"We *are* soldiers."

"How about the one about the beginning of magic?" Felias said. "I've heard it told the Silas' Hill version—they call it 'The Blessing' here—but I reckon they tell it different where you're from."

Murmurs of agreement from the rest of the squad settled it; it was a popular Tale, since it told of the five heroes.

"They call it 'The Chalice' in House Kyra–Bendekan." Tobin cleared his throat. "And this, dear friends, is why…" With the last line, Tobin changed his voice to the lilting rhythm of a teller and began speaking words he had memorized years ago over the course of many tellings.

"Once, long ago, on the far side of Theold's Mountains, there lived five good friends in an old city called Praeta, the city of bridges. They had been brought together at birth and raised in one house, being taught in all aspects of combat, knowledge, and consideration, because it had been prophesied they would face a grave danger that would threaten the land.

"The first was Bendekan, a fighter of great renown even as a child. He carried twin truncheons of ash held in sheaths on his back, and his boots were of the darkest black, rumored to be the hide of some monstrous crea-ture he had slain in his youth.

"The second was Yoel, black-haired and lean, and darkly handsome. He wielded breaksteel daggers kept in arm and leg sheaths and used his speed and strength to overwhelm opponents as only the most skilled of knife fight-ers can.

"The third was Tabitha. Gentle and kind to those who called her friend, she was yet fierce and fearsome in battle. Though many praised her skill with a sword, her greatest strength was her ability to read her opponents and dictate the flow of a battle. Her tactics kept the five together, and her quest for knowledge was as relentless as her determination to apply it. Aware of the responsibility she carried in keeping not only herself but her friends safe, she kept to herself, even hiding part of her face behind a veil.

"The fourth was Neri, whose natural empathy and way with people made her memorable to all she met. She was intelligent and strong, and she was known for her incredible skill at archery, wielding a longbow and crow-fletched arrows.

"The last, and youngest of the five was Ibram, a boy of great knowledge who grew into a man of great wisdom. He wielded a teak quarterstaff and was proficient in every fighting form and discipline known to man. His reputation preceded him wherever he went, even though by his age he should have been counted least among the five.

"The friends grew up together, receiving the peoples' admiration for their feats of strength and cunning and knowledge. They knew that in return they would one day have to perform a great task. It happened that when they came of age, a fresh spring was discovered in one of the nearby mountains. The spring's waters were filled with magic so strong it drove men mad and caused them to become reckless, killing and plundering for pleasure.

"The five young heroes took up their weapons and fought the plunderers. Though they were at a disadvantage to the evil men's magic, their skill and careful planning allowed them to defeat their adversaries. Tabitha directed their tactics and led Yoel and Bendekan in a frontal assault, while Ibram crashed into the enemy from the side. Neri watched Ibram's back, shooting those men who tried attacking him from behind. After a short and ferocious battle, the five friends had beaten their adversaries into submission.

"When the threat had been vanquished, a creature made of mist, the very guardian spirit of the land, came down to the five and offered them a reward for the task they had completed: It would give them magic of their own. Magic would come with a price, however: It was dangerous to attain, and once it had taken root in them, it would compel them to act forever as the guardians and servants of those people who dwelt in the land.

"The five heroes accepted the price, and the guardian spirit called up five spirit creatures to draw water from the magic spring. A forest guardian was sent for Bendekan, a water sprite for Tabitha, a wind dragon for Ibram, a fire imp for Neri, and a spirit stallion for Yoel. The five creatures pooled the water they drew into a beautiful chalice, hammered from the purest of metals, which altered the magic so as not to drive the heroes mad as it had the plunderers.

"With a final warning about the dangers of receiving magic, the guardian spirit handed the chalice to Bendekan, who drank deeply. He passed it on to Tabitha, who passed it on to Neri, who passed it on to Ibram, who passed it on to Yoel. Yoel saw there was still a large amount of water in the chalice and drank it all, hoping it would give him more magic than it would the others.

"After they had drunk from the chalice, the five felt magic expand inside them, giving them power. Bendekan received magic that came from the woods, Tabitha that which came from water, and Ibram that which came from air. Yoel, who had taken the biggest sip of the spring's water, gained fire magic more powerful than the magic of the other four.

"Neri's magic, however, did not take, and she became deathly ill. Yoel, who loved her, pleaded with the guardian spirit, who told Yoel he now possessed the power to save her. Using his magic, Yoel was able to restore

Neri's health.

"Though the five were no longer balanced in their power, their combined magic let them restore peace to the land. They knew their work was to protect the land and the people, and to act for the guardian spirit who had granted them their power. For years, peace reigned under the five, and the people of the land prospered."

Tobin stopped, breathless, eyes focusing once more on the flickering fire, and then on his friends sitting around it. A few, including Timothy, had their eyes closed as if falling asleep. Others stared at the fire, unseeing, or out into the darkness of the night. One pair of eyes looked straight at him. He couldn't see who it was with the fire between them, but he could see the eyes reflecting the flames.

He was about to clear his throat and ask who it was, when the person stepped towards him, becoming a uniformed soldier in the dark colours of the combat group Bright Midnight. She—it was definitely a woman—had the twin blue bands of a second's badge on her arm.

Bendekan! Tobin jumped up from his seat, saluting, and the rest of the squad followed suit.

"At ease," the woman said. "I'm Runie Shadewalker, second in Bright Midnight. I have a message here for Squadleader Tobin vinn Baorock. That must be you."

Tobin swallowed at her direct gaze, then accepted the letter she held out to him. *Must be incredibly skilled to earn a name like Shadewalker,* he thought. That was one of the downsides of being a noble. He got a name handed down to him, whereas others got to earn their names.

"Quite young to lead a squad, aren't you?" She regarded Tobin with an abstract sort of interest.

"Yes'm. The youngest in my combat group."

"Ah, yes. Yoel's Atonement."

Tobin scowled slightly at the name. Runie's comment wasn't degrading exactly, but there were soldiers who took savage pleasure in pointing out his combat group's connection to Yoel and his shameful legacy.

"You tell a good Tale, Tobin. Anyway, the missive's to let you know my squad will be accompanying you on your mission."

"What?" Tobin had to fight to keep angry disappointment from his voice. "But—Second, this was our mission."

"It still is. But there's been word of bandit activity in the western plains. The council decided to send a second squad."

Tobin's mouth curled, but he didn't dare voice more of a complaint than he already had. *That isn't fair,* he thought. *There's word of bandits and suddenly other squads want in on the fun.* It meant they might get some real experience on the mission, but he didn't know if that was worth it. He'd be under Runie's authority, since she outranked him. She'd like as not keep the squad tucked away and safe.

Runie's expression softened, as if she guessed at his thoughts. "Don't worry, Tobin. You'll still see action, if there is any. But now you'd better head to bed. We leave at first light."

When Tobin was shaken awake by Felias, who had been on watch, both excitement and dread bubbled up in his stomach. *This really is it.*

Squad Fourteen dressed in the dark, gathered their packs, and left the barracks in silence. Runie's squad—Squad Three of Bright Midnight—met them at the bridge. Tobin looked at their faces, indistinct and shadowed by their dark hoods, and shivered. *They look like a real squad.*

Bright Midnight wasn't a traditional choice for guarding a bunch of diplomats, but they specialized in night work. That was likely why they'd been added once Silas' Hill had received word of bandit activity.

Tobin half-expected Runie to barge in and take the lead, but she motioned him forward. "Your command, Tobin," she said without a hint of sarcasm. He smiled at that.

The group of twenty followed the bridge to the northern hill, then jogged down to the north-eastern stables. They didn't speak, but Tobin could feel the anticipation well up in his squad as they saddled their horses and arranged their gear. He grimaced at the sight of Spiffy, his small, rather potbellied horse, next to some of the others' sleek chargers, but his back was straight as he led the group towards Caleb's Gate.

"Here comes the relief." The guard waiting for them at the gate bore the blue and white uniform and tower insignia of Bendekan's Bastions, a large combat group charged with keeping the borders.

Tobin saluted. "Squadleader Tobin of Yoel's Atonement."

"Uptight one, are ya. First mission?"

"Yessir." The soldier had no ranking on his uniform, but he was older than Tobin which demanded respect, though not obedience.

"Don't you worry, Mirren, we'll take it from here," Runie drawled from behind Tobin's shoulder. She nodded towards the cluster of riders and carriages outside the gate. "Those are our charges, I presume?"

"On the mark. A nice enough bunch, seeing as they're from the Republic and all, though they made a fuss when they first saw Kane and Fellin soldiers. Wouldn't mind some of the Republican ladies myself."

He winked at Runie, and her face hardened into a scowl.

"Just because you're on morning shift doesn't mean you get to be smart with me."

"Yes'm." Mirren straightened into a salute, his right hand curled into a fist above his heart. "I meant no disrespect, Second."

"Right." Runie's voice was heavy with sarcasm, but she turned away from the guard and towards the group awaiting them. "I'll make the introductions, Tobin, and from there you can take the lead."

Tobin nodded nervously and followed Runie towards the other riders. There were thirty of them in all, he knew, though only eight were actual diplomats. The others were largely servants and packmen, and a few were family to the chief Republican ambassador, Lord Kile Briar. Why they still used titles like lord and lady when they prided themselves on being a Republic, Tobin didn't know. *Then again, it's not like they're a real Republic anyway. Everyone knows the Service holds more power than is good for them, and Bendekan knows they hardly answer to the actual government.*

It was funny, in a way. The Saint Brazen Republic and Ideon had warred for centuries, and yet here they were, pretending everything was dandy, sending diplomats back and forth to discuss the continuation of the unprecedented peace they were having. And then there were the rumors from the border, whispers warning of increased troop movement and smuggling activity. Tobin supposed the threat of bandits was all part of it. *Leave it to us nobles to make things complicated*, he thought, chagrinned. *Lords and ladies indeed.*

Runie and Tobin made their introductions before dividing up their squads. Tobin's soldiers formed a loose perimeter around the group, while Squad Three dissolved into the woods. They weren't needed yet, but they would look for signs of those bandits once they hit House Beater's Plains in a day or so.

Riding at the head of the column, Tobin couldn't help but think back to his departure from Kyra's Hold two years ago. He'd ridden out with a head full of hazy visions of heroism, imagining himself leading scores of soldiers into battle. He fingered the tonfa at this side, the wood still smooth. Somehow, he'd hoped to earn a carving before that first year was out. He'd scraped his cheeks raw, trying to procure some whiskers to burn before the hall of statues as proof of his adulthood, and he'd figured the heroism would just kind of follow.

Kind of embarrassing to think back to, Tobin thought. *I didn't know a thing.* He'd made it to Silas' Hill fine, of course. He'd even met a cantankerous wind spirit on the way. Other than a safe journey, however, he hadn't accomplished much. *I guess there's time for that still. This is how I start proving myself.* He straightened in his saddle, catching Runie's eye as he did so.

"Don't worry, Tobin. You'll do fine."

"Were you nervous? Your first time, I mean?"

Runie barked a laugh. "Scared out of my mind, actually. I mean, I didn't have any command my first mission, but I did get caught in a border skirmish."

Tobin's eyebrows shot up. "Thought they don't have those anymore."

"Not usually. But occasionally you get a few Servicemen forgetting the government leash on them. Or smugglers. I went down in the fight right away. It was a good thing we had a healer with us, or I might've lost my leg. Earned myself a carving though, a little one." She reached to the opposite side of her saddle and unfastened a beautiful wooden cudgel, with a stone head and a carved handle.

Tobin's breath caught as she handed it to him—weapons were *personal*. He almost dropped it, surprised at the weight, before catching it securely. "It's beautiful."

The cudgel wasn't completely covered in carvings, the way a veteran's weapon would be, but it still held a myriad of intertwined images and symbols, enough to show she was a formidable soldier. He recognized some of them—a stylized wolf which signified an espionage mission, a cluster of stars marking her as an excellent navigator, a forest guardian's face for having protected something. A weathered carving of a beehive-shaped tomb was etched near the bottom. Born and raised in House Silas' Hill, then. Descended from a family of warriors.

"See that?" Runie pointed to a small carving on the handle's edge, a crossed pair of knives. "You get that for surviving your first battle."

Tobin ran his hand over the mark, then handed the cudgel back to her. "Thanks for showing me."

"You'll get your own carving soon enough. Probably sooner than you're ready for."

Tobin smiled and turned his attention back to the road. Maybe it wouldn't be so bad after all, having her with him. She seemed nicer now that they were moving. He looked back to see the columns of horses following him. It wasn't quite like what he'd imagined, of course, but it was still good. *I bet some of the Tales' heroes started out like this. Like me.*

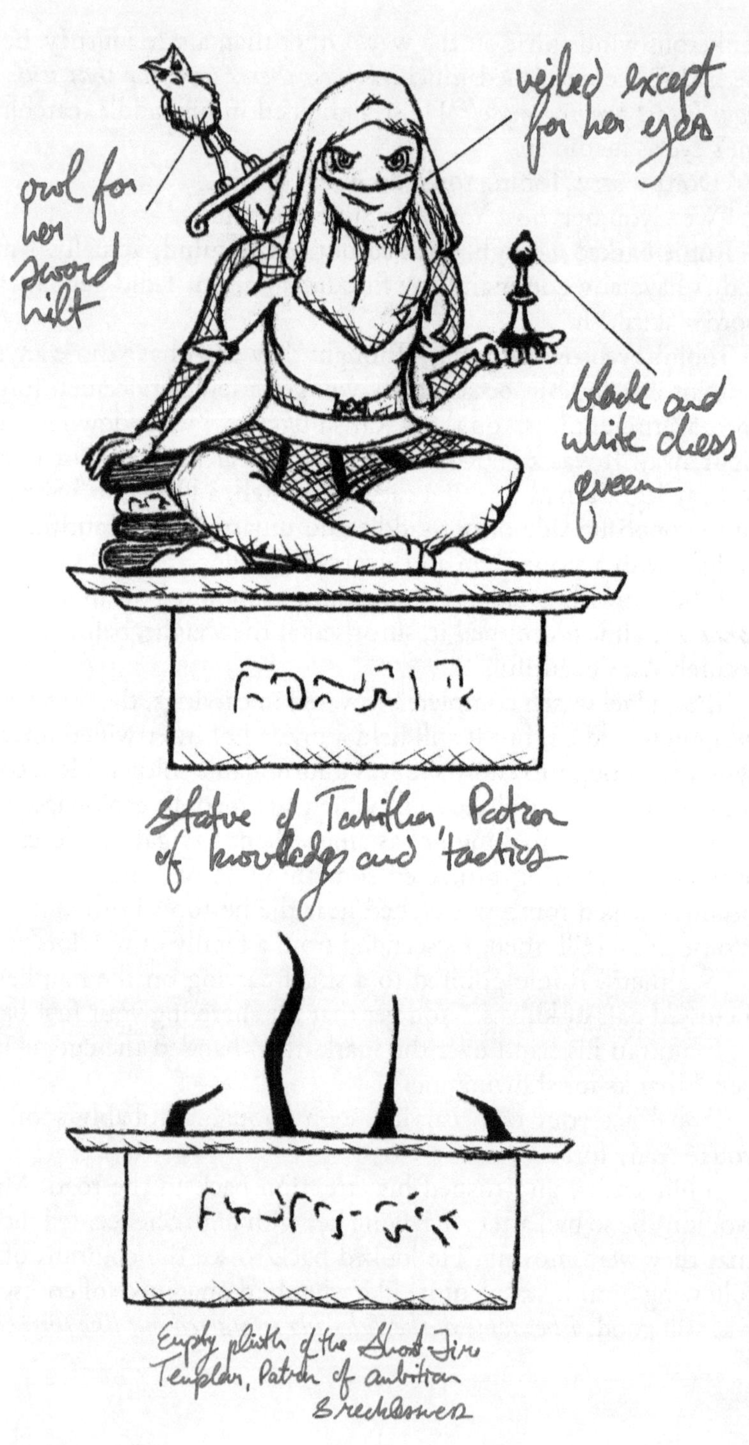

Statue of Tchitha, Patron
of knowledge and tactics

Empty plinth of the Short Fire
Templar, Patron of ambition
& recklessness

3

THE NICEST CROOK

Six Years Ago
Wrovetown, in Arahill, Saint Brazen

The pictures had gotten clearer lately. Mesmerized, Imp stared into the white lights that rose from the fire with a hunger that had nothing to do with his growling stomach. His memory was already fading, but this was what he had left of her.

He realized now that no one else saw those little white lights. Maybe Mama hadn't seen them either. *Mama always said I was special.* She had been special too.

Today they didn't form any clear pictures, and the noises he heard were jumbled. Vague figures moved back and forth between the lights, but nothing stood out. The bigger the fire, the less the pictures made sense. Today's fire was huge. The biggest he'd ever set.

He backed away from the flames and dug a grubby hand into his coat, pulling out a thin roll of paper-wrapped leaves. He stuck the end in the fire, then sucked on the other end, inhaling the smoke. The other street urchins seemed to think these were good.

Puffing half-heartedly on the cigarette, Imp ducked away from the burning timbers and into an alley. *Get out before anyone finds me.*

A blur of movement caught his eye, and he spun around, excited. *Fire imp?* They sometimes came to his fires and danced, but they didn't like it much out in the open. Imp didn't know why. When he couldn't spot anything, he turned back, disappointed.

"Hey you! Stop!"

Oh no. Imp threw the cigarette to the ground and ran for it, ducking between garbage heaps and piles of rotten wood.

"Fire! Fire!" More and more people joined in the cry. A crowd was forming. *Not good.* People might think he'd set the fire if he ran right out of it.

Careening to the side, Imp tried to think as he ran. More shouts sprung up both behind and ahead of him, and he bit back a cry of frustration.

Suddenly, a man appeared in front of him, grizzled and dirty, with a staff in hand. Imp backed away, but the man grabbed him in an iron grip and towed him to the side.

"Hey! Lemme go!"

"Quiet, boy," the man hissed in a rasping voice.

They reached the end of the alley, where a wall of people had formed, shepherded by several Servicemembers. They turned, eye insignias glinting. *Everyone's looking at me. Even the coats.*

"And where in the shades are you coming from?" one of the Servicemen barked.

"It's my nephew," the old man rasped, keeping a firm hold on Imp's arm. "He likes to run out to play near the Chisel." He gestured to the flaming building. "Got caught in the fire."

"Yeah, yeah, move along already." The Serviceman seemed more annoyed than suspicious. "Get the kid outta here." He turned to the crowd. "Can we form a waterline please!"

The man dragged Imp through the mass of people until they reached a different alley, where he deposited Imp onto a crate.

"What'd you do that for?" Imp asked, scrambling to his feet.

"Thought a stupid boy like you could use the help. What's your name?"

"Imp. Well, it's Peter, actually."

"Imp. I take it you're the arsonist that's had this town up in flames?"

"The what?"

"You set a lot of fires?"

Imp hesitated, then nodded.

The man studied him, a quizzical expression on his face. "Name's Old Man Bento. Least it's what people around here call me."

Imp could see why. The man's hair stuck out from his head in crazy tufts, and his skin was cracked and wrinkled, like old leather.

"You've got interesting eyes, Imp."

"What?"

"Your eyes. Unusually pale, aren't they?"

"I guess so." People often said his eyes were strange. He hadn't ever met anyone else with light grey eyes.

"You have any parents?"

Imp shook his head. "Not anymore."

The man looked back at the Chisel. "Well then, Imp. What was all that about?"

Imp smiled, seeing the tall building still wreathed in red and yellow and orange flames. *Looks like the water isn't doing much good.* He shrugged at the old man's question. He couldn't explain why he set the fires. He just liked them.

"Not the fires," the old man, Bento, said, as if reading Imp's thoughts. "You see things, Imp. Don't you." It wasn't a question.

How would he know? Unless… Imp's eyes grew big. "You see them too?"

"No."

"But you said—"

"I don't see them, Imp, but I know when someone else does."

Imp could feel the fear creeping in. He wasn't supposed to see things in the fire. He didn't know why, but he knew it was bad. "Is it true what people say? Does it mean I have magic?"

"Magic?" Old Man Bento barked a laugh. "Hardly. What you have is a whole lot rarer than that."

Present Day

Two days later, Jenna was still cooped up in her library study, searching through old books and reports. If any place held a record of magic settling late, or of her particular type of magic misbehaving, the tower would be it.

She flipped through *A History of Elemental Magics*, rereading the introduction to the passage on soul and aether magic for the third time that morning.

> Aether and soul constitute the newest discoveries in elemental magic and trace their origin back to 'The Tale of the Ghost-Fire Templar,' early versions of which first surfaced around 425, which seems to refer to a point in time between year 380 and year 415. Though scholars disagree on the origins of the Tale and how much truth has been preserved

in its modern telling, it is certain soul and aether were not part of the original elements wielded by the five heroes, and it is equally certain the two were discovered together and have never appeared separately within a mage (see Hera vinn Hearas).

None of it was new information, and none of it helped with her present dilemma. Sure, the text and others like it agreed that soul and aether magic could sometimes act differently due to their separate history, but none of that told her how to control the magic.

Another quality unique to soul and aether magic, is its frequency in magic users who draw their energy from nature. Though body and object mages do occasionally exhibit soul and aether magic, it is usually weak and unimpressive compared to that of nature mages.

This differs from the distribution of all other elements, save perhaps for that of fire, which seems to marginally favour the nature mages of House Weathslayer's Grave (resulting in lower numbers of water, earth/wood, and air mages in that House). This, however, can be explained by heritage alone, as the House's original Patron, Yoel, claimed a greater amount of magic than his four companions. (See pg. 436 for more on magical ancestry.)

The passage went on to specify the exact powers of soul and aether magic, as well as common sources. Jenna's source wasn't there, of course. *My magic had to be different from everyone else's.* She skimmed over some of the sections anyway.

One of the most practical aspects of soul and aether magic is its unique ability to be shaped into a myriad of forms depending on the needs of the wielder, the strength of the magic, and the mage's available power or energy source. Unlike the other elements, which rely on being used as they are—for example, earth can be moved, shaped into structures, and manipulated in form, whereas air is often used to push or pull objects, or in advanced cases, manipulate breath (see pg. 56 for discourses on the tasks most suited to elemental magics)—soul and aether can be used to create almost anything, provided the object in question reflects some element of 'darkness' or 'light.'

Aether is primarily used as a battle magic, suited as it is to forming energy blasts or being shaped into weapons. Traditionally, the very first object aether mages learn to shape is a small triangular blade, a tribute of sorts to the magic's destructive power. Soul, on the other hand, is the elemental magic most suited to protection or healing. It can be formed into shields, bandages, or similar items, which often retain magical properties and are near-indestructible when formed correctly. It has been suggested that aether and soul wielders practice using this creativity inherent in their magic.

There are, however, several taboos that govern the use of shaping objects which, if broken, can result in dire consequences. Foremost among these is the limit on copying exactly any living being known to the mage. Although it is, in most cases, easier to work from a mold well-known to the wielder, creating a magical copy of an existing living being remains a most dangerous endeavour, since exact copies tend to gain some form of sentience which prevents the mage from controlling them.

Further taboos…

Jenna skipped past the rest of it, including the passages that recounted famous soul and aether mages throughout the Legends, and flipped to the small list of references at the end of the chapter. She cross-checked them against her notes. *One more.*

The book was one she'd never come across before. *The Search for a Source.* There was a note beside the reference:

Though this volume has proven valuable on tracing the origins of soul and aether magic, much of the book is written purely from Tales and other stories, to the extent that *The Search for a Source* has been widely contested by theorists of solid repute.

Mentally making a note not to trust whatever hearsay she read in the book, Jenna grabbed her crutches and hobbled out to the library proper. Passing towering wooden shelves laden with books, scrolls, and ions—sheaves of cured animal hide folded into a sturdy pyramid-shape—she reached the index, a massive tome that sat on a reading pedestal. Jenna consulted its pages: Kalaaman Tower held a single copy of *The Search for a Source*, stored a floor above the main library.

Jenna inched up the winding stairs, each step a precarious balancing act, and made her way through the familiar hallways and atriums until she reached the small storage room the index had indicated. She found the book collecting dust in a corner and picked it up, running her fingers over the dirty cloth cover. *I suppose I should be glad they had it at all.*

Tucking the book into her belt, Jenna started walking back to her study. She was almost to the stairs when a voice gave her pause.

"—heard about her getting released from her studies," a woman was saying.

"Quite right what the elders decided, if you ask me," a second woman said. "There's no amount of war-research as measures up to our safety."

They were talking about her. And they were coming closer. Jenna ducked behind a carved pillar, wanting to hear the rest of their conversation. One of the voices belonged to Alianne, a theorist who had helped her with her analysis of the Second Magewar, but the other was unfamiliar.

"I hardly think any of it will be necessary," Alianne said. "We finally have some peace, and I think we should set about trying to keep it instead of hankering after another war."

Jenna scowled. *Researching the wars has nothing to do with wanting more of them.* She gripped the handles of her crutches, hands whitening.

"Well, either way, we won't have to worry about it anymore. Without that gravemaker around we'll have time to devote ourselves to some proper study."

Jenna's breath caught in her throat at the insult. Her insides seething with anger, she stepped out from behind the column as the two women passed by.

"I beg your pardon," she said through clenched teeth. "What did you call me?"

Alianne had the grace to look ashamed. "Nothing. Nothing that was meant anyway."

The second woman, short and plump, retreated a step, paling. "Nothing at all, Jenna Brightshade. Nothing at all."

The two women all but ran from the room with apologetic mutters, but Jenna hardly heard them. *She was scared of me.* The second woman had acted genuinely afraid. *I don't want to hurt anyone. What did I ever do to warrant that kind of treatment? Dangerous magic and Yoel's cursed House—my House. I didn't ask for any of it.* Confused and angry, Jenna made her way back down the stairs. *I need a place to think.* She didn't return to her study but descended a further round of stairs to reach the tower's hall of statues.

The hall, more of a chapel really, was dimly lit by torches on the walls, as well as a round skylight set into the room's center. The skylight showed off the cylindrical shaft that ran through the middle of Kalaaman Tower, from the ceiling of the chapel to the uppermost story. No one came here much anymore, which suited Jenna fine. The place had become a quiet refuge for her, a place for reflection and silence.

The tall statues that ringed the hall on plinths of stone were featureless in the soft lighting, their faces swathed in the shadows cast by the ceiling's wooden gables. Jenna made her way to one of the hard-wooden benches set in between the statues and sat down. She glanced to her right, where the hall's only empty plinth lay. It represented the Ghost-Fire Templar, Patron of ambition. Though she couldn't make out any detail in the dim lighting, she knew the statue of Tabitha, Patron of knowledge, lay to her left. A hooded statue of a man clutching a staff stood directly across from her, depicting Fate's Hand, a minor Patron symbolizing daring and discretion.

Jenna's legs cramped in pain, worn out from the stairs, and she went to massage them when she realized she still had the book tucked into her belt. *The Search for a Source.* Forgetting about her aching legs, Jenna pulled it out and flipped open the dusty cover. She closed her eyes, breathed in the vanilla-like smell of well-used pages, and smiled. It smelled like home. *A home I'll be forced to leave.* The thought returned a scowl to her face. Perhaps the book would have some answers.

As Jenna began to read, she noticed scribbled notes in the margins, faded with age. Many pages were dog-eared or creased. She flipped past the first few chapters, since they seemed to be concerned with Tales that originated before the first records of soul and aether magic; the book followed a rough chronology. When she reached the fifth chapter, she paused, curious at the title—'Ghost-Fire.' This was the part that *A History of Elemental Magics* had referenced. Jenna read:

> Over time, many figures, creatures, and heroes of legend have been associated with the most elusive of magics—that of aether and soul. From Yoel, Patron of a cursed House that seems to possess a great affinity for aether and soul magic, to The Monk, who was rumored to possess an especially volatile form of it, to the very spirits of the land, creatures rumored to bond with the magic and make it their own.

Jenna's lip curled in amusement. She could see why the book was considered unreliable. Spirit creatures were real enough, of course, but their supposed connection with soul and aether had never been properly studied, much less proven, and they certainly couldn't 'make magic their own.' Even worse, the book managed to repeat the word 'rumored' twice in a single sentence, which didn't bode well for its credibility. Still, it was true House Weathslayer's Grave—and presumably Yoel's legacy—was tied to soul and aether magic. Jenna set her doubts aside for the moment and continued to read.

> One such figure has, however, surpassed all other associations, since he is held to be the first wielder of aether and soul magic. This figure is, of course, the Ghost-Fire Templar.

A note was scribbled into the margins next to the paragraph. It took Jenna a few moments to decipher the cramped hand: *Answers at the shrine? Silas' Hill.* Jenna frowned at the writing, in part because she had been taught never to deface something as valuable as a book, and in part because the writing seemed like the sort of thing that would answer her questions.

A shrine could help me… but whose shrine is this referring to? And what's the connection with the Ghost-Fire Templar? The link between that particular Patron and her particular brand of magic had always seemed curious to her, since the Templar was associated with House Heron–Neminia, while her magic was associated with House Weathslayer's Grave. Could it be a shrine to Yoel? That didn't make any sense.

Jenna scanned the next few pages but found nothing related to a shrine or controlling the magic. The volume transitioned into the soul-and-aether-related Tales, and the snippets of handwriting degenerated into the unintelligible. She snapped the book shut in frustration. *Useless. Just like the reference warned.* Then she noticed a fold of paper sticking out from around where she'd been reading. Her curiosity got the better of her, and Jenna opened *The Search for a Source* again. A piece of paper was stuck between two of the pages. She worked it free.

A map. Excitement swelled in her chest before suspicion replaced it. *How convenient.* The map wasn't like any she'd studied before, but the lines on it were familiar nonetheless. It depicted House Silas' Hill, without any of its cities. Several geometric shapes were marked on the map, some of them outside the House's borders. It was a small, triangular mark that caught her eye, drawn just within the south-eastern border line. It was labeled 'Ghost-Fire Templar's shrine.' Jenna stared at it. *Impossible.*

A clatter from the stairs made Jenna look up just in time to see Castor walk into the domed room.

"Thought I'd find you here." He approached the bench where she sat. "Doing okay?"

She nodded absentmindedly. "I think… I think I may have found something."

"Really? You've found out what's wrong with your magic? Or how to control it?"

"No, nothing like that. It's just… The Ghost-Fire Templar. He keeps cropping up."

"Why wouldn't he? Tales make him out to be the first soul and aether mage."

"Exactly. If anyone would be able to tell me how to control soul and aether, the Templar would."

"I don't understand."

He looks kind of cute when he frowns, Jenna thought, before trying to explain herself. "The shrines. They're meant to give guidance to those seeking a Patron."

"Okay…? Don't tell me you're not satisfied with pledging yourself. Or are you saying you want to ask Tabitha for guidance?"

"Not Tabitha. The Ghost-Fire Templar."

Castor paused, confusion flickering across his face. "I don't follow, Jenna. There *are* no shrines to the Ghost-Fire Templar."

"Not according to any reputable documents, no. But according to this," Jenna held up the map, "there is a shrine to the Templar at the eastern border of House Silas' Hill."

He raised an eyebrow. "That map looks like it was drawn by a child. You think… that could be an actual shrine?"

"It's ancient magic. Scholars agree a lot of shrines have been lost throughout the years, and if there really is a shrine to the Ghost-Fire

Templar—"

"—then the border by Theold's Mountains would make sense." Understanding dawned in Castor's eyes. "You want to go."

Jenna nodded. "I can't stay here either way. And this is the best lead I've had in weeks."

Castor tilted his chin as if deliberating with himself before looking back to her. "It doesn't seem like a lot to go on." He paused, and she thought he would tell her off, but he continued. "I'll need to let the master founder know, but I don't see Marcus refusing any extra hours, so I should be able to get a few weeks' leave."

"You'll come with me?"

"Of course I will. Lowly tradesman like myself pass up a little adventure?" Castor smirked. "Wouldn't miss it."

Jenna smiled and made to stand up, but then grimaced in pain. She'd forgotten about her legs. The hard-wooden bench certainly hadn't done them any favours.

Castor put a hand on her shoulder, concerned.

"I overdid it with the stairs today is all." Castor helped Jenna massage the cramps out of her legs, but when she tried to stand, her legs still buckled. "I hate being useless," she growled, frustrated.

"You're not useless." He pecked a kiss on her forehead. "Here. I'll carry you back home, and you can start packing while I arrange for that leave of mine."

She let him pick her up, grabbing the book and crutches as he did so. She wouldn't mind her legs so much if she had her magic back. Not that she didn't enjoy Castor carrying her every now and then. It was the fact that she couldn't choose it. Sometimes she was simply helpless to move.

"I'm glad you're coming with me," she said into his shirt, her voice muffled.

"Me too." She could hear the smile in his voice. "Someone's got to keep you out of trouble."

A week later, Jenna and Castor left Renforth at daybreak, their saddlebags heavy with supplies, some of Castor's tools, and, in Jenna's case, borrowed books and scrolls.

Castor had received a journeyman's travelling leave from his master. He'd be able to work for up to a week in any town large enough to contain a foundry, earning them enough to get by. His work would extend their travel time, but at least it offered financial security.

Jenna was glad to be in the saddle again. City life didn't lend itself to much riding, and she had missed going on excursions with her dark grey mare, Silverphile. The horse had been a parting gift from her father and uncle when she'd passed the theorist examinations and left the family's merchant estate in House Weathslayer's Grave to make her way to Renforth. That had been over two years ago. Her magic had been underwhelming and about as safe as soul and aether magic could be, and she'd welcomed the chance to study, to help her nation in some small way.

They were silent for much of the ride, Castor studying a map of the countryside and Jenna lost in thought. They took breaks to eat and to water the horses but didn't stop for good until they reached a small town called Hemsford where they planned to stay for the night.

Castor managed to trade a few hours' work for a bed at The Blank Spot, the larger of Hemsford's two inns. Jenna was glad for the comfortable accommodations; her legs ached terribly from riding all day. Though her saddle had been designed specially for her—there were straps to hold her legs in place, as well as straps for her crutches—and Silverphile had been trained to be directed with reins alone, Jenna knew she'd pushed herself too hard.

As she rode into the stable to take care of Silverphile, Jenna kept her shoulders straight, hoping Castor wouldn't notice her exhaustion. She undid the buckles strapping her legs down and slid over the mare's back, deftly catching her arm in the stirrup to keep herself from falling. If she hadn't taken months to perfect the trick, she would have collapsed, she was that tired. She was about to grab her crutches when Castor reached over and unfastened them for her.

"Don't pretend I don't know you overdid yourself," he muttered into her ear as he helped her to the door connecting the stable to the inn. He tossed a coin to the stable boy who had grabbed Silverphile's reins. "You don't have to push yourself you know. I know you're tough already."

"I'll keep it in mind. It's just been a while since I've ridden an entire day." She shook off Castor's helping hand and grabbed her crutches while he got their packs. Together they entered the inn's common room, where dinner was about to be served. The smell of food and the crackling fire made Jenna feel much more alert, and her legs seemed to ache less as she made her way to a table and sat down.

A young server set food and drink before them. Castor began to wolf down his meal—*you'd think we'd had no lunch*, Jenna thought bemused. She, on the other hand, ate slowly, taking time to observe the inn's other patrons.

Most of the people were dressed in simple, homespun garb, though a few sported the brighter fabrics and finer clothes of merchants. A teller stood in front of a group of rapt listeners in the corner. *Right. Tales' Night today.* Jenna listened briefly and recognized the Tale as 'The Blessings of the Markois,' one of the Tales in *The Cycle of the Magewars.*

One gentleman stood out among the small crowd, the fur on his face and the cat-like tail sneaking out from behind his back marking him a Fellin. Though Kanes were quite common this far to the east, Fellin were a rare sight as they tended to stick to Ideon's north and west. The man noticed her gaze and gave a tiny nod, as much for Castor as for her. The tribes might not be as formidable or united as they once were, but they still respected each other. She nudged Castor, who noticed the man and nodded back.

As she turned her gaze back to the room, she picked out snippets of conversation.

"…melon crop coming along nicely now, so glad I planted some…" boasted a farmer, sharing a mug of ale with a friend.

"Fall rains ought to be coming soon."

"…new cartload of pots—through—forest is going to be interesting…"

"…and I said to him, 'I'd pack a better staff if I were you'—" the voice dissolved into cackles of laughter.

The talk that drifted her way seemed to consist mostly of farmers' and herders' easy chatter, with a few merchants' and travellers' words mixed in, familiar to her from growing up on a merchant estate. It was comforting. Even the quiet tower library couldn't match the comfort and safety of a simple town inn. *I've been so stressed the last few weeks, I almost forgot what it's like to relax,* she thought.

Suddenly a different voice, spry and tinged with worry, bored its way through the comfort of mundane chatter.

"Heard the tension is rising. Republic—technology gained supporters in the east…" Jenna looked over to see a wiry woman talking at a table of farmers. One of the men made an indistinguishable reply. The woman chuckled hoarsely. "…Not if they know what's good for them. Best stay down—of Beater's Plains… will have a fit."

Jenna felt an uncomfortable tingle at the back of her neck, as if someone was watching her. She turned around, and sure enough, saw a dark-clad man sitting in a corner booth by himself, glancing in her direction—though whether he was looking at the woman who had spoken or at her, she couldn't tell.

Jenna turned back to listen to the woman, but the discussion at her table had gone back to the farmers' crops and the load a visiting merchant was carrying. However, as Jenna finished her food, she heard other harmless conversations occasionally punctured by a worried remark about technology or uncertainty.

Tensions between the Ideon Nation and the Saint Brazen Republic had been rising, true, but the peace had lasted over sixty years this time, and no one wanted another war. While the talk worried Jenna, she was certain the two countries' conflict could be resolved peacefully. If there was one thing her research into the wars had taught her, it was that they could have been avoided through peaceful negotiation. *As long as Eleszan still stands by as a neutral party, I don't see any of this being cause for worry.* Still, the tension was there. The people felt it.

Jenna stiffened. She sensed something die behind the tavern bar, and her vision changed, everything tinted purple as a pinprick of energy hit her, then another. The energy built up pressure inside her as if it was boiling water and she the bursting kettle.

"Castor," she hissed.

He turned to her, and understanding dawned in his eyes. "What do you need?"

"The stable—"

Castor jumped to his feet and helped her out of her chair. Together, they stumbled the few steps to the connecting door. Jenna clench her fists. Her muscles flexed and tightened as she fought to keep the magic from bursting out of her.

Once they entered the stable and the door closed behind them, she focused on the energy, allowing it to manifest as magic.

Elemental magic could be complex, but the basic principle was simple: The mage drew in the energy from their source, stored it in their body for a short time, then released it. Depending on the wielder's mental focus and practice, they could shape it into different forms suited to the magic.

Jenna's magic seemed to manifest as aether more than soul, but a blast of aether might light the stable on fire, so she forced the energy to become soul magic. The pressure inside her lessened, and her vision faded back to normal. Glowing white tendrils appeared around her arms, rising in and out of her skin and wrapping around her fingers. She released them, and they dissipated into the air.

"That was close," she muttered.

"You did it. You had it under control that time. What changed?"

Jenna thought for a moment. "I've tried to simply hold it in, like Master Raver suggested, and it's never worked." Master Raver was the soul and aether mage who had first attempted to help her with her magic. "But maybe I've been doing this all wrong."

"What do you mean?"

Jenna turned back to inn, hobbling inside.

Castor followed. "Jenna?"

She reached their table and grabbed her saddlebags from underneath it, digging out *A History of Elemental Magics* and flipping it open. "Here, Castor." She kept her voice quiet so as not to disturb the inn's other patrons, some of whom were looking towards their table, no doubt curious about their abrupt exit and re-entrance. "There's a technique in here referred to as casting out, used by elemental mages who draw their magic from nature. 'Rather than focus on the energy within a physical entity, as both object and body mages do, nature mages must cast out in order to ascertain whether any sources of energy lie nearby. Most mages do this every waking hour without conscious thought, but a focused cast will increase a mage's range dramatically, within the constraints set by the type of magic and the strength of the wielder.'"

"And that's what you did? You cast your magic out?"

"Not on purpose. The more my magic has sparked out of control, the more I've prevented myself from casting out for sources, partly to try and control it, partly because, to be honest, I'm scared of it. Ever since the problems started, I've been blocking off my range. But I was so relaxed in there, I think I accidentally cast out again, which let me anticipate the energy. I keep feeling like I'm being bombarded, but maybe if I cast for sources it'll prevent me from being taken off guard when the energy hits me."

Castor nodded. "Maybe that'll also prevent the energy from being automatically used up," he mused.

Jenna hesitated. "I hadn't thought of that."

"Well, you're the theorist with experience in magic, but I definitely remember you being able to tolerate cats killing mice before your magic started to... you know."

"I guess the energy was still there, but not strong enough to warrant the need to use it...?" Jenna drifted off into silence, her thoughts whirring. "I need to do more research."

Castor handed Jenna her crutches. "May I suggest some rest before you dive back into your books?"

She blinked at him, startled from her thoughts. "Rest? Oh, right. That's probably a good idea."

Gathering her books, Jenna rose and shuffled towards the bar. Castor picked up their bags and followed her. The innkeeper handed them a simple pewter key and gave directions to their room, which was down the wide hallway that led off the common area.

Castor opened the door for Jenna, and she looked back at the tavern before hobbling through the doorway. Most of the farmers were beginning to leave; no doubt they would be waking early the next morning. The merchants still sat at their booths, talking and drinking. The teller had finished the Tale and was settling back with a heaped plate.

Jenna glanced at the corner booth where the dark-clad man still sat, nursing a drink. His head twitched back, as if he'd shifted his gaze. Had he been… watching her? Castor nudged her, wanting to get into the room, and Jenna put the thought from her mind. *Of course he wasn't. Why would he be watching me?*

Adriane walked along Cain's streets, winding paths that led further and further into the Poors Quarter. A street sign caught her eye. Abel Way. She liked the sound of it, so she turned left, entering a narrow alley that crept towards the city's edge.

How much did that Serviceman really see?

Adriane had spent the evening at Henderson's shop, stocking the meat and then cleaning. After the night's shadows had begun overtaking the city, she had retreated to her room before slipping out of a rickety window and into the alley at the shop's rear, fearing that the Service might be watching the entrance. She'd left a note for Henderson, in case she didn't come back.

She sniffed the air, smelling traces of soot, blood, rotten food, and garbage. *It's a good night for a murder*, she thought. *That's what this place feels like anyway.*

Abel Way was deserted, filled only with cracked barrels, rotten crates, and scraps of wood and metal. Piles of spongy refuse squelched underneath her booted feet. A punctured pipe hissed steam ahead of her. As she walked, Adriane kept a wary eye out for people. She needed to find herself a place she could hide away, some place safe and far from the city's regular folks. If that meant traipsing around after dark when thieves came out to play, so be it. She fingered the side of her knife where it stuck out of her boot. She could take care of herself. *And whatever I can't do my magic does for me anyway.*

A crackle pierced the night. Adriane froze, her hand poised to draw her knife, but nothing moved. There was no sound besides the hiss of steam. Thinking she must have imagined it, she inched forward, heart pounding.

A snapping sound, a burst of adrenaline, and Adriane was on the ground, a man gripping her shoulders, pressing her down into the dirt. Suppressing a scream—no use drawing attention to herself in this part of the city—Adriane grappled with the man, using all her pent-up frustrations, her anger, to try getting him off her. An eye-shaped badge, blue iris, crossed her sight, pinned to his chest. *A Serviceman,* she thought, panicked. *Did I give myself away back at the shop? Did they follow me?*

The man forced her into a headlock, squeezing the breath from her lungs. If ever there was a time to try using her magic, this might be it. Letting her emotions go as far as she dared, Adriane tried to get her magic to kick in. She felt the shadows flicker around her, the cold surround her, and almost managed to make it work, but the man threw her down hard, and the moment was gone. Mist rolled off her skin, and the magic escaped her grasp. The man grabbed a pair of leather ties from his belt and went for her wrist, cuffing her face as he did so.

Struggling wildly, Adriane managed to draw her knee up, kicking the man in the chest and drawing her knife at the same time. The man heard the hiss of cold steel and clamped large fingers around her knife hand, trying to take the weapon from her.

"Get off!" She tried to free the knife. "I'll gut you."

He laughed, a hoarse, throaty chuckle that made her skin go cold. "I doubt it," he said, calm as if he were strolling around a meadow. "You don't look like a killer. Just a lost little—"

Thkkk. A throwing knife sliced through his coat and grazed Adriane's side. It quivered where it stuck up between two cobbles.

Before either of them could react, another knife spun through his neck, cutting him open and spilling blood all over Adriane's startled face. As Adriane gasped for air, the man gave a cough—half scream, half groan—and collapsed to the side, dead.

Adriane jumped up, ignoring the gore and the pain in her side, and rushed into the shadows, brandishing her knife, ready to defend against a new attacker. A silhouette detached itself from halfway up one of the surrounding buildings. It dropped and rolled as it hit the ground, then walked up to her.

"Looked like you could use a little help."

"I had him," Adriane hissed through gritted teeth. "Stay back. Who are you?"

"Oh, me?" The silhouette gestured with its hands as if it had just noticed itself. It stepped out of the shadow and into a patch of moonlight. Tall brown boots. A dirty coat. Long, dangling arms and a clean-shaven face, glinting palely under a mop of dark hair. He looked about her age. "Nobody much. Just the owner of this lovely little street. Been following that piece of Service trash for an hour or so. Saw him camped out behind a butcher's shop."

His manner didn't seem threatening but calm and easygoing, as if he were trying to be funny.

Adriane kept her guard up. "Then why didn't you kill him for me earlier?"

The young man looked embarrassed. "I… uh… I lost him. But—I found him again, sure enough. Would've helped if you'd screamed a bit though. Still, nailed that bastard right down to the ground, and speaking of which…" he walked the few steps to the body and retrieved his two dripping knives. "Are you okay? I think I nicked you by accident."

As he cleaned and sheathed his blades, Adriane caught the blue glint of indobalt and pushed further back against the wall. "I'm—I'm fine. Leave me be." It was said the metal could nullify magic. As much as she hated her magic, the thought terrified her.

The street spun around her, and her knife clattered out of her hand. She fell back against the nearest wall, dizzy and sick, all the adrenaline emptying out of her.

The man edged closer, as if approaching a hurt animal. She tried to stand, but he gently took her arms and lowered her to the ground.

"Easy there. That's just the shock talking. I'm not gonna hurt you. Never seen a man killed before, have you?"

She shook her head. "Once," she whispered. She'd thrown a temper tantrum about something menial, couldn't even remember what, then had run away to cool off. Her parents had come after her. *The woods were dark*—she could see the scene in her mind. Her parents found her, talked to her. Then a figure jumped out of the night, wielding a knife, and Pa yelled at her to run…

"Hey." The voice broke through her thoughts, shaking her from the memory. "It's okay. There's nothing to killing. A Serviceman like that, it's no different than gutting a pig. Here. We'd better go inside and get the, uh—let's get you cleaned up." He seemed to think the words 'blood on your face' would be too much for her.

Sensing his sincerity, Adriane shook off his helping hand, fumbled for her hunting knife still lying on the floor, and stumbled to her feet.

"Going to throw up?" he asked.

She shook her head.

He offered her his arm—which she refused—and then walked to a small wooden door set into the side of an old building. The storied structure looked dilapidated and abandoned, but Adriane registered hidden iron bands reinforcing the door, which opened on greased hinges.

"Now the great thing about owning a street," the man said, "is you own the buildings too." He held the door for her and beckoned.

Making up her mind, she sheathed her knife and entered. Inside was what looked like an empty tavern, chairs and tables scattered about the floor, a bar on the side, and swinging doors leading to a kitchen.

The man came in after her. Though the hallway was wide, he walked so close that his arm brushed hers. Adriane jerked away at the touch, but he merely passed her and turned right towards an ancient-looking staircase.

As they ascended, Adriane heard voices growing closer. At the top of the landing, a hallway led to a sturdy door, light shining out from behind it, and the sound of conversation became even louder. He led her to the left, to a different room, where a table, a chair, a cabinet, and a bed were set out.

"Here, sit." He gestured to the bed, then took an oil lamp from the cabinet, lighting it. "I've a gathering of friends here tonight. Mistress Gera deals in—ah—herbs, and I'll ask her to see to that scratch of yours. I'll be right back."

The man left, and Adriane heard him enter the adjoining room. The noise swelled when he opened the door, greetings being shouted his way, then shut off when he closed it behind him.

She looked down at the rip in her coat, seeing a small red stain ooze through the worn material. *Some knife thrower he is*, she thought. Then again, he had been shooting knives down from eight paces up a building, perched on a tiny ledge. Perhaps she should simply be thankful he hadn't accidentally killed her.

A few minutes later, an older woman entered the room carrying a basin of warm water, a cloth, and a small bag. She smiled at Adriane.

"I'm Gera. I hear you got yourself into a bit of trouble." Setting her burdens down on the table, she pulled out the chair and sat. "Now, dearie, if you wouldn't mind lying down and taking off that coat of yours."

Adriane followed her instructions, putting her coat to the side and pulling at the slit the knife had made in her shirt. The cut stung, but the blood was dripping slowly, so it couldn't be deep.

Gera washed the cut, hemmed and hawed over whether or not to do any stitching, put a salve on it to prevent infection, and bandaged it smartly.

"I've told him a million times not to throw with his left, you know," she said. "Has much better aim with his right."

A knock sounded on the door, and the young man from earlier entered. A hand clamped over his eyes, he waved his other arm about dramatically.

"It's fine," Gera said, her voice resigned as if used to his theatrics. "You can look."

The man took his hand away, then grimaced at seeing Adriane. "You still have blood all over—I mean—you're still a bit dirtied up."

"I can take it from here, thanks," Adriane said. Gera pressed the washcloth into her hand, and she proceeded to wipe grit and caked gore off her face.

The man gave Gera a look, and she gathered up her things and left.

Adriane made to get up, but the man leaned over and pushed her back. She looked up, startled.

"I can't help but wonder," he said, "what you were doing wandering about the Poors Quarter this late at night."

"It's my business." Adriane said, instantly on guard again.

"I couldn't help noticing that the Serviceman seemed to be following you specifically. I thought at first he was after some of my, um, friends, but it seems you were on Abel Way by accident."

Adriane said nothing.

"And I also couldn't help but see that while you were fighting you almost dissolved into shadows." He paused. "Literally—in case that wasn't clear."

"I—I can explain," she said, grasping for some sort of way out, suddenly scared of him, of being in a strange place, of having been maneuvered out of the street to a forgotten house where no one would find her. Her fingers itched for her knife, reaching towards her boot.

The man grinned. "Looking for something?" He flourished her knife. "I may not be the best tracker, but I'm one hell of a pickpocket. Now, care to explain what was going on out there, *mage*?" He said the word strangely, with a sense of weight and familiarity, as if being a mage made her inhuman, just like him. His fingers flashed at his waist, and one of the bluish knives appeared in his hand.

"My name is Adriane," she said. "Not mage. I'm not a mage, I'm—I don't know. Different."

"You have magic?"

She nodded, eyeing the knife. Denying it wouldn't make a difference now.

"The Service has been following me for a while, trying to catch me. I thought I lost them, but I guess I was wrong."

"Well," the man said, "if it makes you feel better, the Service doesn't like me much either."

"You're a thief I suppose."

"A thief?" The man seemed incredulous. "A thief!? Of course not! I'm not a common thief. I've got a whole guild. That is, I'm a guild sponsor, a guild leader. Much more intimidating than being a simple thief, thank you very much." He smiled.

"Are you going to kill me?" Or hand me over?"

"No, I don't suppose I am. I mean, I could. But to be honest, I like you. And I don't much like having to kill people I like."

"Right," she mumbled. *Some logic that is.*

"What I want to know is why you are here."

She thought for a moment, then decided to tell the truth. "I'm hiding out. Or trying to. They'd have killed my family if I hadn't left."

"Left?"

"I'm from one of the hamlets."

"I see."

The man sighed, and the knife in his hand turned from weapon to theatrical prop. "Well, you've put me into a bit of an awkward situation. I've let you in our headquarters, and I can't let you run loose and get captured by the Service and give away where me and my guild are hiding out, you know?" His manner was easygoing again, as if he were trying to be nice.

"What are you saying?"

"I'm saying maybe you could hide out here with us." His fingers flourished the blade, making it disappear into a hidden sheath.

Adriane felt anger welling up, for no reason at all. "Stay? And what, trust your word? Trust that you won't sell me out?" *This wasn't part of the plan. No one was supposed to know about my magic.*

"Whoa, easy there." The man threw up his hands, startled by the outburst. "Only if you want to. And yes, you'll have to trust the word of a thief and a murderer, but I'm as human as you are, darling."

"It's Adriane."

"Yeah, that. Think about it, alright? Go back to that butcher's shop you're staying at and mull it over. Either way, I'm gonna be sending someone to tail you."

"Spy on me? Make sure I don't go running to the people trying to capture the both of us?"

He raised his hands in exasperated surrender. "No. To make sure you don't get jumped again."

"Oh."

He smiled at her. "You're great with people, aren't you?"

She frowned, suppressing her anger. *He's being nice*, she thought, *when he has absolutely no reason to be. No* right *to be.* "I'll think about it," she said. Then, forcing the words across, "thank you."

He grinned again, then turned to the doorway and shouted, "Jacob!"

A door opened and closed, and a tall, freckled boy in a dark coat entered the room.

"Adriane, this is Jacob. He'll be tailing you. Don't gut him with your knife. Please." He handed the hunting knife back to her as the youth raised an eyebrow. "I'm kidding," the man muttered. "If you decide you want to come, let me know. You can tell Jacob, or you can make your way back here. I'll make sure whoever's on guard lets you in."

Confused at his offer, but grateful nonetheless, Adriane gathered her coat and sheathed her knife. He held the door open for her, then strolled to the other room, rejoining his friends.

Adriane walked down the staircase and out of the building. Jacob followed silently a few steps behind her. Back in Abel Way she paused, noting that the Serviceman's body had been quietly disposed of. She supposed the man had sent someone to move it.

"I never asked for his name," she said to herself.

"Him?" Jacob said. "You don't know?"

Adriane looked up, startled. "No idea."

"His name is Lancaster. And he's the nicest crook this city's ever seen."

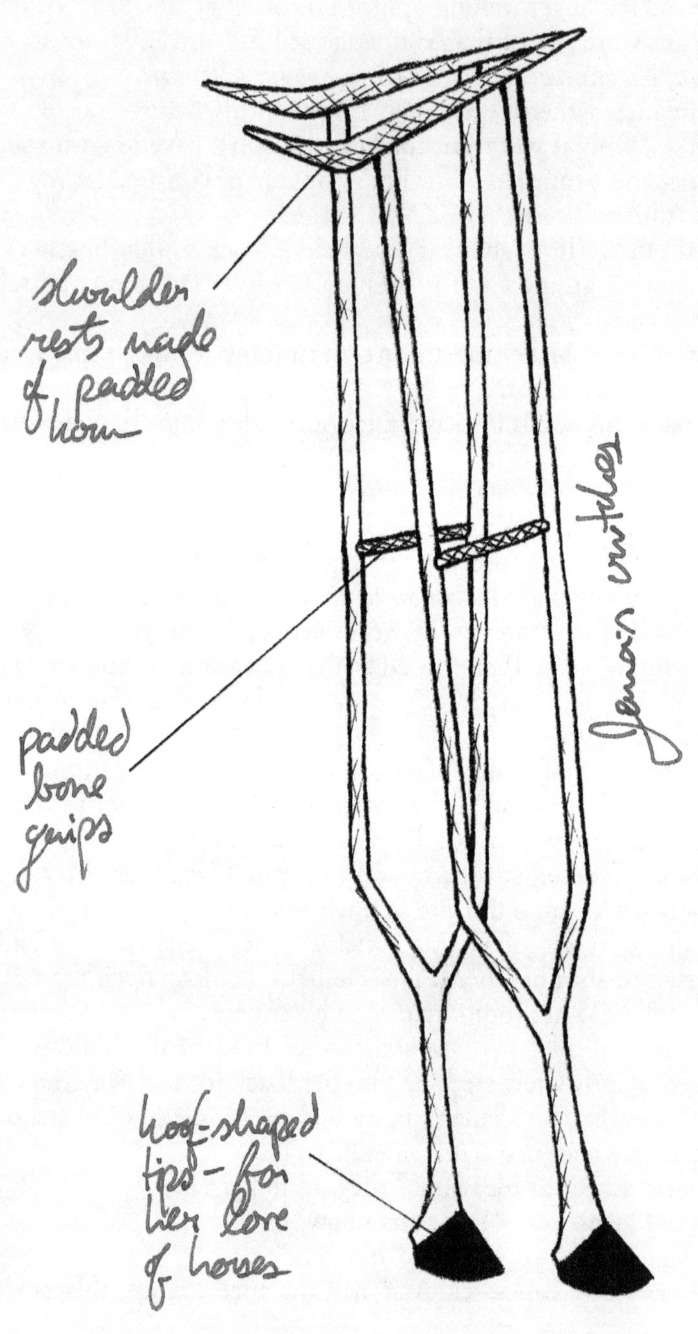

shoulder rests made of padded horn
padded bone grips
hoof-shaped tips - for her love of horses
Jenwin crutches

4

SOUTH AND EAST

Four Years and Eight Months Ago
Cain, in Arahill, Saint Brazen

"What do you think you're doing, Rise?" Daniel bellowed. Rise hadn't seen his brother this furious in years. "What's it to you? Doesn't matter."

"Doesn't matter? Doesn't matter? You've been running information to the Service, let alone the fact that you're running with a gang! Have you even thought about what would happen if Pa found out?"

"What he doesn't know carn't hurt him. And it's a *guild*, not a gang." Rise moved to close the heavy wooden shutters. In this part of Cain, neighbours might be used to hearing each other through the thin walls and unglazed windows, but if word got out that he worked for the Service now...

"You don't think this has consequences? Think for a moment, Rise." Daniel gripped him by the arms and shook him. "What happens if the Scroll Brotherhood finds out? You think they're gonna be happy you've been selling them out to the authorities?" He forced open Rise's left hand, revealing the gang's tattoo, a triangle with a curl coming out of one corner. "They didn't give you *that* for being some lowlife. You walk with them, eat with them, you even sound like them. They think you're one of them. They'll kill you if it comes to it."

"They don't matter, not compared to the Service."

"And what? The Service'll protect you?"

Rise smirked, pushing Daniel off. "Sure they will. One thing they know is how to take care of their investments. How do you think I got the money?" As it turned out, the ring he'd first stolen to prove himself and several other items the Brotherhood had their eyes on were magicked in some way. The Service paid well for that sort of information.

"Shade and flame!" Daniel swore. "Feeding our family with the Service's plaits is hardly better than starving."

"Maybe, but hardly better is still better," Rise said. "Better than losing Pa's farm. Better than being just another poor thief on the city streets. In case you'd forgotten, we wouldn't even have this place without the Service's shades-forsaken plaits. They're not so bad as you think."

"What, you think those bodies hang themselves off the walls? You think the Service doesn't take whatever it wants?"

"The Service does what needs to be done to keep order. I don't care if you see it otherwise." He turned to exit their apartment, but Daniel moved to block him.

"And what about her?"

"Lena? What about her?"

"You're doing all this for what—money and a girl?"

Rise scoffed, trying unsuccessfully to get past his older brother. "I'm doing it curse I carn. Doing it for myself." Daniel let him go, and he pushed past the door, hurrying down the dilapidated brick hallway beyond it.

"Be sure you are, Rise," Daniel yelled after him. "Cause once they have you they won't let you go."

⚬⚬⚬

Present Day

The next morning, Jenna slept in while Castor rose early to work for the innkeeper. After waking, she spent the morning relaxing in the inn's common room, reading and conversing with Hemsford's residents. Castor joined her for lunch, and after that, they packed their things and rode to the village shrine.

It had been Castor's suggestion to check the shrine. It was said the words written on shrines were messages from the Patrons themselves, messages specific to those who approached the shrine, trying to decide which Patron to pledge themselves to.

"The messages still appear to those who have already pledged themselves," Castor had said. "You never know—since it's a shrine we're seeking, maybe you can find help from another shrine." Jenna agreed they might as well try it.

Hemsford's shrine was situated in a small square a few blocks from the inn. It consisted of a simple pedestal and statue covered by a roof and surrounded by a low wicker fence with two openings. As Jenna and Castor approached, people moved away, no doubt thinking they were looking for a Patron. Castor stopped his horse at the wicker fence, and Jenna dismounted, entering the shrine alone.

She hobbled towards the statue, which was carved into the shape of a man wearing a flowing hooded cloak and carrying a lute—the shrine was pledged to the Monk. The stone plinth the statue rested on held a carved inscription. As she approached, the letters blurred, rearranging themselves.

Patron inscriptions were carved into the stone by carriers of a specific type of transformational magic. The magic allowed the letters they carved to shift depending on who was reading them.

The messages only worked for one person at a time. Had Castor entered the shrine with Jenna, the stone would have read its original inscription, most likely a Tale or legend about the Patron. Since Jenna alone had entered, however, the statue would deliver a message meant only for her. Scholars didn't agree on how this worked, but it was generally held that the words were meant to help people pledge themselves. They were words of wisdom, words of guidance.

Jenna also knew the inscriptions could be imprecise. Since they depended on the person approaching the shrine, they were only as defined as the seeker. After all, if you didn't know yourself, how could the magic perceive enough of your character and your goals to know what to write?

As for the words being Patron-inspired, she didn't know. They could be, considering the strength of the magic. It had been honed for centuries, cultivated by a small group of House Kyra–Bendekan's object mages. But then again, many of the Patrons had been dead for centuries as well, with only Tales remaining. Those who weren't said to be part of the Markois anyway. Could any magic, even an ancient and powerful one, know the minds of the dead?

Jenna shook herself from her thoughts and bent to read the words that formed on the plinth.

> The way of peace lies to the south.
> The way of war lies to the east.
> Your way of peace is the way of war.

She gazed up at the hooded figure, wishing the Monk—or whoever decided on the words—could be more specific. "I know I haven't exactly been myself lately," she muttered, "but some more clarity would've been nice." Still, it wasn't as cryptic as some inscriptions she had come across in her research.

Jenna returned to Castor and mounted Silverphile.

"So? What did it say?"

Jenna repeated the words for him. "It does sound like it's saying we're on the right track. I mean, south and east—that's where we're heading to find the shrine."

"That war bit though." Castor looked worried. "War to the east sounds a bit too much like the Republic to me."

"There's always something going on with the Republic. It's not like we can do much about it."

"I suppose not. And it did mention peace. Peace is good."

"Peace and war," Jenna mused. "Or maybe peace through war? Or war because of peace? I don't know. We don't have enough information to be able to interpret it."

"Either way, we know where to go. Let's take it as a good sign."

With that, Jenna agreed. They turned their horses and rode onto the East Way, a major highway that went right through the heart of the town. It would turn south and east once they passed Hemsford's borders. Towards the shrine, hopefully. And towards who knew what else.

Tobin rode silently for the first shift, happy to watch the sunlight creep over the rolling terrain and listen to the steady rattle of the horses and carriages behind him. Runie stayed with him for a half-shift, before moving to the back of the column. The other riders changed positions occasionally but mostly stayed in order.

Once they left Silas' Hill and the hamlets surrounding the city, all signs of civilization ceased, save for the road and the few statues and shrines stationed along it. They didn't stop, since the Republicans didn't care for any of the Patrons, but Tobin looked at each chiseled figure as they passed—Silas, Denia of the Heartwings, Martin the Guide. There was a tiny shrine dedicated to a minor Patron he didn't know, and he scribbled a note on a scrap of paper; he'd look it up once they reached the next city.

When Timothy came to relieve him after noon, Tobin rode back to their supply wagon, tied his horse to it, and lay down atop of a barrel of water and several parcels of dried meat. It wasn't the most comfortable bed in the world, but he was tired enough from waking early that he fell asleep anyway.

He woke up to someone rustling through the wagon's contents. Tobin blinked groggily, uncertain where he was for a moment, before remembering. *On a mission*, he thought with a smile, before stretching and sitting up.

He'd assumed one of his squad was rummaging through the wagon, but instead, he found a young woman dressed in a burgundy riding skirt and a light grey blouse—the clothing gave her away as one of the Republicans. They were the only people mad enough to have women ride in skirts. He cleared his throat, and she jumped.

"Anything I can help you with?"

"I didn't see you there, sir. Please, is there any place I might find some wine? Lady Kesma is tired of drinking water, and she told me not to return to her side until I found something more suitable for her to drink."

Tobin raised an eyebrow. He'd dealt with nobles all his life, but the Republican sort had always seemed a bit off to him. *Not that there aren't any rotten apples among the Ideians.*

"We're not carrying any wine," he said. "The water's all spelled clean, so your mistress needn't worry about it being unsafe to drink."

The young woman twitched at the word 'spelled.' "I think that's precisely why she wants some wine. I don't dare tell her there isn't any."

"Here." Tobin clambered out of the wagon and re-mounted his horse. "Why don't I come with you to tell her. Can't be all that bad coming from a squadleader."

The young woman eyed him. "I guess we can try." She remounted her own horse, and Tobin followed her to a small cluster of riders at the back of the column.

Judging by the sun's position, he'd slept well into the afternoon, but that was alright. He wasn't on duty until the evening. The young woman nodded discreetly towards the group, and Tobin was about to ask which one of the riders was her mistress, when his jaw dropped.

Only one of the riders was a woman, and she was about as beautiful as they came. She had pale skin the like of which was rare in Ideon, blue eyes much lighter than any he'd ever seen before, and black hair with a few reddish strands twisting through it. He'd have guessed she was a few years older than him. Tobin tried calling a greeting but found he had to clear his suddenly-dry throat before any sound would come through it.

"Good afternoon," he finally stammered, annoyed at how flustered he felt.

The riders—all five of them diplomats by the quality of their attire—turned to face him. Annoyance flickered across the lady's face at the interruption.

"What is it?" The man who spoke had an arrogant sort of voice, a voice that commanded respect.

I'm in charge here, Tobin thought, trying to feel confident. He introduced himself as one of the squadleaders and gestured at the young woman who'd brought him. "I understand you sent for something besides water," he told Lady Kesma, trying not to wither under the intense gaze she directed his way.

"You understand correctly, and yet you're here without anything else to drink." Her voice was as beautiful as the rest of her, but harsh too. Unyielding.

"Er, yes." Tobin swallowed. "Unfortunately, our supplies are limited to water until we reach the next village."

She kept her eyes locked on him for a moment, before turning back to her companions with an air of indifference. "I see."

"I told you it's barbaric here," one of the young men said, dragging his horse's reins to the side with a derisive gesture.

Tobin winced at that; the horse masters back in Silas' Hill would have had them running punishments for hours if they treated one of their horses that harshly. He knew he shouldn't respond to the taunt, but he couldn't help himself.

"It's not barbaric at all," he said, wishing Spiffy stood as tall as the diplomats' horses. "We spell our water clean, so there's no risk of catching disease from it. It's more than you can do, I'm sure."

"Whatever." The young man jerked his horse away, followed by the other men. To Tobin's surprise, Lady Kesma stayed, her lady-in-waiting hovering behind her.

"You do this with all your water here?" she asked, her tone neutral.

"Sure." Tobin felt heat creep into his face. "There's a type of transformational magic that can do away with disease."

"Transformational magic." Lady Kesma said the words as if unsure what to do with them.

Tobin wasn't supposed to reveal too much about Ideon's mages to any of the foreigners, but he thought a bit about disease-reducing magic could hardly be dangerous information. "The magic turns soiled things clean, if they aren't too bad," he said. "It's not perfect, but Bendekan knows it's better than dealing with epidemics from bad food or drink."

Lady Kesma's face twitched when he mentioned Bendekan, but she remained impassive otherwise. *They don't have Patrons there*, Tobin chastised himself. *You're not gonna keep her interest by talking about them.*

"Is there any other magic that can—" she began, before a shout interrupted her.

"Tobin!"

Tobin nearly dropped his reins in surprise. He glanced back at Lady Kesma, only to see her riding back to the other Republicans. *And here I thought that was going well.* Tobin shook his head and spurred Spiffy forwards.

"What is it?" He looked for the person who had called and found Era, one of his squadmates, riding towards him.

"Runie needs you at the front. Now." Era swallowed. "You'll want to see for yourself."

Tobin guided Spiffy to the edge of the road where the way was clear and cantered towards the front of the column. He could tell something was wrong as soon as he got ahead of the wagons—smoke was curling up in the distance. He'd been too distracted to notice it.

He spotted Runie further up the road, on the lip of a small hill, and urged Spiffy towards her. "What's going on?"

Runie's mouth was set in a grim line. "See for yourself, Tobin."

She gestured down the hill, and Tobin turned to look. The land opened up into wide, sprawling plains, and the trees that had dotted the hills they'd been riding through receded. The smoke he'd seen was swirling in the distance, concentrated around a spot several miles down the road. Tobin thought he could see walls and buildings through the smog.

"Is that—"

"Yes." Runie scowled. "That would be Martin's Grace, the town we were to stop in for the night. It looks like we've found those bandits Elder Iram mentioned."

As they left the town, Jenna cast out her senses, letting her magic pick up on nearby sources of energy without trying to block it all out. The green of fields and forest occasionally flashed purple, but the energy didn't consume her, didn't rush inside her and then try to force its way out. The only close call came when they passed a butcher's shop. The building was brimming with residual energy, but Jenna managed to keep her magic under control by focusing, then releasing the energy as soul tendrils from her hands, much like she'd done in the stable.

"Well, it's working so far," she told Castor when they'd gone a few miles without any incidents. "I've noticed the energy, but it hasn't sparked out of control, not even when the energy came from death."

"You know, if you were a regular mage, they'd say it'd be quite practical, drawing your magic from death and destruction. There's plenty of that around no matter where you go."

Jenna frowned. "I guess so. But it doesn't exactly make for a pleasant experience, knowing whenever something dies around you."

They kept straight on the East Way, entering the northern reaches of the Monkswood, a large forest that covered much of southern House Silas' Hill and reached all the way down to Connac's Garden and Weathslayer's Grave. It was thick and twisted, full of thorn bushes, lush trees that shone in the late summer sunlight, and rough boulders, logs, and roots that rose through the forest floor. It was, in a word, massive, and in a second, beautiful. It reminded Jenna of home.

They rode for the remainder of the day, before camping in a sheltered clearing. Waking late, they set out well after sunrise in companionable silence.

Suddenly, Castor jerked up straight, nose twitching. "Do you smell that?"

Jenna turned, surprised. "Smell what?"

Castor sniffed the air. "Something dead." He grimaced, pointed teeth flashing. "Do you sense anything, Jenna?"

"I—yes, there's something…" Jenna could feel a distant sort of energy emanating from a spot further down the road and off to the side, just out of her range. She spurred Silverphile towards it, Castor following. "I think—" Like a floodgate being drawn back, a rush of energy hit her like a physical blow.

"Jenna!"

She reeled in her saddle as white and purple spikes of magic shot out from her hands and feet, narrowly missing her mare, leaping up into the air like sparks.

"Jenna—Jenna are you alright?" Castor rushed to her side.

A shout burst from her lips, and she felt herself crumpling sideways, held up only by the straps that tied her legs to her horse. She could see the trees still, but a face appeared within them, hemmed in by leaves and roots and withered bark, blending into the mottled purple and gray foliage ahead of her.

It was an ageless face, so withered it seemed hardly a face at all. It was carved along the same lines as the craggy trunks of the trees, and neither mouth nor nose were apparent in its features. The only thing that convinced Jenna that what she was seeing was indeed a face, were the eyes. They shone out bold and yellow, as if in defiance of the strange quirk that made her see in shades of purple whenever her magic activated. They glinted intelligently. Then they were gone, and Jenna realized she was still half out of her saddle, bent awkwardly, and gaping at an empty tree line full of leaves, plants, and forest-scape, but lacking a face of any kind.

"Did you see that? The face?"

Castor pulled her back up into her saddle. "See what? What happened?"

Jenna shuddered. "That was more energy than I've ever felt before. And that face in the trees—"

"What face, Jenna?"

She breathed deeply, trying to calm down. "I saw something, right after my magic exploded. A face made of bark, with bright yellow eyes." She didn't know why, but she felt she should've recognized it.

Castor paused. "Like... a forest guardian?"

Jenna's eyebrows rose. "Exactly like that. Like the Tales describe them anyway."

"But what set off your magic?"

"I don't know."

"Let me find out." Castor wheeled his horse around. "I told you I smelled something dead, but it doesn't smell... right. I don't know." He turned down the road, nostrils flaring.

"The energy came from beyond the road, over there." Jenna pointed, and Castor disappeared into the forest, following her direction.

Jenna waited for a few minutes before nudging Silverphile forward. "Castor?"

He emerged from the bushes, face pale. "There's a man there. A body."

"Let me see." Jenna turned Silverphile, but Castor's arm blocked her path.

"I'm not sure you want to."

"I'm not squeamish. I'll be fine. Show me."

Castor nodded and led her through the trees. She noticed the smell then, the metallic scent of blood and the stench of rotten meat. Castor had pulled his shirt over his nose; she couldn't imagine how awful it must smell with his amplified senses.

"Here," Castor said. He dismounted by a fallen log, which he nudged to the side.

For a second, Jenna didn't see a thing. Then, she noticed a face staring out from beneath the log, eyes crawling with maggots. She followed the face to a neck, which led to a torso, bloodied and half-buried in loamy earth. Jenna swayed in her saddle, suddenly nauseous. Somehow the smell seemed a thousand times worse now that she saw where it was coming from—not from a slaughtered animal or a rotting heap of garbage, but from a man.

"How…" She had to swallow before being able to continue. "How did he die? Can you tell?"

"I'm not sure," Castor said gently. "But I can tell it wasn't an accident. See this?" He pointed to tattered remnants of skin on the man's back. "That's a whip mark. But it burned him where it hit." He pointed to black and white streaks mixed in among the whip marks. "I've never seen a whip burn like that before."

"What do we do?"

"Head back to the road, Jenna. I'll—I'll search his body and see if I can find out who he is. We'll tell the elders in the next village. They'll know what to do."

Jenna nodded, then complied. She waited anxiously for Castor, who joined her after a few minutes, wiping bloodied hands on a rag.

"Found anything?"

Castor passed her a cloth satchel, which she opened, revealing a pendant on a ruddy cord, worked in bronze and molded into the shape of a maple leaf. It was a common design—many Ideians wore jewelry that connected to their Houses, and the maple leaf was associated with House Weathslayer's Grave. The satchel also contained a simple silver wedding band and a slit purse which had been emptied.

"Looks to me like he was a traveller who got murdered for his money," Castor said, "though the pendant and ring don't look rich enough to warrant him having much."

"The wedding ring could help someone identify him though," Jenna said. "I'd hate it if no one knew who he was."

"I'm sure the elders will know." Castor reached over to take her hand. "They'll find whoever was responsible."

They continued down the road, but the forest seemed somehow less beautiful now. Jenna had grown up around nature, had always enjoyed the outdoors and riding, but suddenly the trees' shadows seemed to slink together and leer at her. She recalled the face she'd seen in the trees and shuddered. The way it had appeared right as they'd found the dead man… *Was it connected to my magic somehow? Or to the man's death?*

Though she knew the vast expanse of verdant shadows would not harm her, especially not with Castor by her side, she still nudged Silverphile closer to Castor's tall gelding so she could keep holding his hand. Riding this close to him, she could see his dark, human-shaped nose quivering. She was glad his senses were Kane-inherited. If there was danger ahead, he'd sense it coming.

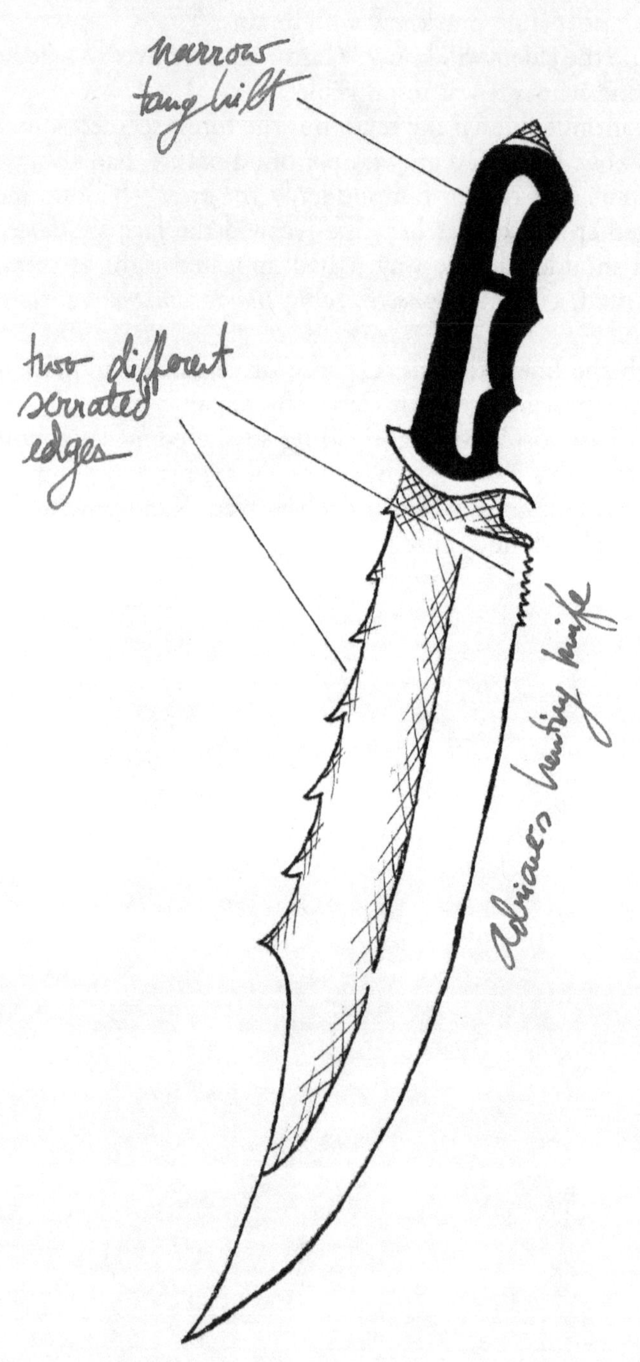

narrow
tang hilt
two different
serrated
edges
Adriana's hunting knife

5

THE ABRAHAM GUILD

Four Years Ago
Wrovetown, in Arahill, Saint Brazen

Imp crumpled, opened, and re-crumpled the paper slip in his hand. He had memorized the words on it and now repeated them to himself as he ran.

He passed the houses of the East Quarter, heading towards the Wine Quarter, which lay directly opposite. It was an area he rarely visited since it housed the Service's headquarters. He was headed there now.

He didn't see how he had a choice.

The Service hadn't known he and Uncle Bento had moved into the Chisel after the fire had gutted the building. They'd been doing alright, living off the money Uncle Bento made telling stories in the square. He'd cared for Imp, shown him how to scavenge for food and steer clear of the guards. They'd been a team. But no matter how often Uncle Bento had cautioned against it, Imp continued to set fires.

Then the Servicemen had shown up at their doors, looking for him. They'd seen him set a fire, then followed him home. *At least they didn't see the lights*, Imp thought. *If they'd seen what I see in the flames they'd hang me off the walls instead of askin' me to help.* That was something at least.

Uncle Bento had said Imp needed to make his own decision, whatever that meant. He hadn't stopped the Servicemen. How could he have? *He'd have found a way*, Imp thought angrily. *He always knows something, some way to get out.* Why hadn't he saved Imp this time? *Dunno if I even need saving.* The Servicemen hadn't come by to kill him or take him in. It was better than that.

Imp skidded to a halt once he reached the low brick building that served double duty as Wrovetown's Service and Standard Force headquarters. The Service didn't like having to share it, he knew, but Wrovetown wasn't big enough to warrant separate buildings for the authorities. *They're one and the same in a way. Except the Service is offerin'.*

Imp glanced up at the bricks, gulped a breath in for courage, and ducked inside the main entryway. The two guards at the front, both Service and Standard Force, sneered at his dishevelled appearance but let him in without further delay.

"Peter Berahsson is it?" One of the Servicemen who'd paid him a visit stood in the main atrium, hair as black as his immaculate coat, boots so polished Imp reckoned he could use them as a mirror.

"Yeah," he said. *Stay calm.*

"So, what'll it be. Come to accept the governor's most generous offer, I expect?"

Imp licked his lips. He knew what would happen if he said no. *I'll get my arm cut off for fire-setting, if they don't leave my body rotting in an alley somewhere.* He wasn't sure which would be worse. "I am."

"Thought you might, thought you might." The Serviceman gestured to a door that lay off to the side. "Right this way then, Peter. My name's Nero. I'll take care of you from here."

Imp followed the man, heart thumping in his throat. He looked down at the paper in his hand one last time, before tearing it in half and stuffing it in his grubby pocket.

Peter Berahsson, the paper read. *Service Headquarters, Greatroad in Wrovetown. Noon appointment.* The paper was delicate, and the handwriting swirled across it in fancy loops.

Imp put on a grin full of a confidence he didn't feel. *This is what it's come to. Can't be worse than scroungin' for scraps on the street.* As long as they didn't find out about what he really was.

⸎

Present Day

After returning to the butcher's shop, Adriane lay in bed, awake. Lancaster had assured her that Jacob would watch the shop that night, ensuring no Servicemembers were near, but still, she couldn't sleep. Instead, she contemplated his offer. In the end, she knew she would have to accept his proposal. It posed a risk, especially since trust was involved, but it seemed better than her other options. She would be hidden, and her family would be safe—uninvolved in whatever chase the Service was hoping to pursue. Even if Lancaster did know about her magic.

Adriane frowned. *That can't be helped now.*

When the dim, gray light of dawn filtered through the wooden shutters covering her bedroom window, Adriane got up, tidied the room, and picked up her bag. After a quick meal, she said goodbye to Henderson. Although he was surprised to see her leave so abruptly, he seemed to understand her desire for secrecy.

Stepping outside the shop, her bag on her back, Adriane looked to the building's street-cast shadow where a dark figure detached itself from the wall. *Jacob.*

He poked his head into the dim sunlight. "Made up your mind, I guess? Leaving? Or coming with me?"

"I'm coming."

"Righ' this way."

She glanced at their surroundings, wanting to make sure no more Servicemen lay in wait to follow them.

"Don't worry," Jacob said. "They sent another Serviceman to watch the place, but he got mysteriously doused in horsemanure." He grinned impishly, revealing several knocked-out teeth. "It's safe to go."

Jacob set off at a job, and Adriane followed him through the maze of streets. No telling if she could've found her way back by herself. Cain's Poors Quarter was a rat's den, a hopelessly zigzagging run of dingy streets and alleys twisting across each other.

They turned and wove their way about. People. Horses. Dung and grit. Shops. Smells: frying meats, fresh bread, reeking heaps of refuse, steam.

They reached Emboss Street, turning where a gold-filigree worker had laid out his tools. Next was a right onto Kerabant Street and then two lefts in quick succession. Adriane lost herself in the maze, focusing on her feet and Jacob's gray-coated back leading the way. Her thoughts kept jumping around, but she let none of the nervousness show on her face. They continued for half an hour, sometimes walking, sometimes running, ducking into an alley once to avoid a black-coated stranger with that same slashing blue-eyed mark. Back and forth they trod through alleyways until they reached the familiar snake of muddied cobblestone marked Abel Way.

"Here we go," Jacob said. "We'll take the regular entrance this time.

Well, one of them anyways."

He led her down the lane, past the door that led to the ground-level inn. Sounds were coming from beyond it, and she guessed the inn was a front to hide whatever Lancaster and his guild did upstairs. They approached a rickety wooden staircase that sat recessed in one of the gray building's many niches. The stairs led to a door set into an arch of crumbling concrete, reinforced with wooden beams. The steps didn't creak, and the door turned on well-oiled hinges as they entered.

"So—"

A bolt of adrenaline shot through her before she recognized the voice as Lancaster's.

He stepped out of a niche in the wall. "Seems you made the right decision. And a good thing too—otherwise I'd have gathered my little guild together for nothing."

He smiled at her, and a shiver traced down her spine, whether from fear or anticipation, she couldn't tell.

"Follow me," he said.

The hallway was dark and smelled of dust and rust, as rundown as the rest of Lancaster's place seemed, on the surface at least. As always, Adriane's eyes were wide and alert, observing what detail she could.

Lancaster led the two of them to the wooden door which had hidden the voices and light on her last visit. Once again, light blazed from the cracks in the doorway, and a murmur of strange voices assaulted her ears in a wild cacophony. Lancaster entered without knocking.

"Hey, Sponsor's back," a voice yelled.

"Lancaster, we've just been thinking, if the Hobiars—"

"—and curse we can upturn the whole dish, I say, but—"

The voices washed over Adriane as she slunk to the open door. She counted twenty-one people sitting, standing, talking, walking, eating, and drinking in the room before her. Most were clumped together in twos and threes, but two larger groups gathered around tables with dice and cards. Many shouted greetings to Lancaster or raised tankards in his general direction as he entered, but there were a few loners too, watching from the room's edges, sticking to the shadows like Adriane herself preferred.

Jacob nudged her from behind, and she entered, stepping into the light.

The room itself was large and roughly square, with various nooks and crannies, hallways and doors opening up on all sides. A counter was set into the floor on the right, heavy wood bedecked with earthenware bowls and cups. Many of the cups were filled with drink, and several pitchers of the same were scattered throughout the room. All manner of chairs, tables, and stools filled the rest of the floor.

The air was refreshingly clean after the dingy hallway, and the space well-lit by a beautiful chandelier set into the sloping roof. Carved of complementary shades of wood laminated together, it depicted all manner of creatures straight from legend. An imp writhed in a wooden tongue of flame, carved into a light piece of pine, juxtaposed with a dark depiction of a stone sprite. A half-human half-cat creature stalked its way across a sanded piece of red oak, while a wooden mask floated behind it.

"Like the chandelier?" Lancaster said. "My grandfather made it, crazy man. All that lovely rubbish about dancing spirit creatures or something."

"Like the shades."

"Yeah, those. So…" Lancaster nodded towards the room. "You ready to meet these fools, or are you going to spend all evening critiquing my décor?"

Adriane grimaced, eyes seeking out the people, looking at their faces and necks, shoulders, arms, legs, wondering how many of them she would be required to meet.

"I'm ready." She glanced wistfully back at the door, then followed Lancaster to the first table, where two women—one young and one old—sat, drinking mead from clay cups. Adriane could've spotted many of the room's occupants as thieves and crooks from far off, but the two women were part of the few who didn't quite fit the mold.

The older woman wore an unremarkable hat and a coat of indistinguishable colour. Her feet, which stuck out of a wide wool skirt, were booted in soft leather, the kind that made no noise on cobbles and could be worn comfortably for hours on end. She was hunched over so her face was hidden, but Adriane could see her eyes darting across the room, observing everyone. Her gaze landed on Adriane as she and Lancaster approached the table. The look she gave her was sharp as a knife, and Adriane's mouth felt suddenly dry.

"Evening Mistress Brewer. Mia," Lancaster drawled.

The older woman bobbed her head in greeting, and the younger woman beside her looked up from her cup. Though their faces were different, their matching black hair and dark eyes gave the immediate impression the two were related.

"Might I introduce you to Adriane?" Lancaster beckoned her forwards. "Just want to make sure you don't slit her throat when either of you's on watch."

The younger woman smirked. "Curse I wouldn't dream of it, a beauty like her." She turned to Adriane. "I'm Mia. This here's my aunt. Everybody calls her Mistress Brewer."

Adriane nodded, refusing to meet her eyes. Instead, she focused on Mia's clothes: a dark shirt and loose breeches that failed to obscure her beautiful figure, leather boots like her aunt's, thin lines standing out against her arms—knife sheaths more like than not.

"Observant but not talkative," Mia said drily. "I like you already."

Adriane reddened and looked up. "Just quiet."

"That's okay. Most folks here are." Mia nodded towards one of the rowdier tables that hosted a dice game. "Except when drink's involved, of course."

"Can't judge a thief as likes a good reward at the end of his day," Lancaster put in with a quick glance to the side. "Or at the end of *her* day—not that I'm making distinctions." He flashed a grin at Mia, who rolled her eyes.

"Here, I'll introduce you to the lot," Mia said, turning to Adriane. "Seems Lancaster is pining after his good reward."

"Hey now, I didn't mean—" Lancaster began, but Mia had already grabbed Adriane by the arm and dragged her over to another table.

"What was that all about?"

Mia raised an eyebrow. "Did you see how he was looking at you?"

"Looking at me?"

"No you didn't, did you," Mia muttered. "Never mind. Here, have you met anyone else yet?"

Adriane pointed out Jacob, who was sitting with Gera, the woman who'd tended to her cut, and a man with only one arm. Mia whisked her over and tactfully inserted herself into the conversation—they were arguing about the right way to poison a guard on duty, and Mia had a great deal to say on the subject. She introduced Adriane while she was at it, teased Jacob about the scruffiness of his hair, and told Gera about a cartload of herbs that was due to come in the next week.

She's good, Adriane thought with a touch of admiration. *Fits in perfectly*.

As the evening progressed, Mia steered Adriane from table to table with an expert hand, making introductions and exchanging jokes and stories with the other members of the Guild. Two of the younger men at one of the dice tables—brutes or killers by the looks of their muscles and the knife-scars on their arms—puffed up as Mia approached and spent the time she sat at their table each trying to outdo the other with boasts about their exploits. Mia all but ignored them.

When they'd completed their circuit of the room, finishing at the counter where a richly clad young man introduced himself as Terrasin Berrar and offered them a drink, Adriane's brain was rattling with names and faces she doubted she'd remember. Mia led her back to Mistress Brewer's table where Lancaster sat.

"That wasn't so bad now, was it?" Mia said.

Adriane shook her head, more in an attempt to stay focused than in agreement. She was feeling the lack of sleep.

"Adriane?" Mia sounded concerned, and Adriane realized she had stopped walking.

"I'm tired. Sorry."

Lancaster all but jumped up from the table and sauntered towards them. "Couldn't help but overhear your predicament. Allow me to show you to your room." He gestured towards a narrow hallway that ran out next to the counter.

Adriane took a step towards it but stumbled on a discarded cup. Lancaster caught her up in his arms before she could growl a protest.

"Typical," Mia muttered, disgusted. "If he tries anything stupid, I'll gut him for you," she told Adriane before heading back to her aunt.

Lancaster went down the hall and through a door and then deposited her gently on a cot in a simple bedroom. She was too tired to complain any further.

"Lancaster?" she asked, instead.

"Now, don't ask me to stay. It'll take a few more visits before we can get to that stage," he joked, throwing a blanket onto her head.

"Your... guild." She pulled the blanket away from her face. Fear clamored at the back of her mind, but there was something else there too. Her heart beat faster when she looked at him. "They can be trusted? I'll be safe here?"

"My people?" He sat on a corner of the bed. "Not really. Not as far as your magic is concerned anyway. What do you expect from a thieves' guild? As for myself, however, that's a different matter entirely. You'll be safe here, and you can trust me, darling."

"Can I?" The thought escaped out loud before she could rein in her tongue.

Lancaster grinned and handed her a brass hairpin with strange wire swirls at one end. "That's the key for the door lock. It's not your regular tumbler lock either—most wouldn't know how to pick it. The floorboards outside creak, so you can hear anyone coming, and if you lift the mattress, you'll find a trapdoor that leads outside. If you still don't feel safe, just let me know, and I'll figure out a solution, darling." He pulled the blanket teasingly over her head again before stepping out of the room. She could hear him whistling in time to the floorboards creaking as he walked down the hallway.

"It's Adriane," she said, her voice muffled by a fold of soft cloth.

Jenna and Castor rode the rest of the day in relative quiet. They reached Stillbrook, a small village situated in a series of clearings, late that evening and decided to stay the night. Their original plan had been to ride further that day and camp in the woods, but Jenna admitted to Castor she'd be glad to sleep surrounded by walls and a roof after the day's events, and he agreed.

As they entered the motely collection of small buildings that flanked the road and a gurgling stream, Castor dismounted.

"Right. I think I'll approach the elders right away and inform them of what we saw." He nodded towards a small cottage that had a banner planted in front of it—a beehive-shaped tomb on a purple background, the coat-of-arms of Silas' Hill. The banner denoted the residence of one of Stillbrook's elders.

As Castor turned towards the cabin, Jenna continued down the road until a farmer called out a greeting to her. She exchanged pleasantries with the woman, who informed her that Stillbrook was too small to boast even a tavern but offered the two of them her barn in which to stay the night. Jenna accepted, thankful, and followed the woman to a sturdy wooden barn at the village's edge. Castor found his way there shortly after.

"He's not one of theirs," Castor told Jenna. "I told them where we found the body, and some of the men went out to get it. The deathsayer is preparing his rituals, so at least the man'll get a proper burial."

They went to bed soon after Castor returned, but it was a long while before Jenna slept, and when she did, it was a restless, uncomfortable sort of sleep. They rose early the next morning as if by some silent agreement, wanting to put some distance between themselves and the murdered man they had discovered.

Another day's ride brought them to Hartglen, a good-sized village which boasted both a tavern and a small shrine to Fate's Hand, another one of Ideon's minor Patrons. Here, Castor once again asked after the unidentified man, and this time he got a name.

"Michael Grassman. He's a farmer from Weathslayer's Grave who moved to the area recently," Castor explained when he returned.

"Does he have a family?"

Castor nodded. "His wife died some time ago, they said, but he has a daughter named Zenia who lived here with him, as well as a son who's training up in Silas' Hill." Castor's face darkened. "No one's seen the daughter, Jenna. Last they heard, she'd been with him. Apparently, they were heading to Renforth, seeking an apprenticeship at the Tower for her."

A difference of a few weeks and I might've met her, Jenna thought. "That's awful. No one knows where she is? I wonder if she knows about what happened to her father."

"I don't know." Castor put his arm around Jenna. "There's something else."

"Good news?" Jenna asked before seeing Castor's face. "Oh. More bad news."

Castor nodded. "The elders weren't as concerned about the man as I thought they would be. I asked them about it, and they said they had a bigger problem. One of their trappers had seen a party out in the woods. Could be nothing, of course, but the trapper said he thought he saw a Service brand on one of them."

"Border raids? But—there's been a fresh exchange of diplomats."

"No one's saying it's a raid yet. But you've heard the talk in some of the villages. Things don't sound so good. Everyone's on edge."

"Let's hope it's nothing then," Jenna said. "It could be a party of hunters, or some of Bendekan's Bastions border patrol."

"It could be." Castor didn't sound too sure.

"Any other news you picked up from the elders?"

"Actually yes, I almost forgot. One of the elders here is a mage. A soul and aether elemental, though he draws energy from his body instead of from nature. He's invited you to come see him tomorrow. Said maybe he could try to help."

"That's brilliant." Jenna smiled for what seemed like the first time in weeks. "I was beginning to think it was all bad news today."

"There's always something good if you look hard enough. Most of the time, anyway."

They spent that night in another barn, and Jenna found she felt much better about the last few days now that she had something good to look forward to. Her magic hadn't sparked out of control either, since the dead man anyway, and though she occasionally felt flashes of energy around her, she was able to control herself. Even sleep came easier that night, and Jenna drifted off within minutes of lying down. She dreamed of riding through a beautiful forest with Castor. The only thing amiss was a craggy face that appeared in the dream's background, its yellow eyes glinting with some unfathomable emotion.

⸺ ⧜ ⸺

"So," Lancaster said, "I think it's time I find you something to do around here."

Adriane had spent a day cooped up in her room, alone with her thoughts, until Lancaster brought her back into the common area.

"You know, you can come out anytime you like, darling." He smiled. "We don't bite—well, most of us anyway. You probably shouldn't come along on raids just yet, but I figure it'll get boring if you just sit around all day. So, what are you good at?"

"I can trap and hunt," Adriane said, before remembering that wouldn't be much help in a city. "And I'm a right hand at skinning and butchering. I can read, too."

Lancaster raised his eyebrows. "She reads," he said to Mia, who was just walking over from the neighbouring table.

"Finally!" Mia said. "Trying to talk to anyone here about books is about as hopeless as getting locked in a Service dungeon."

"Hey—" Lancaster began.

"Okay, fine, you're not bad. But sometimes talking to a man just doesn't cut it."

"Well," Lancaster said, puffed up with a mocking display of wounded pride, "in that case, I'll let you two sort out your schedule without my help." He got up to leave. "Oh, and have Jacob teach her how to handle that knife of hers."

"I can handle myself just fine," Adriane called after him, but he simply waved with a flourish and left. "Is he always like that?"

Mia laughed. "He's worse around you."

Chairs scraped across the floor, and Adriane jumped at the noise. The other guild members headed out, following Lancaster's lead. Some carried weapons while others were outfitted with steel contraptions that looked uncomfortably like her hunting traps.

"Where are they going?"

Mia tipped her head towards one of the shuttered windows. "It's dark out. Safest time to take out a few Servicemen."

Is that a joke?

"You said you carn skin and butcher, right?"

Adriane nodded.

"You'll forgive me for asking, but is that limited to animals, or can you…?" Mia stopped, seeing the look on Adriane's face. "Ooo-kay. Sorry, just needed to clear that up. Anyway, you carn help butcher the chickens for tonight's stew. Well, the morning's stew technically, since dinner's in the morning… it's all a bit confusing, but you'll get used to the backwards schedule. For now, come with me."

"Are we following the others?"

"Not tonight. Lancaster said you're in trouble with the Service, so there's no way you're going anywhere near their headquarters."

Adriane fought to keep her expression neutral. How much had Lancaster said? Then she realized the other meaning behind Mia's words. "You don't mean—they're really going to kill Servicemen tonight?"

"Shades willing. Servicemen are a right plague, and though we're on good enough terms with the Guild of Blades and the Scroll Brotherhood, neither they nor the other guilds want to play exterminator. Lancaster's taken it on himself to clear the streets when he carn, as long as Lukhas Bladeeye—that's the thief king—allows him to."

"And if he puts a stop to it?" Adriane asked, curious.

Mia shrugged. "My guess is Lancaster will still find a way."

Adriane followed Mia out of the common room and down another hallway. Suddenly, something struck her side. She reeled to keep on her feet as someone crashed to the ground beside her.

Mia spun, twin knives appearing in her hands. "What the—oh. Hello, Jacob." She rolled her eyes skywards and sheathed the blades in her sleeves. "Good thing I'm the one who'll be teaching the silent movement lessons."

Adriane gave the boy a hand up, and he blushed. "Thanks. Sorry, I didn't mean to walk into you."

They went on, Jacob following. "Sleep okay?" he asked Adriane as they walked past her bedroom and down a flight of stairs.

She shrugged.

"Still got your knife?"

She reached for the boot-liner, but her hand closed on empty air. "What in the shades—"

Jacob grinned with a decent imitation of Lancaster's infuriating smile and drew her hunting knife from his sleeve.

Mia sighed at him without turning around. "Give the knife back," she commanded, which Jacob did. "Sorry, Adriane. He's been insufferable ever since Lancaster taught him that trick. Anyway, here we are."

Mia opened a heavyset wooden door that was covered with an intricate array of glass tubes. Behind it lay a cobbled courtyard with an open roof. A few racks of weapons, mostly knives, stood in the corners, and a patch of ground had been cleared of cobblestones and filled with packed dirt; Adriane guessed it served as a practice yard. Several steam pipes and a water tank flanked the courtyard, attaching to some sort of cog-driven mechanism that led to the door's glass tubing. *A lock of some kind?*

Jacob pushed ahead of them, running to the knife-racks, while Mia lit two torches set into wall brackets. Adriane stood in the doorway, observing, until Mia beckoned her closer.

"Lancaster's asked me to help you memorize some of the city streets and roofs and to teach you about moving silently and the like. Jacob's gonna show you some knife skills and pickpocketing."

"I told you, I can handle myself," Adriane said. "Besides, I trap and hunt. I can move silently if I need to."

"I'm sure you carn—in a forest. But the city's a bit different. Trust me, we're not teaching you out of belittlement. Every new member gets at least a few lessons. I carn tell you're sharp, Adriane. You'll learn quickly."

"You'll be pickpocketing me instead of the other way around before you know it," Jacob chimed in, his childish features and bright smile at odds with the assortment of throwing knives now tucked between his fingers.

Over the next few days, Jacob and Mia taught Adriane the basic skills of a rogue. Mia also provided her with related books, maps of the various city districts, and a chart explaining the complex hierarchy of guilds and thieves. Cain's nightfolk operated under the thief king's loose leadership which resulted in intricate relations between Lancaster's people, the Abraham Guild, and the other criminal organizations.

Every morning after dinner, Lancaster took her out into the city, providing a practical application for the new skills she was learning. Though she still felt shy and nervous around him, she began to rely on these quiet mornings, on his steadfast companionship. They were a way to escape the dark thoughts that all too often filled her head.

"Why do you do it?" she asked Lancaster on one of these escapades. "Go after the Service especially? None of the other guilds do, not even the dangerous ones."

Lancaster smiled his easy smile. "I have my reasons."

"Well?"

"I'll tell you the day you admit that you like me, darling." He never did explain himself. And he knew how to stop her from asking him any more questions.

It didn't take long for Adriane to adapt to a thief's schedule—sleeping by day and working by night. Though Lancaster kept her from active involvement in any of the Guild's activities, he showed her the city and seemed intent on introducing her to every single one of his people, even when she insisted she'd rather avoid them.

"The Abraham Guild needs intimacy," he told her. "We need to know each other, need to know which faces are in and which faces are not."

"I'm supposed to be hiding," she said, and the fear crept back into her head. She felt safe around Lancaster, Mia, and Jacob, but the other guild members weren't the same. "I'm supposed to be invisible here."

"You'll be fine," he assured her. "No one will hurt you as long as I'm around. And even if I'm not… I know you've got your fire inside."

She didn't know whether he meant her magic or something else.

On those occasions when Lancaster and his people raided food stores, robbed merchants, or set ambushes for lone Servicemen, Adriane continued practicing knife skills and silent movement with Jacob and Mia.

"Curse you might be able to act as a lookout soon," Mia said.

"But first," Jacob interjected, "Practice. Now try again."

Adriane glanced at the knife in her hand. It was smaller, more delicate than her hunting knife, but razor sharp. Apparently, thieves didn't believe in using practice blades.

She thrust the knife forward, but Jacob sidestepped with ease, deflecting with a knife of his own. "You're still not aiming for the sweet spot," he said. "You carn't just pretend. You've gotta mean it."

"You know, I really don't want to kill anyone," she said.

"Yeah, but that's kind of the point. At least *try*."

Adriane rolled her eyes. *If Hannah could see me now.* She realized she was gripping the hilt far too tightly and relaxed her hand. Taking a deep breath, she emptied herself of emotion like she did when fighting her magic, then stepped forward with a purposeful but relaxed strike.

Jacob sidestepped, but something was different. His face widened in surprise, and she felt her knife meet a hint of resistance.

"Jacob!" Mia rushed to his side, and Adriane dropped her knife, seeing the crimson stain against his side.

"Shades, Jacob, I'm so sorry." Fear welled up, and Adriane fought to keep it back down, feeling it call to her magic. *Again. I've hurt someone again.*

"No, no it's okay." Jacob was… smiling? "That was good that time. Don't worry, you only grazed me."

Lancaster chose that precise moment to walk into the courtyard. "Lunch is—shadows, are you okay, Jacob?"

"Just a scratch." Jacob lifted his shirt to reveal the shallow cut over his hip.

"It's about time you accumulate some scars," Lancaster said. "You look far too pretty like that, you gotta give the rest of us a chance with the ladies." He turned to Adriane. "Right, darling?"

She gave him her best straight-faced glare.

"Wonderful," he exclaimed.

"What?"

"How you do those—perfect glares and all with the blandest face I've ever seen. Not that your face is bland, of course not, it's ama—I mean, it's impassive." He stopped himself, and Mia nudged Adriane, shooting her a significant look. Adriane still didn't know—or at least, refused to admit she knew—what Mia meant.

Jacob cleared his throat. "I'm still injured over here."

Adriane turned back to him, away from Lancaster. "You sure you're okay?"

"Curse I am. Whatever you did there, you were way more concentrated when you struck. It was perfect."

She helped him up, and they put away their knives and went upstairs for a midnight lunch. Gera, who was never to be found without her healer's bag, whipped out a vial of clear liquid and a bandage for Jacob, who showed off his new wound to some of the more grizzled knife fighters.

"Adriane gave me that," he said proudly, gesturing at her from across the room.

Adriane frowned and dropped her head to hide her face from view. *It was… easy*, she thought. The hint of resistance against the blade had scared her for a moment, but then she'd realized it was no different from hunting or from butchering her kills. *Something I'm good at.* She shuddered at the thought.

Riah
Sean
Kanbar
Tellin
Oren
Camorin
Kane
Ukan

6

THE WRONG WAY

Four Years Ago
Cain, in Arahill, Saint Brazen

They'd offered him a job. An actual job, more than passing information. Rise had half a mind to accept it; more than half, in fact. He'd argued with Daniel about it again. *That fight certainly didn't end well.* Rise had left the apartment with a packed bag and a promise never to return. He'd write to Pa later, explaining his side of things before Daniel spread too much bile. *He was always Pa's favorite anyway. Never mind that I saved our necks and put food on the table time and time again.*

Rise turned down Flames' Road, whistling to himself. The Service's headquarters loomed up ahead, all finery and steel, with steam hissing from vents in the roof. The doors were painted indobalt blue, a not-so-subtle reminder of the Service's might. *We'll protect you*, those doors seemed to whisper. *We can neutralize any threat—even magic. So why not walk in?*

I could have it all, Rise thought. He stopped in the street, taking a moment to think.

Daniel would remain furious at him, but that wasn't much different than before. The two brothers hadn't gotten along in years, not since Rise had started running jobs for the Scroll Brotherhood three years ago. Now Pa—he would be disappointed. But not angry, surely. *Pa always taught me to follow my own judgement.* That was all Rise was trying to do.

There wasn't anyone else to worry about, not unless he counted Lena. Her opinion on the matter was clear. She was the one who'd gotten him the offer. Rise smirked to himself. He'd started taking her to bed about a month ago. Not that it was serious. *Curse it won't last, but it's good while it does.*

Rise realized he'd been standing in the near-empty street for a few minutes without making a move either way and shook himself out of his reverie. *Shades take it*, he thought. *Curse myself if I don't take the gamble now.* He walked towards the Service Headquarters' main door. A guard was posted, more for the sake of image than anything else. *Been runnin' with thieves for too long*, Rise thought. *Might as well do some good while I carn.*

As he entered the impressive building, Rise squared his shoulders. For once he was doing the right thing.

Present Day

Adriane had become well-acquainted with the Abraham Guild's small but well-organized meat cellar. Having finished a lesson on knife-work with Jacob, she now regarded a deer's carcass with a hint of a smile. *Finally, something familiar.* She chose a knife from the rack and began extracting the animal's guts, her motions careful yet sure, her mind sunk deep in her memories.

"I've never seen a girl skin a deer so fast." It was her father.

"Let alone anyone." Max chuckled. "I think we all know who'll take over trapping from you, Pa. I'd better stick to my grain fields."

His friends called for him to hurry as he left the hut, sickle hanging from his belt.

Pa motioned for her to come. Adriane exchanged a grin with Hannah, who was busy gathering her sewing, before turning to follow him outside.

"Wait, Adriane." Her mother pressed a lumpy package into her hands. "Don't forget your lunch again."

"Thanks, Ma." Behind their mother, Hannah stuck her tongue out at Adriane. Adriane pulled a face in reply.

She and her father carried their skinned and cleaned deer's carcass over to the butcher.

"Stay here today, darling," Pa said. "Master Adner'll teach you to butcher the deer. No use in knowing how to hunt and skin without having some idea of the butchering as well." He ruffled her hair as he left, whistling a tuneless melody.

Someone coughed, and Adriane jerked out of her memory, falling automatically into the knife-fighter's stance Jacob had taught her.

"Looks like Jacob's doing alright at teaching." It was Lancaster. "Or you're just a quick learner."

He smiled, and Adriane found herself blushing. She must look ridiculous. She put down the knife and went to wash the blood off her hands.

"I've never seen anyone gut a deer that fast."

Adriane screwed her eyes shut, then relaxed her expression before turning to face him. "How long were you watching?"

"Ahh." His face reddened. "A little while. You just looked so focused, I didn't want to interrupt. You're a frightening sight with a knife, darling."

"It's Adriane."

He reached over to sort through a few crates of packaged vegetables. "No lessons this evening?"

"No, Mia's aunt needed her, and Jacob's on lookout duty. You?"

He fished a sack of potatoes out from under a heap of carrots and rummaged through a second crate. "Got conscripted to get some ingredients for the stew. Cook wants it to be simmering all night."

She raised an eyebrow.

"Even guild sponsors have to humble themselves occasionally," he said with a self-pitying look. "But truth be told," he lowered his voice, so she had to lean closer to hear him, "I'm as terrified of Cook as everyone else, so it's not like this is a voluntary humbling."

The chagrin on his face managed to draw a chuckle out of her.

"Anyways, when you're done with the deer, breakfast is in full swing upstairs. If you're quick, I may just let you sit at my table."

She gave him one of those glares he found so amusing. "I'll think about it."

He left, toting a few bags of vegetables, and Adriane returned to her task, finishing the deer and delivering the cut meat to the Abraham Guild's rather cantankerous cook. She made it upstairs just as everyone was leaving, no doubt heading to their usual nightly activities. *I guess Lancaster's already gone then,* she thought, disappointed, before mentally kicking herself. *Not that I care. I don't even know him. Just because he reminds me of Pa doesn't mean he's anything like him.*

"Hey, over here." Lancaster waved from his usual table in the back.

Or... he's still here. She passed Mia pulling a complaining Jacob along by the wrist as she made her way towards Lancaster.

"I thought you had lookout duty?" she asked him, but before he could open his mouth to reply, Mia pulled him away with her, shooting Adriane a significant look.

Okay. Something's going on.

"What's up with Mia and Jacob?" she asked Lancaster.

"Nothing." Seeing the question in her eyes, he grinned, then offered her bread and butter. "Well, nothing really. I won't be joining any of the raids tonight, but Jacob wanted me along, I think."

Silence fell as the last few guild members cleared the room. Adriane realized they were alone together.

Lancaster cleared his throat. "Tonight, I thought I'd make a night just for us. You know. Casual, friendly quality time. Up for it?"

She glared at him, and he laughed, prompting her to smile.

"I'll take that as a yes."

He told her of the Guild's latest shenanigans involving a dispute with the Hobiars, a rival guild, as she ate her breakfast. When she'd had her fill, he got up and held his arm out to her with a ridiculous bow. Gingerly, she took it, letting him lead her out of the main room and to a back staircase which she knew led to the roof. They stepped onto the rattling wood, climbed up, and soon reached a heavy trapdoor which Lancaster held open for her.

She stepped into darkness, feeling for the rough shingles under her feet, waiting for her eyes to get accustomed to the night.

The view was beautiful. Adriane took in the bright stars, the glowing lights flickering here and there in the city streets, and the sheer volume of inky black air between each glowing pinprick of brightness. It made her breath catch in her throat.

"Beautiful, isn't it?" Lancaster stepped next to her and closed his eyes.

Somehow it made her sad. She could remember a clear night like this with her father, lying on top of a wooden cart, stargazing. Even after his death, the stars had still been a solace for her to turn to, companions who would not condemn her for the things she could not control. It hadn't been her fault, not exactly, but she knew she carried part of the blame. *If I hadn't gotten angry and run away, they wouldn't have died.* That same night had been the first time her magic appeared. *And then I hurt Hannah. I made her fear me, if only for a moment.*

She realized she was still standing next to Lancaster, on a rooftop in Cain, far away from the places in her memories. It felt wrong, somehow, for him to be there, intruding upon her thoughts. Adriane stepped away from him.

"I'm here, darling," he said, misinterpreting the gesture, "and I'm not going anywhere."

"It's Adriane." She didn't know why she was suddenly angry.

A smile tugged at his lips, and then he did what she had unbeknownst been waiting for since that first night: He said her name.

"Adriane."

He said it slowly, with black air and starlight in his mouth, and she found the sound reminded her of something she couldn't quite place but nonetheless, would never forget.

"Adriane." As Lancaster said it, he stepped towards her again and stretched out his hand, smoothing a strand of long hair behind her ear with a delicate finger, offering her his share in the moment.

His touch was a spark of electricity, and she was angry again, angrier than she could ever remember being. Lancaster started to speak, but before she knew what she was doing, she had grabbed the front of his coat and dragged him the quick step to the roof's precipice. Her knife was at his throat in a heartbeat.

"Hey, okay. If it bothers you, I won't call you by—" his voice cut out with a wheeze as the coat tightened around his neck. Her knife descended mechanically to his throat, ready to cleave his soul away as easily as it had slain the game back home. She would kill him, kill him for simply daring to reach out to her.

Adriane did not have a chance to let go or even fully realize her actions. Another sensation crept over her, not unlike the rush of anger she had felt but colder and more primordial. Her magic called to her, and she surrendered herself to it, for once uncaring, knowing only that the overwhelming surge would prevent her from feeling anything else.

All semblance of the control she'd managed to build up disappeared. Her magic washed through her, and the distant seconds it bought her felt like unchained minutes, hours, days, even. *I need to stop*, she realized. She didn't know what she had felt and didn't want to know because it hurt to feel at all. But no matter what she felt or did not feel, she could not kill Lancaster, could not murder the only friend she'd made. The shadows called to her, and as her knife descended towards his throat—too far gone for her to stop—she looked at his eyes and saw both fear and deadly calm reflected there.

In that moment, she knew he could have escaped her stranglehold. He was bigger and stronger than she and could have wrenched himself free. She saw the abandon in his eyes and knew this, knew he had chosen to trust her with his life for no reason at all. The realization threatened to drag her back, but with a monumental effort, she dove into her magic and dissolved into cold shadows, the echoes of reality following in her wake.

"Adriane," she heard him whisper.

The magic bounced around her, and her senses seemed to sharpen. Little details stood out. A dribble of blood snaked down from Lancaster's neck. His body teetered on the roof's edge and fell back. The whisper of steel sounded from a street, and a bird startled from a nearby chimney.

Halfway across the roof, Adriane felt her magic let her go, and she materialized out of the shadows. Something struck her across the head, and the last thing she felt was a new kind of darkness embracing her.

Her eyes snapped open. She was lying on a soft down mattress. Her head aching, she tried sitting up and saw Lancaster's face swim into focus above her.

"Thank the shades," he said. "You're awake."

Her head throbbed, but nothing else seemed to be wrong with her. "You didn't fall. I—what happened?"

"Well, I caught myself on the ledge. And then you sort of… um. You materialized into a chimney. I was worried you'd somehow gone through it, but it looks like you're okay." He paused awkwardly. "I guess I'll let you rest. If you need anything, let me know."

Lancaster turned to leave, a little too quickly.

"Wait," she began. "About earlier—"

"It's alright. It was my fault. I shouldn't have—"

"No, listen," she interrupted him. She had to speak her mind. *If this ruins our friendship, I'd at least like him to know why.* She could see the dash of crimson still bright against his throat, and her own throat constricted guiltily. "I'm so sorry," she murmured. She'd almost killed him.

He must have seen something in her eyes, because he sat down on the bed and reached out to her again, saying her name softly, the way he'd done on the roof. "It's not your name, Adriane, that bothers you, is it?

My name. He says it like Pa used to. "No." Her voice seemed loud in the air, and yet she knew she spoke barely above a whisper.

"Then what is it?"

He cares, Adriane realized. *He cares even though I hurt him.*

She had a choice to make. The safe option would close the door he had dared to open, perhaps close it forever. The alternative? Open that door further, throw it wide and let whatever ugly thing hid inside her out. *Whatever keeps me safe*, she thought, then hesitated. *What do I have to lose? What am I risking?* She knew she was weighing this chance at intimacy against her own fear, nothing more. He already knew about her magic. He'd already kept her safe. He'd proven he trusted her with his life.

"I'm afraid," she said, her voice behaving normally again. "I'm afraid of what will happen to me and to my family. I got caught up in my memories, and you intruded on that. I didn't see it coming." It wasn't enough. "I didn't mean to—" she paused, gathering her thoughts. "I never meant to make friends or be around people. I need to hide and find a way to stop this madness. I don't—I don't know what to do. I don't know what to do with you, with anyone. I don't know what to do about leaving. I don't know how to keep anyone safe. I have all these conflicting feelings, and I can't control them. I don't know how to stop being afraid."

"It's okay to be afraid," Lancaster said. "You know, I… I wasn't always a guild sponsor—a criminal, if you prefer that term. But when I joined this world, I was terrified. Everything was so different than at home. Then I founded the Guild. I didn't mean to intrude on your memories, but—" he paused, seemed to make up his mind, then forged ahead.

"Look, you're not some sort of hermit. You need someone around to take care of you too. I know what it's like to be completely out of your depth and not know what to do. I had no one to help me at first, but I'm just trying to make sure you don't have to go through that same experience. And… it's more than that with you. What I feel for you has nothing to do with your family or your magic and everything to do with *you*. The way you pick up new things as if you'd already learned them. Or those straight glares you give. That look in your eyes, when you think no one's watching, and you allow yourself a smile. I love you, Adriane. There, I've said it. I love you, and I think maybe you love me too. In one way or another."

Is he really doing this? She beat the thought away. He was sincere. He'd already proven it.

"Well… I don't hate you." The tiniest of smiles threatened to tug at her lips.

"See, darling?" He laughed. "Easier already. Look, I know your family's gone. Right now, or maybe forever, okay? But there's a new family here, and the Guild takes care of its own. *I* take care of my own."

"By telling them to go rob the Service treasury."

He scoffed, thrusting an arm into the air with the panache of a seasoned actor. "I certainly do not! I suggest it, and they decide what they will or won't do. Besides," his voice became serious, "I would never ask anything of you. I would never endanger you for the sake of some revenge. Never."

Adriane believed him.

"You've noticed this too, I know you have, in the whole month or so we've known each other. There's something about you—about us—that just works." His smile was inviting. "Even if you'll just be my friend, I can promise I'll take care of you. Nothing will happen to you. I swear it."

Adriane couldn't understand how a few weeks spent in this man's company, coupled with the revelation of her magic and his near-death trust exercise on the roof could amount to anything substantial. *And yet*, she thought, *there is something here. Something I thought disappeared when I left Hannah and Max.* She didn't truly want to be alone. She wanted this. She wanted him.

"What are you saying, Lancaster?" It felt strange, addressing him by his name, as if it held more now than it had held before.

"I'll keep your secrets is what I'm saying. And I'll tell you a secret of my own." He paused for dramatic effect, then whispered: "Lancaster is my last name. My first name is Abraham." He grimaced. "Don't tell anyone. They'd laugh themselves silly if they knew the Abraham Guild was named after me. Too much of a mouthful for any respectable crook, you know?"

He grinned so roguishly that she found herself smiling, and suddenly they were both laughing—at the silliness of his name and the fact that people cared about little things like that.

Before she knew it, Lancaster's arm snaked around her shoulders in a comfortable embrace, and his lips were on her forehead and her head rested on his chin. They held each other; she could feel his racing heartbeat through his shirt.

Lancaster kissed Adriane's head and the tip of her nose and then drew back abashed, his cheeks glowing red.

"I suppose I'm much too forward, but I think I should like to kiss you properly." He turned an even brighter shade of pink.

The temptation to turn away and leave was as great as the temptation to say yes. For once, however, Adriane let her fears and worries slip away. Turning at least as red as Lancaster, she nodded and searched his eyes with hers.

With a slowness that bespoke extreme care, he lowered his face to hers. Her mouth went dry, and his wasn't much better. Their lips met briefly, before Lancaster pulled back again.

He grimaced. "Somehow I thought that would be less awkward."

Adriane raised an eyebrow at him. "Try again?"

He smirked. "I suppose we just need some practice."

Squad Three had canvased the town and its surrounding fields and forests but found no sign of the bandits. They'd hit hard and fast and gotten out just as quickly. The townspeople remaining were devastated, burying their dead and counting their remaining possessions. The bandits had been after food and livestock, though they hadn't balked at taking the money too.

Ignoring the diplomats' insistence of stopping in a proper town for the night, Runie had ordered they ride on, hoping to catch the bandits before they could strike another village. Once it had gotten dark, they'd set up camp in a field soft with grass, though the Republicans had complained about the hardness of the ground.

Tobin was helping Felias with the fire while Yemena and Horse—his name was Phillip, but everyone called him Horse after he'd showed them how to jump on and off a galloping horse—showed some of the Republicans how to rig a tent. He could tell from their clipped tones that the diplomats weren't at all pleased. Perhaps it had to do with both the Ideians being Fellin. Tobin sighed, then got up to help his squadmates sort it out. Perhaps the fool Republicans would listen to him if not them.

"Is there a problem?" he asked, approaching a complaining group of diplomats that included Lady Kesma and the man who'd been so harsh on his horse earlier that day. *Lord Herod Irratus, if I remember correctly.*

"You can tell your shades-forsaken cat-folk that we refuse to camp in this—this filth for the night," Lord Irratus spat. "It's bad enough you consort with half-breeds, let alone force us to—"

"You're welcome to ride on if you like," Tobin interrupted, trying not to show his anger at the Republican's words. *No one talks to my squadmates that way.* "But the squads are staying here. It's a good campground. If it's an inn you want, I'm afraid you'd have another half day's ride ahead of you."

The man scowled at Tobin, then sniffed derisively. "Come on," he said to the others, before stalking back to his horse. Tobin almost thought he was going to leave before seeing him grab his packs and yell at one of the servants—something about finding a spot of ground that wasn't 'soaked in dung.'

I suppose that could've been worse, Tobin thought.

He looked back at the Republicans who hadn't gone with Lord Irratus and had an idea. "You're welcome to join us by the fire," he said. He remembered how intrigued Lady Kesma had been by Ideon's magic. "We'll tell some Tales, if you like. I know this must be different than you're used to. A good Tale and you'll forget all about the—ah—less than comfortable circumstances." It's what he would've wanted had he been stranded in unfamiliar territory. Of course, the Tales weren't familiar to them like they were to him, but who didn't like a story?

Tobin turned back to the sizeable fire Felias was building. Timothy could have used his magic, of course, but that would've really got the Republicans going. Their dislike of both the tribes and magic went back years, to the First War, and he figured they couldn't be undone by a single night of storytelling, however well the Tales were told.

When they gathered around the flickering flames, Tobin was relieved that some of the diplomats and most of the servants joined them. He couldn't tell if Lady Kesma was among the shadowy figures, but he decided to pretend she was.

His squad looked at him expectantly. Timothy nudged him to begin already.

"Any suggestions?" Tobin asked.

His squad threw out names while the Republicans looked on, confusion and curiosity mingling in their eyes. Tobin dismissed all Tales that dealt with the wars—that topic would be too sensitive for their company. He'd heard Republicans refused to even admit some of the wars had happened, and that was a kettle of fish he'd rather not delve into. *Especially if I'm going to impress Lady Kesma.* He'd never met anyone with her unique combination of beauty and imperiousness, even among the Ideian noblewomen.

He must've glanced at his listeners one too many times, because Timothy leaned over conspiratorially. "You know, I'm pretty sure telling a Tale's the wrong way to woo a Republican lady."

"Shut up," Tobin hissed, mortified. "Alright," he said to his audience.

"Tonight I'll tell you of a time long past, when the tribes still roamed the lands and spirit creatures wandered about freely, without fear of humans."

He figured it was a safe enough topic. The Republic had killed off most of the tribes, but that had been years ago, and he knew that they refused to admit the massacres, just as they doubted some of the wars. If he was lucky, the Tale might even contribute to their understanding of the Fellin and Kane soldiers among them and prevent further insults to his squadmates. Besides, the Tale involved less magic than some of the others, and it stayed away from topics of war.

Tobin cleared his throat and began telling 'Rehu's Gifts,' an old Tale that had been passed down to him by a distant relative who had been part of the near-extinct Riah-Own tribe:

"Long ago, before the age of Tales and stories, before the Legends them-selves came to be named, in days known only as the Ancient Times, there dwelt in the land eight tribes of a single mind and a single heart.

"Though the pursuit of each tribe's trade and living was aligned with that of the other tribes, each tribe held one particular thing, one particular value above all else. The people of the tribes lived their lives peacefully, striving towards these ideals, and it happened that a spirit creature called Rehu noticed how the tribes lived in harmony and decided it would reward them for their dedication.

"One year, as the tribes gathered together in a celebration of their unique gifts and strengths, the creature Rehu appeared to them as a blue mist ma-terializing in the midst of their revels. It told them how it had noticed their unity and offered them the opportunity to ask for a gift, one gift for each of the eight tribes.

"The tribes wondered at this and conferred among themselves. As they saw it, they merely lived according to their values and needed nothing further than to stay rooted in their beliefs. They turned to Rehu to tell the spirit this, one tribe at a time.

"The first tribe to approach Rehu was the Camorin tribe, the eldest tribe, and one of the largest. The tribe's elders told Rehu that they sought to live a life of responsibility—both to each other and to their sister tribes, and they would ask nothing more than to never stray from that path.

"Rehu told them they had chosen their gift wisely. It directed their atten-tion to the south, to the unyielding oceans and tides and the great creatures that lived in the southern seas. It told them to look to the whales and their unceasing devotion to their young as an example of responsibility, and that they would find their assurance in the depths of the southern sea.

"*The second tribe to approach Rehu was the Seer tribe, the smallest of all the tribes. The Seer elders told Rehu that they sought wisdom above all else, and they asked for a way to better follow the wisdom they sought in order to help guide the other tribes.*

"*Rehu told the Seers to look to the southwest, where the spirit creatures were plentiful and varied. It told them to look to the spirits for guidance in matters of wisdom, as they showed a depth of understanding far beyond that of the animals.*

"*One after another, the other tribes approached Rehu with similar requests. They asked the creature to give them the strength to pursue their chosen value with integrity.*

"*The Own asked for knowledge, and were directed to the west, where all manner of birds and winged creatures stored up knowledge. The Riah asked for ways to fulfill their great ambition and were directed to the snakes that ruled over the marshes in the northwest. The Fellin tribe sought to further cement their independence and were shown the great cats that reigned free in the continent's northern reaches.*

"*The Kambar tribe asked for bravery, and Rehu directed them towards the great northeastern forests, where cave bears marked out their territory. The Kanes sought greater loyalty and were shown the packs of wolves that roamed the eastern grasslands, always working and remaining together. Finally, the Wears asked for better ways to express their creativity. Rehu told them to look to the southeast, where all kinds of lizards populated the mountains, each group more diverse and colourful than the next.*

"*Rehu praised all the tribes for having chosen their gifts well and instructed them to seek out the land and creatures it had pointed out to them. Finishing their celebration, the tribes did so, and each tribe learned from the beasts and creatures of the land and sea.*

"*As they learned the ways of responsibility and wisdom, the ways of knowledge, ambition, and independence, the ways of bravery and loyalty and creativity, the tribes discovered they were changing, becoming physically more like those creatures they sought to emulate.*

"*At first the tribes thought they had been tricked, that Rehu had called some curse down upon them. Soon, however, they realized their changing appearance was not a curse but a blessing—an outward manifestation of their ideals and values.*

"*The Camorin took on the semblance of whales and became the first humans to be able to live a life in the oceans. The Seers took on the characteristics of spirit creatures, untethering themselves from the physical world in order to gain powers of foresight and wisdom. The Own grew feathers and wings and soared above the land, gathering more knowledge. The Riah gained snakes' scales and tails as well as the gift of quick movement, which allowed them to pursue their ambitions with renewed vigor. The Fellin took on the characteristics of the great cats, each one different and unique. The Kambar became similar to the bears that dwelt in the east, their appearance and strength matching the bravery they had so carefully cultivated. The Kanes became more like the wolves, an outward manifestation of their pack-minded loyalty. And the Wears became as diverse and colourful as the creative creatures they sought to emulate.*

"In this way, the tribes became more than fully human, unlocking the truth behind their pursuit of ideals. Their appearances would forevermore stand testament to the strength of their beliefs and their devotion to a life of peaceful coexistence and harmony."

A minute of silence passed, the only sound that of whispering fabric as a few of the listeners shifted positions. Tobin smiled, knowing he'd done his job well. He absentmindedly rubbed a rough spot on his right shoulder, where scales and a few half-formed feathers disfigured his otherwise smooth brown skin. It was the only reminder he had of his distant Riah-Own ancestor, of the fact that his family, like so many others, was in part descended from the tribes.

"Tell another?" came a quiet female voice from the side.

Startled from his thoughts, Tobin turned, half-hoping it would be the beautiful Lady Kesma before realizing the voice had been quite unlike her; it was her servant girl, the one who had tried to fetch her wine.

"Sure thing."

Keen to keep the Tales' flow going, Tobin began a rendition of 'The Ghost People,' as told in Silas' Hill, keeping 'Tales of Madness' at the back of his mind, in case the squads or the Republicans wanted another Tale after. Both dealt with the tribes, providing continuity, and they also stayed away from sensitive issues, which was just as well.

As it turned out, the darkness of the night and the strangeness of the day's events lent themselves to a perfect evening for telling. Tobin's audience was attentive, eyes shining with the fire's light, and he and some of his and Runie's squadmates told Tale after Tale until well into the night.

The next morning—or afternoon, rather—dawned like a dream. Adriane awoke in a misty sort of brain fog, gathering her thoughts together like untangling bits of snarled string on a snare. She was full of an electrifying lethargy, sleepy and tired from staying up late, yet wide awake with the knowledge of Lancaster's promises, his words, his reassurance.

Adriane felt a hand squeeze her own and resisted the urge to jump up. Instead, she opened her eyes and saw Lancaster on the floor, wrapped in a blanket, gazing up at her with a lazy smile. They were still in his room, and he'd offered her the bed for the night, retreating to the floor to make his intentions clear. Commitment and companionship was the name of his game, not fast love and easy romance.

She found herself smiling back and, to her surprise, realized she was genuinely happy. Shadows gathered around her vision, not in the violent way her magic usually used, but in a simple and peaceful sort of dance. She felt right and, in that moment, knew her magic would take her anywhere she desired if she but commanded it to. It felt controlled, and the stab of anxiety that had briefly surfaced with it disappeared. Her magic ran off pleasure too, it seemed. However, there was no place, in that moment, where she would rather be. She let the sensation slip away, like sand shifting through a sieve of fingers. This was okay.

"I'm afraid I've got to go," Lancaster said, still caressing her hand. "The Guild calls."

"Alright."

"Feel free to stay longer though, Adriane." He got up and pulled on a fresh shirt, his back turned to her. She averted her gaze, but not before she noticed the many scars crisscrossing his back. He turned and smiled at her one more time, then left.

The sweetness of her name, the way he'd said it, still lingered in her ears. It made her seem strong, not like the fearful child she felt like sometimes. She'd heard city boys were forward and wild, not at all used to the slow, traditional courtship of the country, but Lancaster was something else entirely. Not slow, but not all too fast and, considering that he was a thief, strangely disapproving and innocent of the ways of the world. *The thief and the mage. Sounds like some sort of legend.* She couldn't quite decide if it sounded like a good one.

What if Mia comes looking for me? Adriane bolted upright at the thought and pulled on her boots, deciding she didn't want to be found in Lancaster's apartments. She hadn't meant to fall asleep there at all, really. It had merely been the place Lancaster had brought her to after she had knocked herself out with her magic. She blushed at the memory. In a way, it seemed funny that it had been the same night they'd kissed and talked of happy things.

Adriane crawled out of the bed and immediately had to hold on to the wall as the room spun around her. She felt at the back of her head and discovered a large and painful bruise spreading underneath her hair. Perhaps the bump had made her giddier than usual.

After grabbing hunks of bread and cheese set out on a table, Adriane left Lancaster's apartments and found herself in an unknown part of the Guild headquarters. She turned down the hallway when a door snapped open in front of her, and she nearly rammed into a slight and dark-clad figure hidden behind a stack of books.

"What the—what shadows-cursed idiot just wanders about the—oh. Hello, Adriane." It was Mia.

Adriane smiled awkwardly, picking up a fallen book.

"Thanks. Looking a bit happier than usual, what?" Mia's eyes glinted mischievously.

Adriane shrugged. "Can you show me how to get back to the common room?"

She was sure Mia would ask her what she was doing there, but she simply gave her directions and remarked that Cook had a bunch of skinning for her to do. Adriane got the impression Mia held her tongue because she was being considerate, not because she didn't guess where Adriane had been.

She soon reached the common room, where she was surprised to find Lancaster having an intent conversation with Mistress Brewer and a burly man she didn't recognize. Jacob was also there, hanging back with the air of someone waiting for the opportune moment to deliver a message—presumably he didn't want to disturb Lancaster's conversation.

Something's wrong. Lancaster nodded to her as she entered, then turned back to the others. A slight flush rose on his cheeks, but otherwise his face was drawn and concerned. His hands trembled where they grasped the back of a chair.

Jacob greeted her with an enthusiastic side-hug, which she tried—unsuccessfully—to dodge. She looked at the boy and found she had a smile for him too, though it didn't come effortlessly.

"Lancaster been talking since he came down?" she asked. *He's usually out on the streets by this time.*

"Yeah. He was late though."

She tried to get Lancaster's attention by shifting into his field of vision with all the subtlety Mia had taught her, but he turned away and studiously continued his conversation, the frown growing on his face.

"He'll be busy for a while," Jacob remarked tactlessly. "I'm sure he'll get to you if he carn, but I've been waiting half an hour already."

"Is something up?"

He shrugged. "My group's raid went wrong last night, so maybe it's that. Shades-forsaken Servicemen knew we were coming. We lost Hanker," he said, naming one of the Guild's knife fighters.

"Dead or captured?"

"Dead." Jacob's smile dimmed. "Thank the shades."

She nodded grimly, then excused herself and went to find Cook, who seemed surprised that Mia had sent her.

"But lambs carn't skin themselves true enough," Cook said, without even cursing or waving his favorite wooden spoon about. He directed Adriane to one of the storage cellars.

I guess everyone is downcast today, Adriane thought, hooking several sheep carcasses to the ceiling beams. Her own joyful mood hadn't lasted long either, what with Jacob's news and Lancaster's silence. That silence stayed with her as she began to skin and butcher the sheep. *Is it just the failed raid? Is he regretting last night? Ignoring me?*

It didn't seem like something Lancaster would do, but over the next few days he continued to avoid her. Mia took over a silent movement lesson he'd promised to teach her, and Jacob stopped by often—whether on his own initiative or Lancaster's she wasn't sure. On the second day, Jacob told her she wasn't to go on any more forays or raids outside headquarters. Though the rest of the Guild seemed to return to their nightly activities with renewed bravado after the failed raid, Adriane remained confused and alone.

Lancaster's erratic behaviour continued to the point where Adriane wondered if she'd done something wrong or misunderstood his intentions entirely. She debated confronting him about it, but the one time they were very nearly alone together he turned away, frowning, and sent Jacob to take her to the kitchen so she could eat dinner in peace and quiet. It was a kind gesture, since he knew she disliked the loud, sometimes drunken dinner conversation in the common room, but all the same, she felt like he was hiding her away and avoiding her company.

Adriane's nights were now spent solely in Abel Way and the buildings surrounding it. She found herself growing increasingly moody and silent, that wonderful night with Lancaster growing ever dimmer in her mind. *He has to have a good reason for avoiding me like this… doesn't he?* The thought wouldn't let her go, so she decided to ask Mia.

"There's been bad news hanging in the air," Mia said. "Several raids and robberies gone wrong and the results worse than they should've been. He's just got a lot on his mind is all."

"You don't think… maybe there's a Service informant in the Guild?" Adriane felt almost silly voicing the concern—she didn't know most of the Guild's members as well as Jacob and Mia, but surely Lancaster vetted his people?

"It's not just the Service," Mia said. "If an informant's the problem, they would have attacked headquarters already, taken Lancaster out. But Abel Way's been quiet as a grave."

Too quiet, Adriane thought, *like the quiet breath before the snare snaps shut.* She said nothing, however, all too aware that a hunter's instincts were at odds with the intricate balancing act purveyed by Cain's night-folk.

Mia switched the subject, trying to make her laugh at Jacob's most recent pickpocketing antics, but a sudden wave of emotion hit Adriane, and she turned away, fighting to keep her magic from pulling her into the shadows. It hadn't shown itself since that morning in Lancaster's apartments, but her confusion and anger meant it was only a matter of time.

Somehow it all comes back to that night we spent together. She didn't understand his actions, didn't understand her own feelings. *Something changed—but not in the way I thought.*

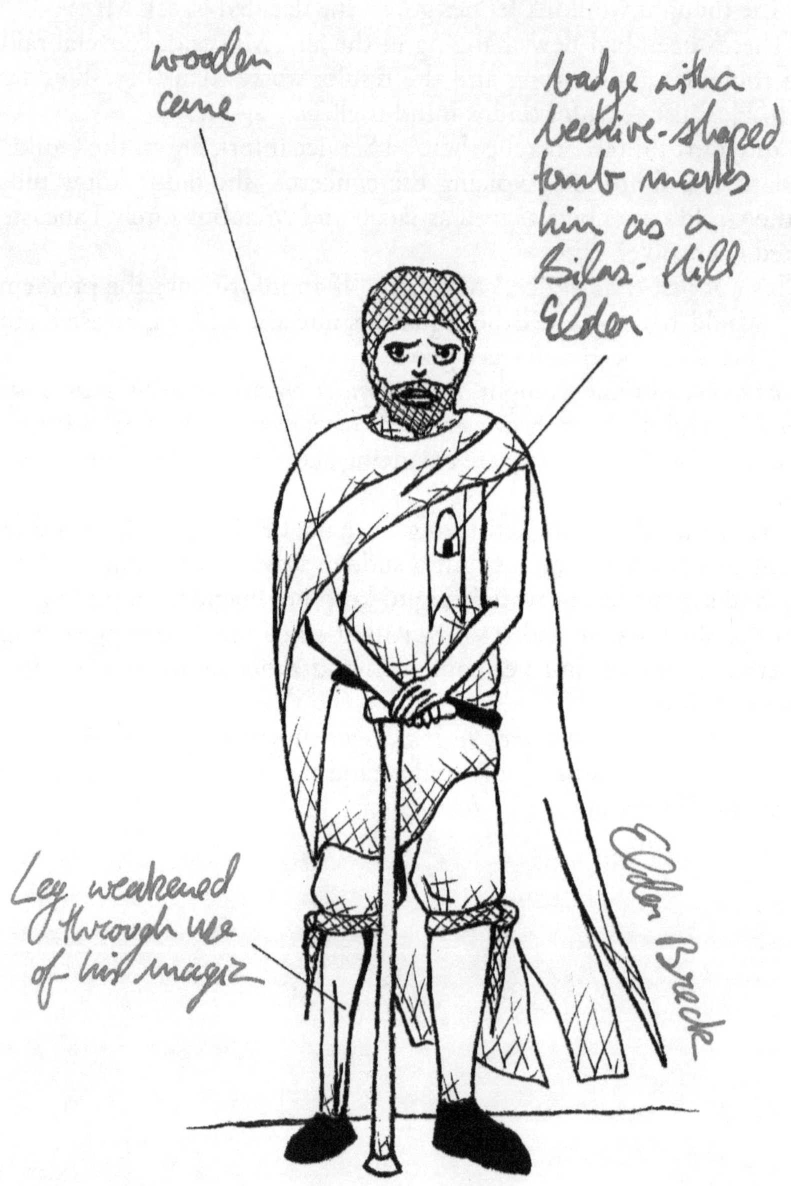

wooden
cane
badge with a
beehive-shaped
tomb marks
him as a
Silas-Hill
Elder
Leg weakened
through use
of his magic
Elder Breck

7

GHOST-FIRE

Two Years Ago
Salisben, in Escava, Saint Brazen

Imp could vividly remember the first fire he'd set for the Service. It had been a merchant's villa on Wrovetown's outskirts, all stone facades and marble arches, beautifully challenging to light. The only real tinder had been the wooden furnishing, the door frames, and a few of the inside walls, but he'd used plenty of kerosene soak, and the heat from the fire had cracked the cement keeping the heavy stone slabs together. *Guess they should've gotten the high-quality stuff,* he'd thought, delighted at his success. It was part of why he was so special. He could light *anything.*

The Service needed him because of his skills. Anyone could set a little fire or watch a building go up in smoke, but only Imp was precise enough to smoke out criminals from their dens, to punish the Service's enemies without being traced back to them, or, in the case of this first fire, to scorch the villa of a merchant who'd betrayed the Service while leaving neighbouring buildings untouched.

Of course, it was only afterwards that he'd learned the merchant and his wife had still been inside. The intelligence that said they were on a business venture had been wrong, and his fire had cost two innocents their lives. It had been a mistake. Afterwards, he'd been more resolved than ever to stay professional and thorough in his fire setting, to never again make such a terrible blunder. Of course, you'd think he would've heard their screams from the outside or noticed them trying to put out the blaze or something. Perhaps they'd died in their sleep, from the smoke. *Yes, that must have been it.*

Returning to the present, Imp blinked bleary-eyed at the bleak wooden carriage roof that had been bumping up and down in front of his eyes for the past few hours. He always thought about his fires. He saw them behind his closed lids and set them again and again in his dreams.

Every fire was different. Just like every city. The Service moved him every few months—they'd seen how good he was, and it seemed like they needed him everywhere. He'd been to Indcity, Korrstone, and Ellaketown. He'd even had a brief stint in Brane, the Republic's capital.

This time, Imp was heading towards Salisben, a city perched on the eastern end of Brazen Pass. He'd been on the road for three days already, jolting about in an endless monotony of hoof beats and bumpy roads. They'd switched horses every few hours, of course, but there was no need to leave the carriage for that, so it all felt the same to him. He supposed he should be thankful for the stables. He'd heard that Ideon and Eleszan didn't bother nationalizing their supply of horses, which seemed silly. Why own a horse when you could ride hard for an hour, then trade it and ride on just as fast?

"Awake?" Herald interrupted his meandering thoughts. He'd been lounging on the seat opposite him. He was another young Service protégé from what Imp gathered, not that he knew him well.

"Hmm? Yeah." Imp half-rose from his stretched-out position. "Mostly."

"Thinking about fire again?"

"How'd you know?"

Herald grinned. "That faraway, brooding kind of look."

"Whatever." Imp slumped back down. "I'm always thinking about fire."

What he didn't say was why he always thought about fire. Sure, it was everything he did and had, but it was also his only connection to his past. He hadn't seen fire imps in a few years now, and the white lights in which he saw stories unfold hadn't grown clear in a long time either, but he still remembered them.

He remembered when it had all confused him, when Uncle Bento had said Imp had something more special than magic. It wasn't about what he *had*, really. It was all about who Imp *was*. His mother too.

The driver tapped their window, and Nero, who'd been snoring away next to Imp, jerked up. He rubbed a thick hand across his eyes, then looked outside.

"We're almost to Salisben, Peter."

Nero's official title was Imp's senior mentor, but he felt more like a chaperone most of the time. He made sure Imp did his duty, followed orders, and thought what they wanted him to think. The Service was like that. It gave you everything, pain included. *And Nero is more of a pain than anything else.*

"Did you know Salisben contains one of the oldest Service headquarters?" Nero continued. "I was stationed there myself once, back when Michael…"

Imp made noncommittal noises at appropriate intervals, trying to drown out Nero's prattle. The carriage's motion changed, becoming smoother. After a few minutes, they stopped. The door opened. Daylight.

Herald stepped out, followed by Nero who stretched and yawned. He then adjusted his coat importantly and brushed it flat against his side, the brass buttons shining in the evening light.

Imp got up and followed him, jumping off the carriage's wooden step and onto stone tiled ground. He absorbed the view in the few seconds it took him to walk to a gate set into a concrete wall.

Tall brick buildings, some stone and concrete. Cobbled streets, but no one out. An eerie calm for a city. Green in pots and on trees. Brown for earth. Red tile roofs mostly, some gray and yellow thatch. Blue and pink splotches on the side walk—stains from chewed carry-bush leaves and spit. Warm steam from pipes along the walls. Creaks from the gate, its mechanical parts spinning it open.

The gate was a nice, reddish cherry wood. Imp knocked on the timber as he passed. *Plenty of sap still.* It would crackle and spark beautifully if lit.

They met the Gaunt and a few other Servicemembers inside. The Gaunt wasn't his real name; his name was Mr. Kurtis Jesaisah, just like Imp's was Peter Berahsson. But the Gaunt had a pinched face and a cruel way with people, and those two things had earned him the name. Not that the Service let you use nicknames.

The Gaunt was part of the Board, the group that led the Service, and his presence told Imp this wasn't some ordinary mission. Even Nero brought it up later that evening.

"We're spending a night in the elite building. Think of that, Peter!" Nero bubbled. Imp had tried to get the man to stop using his real name, which he disliked, but Nero never gave in. "This is the Protectorate's headquarters—mighty special bringing you in just to set a fire."

Imp shrugged. "Does it matter?"

"Matter? Of course it matters, Peter. Remember that businessman you smoked out last month?"

Imp smiled. How could he forget?

"It turns out he was hiding a shipment of indobalt in that warehouse, blatantly ignoring the Service's new trade regulations. He hadn't even paid the indobalt tax."

"Guess that ruined his business." Imp didn't care. *It's his own fault if he hides something like indobalt from the Service.*

"Not only that. It brought you to the attention of some very important people—one of them being Mr. Jesaisah. And it's no accident that Herald is here. I've heard they're considering him for the Protectorate after he pulled a daring bit of undercover work with the Guild of Blades. They might consider you too if all goes well here."

Imp knew Nero really meant both of them. *Thinks I'm gonna get him into the elitists.* The Protectorate was a special division of the Service, and they enjoyed even more free rein than regular Servicemembers. *If I were an elitist, maybe I could set fires wherever I wanted to.* The thought brought another smile to his face.

⸙

Present Day

When Jenna awoke that morning, it was still cool out. Castor didn't stir when she got up, so she decided to head into the village to surprise him with a hot breakfast. Her legs were stiff and sore from sleeping in the barn with nothing but blankets and some packed straw between her and the ground, but she would be fine if she rode.

Grabbing her crutches, she washed up in a small outhouse, glancing at herself in the cracked mirror that hung from a nail in the wall—a testament to the farmer's wealth; mirrors and glass were expensive. She paused to examine her reflection. Her dark complexion and dreadlocked hair were familiar, but the rest of her seemed stronger, more lithe than she remembered. It seemed she was getting used to days spent riding and walking instead of researching behind a desk. *Though travelling and sleeping rough seem to be having the opposite effect on my legs.*

She found Silverphile lipping hay from a trough, and a farm boy turned from his chores to help her saddle and mount. Jenna rode out onto the village's main street, a small lane flanked by a motley collection of homes and stores and shrouded in a gentle drizzle, the first in weeks. Though few of the tiny establishments were open, she soon spotted a bakery whose ovens were already steaming at full capacity and rode up to it.

Getting out of the saddle and limping to the door with the aid of her crutches took an enormous amount of effort, but the delightful smells awaiting her inside the building were worth it. The baker and her husband, both Kanes, cheerfully gave her a basket of sweet-smelling rolls and fresh bread, charging her modestly. They even sent their son out with her to help her mount again.

Her legs swinging back and forth as she rode—she had little control over them at the moment—Jenna made her way back to the barn. She caught a glimpse of a man ducking into one of the village's few side streets and paused. The roads were otherwise empty, and the man's appearance piqued her curiosity. *He seems… familiar somehow.*

Jenna turned Silverphile after the man but kept her distance. She couldn't say why, but something seemed off about him.

The man crept southward, approaching a small building perched on the village's edge. He stopped at the door, knocked, and entered without preamble. As he did, his head turned to the side, and Jenna realized why he appeared familiar. *It's him. The dark-clad man from the Hemsford Inn.* The one who'd seemed like he was watching her.

Thankful for the beaten-dirt road that muffled her mare's hooves, Jenna approached the purplish building, undoing her leg straps and dismounting. She hobbled the last few steps to the door.

The house felt… full, somehow. Leaving Silverphile's reins trailing in the dust, Jenna redoubled her grip on her crutches and pressed her ear against the rough wood.

"—taken too long already, so I suggest we leave today. We can continue north before we head back. We've got near enough of 'em already."

"But I'm telling you," a second voice said, "this is the one that's gonna get us noticed. Vinnick said she needed—"

"I know what Vinnick said, but there's a difference between taking risks and being stupid. I'm not risking my neck or yours any further, and I'm certainly not risking anyone finding we've been crossing without sanction. The Service doesn't need that kind of trouble. Things are shaky enough as it is."

Jenna couldn't stop herself gasping in astonishment before she caught herself. *The Republican Service—here, in Ideon?* This was bad. There were rumors, of course, but then, there were always rumors. This—this was proof. Her heart pounded, but she stayed by the door, determined to hear more. She remembered the corpse they'd found—these two men could be the ones responsible for the man's death.

"—for now, and we can come back once they've explained away his death." The voices seemed to echo her thoughts.

"Alright," the second voice said, "but we'd better stay close. The girl is…"

Jenna realized the voice was approaching the door. She rushed back to Silverphile before realizing she had no way to mount with her legs as limp as they were. She glanced back as the door opened. A man's cloaked back appeared in the doorway. In the oblivious moment he took to say goodbye, she managed to hoist herself into the saddle with the silent speed and strength that came from being terrified.

"Hey! You!" the man shouted. He'd turned and seen her. Another man ran out from inside the house. He spotted her in a heartbeat and ran. The first man drew a short sword that had been concealed inside his cloak.

Jenna cast out for an energy source and felt a rush of strength flow into her from the building the two men had vacated; it was brimming with the destructive energy that fueled her magic. She wondered that she hadn't noticed it before, when she realized that she had. The house had felt full—full of energy. She hadn't noticed her vision tinting purple because she'd assumed the colour was due to the house's paint.

Gathering the energy together, she wove aether into the first object that came to mind—a little triangular blade called a splinter, traditionally the first object a soul and aether mage was taught to form. She could produce them almost instinctively. Eight purplish-black splinters appeared as she visualized them, and she thrust them between herself and the swordsman. It was just like practicing with one of her teachers back at the university—except her magic had grown even stronger. She'd never before managed to procure more than two of the blades.

"So that's…" the man in front of her began, when the second man, now mounted, crashed over a low fence.

Her attention wavering—she couldn't face both of them—Jenna hesitated before turning back to the swordsman. *Let the other escape. I'll still capture this one.*

Jenna concentrated on the splinters and urged them forward. A glint flashed in her peripheral vision—she jerked as an arrow streaked past and buried itself in a fence post. Ducking behind her mare for cover, she spotted the second Serviceman down the lane, a cavalry bow in his hand. The seconds it took for her to process what had happened were enough for the first man to vanish behind the building. He appeared on a horse of his own and galloped towards his comrade.

Hoping not to lose them, Jenna urged Silverphile into a canter, ducking between the buildings that remained between her and the forest's edge. The two men were only a few horse-lengths ahead of her. She could do this; she could reach them. *But what will I do once I catch up?* She'd lost the aether splinters the second her concentration wavered, and she was unarmed.

The two men seemed to be having similar thoughts. They wheeled as one, galloping towards her. Silverphile balked as they approached, and Jenna lost her grip. She fell from her horse with a cry, but before she could hit the ground, a mass of white tendrils appeared out of nowhere and caught her in midair. The two horsemen saw the magic and hesitated. Then they raced back towards the forest, disappearing into the foliage.

The magic that had caught Jenna released her, and she floated gently to the ground where she lay still for a moment, panting. *That was stupid.* She grimaced, then pushed herself up on her elbows. She tried her legs, but the fall hadn't exactly improved their condition. The sickness that prevented her from walking was inexplicably worse some days, and today she could barely feel her legs at all. They certainly wouldn't hold her weight as they were.

She looked behind her, searching for whoever had cast the magic and spotted a wizened man leaning on a cane, limping towards her. Jenna whistled for Silverphile, who trotted to her side and lipped her shirt in an apologetic sort of way. She could've sworn the horse looked abashed at having panicked and thrown her. The old man arrived as Silverphile did, and he helped Jenna up with a surprisingly firm grip. She clutched her mare's saddle to stay standing.

"Are you alright?" the man asked.

"I'm—I'm fine." The man handed her the crutches. She'd left them on the ground by the building the two Servicemen had vacated. "Thanks."

The man nodded, peering intently at her. "I gather you must be Jenna."

"That's right." She hesitated. "Are you one of the elders here?"

"I am Elder Breck. I spoke with your husband last night. As it turns out, you and I both possess aether and soul magic."

"Well, thank you for catching me, Elder Breck. That fall could have been much worse than it was."

"Indeed." The elder turned back towards the town, and she followed him. "Why were you pursuing those two men?"

Jenna told him about the conversation she'd overheard, and Elder Breck frowned. "That should not be. Unsanctioned Republicans aren't as rare as one would hope, not this far east, but Servicemen are a different matter entirely. Are you certain of what you heard?"

"I'm sure." Jenna spotted movement down the street; someone was running towards them. Castor.

"Excuse me, Elder Breck." She grabbed hold of the saddle, urging Silverphile towards him. The mare, used to her strange ways of riding, trotted forward with Jenna hanging from the saddle by her arms.

"Jenna," Castor called. "What happened?"

She reached his side. "I'm fine, Castor."

"I woke up and you were gone, and I *wasn't* worried, but then some of the villagers said there was some sort of commotion."

"There was a commotion alright. I saw a man I recognized from Hemsford, and I followed him and heard him speaking to another man. They were from the Republican Service, Castor. Spies or something."

His eyes went wide at the news. "That's… not good."

"It certainly isn't." Elder Breck had caught up to them.

"They could be the ones behind that murder," Castor said.

The elder nodded. "They could be, son. We intend to find out."

"Can you send someone after them? Or report it to Silas' Hill?"

"We will report it."

Something in the elder's tone told Jenna he didn't think it would come to much. "What's wrong, Elder Breck?"

The old man shrugged. "We will send news to the House capital at once, of course, but I fear it won't do much. The combat groups are always buzzing for a fight, but the council will explain away our evidence as quick as a water sprite fades."

"Why would they do that?"

Elder Breck chortled humorlessly. "Politics, my dear. Our relations with the Republic are shakier than they've been in years. If we could prove that the Service crossed borders without permission and killed a civilian, well, it would be enough to start another war."

"They'd stop the truth from getting out to save face?"

"Not to save face. To prevent the loss of more life, as they would see it."

Castor placed a calming hand on Jenna's arm, claws catching on her shirt. "It is what it is, Jenna. We can bring news of it again when we return. Maybe they'll listen if they hear it a few more times."

"I must go inform the other elders," Elder Breck said. "But I would still be willing to discuss your magic, Jenna. Castor mentioned that it's behaving abnormally."

They set a time for their meeting, then parted ways. Jenna and Castor gathered their things from the barn they'd slept in. They then found a small shrine dedicated to Fate's Hand, a common Patron this far east. Castor waited while Jenna entered alone.

The statue was grizzled and weatherworn, much like its subject: an old man, cloaked in black, with wild tufts of hair sticking out from his unhooded head and a thick staff in his hand. The Tale carved on the plinth morphed before her eyes, forming three rough stanzas:

> A scholar more the fight becomes
> A soldier more the Tales of peace
> A farmer thieves, a thief recants
> The firebrand unites them all
>
> One blind, one lost
> One doomed to fall
> One leads, one loves
>
> This guidance grants
> An insight given once
> And never again

Jenna stumbled back from the plinth, eyes wide. *I…* She fumbled with the pyramid-shaped ion tied to her belt, crumpling open the cured hide to reveal folded parchment scraps safeguarded underneath. Being a theorist had taught her never to travel without notetaking materials. She scribbled down the words.

I believe the shrines give guidance… but this? The words on the shrine flickered, returning to the original inscription. Jenna shook her head, then hobbled back to where Castor waited. The shrine's message sounded more like some prophecy out of a Tale than any real piece of advice. *If we find the Ghost-Fire Templar's shrine, perhaps it will all make sense.* After all, what relation did Fate's Hand have to their quest? He was a minor Patron associated with territory now belonging to the Republic.

Despite her doubts, Jenna carefully removed the parchment sheet from the ion, which she hooked back on her belt. She tucked the sheet between the pages of *The Search for a Source*.

⁓⦿⁓

Tobin spent most of the week following their discovery of the bandits riding hard and sleeping in the open, with only the occasional stop in a town or village. The diplomats had long ceased deigning to hold a conversation with the Ideians, except to ask when the hard riding would end. That, and listening to the Tales Tobin still told in the evening.

The only two exceptions were Lady Kesma and her maid, for which Tobin was thankful. Though the maid, Yhara, was curious and open-minded, Lady Kesma remained aloof. However, she did occasionally ask him to tell her of Ideon, and Tobin obliged, as long as their conversations didn't stray towards anything to do with the wars, the massacres, any dangerous magics, or the military. *It's a lot to keep track of*, he thought to himself, *but if that's the price to pay for talking to a beautiful lady, I'll pay it gladly.*

"Can you tell me more about Ideon's different magics?" Lady Kesma asked one day, as they were making their way across the fields and grasslands of House Beater's Plains. The road meandered through the pastoral countryside, the party's brisk gait at odds with the lazy, late-summer sun and the sleepy cottages dotting the hills.

"What more do you want to know?" Tobin had already told her about healing magic, and he'd also talked of the transformational magic that affected the shrines they still passed every few days.

"Well," she said, brow furrowing; he'd come to associate the look with a mixture of curiosity and deep thought, "I do not understand how it functions. Is it truly organized in some fashion, or does each mage simply gain a random gift in a certain area?"

Tobin hesitated, glancing towards the backs of Yemena and Rico riding just ahead. The conversation could easily turn to a taboo topic. "It's… complicated. Our magic is organized according to our Houses." This was, strictly speaking, true, though many mages no longer lived in the Houses originally associated with their magic, even if they had studied there.

"That sounds much like the Republican technologies," Lady Kesma said, causing Tobin to startle.

She never talks about the Republic much. I'd think she'd be under the same constraints I am. He thought for a second, and then realized why she was mentioning the Republic. "If you'd tell me more, perhaps it would help me explain the magic systems better. Sounds similar to me." It was a clumsy statement, he knew, but she nodded in understanding. She'd tell him more about the Republic's technology, and he'd reciprocate with some information about magic.

"The Republic's industries aren't specifically confined to our provinces, but we do have locations associated with certain resources and technologies," she began. "For example, my family is from Escava, one of the eastern provinces, and we are known for our copper mines and our timber. We also deal with the dog-folk occasionally."

"The what?" Tobin almost choked. He assumed she meant the Kanes, but calling them dog-folk was an insult as bad as naming someone a gravemaker.

Lady Kesma flashed him a soothing smile. "I meant no disrespect of course. We simply have different names for these things in Saint Brazen."

Somehow Tobin thought she really did mean *things* when referring to Kanes.

"Dog-folk are rare there," Kesma continued, "and we are unaccustomed to them or their ways. It was strange to hear you tell stories of them, truth be told."

Tobin tried not to bristle at the way she said the word—Tales were so much more than mere stories. However, her statement did prove she'd been present at his tellings. He smiled at that.

"What about your magic? Is it similar to the way our resources divide?"

She hadn't talked of indobalt or any specialized technology, but then again, Tobin wasn't planning on telling her anything important either. "In some ways I would think so." He kept his voice low just in case. "Just like resources, there are places where certain types of magic are more common. Each type of magic is associated with the House it is most commonly found in. For example, I'm from House Kyra–Bendekan, which is associated with object-based transformational magic."

"You mean the magic transforms objects?" Her face held confusion.

Tobin sighed. *These Republicans aren't even aware of the things any child here would know.* "Not exactly. Object-based means the mages draw their energy from certain objects. And transformational refers to the category of magic."

Lady Kesma nodded at this. "I have heard of the way energy for magic is gleaned. Each mage has a particular source, which they rely on as fuel. I had thought most mages used their own bodies as their source."

So she does know something. Come to think of it, unlike most Republicans, she didn't sound all warped when she said the words 'magic' or 'mage.' Perhaps the nobles were more used to them, since they had to deal with Ideians on a more regular basis.

"A lot of mages do use a part of their bodies to draw energy from," Tobin said. "Others use objects, and still others use some aspect of the natural world." He hesitated. "Is it true you can do things with steam in the Republic?"

Lady Kesma smiled in a superior sort of way. "Of course, Squadleader Tobin. Think of steam like an energy you can harness to push or pull things. We can use it to open gates, send messages, heat buildings… Steam has a lot of uses."

"I guess technology can be almost as good as magic." Tobin tried a superior grin of his own.

"As I understand it, magic is divided into different categories?" Lady Kesma ignored his attempted jibe. "You have mentioned transformational magic, and I have heard of mages wielding the elements or gaining a skill."

"Yeah." That was obvious enough. "There's lots of little categories within those, but all magic is one of the three. Each of the Greater Houses—except for Silas' Hill—is associated with a combination of source and type of magic."

Lady Kesma said nothing further, and they rode in silence for a while. Her face was blank, but he imagined she must be trying to wrap her mind around magic, just as he was trying to imagine something as insubstantial as steam moving gates.

"Tobin."

He turned his head to look at her. She was beautiful as ever, but her voice seemed different, and she'd dropped his title. "Yeah?"

She hesitated. "Is there any magic that shows the future?"

Odd question. "Not really. Patron inscriptions are the closest to anything like it, but magic can't predict what will happen. No one, not even guardian spirits—what you would call shades, I think—can do that. Why do you ask?"

"Well, I thought magic might be different from technology. From all you've said, however, it sounds like they are different means to the same end."

Tobin supposed they were, in a way. How different were he and Lady Kesma, when it came down to it? Both nobly-born, both working for their countries. Technology or magic didn't matter in all of that. He could see only one important difference.

"Magic isn't just for the elite," Tobin mumbled. He knew he shouldn't have said anything as soon as the words were out of his mouth, but that didn't change the fact that it was the truth. Technology benefitted the rich who could afford it and often as not harmed everyone else. They knew as much from spies and reports of the Republic. Even Eleszan, the Camorin Continent's other country, which tried to remain neutral between the Ideian-Republican rivalry, had problems with technological elitism.

Lady Kesma laughed. "And you suppose magic isn't like that?"

"It isn't just for the rich—"

"That is exactly what it is," she snapped. "Just a different kind of rich. No one can gain magic through any hard work of their own. It chooses some and discards others."

I suppose… she's right, Tobin thought, troubled. *I didn't get any magic when my sisters all did. It isn't fair.* But no—the gift of magic allowed people to work together. *I wouldn't be the fighter I am if I had magic. And the mages help cover and protect us fighters.*

Runie signaled from ahead, and he urged Spiffy forwards, abandoning the unpleasant thoughts. "I'd love to debate you on that another time," he said to Lady Kesma, "but duty calls." Perhaps they'd found a lead on those bandits.

Jenna sat in Elder Breck's single-room cottage, sipping tea from a pewter mug. Light streamed in through the open windows on three sides, and a woven rug rested beneath her feet. The place was by no means luxurious, but it was comfortable and homey.

Elder Breck's magic was only partially like hers. He wielded soul and aether, but his energy source was his right leg. That explained his limp and the cane he'd been leaning on. *In some ways, that makes us even more alike.*

Jenna turned her attention back to the old man, who was sitting on a chair opposite her, lost in thought. He stirred. "I can't seem to remember any instance like it."

"The university's elders said as much. The closest explanation I have is that my magic never finished settling. Perhaps the problems are due to that process continuing longer that it should have."

"I don't pretend I will have any grand solutions for you. I am a simple man after all. But I do know that of all the magics I've seen, aether and soul has been the most volatile. It is a delicate balance, wielding both salvation and destruction."

"That's just legend though," Jenna said, trying not to sound contrary. "Soul and aether don't actually represent salvation and destruction."

"Hear me out, Jenna Brightshade. I am sure you're familiar with the Tales of the Ghost-Fire Templar and his connection to aether and soul magic. Well, in this town there is a particular variation to that Tale. Whenever the man used his aether magic in a destructive way, the spirits of the land would flock to him, haunting him for the harm he had done. Whenever he used his soul magic to preserve or save, however, the spirits of the dead would come to him, and he would put them to rest. The Tale is not completely true—it must have changed countless times over the ages. But if there is one thing all elders know, it is that truth can be found in the Tales we tell. Even if they turn out to be just stories."

"I don't quite follow you," Jenna said, still unsure.

"I am no theorist who could tell you about your magic settling or your particular source. But before I was an elder, I was a teller, and so I can give you the wisdom that all tellers give those who hear their Tales. You've already found some truths in the Tales you've researched. I do not know the answers, but I am certain of where you can find them: in the stories passed down to you."

"That's where I've been looking, but I still don't know what's happening with my magic."

Elder Breck shook his head. "It's not just about your magic, Jenna. There is something different about aether and soul, that much has always been clear. Perhaps by looking at others' magic you will be able to find your answers. And until you do, know that you are not the first to have trouble wielding aether and soul. After all, imagine the Ghost-Fire Templar trying to explain to his elders why the spirits of the dead were appearing to him." He chuckled. "That must have been quite a shock."

Later that day, Jenna and Castor continued on the East Way, heading further into the Monkswood. Jenna was still thinking about Elder Breck's words—about finding her answers in the Tales and the magic of others. Then there was that bit about soul and aether representing salvation and destruction. Such superstitions were common in small villages, especially long-established ones like Stillbrook, but the elder had been right when he'd said the Tales came from truth.

And what about the words from the shrine? They seemed to point towards the Tales as well, especially since they mentioned five individuals. *One blind, one lost, one doomed to fall. One leads, one loves.* 'Blind' could refer to Tabitha, since the Tales maintained her eyes had been the source of her magic. *'Lost' would be Neri, 'doomed to fall' obviously Yoel. Bendekan 'leads,' Ibram 'loves.'* Why did she still feel like she was missing something?

"Castor?"

"Yes?"

"Would you tell me 'The Tale of the Ghost-Fire Templar?'"

"Don't you have it in one of your books?"

"Of course I do. Would you anyway?" It wasn't connected to any Tales about the five heroes, but its connection to her magic was obvious.

"Sure." Castor cleared his throat. "I'm not much of a teller, but here goes:

"*The Ghost-Fire Templar was once a young thief named Jesa who wanted to steal magic. He travelled across the country from the city of Neminia, all the way to Theold's Mountains, crossing them on foot and travelling to the ancient region of Praeta, the birthplace of magic.*

"*There, he met a guardian spirit. It heard his request for magic and asked him why he deserved it. He wasn't as wise as Ibram, as powerful as Yoel, as gentle as Neri, as strong as Bendekan, or as smart as Tabitha. Jesa thought for a moment, then told the creature he was deserving because he was ambitious—he would do whatever it took to gain power.*

"*The guardian spirit told Jesa to travel to the ruins of Canadrel, a once-grand city that had been burned and ravaged by magic until everyone had fled and the forest had reclaimed it. There, he was to seek out the remains of an old temple, the place in which the magical fire had first started, and he was to confront whatever he found there. The spirit also gave Jesa a warning: It told him that magic would cost him everything he had.*

"*Jesa was adamant about completing his quest, and so he made his way to Canadrel. He found the temple easily—it was instantly recognizable by its flame-scorched pillars and blackened, cracked stone. In the temple's center he saw a flame dancing in the twilight, flickering white, then black, then white again. Approaching, he asked the flame for its magic.*

"At the sound of his voice, the flame took on the appearance of a man, who introduced himself as Yus, the fire imp. Yus, flickering black, told Jesa he could gain magic by running through his flames. Then, flickering white, he told Jesa they would both die if he did so.

"Jesa hesitated at Yus' words, not knowing whether to trust his dark side or his light. But after a moment, he decided to take the risk. He gathered his courage, and then he ran through the flame. Immediately, he was over-come by a burning sensation and fell down as if in a fit. He felt conflicting spirits of light and darkness rush through him. Looking up, Jesa saw the fire imp, now a simple red flame, no longer flickering back and forth. Before he blacked out, he heard Yus thank him for releasing him from the magic he had not been able to control. Yus said he hoped Jesa would survive to master the magic and then vanish in a puff of smoke.

"For three months, Jesa lay on the cold stone floor of the temple, strug-gling to survive the tumult of magic inside his body, kept alive without food or water by the energy rushing through him. At long last, he awoke from his feverish sickness, feeling better than ever, and extended his hand. Twin bolts shot from it, one white and one black. Jesa had gained an entirely new type of magic, that of soul and aether.

"Jesa began the long journey home. He performed great feats with his magic, and when he returned to Neminia, he married and started a family. However, not long after reaching his fortieth year, he began to realize he was no longer ageing physically. Food and drink failed to satisfy him, and his body lost its substance, rendering him unable to touch and feel the world around him. He was becoming a ghost, and his magic couldn't help him stop the transformation.

"Jesa thought the guardian spirit had cursed him for his ambition and lust for power. He became isolated from his community, and fewer and fewer people could see or hear him. His wife died, and his children grew up to become some of the strongest mages in the land, but Jesa was forgotten. His legacy lived on only in his descendants and the legends that sprung up, legends telling of the Ghost-Fire Templar and his quest to find magic—a quest that cost him everything he had."

Door into the Abraham Guild's courtyard
steam-powered locking mechanism
glass tubing

8

NOT A SOUL

Two Years Ago
Brane, in Cameron, Saint Brazen

Rise slunk down the dimly lit hallway, lantern light flickering in his peripheral vision. A guard moved to stop him before Rise flashed his left hand open—he'd smeared soot on his palm to hide the tattoo; only the eye-shaped brand was visible. The guard backed away. Nobody messed with the Protectorate.

He made it to the cell and glanced around before producing a rusty key and unlocking the reinforced door. He stepped inside, eyes adjusting to the gloom.

Daniel lay on the floor, eyes shut and breaths steady, his hands chained with manacles that glinted blue whenever a flicker of light reached them. Indobalt. *It's true, then. He has magic somehow, and the Service took him for it.* Rise could hardly believe it, though the proof was right in front of him.

He walked over and nudged him with a booted toe. "Daniel. Wake up," he whispered.

"What..." Daniel stirred and opened his eyes. "Rise? What in the shades are you doing here?"

Rise's mouth twisted. "I'm getting you out."

"You're getting me...?"

"C'mon already," Rise said, more disgusted with himself than with Daniel. The manacles clinked as he unlocked them with a second key, and he glanced back, hoping no one had heard. Thankfully nothing stirred, and he helped his brother to his feet.

"Shadows, Rise. How'd you know I was in here? Why are you doing this?"

Rise shrugged. "Word gets around. And thick as you are, Pa would still kill me for leaving you here like this." He scowled at the state of the cell. "These prisons aren't fit for rats, much less human beings."

Daniel embraced him suddenly, and Rise patted him awkwardly on the back.

"Thank you," Daniel breathed.

Rise realized he was crying. He shuffled his feet. "Okay, okay. Look, I carn get you out of the city, and then you're on your own. But I'm not doing this for you. I'm doing this for Pa. I'm high up enough to get you out, but once you escape, you're on your own. I carn't let them get suspicious of me."

Daniel took a step back, searching Rise's face. He nodded. "Alright. I get it."

"Now c'mon." Rise led his brother through the maze of cramped hallways and tunnels beneath Brane's Service headquarters. Most of the big cities had prisons like this, and they were all laid out according to the same logic. He followed the mental map he'd made, out of the dungeon and into the servants' quarters, then through the complex to an old back entrance.

"What's your magic do?" he asked.

Daniel's head jerked towards him. "Thought you didn't care."

"I don't," Rise snapped, "but if it's something that can help you get out, I need to know about it."

Daniel shrugged. "I can tell truth from lies. But it doesn't always work when I want it to, and sometimes my hands glow when it happens. That's how they found me."

Rise screwed his eyes shut. *He could've known every time I lied to him about where I was. Who I was running with. That's how he found out about the Scroll Brotherhood.* "How long?"

"Started about five years ago."

Rise swore under his breath, then faced the street. "C'mon. Let's get out of here."

Without another word, Daniel followed Rise, and the two of them disappeared into Brane's labyrinthine streets.

Present Day

Tobin rode silently, eyes glued to the hoof prints that marked the narrow path in front of them. Runie's scouts had picked up the bandits' trail a few hours ago, and fifteen of the soldiers, Tobin and Runie included, had split from the diplomats to deal with them.

The trail, mere hours old, had led to a small forest north of the main road, and Runie had commanded they ride on, even though it was getting dark. Thankfully the scout ahead of them had left a clear track to follow.

A quarter-shift or so after entering the wood, the trees thickened around them, and Tobin grew tense with anticipation. Movement caught his eye, and he jerked in his saddle before realizing it was Runie, adjusting her cudgel in its strap. He breathed in slowly to calm himself, then looked back at the hoof prints and the trail. *I have to be on guard, but that doesn't mean I can jump at anything. I've gotta be ready for—*

Thhk. An arrow buried itself in a sapling ahead of Spiffy's nose.

"What the—" Tobin half-turned, but Runie had already spurred her horse forward.

"Tobin! Move!"

Wordless shouts rose from the trees, and Runie ducked as another arrow flew in front of her. *Aiming for the horses,* Tobin thought, slackening his grip on the reins for an instant. Dark shapes rose from behind bushes; a green-clad man exploited his hesitation, leaping in front of him.

"—positions," Runie was shouting. "Don't let them get you out of the saddle. Mages, shields!"

A few more arrows loosened. Two horses reared, hooves flailing. The man in front of Tobin swung a catchpole, and Tobin fumbled for his tonfa, ducking beneath the man's first swing. He glanced back to see another catchpole coming for his throat. He knocked it away, directed Spiffy away from the pair with his knees, and hit a third man in the chest.

Runie was up ahead, cudgel in hand. Tobin glanced back and thought he saw Timothy on foot, facing down a cloaked figure, his sword in one hand, a magical flame in the other.

Something tugged his foot out of his stirrup, and Tobin slipped backwards in the saddle. *Bendekan!* He was off balance and swiped his tonfa uselessly as someone grabbed Spiffy's reins. Snarling, he straightened and smacked his horse's assailant, clearing some space between himself and the men around him. *Where are my squadmates?* He glanced around frantically, seeing struggling figures dispersed among the trees.

"Tobin!" someone shouted as a noose slipped over his head, tightening on his neck. Tobin dropped his weapons and clawed at his throat. Another rope caught his hand. The first noose tightened, and he felt a quick jerk before falling from the saddle. Bright spots danced at the edges of his vision. *Can't breathe!* He fought to stay awake, but the rope constricted, and he fell limp, darkness blooming in front of his eyes.

Adriane shook herself away from her thoughts, trying to recall what Jacob had said. *Some sort of joke about a butcher with too many knives?* She couldn't remember. Mia was laughing though, and so Adriane forced a smile, not wanting Jacob to know she hadn't even listened.

Mia's laughter died as she looked at her. "Seriously, Adriane, what's with you lately?"

"Nothing."

"Oh, come on. You won't laugh, you hardly eat, and you're avoiding people. You're acting as strangely as Lancaster. I almost wouldn't keep you company if my aunt wasn't forever on my back about keeping you safe."

Adriane's head jerked towards her. "What did you say?" Had Mistress Brewer found out about her magic somehow? Had someone else? Could that be why Lancaster was keeping her cooped up?

Mia raised her hands with an apologetic smile. "I'm just kidding. I wouldn't keep you company if I minded. But you've been as frustrated as a Serviceman whose boots won't take a shine. Seriously, what's wrong?"

Adriane grimaced; she hadn't meant to snap at Mia. "Doesn't matter. It's my business."

"I did notice," Mia said sweetly, "that you've been ill-tempered ever since you came out of Lancaster's room, morning over a week ago."

Adriane's face went hot as both anger and embarrassment flared up inside of her. Too late she realized what was happening—she tried to stop the raging tumult of emotions, the confusion and worry about Lancaster, all the pent-up feelings she had for him, the way it felt to be rejected and ignored—but the shadows started flickering around her as her magic tried to take hold of her. Every emotion instantly became extinguished by an overwhelming fear of revealing her magic. Adriane managed to prevent herself from dissolving into the shadows, but just barely.

"Curse you know," Mia said, oblivious to the battle raging inside Adriane's head, "I don't think he's ever kissed anyone before, let alone done anything else." She smiled a hard sort of smile, reminiscent of Lancaster's smirk. "I wouldn't have minded him myself, though shades know he spurned all my advances. He really is handsome, and I carn't—"

Everything was drowned out as a roar of shadows raged around Adriane's body. She lost control. Her magic swept her away, knocking Mia and Jacob to their knees and propelling Adriane along the corridor. She reappeared in the shadows next to a crumbling archway and was immediately assaulted by the loud echoes of her magic bouncing back into the air.

Jacob recoiled. "Oh no!"

"Shadows," Mia hissed. "Shade and flame, so that's what it is."

Adriane felt the last waves of energy bounce back, then dissipate. Her heart beat wildly, and her senses seemed to narrow in on the situation: her friends on the ground, a layer of disturbed dust falling on them. *Thank the shades I didn't hurt them*, she thought relieved, then trembled. *They know now. They know.*

She stood there shaking, her back turned, as Mia helped Jacob to his feet, and they cautiously approached her.

"Well," Mia said in a carefully crafted casual voice. "You know, I was just teasing about Lancaster. Though I do fancy him to be honest." She paused, then continued as if stepping on glass. "So… you have magic."

"Yeah," Adriane said. "I'm sorry—I didn't mean to—are you alright, Jacob?" She looked back at him to see he was shivering, plainly scared witless but making an impressive effort to appear unruffled.

"Y-yeah," he stuttered. "Long as y-you don't do nothin' else." He looked at Mia for reassurance and at her nod bravely placed his hand on Adriane's arm. "You ok-k-kay?"

She looked him in the eye. "I'm fine. And I'm sorry, Jacob. Yes, I have magic."

Knowing she had better explain, Adriane sat on the floor, pulling Jacob down with her. He seemed to be in a mild state of shock, and so she explained that yes, she could do magic, and no, she had never hurt someone. *Except for Ma and Pa and Hannah…* She beat the thought away.

"It's alright," she told Jacob. "I would never use it against someone I care about, okay?" *Not that you know how to use it*, the voice inside her taunted. She snuffed it out angrily. The boy still shivered, but he seemed to calm a little at her words.

"Curse you know, this actually explains a lot," Mia said. "I figured you must have a particular flavour Lancaster liked." The merest hint of bitterness touched her words, and Adriane didn't know what to say.

"You hiding from the Service then?" Mia asked.

Jacob flinched. There was hardly a member of the Abraham Guild who hadn't had trouble with the Service.

Adriane nodded.

"Well, no worries from us, right Jacob?" He nodded earnestly, and Mia flashed a crooked smile. "Not that I know what the Service would want with a mage anyway." She wrinkled her nose at Adriane. "Probably hoping to recruit you."

"I'd rather not find out." Adriane didn't have to guess to know that whatever the Service planned would prove harmful either to herself or those she loved.

Mia seemed to understand and shot her a sympathetic look. "It's alright. I think it's better that we know. You could have told me sooner actually. I understand why you didn't, but you have to trust some people. I'm assuming Lancaster knows?"

Adriane nodded. Mia smiled at that and drew Jacob and Adriane up again, dragging them along behind her. She seemed completely at ease, as if Adriane's magic didn't change anything.

"You won't tell anyone?" Adriane asked, relieved, yet unsure. "Really?"

"Not a soul," Mia said. "Not a soul."

Tobin woke with a groan. He touched a hand to his neck, wincing at the painful welts around his throat. Memories of the bandits' ambush rushed back into his mind, and he sat up with a shout.

"Easy there," a voice drawled.

Tobin looked over to see Runie approaching. She had a bandage wrapped around one arm but seemed otherwise unharmed. He breathed a sigh of relief. "You guys are okay."

Runie smirked. "You'll be well enough too now you've woken up."

Tobin grimaced, rubbing a bump forming on his head. He looked around to see he was in a small clearing, lying on his cloak, with a sack of horse-feed for a pillow. The other soldiers were setting up camp. "Not exactly how I wanted my first fight to go. I—it all happened so fast."

"Always does. You'll get used to it."

"Did you catch them? The bandits, I mean?"

It was Runie's turn to grimace. "No. Not near all of them anyway. We killed one in the fight and caught another three as they were trying to escape, but the rest got away. They knew the forest better, and it looks like they had an escape route set up." She scowled down, either at her boots or at Tobin, he couldn't quite tell. "I have scouts out now looking for anything else, but I doubt we'll find them since they managed to slip past our scouts before. I was stupid to let us get ambushed like—"

"Runie." A soldier from Squad Three was approaching them, leading her horse. She saluted as she reached them.

"What is it, Niecka?"

"We found their camp. Abandoned, but you'll want to see it."

Runie turned to Tobin. "You up for a short ride?"

Though exhausted, he nodded anyway. "Sure."

Runie had their horses brought, and they followed the soldier to a small path that led back into the woods. Before they left, Tobin looked back at the clearing, counting his squad. Timothy and Felias were absent. He swallowed. "Was anyone else hurt?" he asked Runie hoarsely. If the bandits had lost one...

"Not badly. Don't worry," Runie said, correctly interpreting the look on his face. "Your two squadmates are on watch. We had another two soldiers get knocked out, and a few minor wounds here and there, but nothing to worry about."

"Knocked out?"

"Yes. They were trying to take us alive, fighting with catchpoles and the like. Blunted arrows too." Her teeth flashed. "If I can get the ones we caught to talk, I'll have some answers for you."

They continued down the path for a while before Niecka turned down a small goat trail, barely distinguishable from the forest surrounding it. Another few minutes, and the forest began phasing out into a series of clearings. Tobin spotted a few huts between the trees, as well as stacks of crates and barrels. They'd reached the bandits' camp.

Niecka led them to a large hut that looked like it had been used as a storage facility. "Here. You'll want to look at that stack." She pointed to a small tower of crates nestled against the building's side. The lids had been torn off the first few.

Unsure of what she meant, Tobin approached the crates, Runie right behind him. His eyes swept over the first crate's contents. He didn't know what to make of them. *Bracelets...?* The light glinted off them, and he jumped backwards. "Indobalt!"

Runie muttered a curse, then bent to inspect the shiny blue rings. "Looks like restraints of some sort. Some of these are tinted, I think, but others look authentic."

"What are bandits doing with indobalt cuffs?" Anyone caught inside Ideon's borders with the metal could be sentenced to hard labour for smuggling. Most criminals didn't dare mess with the stuff. Besides, criminals relied on mages as much as the army did.

"Must've been trading it," Runie said. "That explains why they weren't afraid of capturing us; they'd have the means to keep us in check."

Timothy was the only mage on Tobin's squad, but Runie's companions included two elemental mages and Niecka, whose magic gave her a marginal advantage when tracking or finding things.

"But why would they try to capture mages—especially soldiers—at all?"

Runie shrugged. "They could've held us for ransom. I would think they'd prefer not to capture a mage, but this way they're prepared no matter what."

"Sounds desperate."

"It's a hard life for some out here. People don't become bandits because they want to, Tobin."

Niecka cleared her throat from behind them. "There's something else."

"More?" Runie turned back towards her.

"Not exactly." Niecka dismounted and entered the storage barn, emerging with a leather bag in her hands. "We searched everything else, and this is the only thing we don't know what to make of." She opened the bag and pulled out a collection of fancy brass buttons, a couple rolls of what looked like bandages, and a crinkled sheaf of paper.

Runie dismissed the buttons with a knowing glance and scanned the paper. Tobin kept his mouth shut while she read, but his impatience still threatened to bubble out of him. Something was scrawled on the side of the paper facing him. *Rise Rezah*, he made out. *Someone's name?*

"What is it?" he blurted out when Runie finally looked up.

"I'm not sure. It's pretty weather-worn, but from what I can tell, a Republican wrote it. A fugitive."

"What does it mean?"

She grimaced. "It means there's another count of murder on the bandits' heads. Even if it wasn't one of ours."

"Are we going after them then?"

"*We* aren't. But I am. My squad will take it from here, and you'll bring those diplomats to Neminia."

"But—" Tobin had to stop himself before voicing a complaint. *But this was the fun bit, and I didn't even get to do anything.*

Runie must've noticed his expression because she gave him a sympathetic smile. "You'll get your chance, Squadleader Tobin. Right now, it's your duty to fulfill your original mission. I've been impressed with you so far, so if you hurry on back to Silas' Hill I might let you tag along for our next adventure."

"You will?" Tobin's disappointment turned to glee, and he straightened in the saddle with a salute. "I mean, yes, Second. I'll get those diplomats to the city, and I'll be back before you know it."

"Then it's settled. You'd best head back to the clearing to get your squad. You'll have to ride hard to catch up to the diplomats and the rest of your soldiers. I'll take things from here."

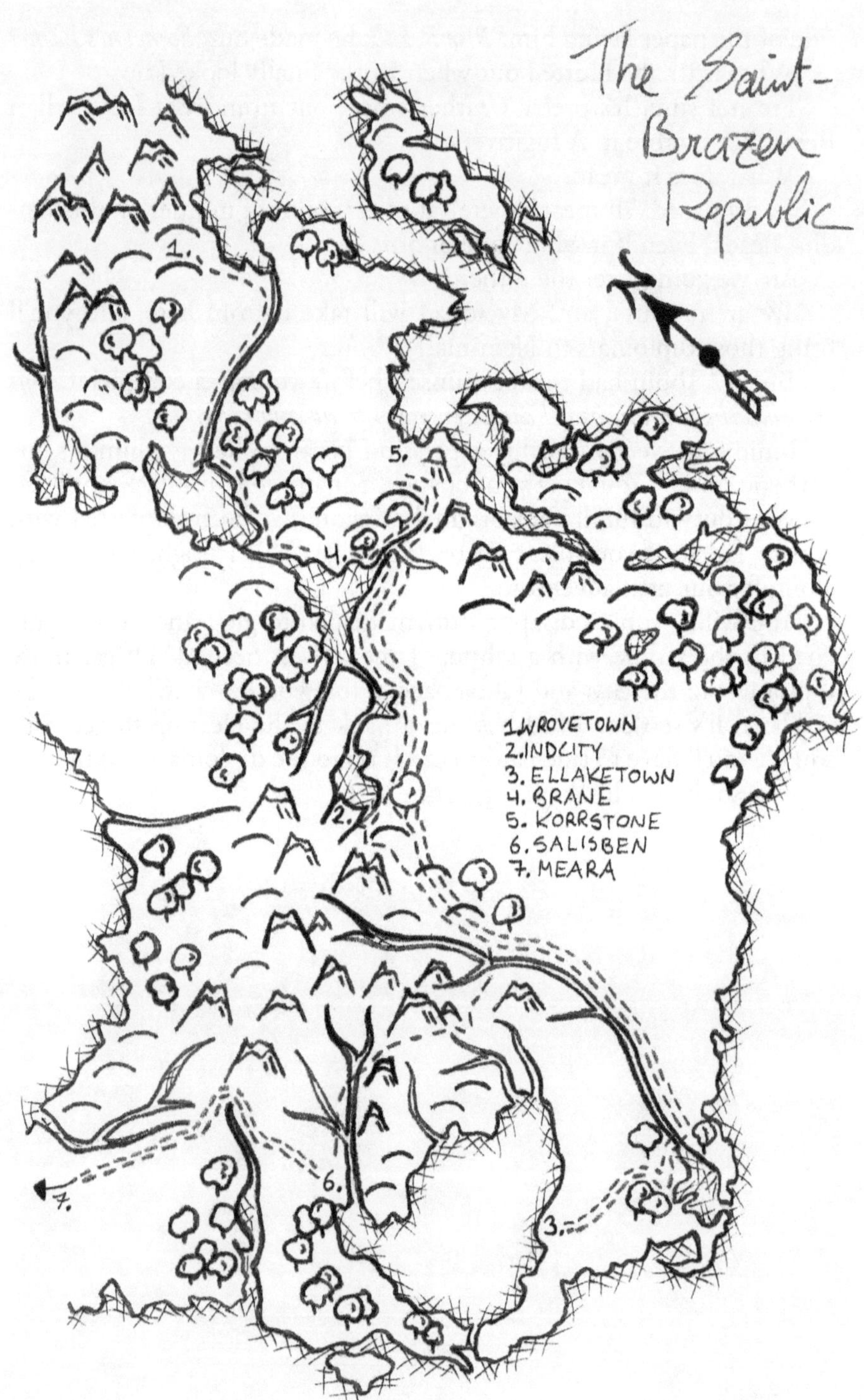

The Saint-Brazen Republic
1. WROVETOWN
2. INDCITY
3. ELLAKETOWN
4. BRANE
5. KORRSTONE
6. SALISBEN
7. MEARA

9

DELICIOUS

Seventeen Months Ago
Salisben, in Escava, Saint Brazen

Imp couldn't believe it had been fifteen months. Fifteen months since he'd smoked out twenty-four members of the notorious Tri-Star gang. Fifteen months since the Gaunt had taken a special interest in him, shipping him off to Meara and now back to Salisben.

A lot of good had come from his last time in the city. After all, twenty-four gang members off the streets from one fire was an impressive achievement. He'd even made a good friend in Herald; the two of them were travelling together now. The problem was the bad memories, the ones he'd buried underneath his success, so he wouldn't have to think about them. They were clamoring for his attention now, clamoring to be heard and recognized.

He remembered Uncle Bento. He remembered the last fire he'd set before the Service had taken him in. There'd been a fire imp dancing in the flames, just a little one, who'd disappeared as soon as cries of another fire had spread through the city and people had rushed to form bucket brigades. That was the last fire imp he'd seen.

Imp had watched the aftermath from the Chisel, the old building he and Uncle Bento had appropriated after it had been decimated by the fire the old man saved him from. He'd saved him then, but he hadn't saved him since. Imp missed him, but he was angry too. *He never came back for me. I made my decision, but I never thought it would be like this.*

Imp was good at following orders, and he loved his fires—but something was changing, something he couldn't quite put to words yet. He knew the Service was right, could convince himself that his fires ultimately did good, but it took its toll. Servicemembers educated him, equipped him, took care of him, but they never told him everything.

Shadows, he didn't *want* to know everything. *Uncle Bento wasn't like that. I really knew him. Until the end, anyways.*

"Peter—Peter are you listening to me?" Nero's clipped voice cut through the thoughts dancing through Imp's head.

"Sorry Nero. 'Course I was. Just thinking." It had always bothered him that Uncle Bento hadn't come back for him, not even to see him. But it could still happen. He wasn't hard to find.

"Good. Now, as I was saying, your skills could come in handy for this particular situation. The Standard Force has agreed to stand back and let us handle things, and I personally think it's an excellent choice on their part. Our elitists can handle the groundwork, but we'll need you to transfer and help smoke out some of the hardier criminals."

They were on their way to some other city again; Salisben was just a cursory stop on their way north. Nero had thought Imp would want to see the aftermath of one of his fires. He didn't often get to return to places. They'd had dinner with some important Servicemen; now the two of them walked along the streets, taking in the city's sights.

"You have word then, on where I'm getting transferred?" All Imp knew was that it was somewhere back in Arahill. He liked to imagine what it would be like if he were moved back to Wrovetown, but he knew that wasn't likely. He'd outgrown his home. His skills were need-ed in the bigger cities.

"I have." Nero smiled ingratiatingly. "But first I have some news to break to you."

Imp fought to keep his face from showing his impatience and tried to focus on the colourful cityscape instead. Nero could prattle on for hours if left unchecked.

"There's a particular reason why you're being moved this time, and I have a guarantee—a guarantee, mind you—that a promotion is due once this is over. They've got problems with some of the local street gangs, and there's reports of at least one known, ah, mage hiding some-where in the city."

Imp finally gave Nero his full attention, mouthing the word 'mage.' "Like… people throwing fire and moving rocks with their minds?" He'd heard the stories, everyone had. He'd even known they must be true from what Uncle Bento had told him. But to actually deal with one? Imp couldn't fathom what that would be like.

"Who's to say? It's no reason to be concerned, and I'm sure you'll find out more in your briefing."

"Okay."

"Oh, and there's something else."

"What?"

"Herald's been cleared to come as well. He's up for a promotion like you, though I wouldn't go spreading that—it's not official yet."

Promotion. Imp knew Nero meant a promotion to the Protectorate, not just a promotion within the regular Service. It would mean more information, more freedom, and more dangerous missions. Imp wasn't sure yet if that was good or bad.

"That's—that's great."

They walked in silence for a while, and Imp counted his steps. Four-hundred and twenty-five. Four-hundred and twenty-six. Ten more minutes' worth of walking, people crowding around them in waves, and then the buildings that had been hugging the streets fell away.

Fine, rich soil covered the sidewalk. Heaps of rubble lined an empty and level salt-and-pepper patch that marred the city's surface. Meander's Quarter. The place he'd set the fire.

A hundred or so paces ahead the blackened ground twisted upwards, gradually blurring into a swatch of wooden skeletons—scaffolding that marked the beginning of the new construction. Beyond that lay completed apartment buildings, still vacant by the looks of them.

"It's so… different," Imp said.

"And it will be better!" Nero said. "They've planned some very nice renovations for several blocks."

A breeze picked up some of the dust and swirled it around Imp's head. The fire had been huge here. He'd leveled more than an entire block, set fire to hundreds of square paces of slum housing and stacked apartment buildings. The Serviceman in charge of the operation had told him that few people were caught in the flames and that the SF had rescued most of the trapped citizens. Only four people had died. According to official reports anyways. *They never tell me everything.* The thought echoed in his head.

Back then, there had been rubble as far as his teary eyes could see. The smoke had still been thick when he'd come back to view his handiwork, with dust and acrid soot in the air. Blackened and charred ruins had been strewn around the block, bricks crumbling and beams dissolving into ash.

"What do you think?" Nero pointed to the framework of a new building laid out on the far side of the burn site. Beside a crane, large pipes lay on the ground in sections, no doubt for transporting sewage and steam, and similar piles of wood flanked the construction. The structure rose four stories into the air and was partially paneled on the lower two floors.

"It's wood."

"Of course it's wood. We've got whole forests available and only so many quarries, Peter. Wood is a splendid building material."

"Except it burns so easily."

Nero chuckled, as if Imp were making a joke. "Of course, Peter, of course. What good would it be if all the houses were made from stone? You'd be out of a job."

"Guess I would be," Imp said. Mentally, he shrugged. There were ways of dealing with stone and concrete. He'd never let a lack of wood stop him.

They walked a little further before turning back towards headquarters.

"You still haven't told me what city I'm heading to."

"Of course, Peter. It's Cain, in the hills district. There's one particular gang there that's been giving the Standard Force quite a few run-ins. They've even hit the Service. Killed at least two Servicemen directly and suspected in the disappearances of four others."

Imp winced. "What idiot goes and messes with the Service straight up?"

"Some youngster who goes by Lancaster. He's the gang's leader."

"A renegade then?"

"No, he's well under the thief king's influence. But he doesn't pay his plaits like the other gangs, and these attacks are bad enough that the Service needs to send a message. We don't just want to take him out— we need to take care of the whole gang. We need an exterminator, not an assassin. Besides, he might've let things slip to his underlings."

"He stole information?"

Nero hesitated. "Well, remember the Ralan scandal back when… no, never mind. I don't suppose you would. You'd've been too young at the time. But this Lancaster fits the descriptions of the man who broke into the headquarters, right in Brane. I'm not even supposed to know, except I was stationed there at the time."

"And now he's over in Cain."

"Yes, Peter." Nero smiled thinly. "And if he's there, we'll find him and make him talk."

Present Day

Following the incident with her magic, Adriane stayed inside more willingly. *Perhaps it's best to stay out of trouble.* It was certainly safer, both for her and for the Guild. Even if the Service didn't know exactly where she was, they'd still be looking for her.

The weather echoed her gloom. Gray clouds blocked out the stars, and occasional showers of rain announced the imminent arrival of autumn. Keeping to her room, Adriane found comfort in the books Lancaster had brought her when she'd first arrived. She rarely ventured far from her quarters, only braving the noisy common room for mealtimes. Jacob and Mia still dragged her out to the courtyard to train though, and she often helped Cook with the skinning and butchering, though she tried to avoid his cantankerous company.

Lancaster continued to avoid her. After another failed raid led to the imprisonment of one of his men, he retreated even further. Adriane observed him from a distance, mentally telling herself it was merely a good way to practice silent movement and observation, nothing more. *Why hasn't he sought me out? Why doesn't he talk to anyone about what's wrong?*

One evening, after a muted breakfast, Adriane found herself with an opportunity to confront Lancaster alone. The Abraham Guild had taken to the streets, but Lancaster lingered by the door, having waited for everyone else to clear out. Before she could approach him, he glanced around the room, not seeing her, and slipped out the door with an air of secrecy about him. Hesitating for a moment, Adriane followed.

Stepping outside for the first time in days made Adriane realize how much she'd missed it. The air carried the smell of recent rainfall, and the mining dust had been subdued by humidity. Still, Adriane wished she was in a field or a forest somewhere—far from the city and all her problems.

It took all her newly-learned skill to keep up with Lancaster and not be noticed. He slunk past the ramshackle apartment complexes shadowing Abel Way with an air of confidence, his nondescript clothes blending in with the city's poorer residents. She followed him through the Poors Quarter maze for several minutes before realizing they were winding their way towards the city center. The streets emptied as they walked on, most people retreating to their homes.

It dawned on Adriane that she was being reckless, putting both his safety and her own at risk. And for what? The moment to speak to him had passed. He might be angry if he noticed her following him, and if a Serviceman recognized either of them, there would be trouble. Nevertheless, the spell of the moment held, and Adriane kept following.

They passed a massive steam pipe, part of a framework of pipes that distributed steam and water throughout the city and served as the boundary between districts. Lancaster turned left, still walking purposefully, and Adriane hesitated. *He's heading towards Left Quarter. Towards the Service headquarters.*

"Shadows keep him," she murmured. "What is he doing there?"

Though night was fast approaching, the sky still provided a hazy illumination. It was much too early for a thief to risk braving Flames' Road, the wide and well-illuminated stretch of pavement on which the main entrance to Cain's Service Headquarters was located.

Something creaked behind her, and Adriane realized she was not alone. She whirled around to see a hand reaching towards her. Adrenaline shot into her, and she turned and ran. A quick backwards glance showed her two pursuers, a man and woman in Service attire.

"Shadows," she cursed, racing back into the Poors Quarter, through the maze of alleys she had begun to memorize. When the pursuant steps faded behind her, she ducked inside the doorway of a rough apartment house. Hoping she'd lost the Servicemen, she eased the wooden door shut behind her and leaned against it, panting.

Hurrying footsteps approached, and someone raced by the door before stopping. A low voice let out a string of curses. The footsteps receded, heading towards the doors of the houses on the street.

Keep moving. Adriane pushed a wooden bench in front of the door, angling it to block the handle, then raced up the building's stairs, heading for the roof. Reaching the fourth and uppermost story, she climbed the roof access ladder and opened the trapdoor, stepping out into the night.

Someone gripped her from behind, and the adrenaline shot back into her body. Hands trapped her arms and legs, and a filthy rope was shoved into her mouth. She tried to defend herself, but there were two of them; it seemed the woman had run to get help while the man had pursued her. She should've known they would think to check the roofs. It was nightfolk territory through and through. She jabbed with her elbows, catching one of them on the cheek, but was forced down within seconds. Her magic was the only thing left, but the fear pushed out the shadows she so desperately tried to surround herself with, and her magic dissipated.

⸎

A day's ride out from Stillbrook, Jenna and Castor tried their hand at rabbit hunting to replenish their supplies. The woods were riddled with the furry creatures, and though they weren't the best-equipped hunters, Castor's nose and Jenna's ability to sense destruction gave them all the advantage they needed.

It was Castor's nose that first alerted them to trouble. Jenna was in the process of ensnaring a rabbit in a cocoon of aether tendrils, when Castor stiffened in his saddle.

"What is it?" She lost control of her magic, and the rabbit made its escape.

"Shh." Castor spun around, nostrils flaring. His shoulder blades rose up, and the hair on his arms stood on end.

"Something out there?" Jenna asked.

"I think it's those spies of yours. It's two men anyway, with a lot of blood on them. They can't be more than a hundred and fifty paces off."

"How do you know they aren't just hunters?"

Castor looked at her. "After finding that corpse… well, let's just say I recognize the smell of decomposing human." He reached into the saddle bag containing his tools and pulled out a large hammer with a blunt steel head. "You'd best stay here, Jenna, in case your magic gets set off. I'm going to follow them. Take Copper for me?"

Jenna took the reins of his gelding as he dismounted. "What if they notice you or you need help?"

"I'll whistle for you. I'm sure Silverphile can get you there in time."

Jenna nodded tersely. He gave her a quick peck on the cheek, then turned and disappeared into the foliage.

Jenna hated just waiting, but Castor was right. Her magic might give them away. Wishing she was with him, Jenna sighed in frustration. *I have magic that runs off bad things happening, and I'm still a useless bystander.* She would have to change that, and soon. *I have to get back to normal.*

Resolving not to waste time, she dug out *The Search for a Source* and flipped through the battered pages. Much of the book recounted Tales and variations of Tales. Some were based on official tellers' renditions, and others were presented without sources of any kind, or with unreliable ones. There was also a section with maps in the back from which the page with the shrines had been torn.

Jenna reached the chapter on the Ghost-Fire Templar and skimmed through a few of the stories. *Wait a minute*, she thought, tracing her finger over a faded title that read 'Soul Creatures.' She'd read the Tale before, dismissing it as unreliable since it talked of a man with magic that caused 'soul creatures' to reveal themselves to him. Considering Elder Breck's words, the Tale gave her pause. *What if it means spirit creatures?* Could this be an instance of soul and aether magic calling ghosts and spirit creatures to the wielder, just like the elder had said?

A beacon of energy hit her, and she reeled in her saddle, fighting to keep her magic from sparking out. She'd only felt this much energy once before—when they found the man in the woods. Her eyes went wide. *Castor. What if he's…?* The shock of the thought was enough to quell her magic, though the energy remained. She could feel it trying to transform into soul and aether, pushing her to do something, to free it. Jenna looped Copper's reins around her saddle horn and spurred Silverphile forwards as her vision flickered into shades of purple.

She rode straight towards the place the energy emanated from, deftly guiding Silverphile down a narrow trail. Her heart raced. *Castor hasn't called*, she thought suddenly. *What if I give him away by riding out into the open?* She hesitated a second, then shook her head and continued. She didn't know what was best, but she couldn't just sit by and do nothing.

Jenna spotted a break in the trees. She nudged her mare towards it, though the energy source was still further off. Something flashed in her peripheral vision. She froze. *What was that?* She scanned the treeline. *There.* Something glinted from beyond the ring of trees encasing the small clearing she was in. Metal reflecting sunlight perhaps? She nudged Silverphile closer.

A quick flash of reflected light, and two mounted men wielding short swords burst out from the foliage. She barely had time to urge her mare to the side to avoid their first pass. *I recognize them*, she realized, noting their dark cloaks. *They're the two men I encountered in Stillbrook.* She opened her senses and let the energy she'd felt flood back into her. This time she had enough fuel for some serious magic. This time they wouldn't catch her off guard.

They tried a second pass, but she was ready for their charge and sidestepped once again, blessing Silverphile's nimbleness. She mouthed a quick prayer to Tabitha before harnessing the energy she'd gathered. She didn't have the training to deal with so much of it at once, but aether was suited to destruction in the same way fire was suited to burning. *It shouldn't be too hard to take them on if I stick to aether*, she thought, concentrating.

Jenna willed her magic to flow into her outstretched arm. Little beads of blackness made bumps under her skin and then rose up out of her pores forming shifting tendrils of aether. The two men hesitated. One sheathed his sword and drew a bow. The other charged. He'd be prepared if she tried sidestepping again.

Jenna took a deep breath. She could feel the power building inside her, wanting to come out. She closed her eyes and *pushed*, forcing it all out through her hand. A burst of dark flame exploded from her fingers, enveloping the approaching swordsman. Copper reared, and Silverphile backed up with a terrified whinny. The blast threw Jenna backwards; she would've fallen if not for the straps over her legs. An arrow that would've taken her in the chest had she remained stationary flew by, embedding itself in a tree trunk. The archer took one look at the mangled remains of his comrade and disappeared into the trees, quick as Denia's wings.

Jenna sat back up, shaking. *Did I... kill someone?*

A creak came from the woods behind her, no doubt the wind bending saplings. Except... no wind on her face or in her hair. The sound came again, and she twisted in her saddle, unsure of what she would find.

The forest appeared the same as before, and for a moment she thought she had imagined the sound. Then she saw movement, and her jaw dropped.

The face in the trees, the face she'd seen when they had found the dead man, was suspended between branches, blending in with them until it moved towards her with big and heavy steps.

Creak. The face jolted with each stride. Still ageless and as withered as if it were carved from bark, still glowing with the yellow light that came from its eyes. Still eerily familiar. *Creak.*

She unbuckled her legs, then dropped down in the clearing's dirt on her knees, head bowed in respect. A low and hollow sound like a wooden flute whispering flowed towards her, and Jenna looked up, astonished. *Is the creature—this forest guardian—trying to talk to me?*

She'd seen sketches of different spirit creatures in books, but they were shy beings. There were only a handful of people now living who could say they had seen a guardian spirit in the, well, flesh. She'd seen smaller creatures, imps and sprites and the like, of course, but never a creature this big or rare or revered. It was said that forest guardians represented the life force of their domain, and that gazing into their eyes was a like catching a glimpse of the universe. Some communities worshipped them, and others held them to the same standard they did Patrons. It couldn't hurt to show proper respect.

One debate that had never been resolved one way or another was that of their level of sentience. The flute-like sounds Jenna heard now didn't sound like anything to her, but the creature's eyes glinted with an eerie sort of intelligence. Jenna had no doubt it was trying to communicate with her.

The guardian took another creaky step, revealing a semi-transparent, bluish sort of body that seemed to exist for the sole purpose of holding up its mask-like face. The face stood at about twice the height of a human, and the guardian's body was lanky and roughly humanoid in shape but devoid of any detail.

"I don't know what you're saying," Jenna called, wondering if spirit creatures—or just guardians—understood human speech. The flute-like warbling continued, and the creature creaked forwards, teetering with each step, until it stood right in front of her. She craned her neck to look at it. Part of her wondered absentmindedly that the horses hadn't spooked.

The guardian leaned down so its face was level with hers and opened its craggy mouth. "Calls." Its voice was still reedy, but the word was clearly discernible. "Dead man. Magic still calls to us. Sometimes." Its mouth narrowed and pursed as if it was sucking something in. "Delicious."

Jenna stared in a mixture of confusion and wonder. Had she… heard correctly? "Delicious?" she echoed.

The giant spirit creature nodded, then started humming to itself. Jenna couldn't help but think its eyes looked like giant egg yolks, soft and friendly. So much for glimpsing the universe.

A rustle sounded from behind the forest guardian, and it lurched to the side, its mask-like head revolving until it faced the other way. It made another noise, something like a low warble, and then its body faded to mist, and its mask-like face dropped to the ground with a clunk where it, too, dissolved. Jenna looked up to see Castor running towards her.

"Jenna! What was that thing? I thought you'd agreed to stay put!" He half-tackled her in a hug, and she realized she was still kneeling on the ground.

"I did, but I felt the energy, and I was worried, and there were the two men—" Jenna tried to explain everything at once, got mixed up, and began again. When she'd recounted everything to Castor's satisfaction, she took a deep breath. "Did… did I kill that Serviceman?"

Castor looked back to the charred heap that had once been a horse and a man. "Yeah," he said slowly. "You okay?"

She thought for a moment. "I think so. It was self-defence. I'm sorry about the horse though. Guess I didn't quite realize how much magic I'd get from that much energy." Now that she wasn't caught up in the moment she could feel how drained she was. "Or how tired it made me."

Castor helped her get up and mount her horse. "Well, I'm glad you're okay," he said. "I made it to that energy source of yours. Another body." He grimaced. "They must've been trying to hide it where no one would find it for a while. This one had his throat slit, none of those strange markings we saw before. I didn't find anything we could identify him by."

They made it back to the road without further incident and continued on their way.

"You know," Castor said, "I was thinking… What if we turned back?"

"Return to Renforth? Because of the Servicemen?"

Castor shrugged. "Them and the two dead men we found. Maybe we shouldn't be out here. We could wait for things to settle before we go find that shrine of yours. We don't have to do it now when it seems there's danger every two steps of the way."

"But we've come so far." A line from the shrine to Fate's Hand came to mind: *This guidance grants an insight given once and never again.* They were so close. *What if this is my only chance?* "I just want to finish this and find out how to fix my magic. You understand, don't you, Castor?"

He sighed. "Of course I do. I just worry."

"It'll be alright. You saw what my magic did to that Serviceman. I didn't mean to kill him, but now they know to stay away from us. With any luck the other Serviceman will have slunk right back across the border with a ghost story to tell about those crazy, magic-wielding Ideians."

"I suppose you're right." He shook his head. "I hope you are."

The Serviceman pushed Adriane to the ground, kneeling on her legs while the Servicewoman pinned her arms down. Suddenly, a roar lit up the rooftop, and the weight on her legs was gone. Lancaster's voice bellowed, "Run!" and she was up again, defending against the woman's punches, trying to see where Lancaster and the other man were. Dodging a kick, she jumped backwards and turned to see Lancaster ferociously beating back the Serviceman, who fell under his vicious assault. Still Lancaster stayed on him, punching his face and torso bloody until his body lay limp. She spotted one of his blue knives curled in his fist.

"Lancaster, stop!" Adriane ran to him and backhanded his shoulder, jerking him out of his rage. He stood panting for a few seconds, then wrapped her up in a tight hug.

"Where's the other one?" he said.

"I think she ran for it." Adriane could feel her heart still pumping wildly.

Lancaster growled a curse. "Shadows. She'll tell them she saw you. This is way too close to our street."

It was then that Adriane realized the other Serviceman must be dead, killed to protect her secret. She looked over at the body, a lifeless and bloody mass.

"I punched him out, then slit his throat," Lancaster said. His voice remained calm, but his hands shook, and tears spilled down his cheeks. "I'm sorry darling, but he would have told them. I couldn't risk that, but the other one still got away." She'd never seen him cry before. It was strange, how out of sorts he was. She felt her stomach heave for a moment, before settling again, his pain allowing her to push past disgust and shock.

"It's alright." She untangled herself from his arms, hesitated, then took his still-bloody hands and wiped them off on his shirt.

"Right. We should go." His quick tears already drying, he took her hand and pulled her down a flight of steps that led to a lower roof. Following a set of ladders and ledges, they reached the ground, then jogged through darkened alleys and back to Abel Way, changing directions often to make certain no one followed.

"How'd you find me?" Adriane asked.

The familiar smile touched Lancaster's face again. "I'd hope six years of being a thief have not been wasted entirely, darling," he said with a hint of his usual flair. "Though you hid quite well right until we reached Flames' Road. Saw you just as the Serviceman came rushing out, and shades, was I ready to give you a mouthful for being outside this early. Speaking of which, what in the shadows' names were you doing out today? All I've done to—"

"All you've done?" Adriane balled her fists, turning to face him. "All you've done, ignoring me and refusing to even talk to me? I thought you lov—I thought you hated me." She saw the glint in his eyes, the shadow of guilt upon his face, and the pieces clicked into place. "You were trying to protect me or something stupid, weren't you?" She was furious at the thought of it.

He grimaced. "Well… morning right after… you know. I got word from Miles about the previous night's work." His eyes held a tinge of fear as he looked at her. "Adriane, every raid that night went bad, every single one. Everything from a small disagreement with the Hobiars to a full-blown robbery that I'd been preparing for weeks. What was I supposed to think? Sure, if it's a couple of incidents it could be chance, but it's been staring me in the face for weeks now."

"Someone's leaking information?"

"And the Service was flexing their muscles to let me know it." He shivered. "I don't like it. If they want me to know that they know, that must mean they have something. I tried to keep the extent of the Guild's failures secret from as many members as possible. I thought… since you're the most valuable person in the Guild, maybe if I distanced myself they'd be satisfied with getting to me and wouldn't find out about you."

"Getting to you?" There was something else he wasn't saying. "The Service, they're not just after me, are they? You're always picking fights with them. They're after you too." It was a statement, not a question.

He grimaced. "Yeah."

"Well?"

"We should keep moving." Adriane hadn't realized it, but they'd slowed and stopped, caught up in the conversation.

"Tell me on the way."

"I will, I will." They walked on, and he gathered his thoughts before speaking. "As you know, I wasn't always a thief. Let's just say I used to have—ah—political aspirations. And they weren't exactly Service-approved. It came to the point where I had to run for it and create trouble a different way." He gestured dramatically. "As you can see, I adapted quite well to the trade. But I've always had it in for them, and I reckon they wouldn't pass up a chance to catch me and get me out from under their feet. Especially lately."

"What do you mean especially lately?"

"Well, you know, I've done a bit of this and that over the past few months, and, er, some of it happened to involve breaking into Service headquarters."

"You did what?" Adriane wasn't sure if she was impressed or just plain shocked. "Why in the shades' names would you do that? If you took anything at all they'd want to kill you and nothing less."

He gave her a twisted smile. "I had to. I was getting so close. I haven't been this close in years."

"Close to what?"

"Look, before I was a thief I had many grand ideas about how this country should be run, most of them absolute rubbish. But I studied too, and it seemed to me the Service was running a bit too wild, so I tried to get something that would be bad enough to make the government reel them in a bit. And then I found out about magic."

He must have heard her intake of breath, because he put his arm around her and pulled her close.

"Yes, Adriane. Magic. Whispers not only of—of *it*, but of the Service keeping it hidden and chasing those few mages still left in the Republic. I've been trying to find out why. I'm convinced it's the big secret that will finally do them in."

She stiffened under his arm. "So… you let me into the Guild because I had magic?"

"No. Well, a little bit. But that isn't why I love you, you know that. Not that I don't love that part of you, it's just—"

"You know, you tend to ramble when you're being sincere."

He grinned. "At least you know I'm sincere."

She hesitated, thinking back to their original topic. "Lancaster… why do you keep skirting around what happened in your past?"

"I'm not, it's just… it was a lifetime ago. I'm not that man anymore."

"What man, exactly?"

He stopped and looked at her, fear clouding his eyes again.

"What's wrong?"

Lancaster grabbed her hand as if for comfort and resumed their steady pace. "I… I was an aristocrat, part of the Ralan family. And I… just… look at this city, Adriane. Look at us right now, running from the Service, stealing and killing to survive. The Republic *built* this system. The Service *supports* it. Did you know all the major guilds, shades, even the thief king himself give the Service payoffs? They get a cut of every shades-forsaken plait we make. People with special skills, talents, even just people in the wrong place at the wrong time—they're forced to join up, helping grow the Service's power even more. It's insidious. It's *wrong*. No organization should have that much power—especially if it isn't even the proper government."

"And those ideas are what got you thrown out on the streets?"

"Yes. My family had to disown me to save face. I was stupid, I didn't think of the consequences of my actions. I'm just trying to do what good I can with the lot I've been given, as dumb as that probably sounds. I used to think I could change the entire Republic, shadows, even the whole continent maybe. I tried to set my sights lower, just protect the Guild, but even if I keep you and everyone else safe, it wouldn't change anything in the end."

Adriane squeezed his hand, unsure of what to say. *Hannah was always the sensitive one. I've never even thought about any of that. All I've been concerned with is myself and the few people I care about.* "Not sure if I'm the one who needs protecting now I've heard all that," she finally said.

"Well, how about this. You guard my back, and I'll guard yours. We'll be a team."

Adriane couldn't help but smile. "Right. A team. Assuming you're going to be honest with me from now on."

Lancaster's mouth twisted sheepishly. "I'm sorry. I promise I will be. It's a relief actually, getting it all out. Guild member have their own reasons for hating the Service, but we don't really talk about it."

"I guess I'm not exactly an open book either," Adriane mused. "But maybe it's time to change that. Eventually."

Lancaster leaned over to plant a kiss on her head. "I'll be there to listen when you're ready."

They walked on in silence until they'd almost reached Abel Way.

"Say Lancaster?"

"Mmm?"

"Before you became a thief, were you rich?"

He gave her a long look. "Not as rich as I am now."

Adriane blushed under his gaze. "But before—"

"Trust me, my ideas might have been grand, but I was still a high-up, no-good bigot. No one you'd like to know."

"That's not what I meant. I was wondering because of your knives."

"My knives?" Understanding dawned on his face, and he laughed.

"They're not indobalt, if that's what you mean."

"But then—"

"Got them tinted blue by the bladesmith who made 'em. Wouldn't fool a smith, of course, but it gives a good bluff for when I need it."

Adriane rolled her eyes at him. "All that for a show? That night you first saved me from getting killed—I was terrified they'd set my magic off or something. I've heard stories that indobalt—"

"You heard stories it works with magic? Kills it? Maybe stops it? Sure it does, but not when it's a simple weapon. Indobalt's best used for shields or chains, things they run a shock through. I'll show you sometime. It can block magic if it's made well, but it won't set it off or kill it completely. And when it's a blade? Nothing to worry about, even if these were real."

Shaking her head, Adriane kept walking. "I guess that's good to know."

"Suppose I should've mentioned it sooner." Lancaster draped his lanky arm around her shoulders again. "But there you go."

"Right." She slipped her hand around his waist as they turned onto Abel Way. It seemed Lancaster didn't care if anyone saw them together. Properly together. Maybe he was doing it to prove himself to her, and that was okay, but she knew that whatever was between them was real.

Several hours later, Adriane sat on the counter of the common room at Abel Way, picking at a bowl of late-summer cherries. Lancaster had retreated to a private room to hear a report from Miles, who had been waiting for them when they returned.

After several minutes, Lancaster came back looking if not grim, at least a little perturbed. He made his way to where Adriane was sitting and jumped up on the counter beside her.

"Looks like Miles is making a habit of himself," he said, quietly enough so none of the other guild members lounging around the room could hear, though Adriane did notice several heads casually turned in their direction. "He's playing bearer of ill news for the fourth time in a row now."

"What did he say?"

"Not here." Lancaster gestured to the hallway. "Let's talk in your room."

They entered the small chamber and sat down on her bed, facing each other, surrounded by dusty shelves filled with books, the few items of clothing she had brought, and the little green pebble she had found in the street the day she'd left home.

"Miles is my eyes and ears near the Service," Lancaster said. "Though you've probably guessed that much already. Anyway, he heard a drunken Serviceman early this morning. Said they're bringing someone special into the city to deal with a gang that's been causing trouble."

"And they mean the Abraham Guild?"

"Well, I'd certainly think so." He smiled, absurdly proud of himself. "No one else has managed to cause them as much trouble in years."

"Are you worried?"

"I don't know. They can't deal with us if they can't find us."

"But what about the informant?"

"If I'm right and this informant's been leaking information for at least a few weeks—which is the only thing that makes sense—then why wouldn't they have revealed the location?"

"Maybe they have, and they're just waiting for this person to come in."

"I've thought of that, but I figure if they knew where we were they'd take us down right away. No sense in leaving us to trouble them. Even with the protection I've tried to throw around this place, a well-thought-up raid could take it if they knew exactly what was in store for them."

"So, what happens now?"

He grimaced. "Much as I hate it, we'll have to wait. Miles will keep looking and listening, and I've posted Jacob and some of his friends on the street. Hopefully we hear of anything before it happens. In the meantime, I'm finding a safe-house for you and a few others, just to be safe."

He paused, and she turned so she could rest the back of her head on his drawn-up knees.

"Whatever happens," she said, "I'm sure it'll be fine."

"Yeah? Seems awfully positive for you. What makes you say so?"

"I don't know. Things feel right again."

"And you're following your feelings now, are you?"

"When it comes to you, Lancaster, I think I'd like to."

"Whatever you say, darling," he teased, and then casually blocked the half-hearted punch she threw in his direction. "Whatever you say, Adriane."

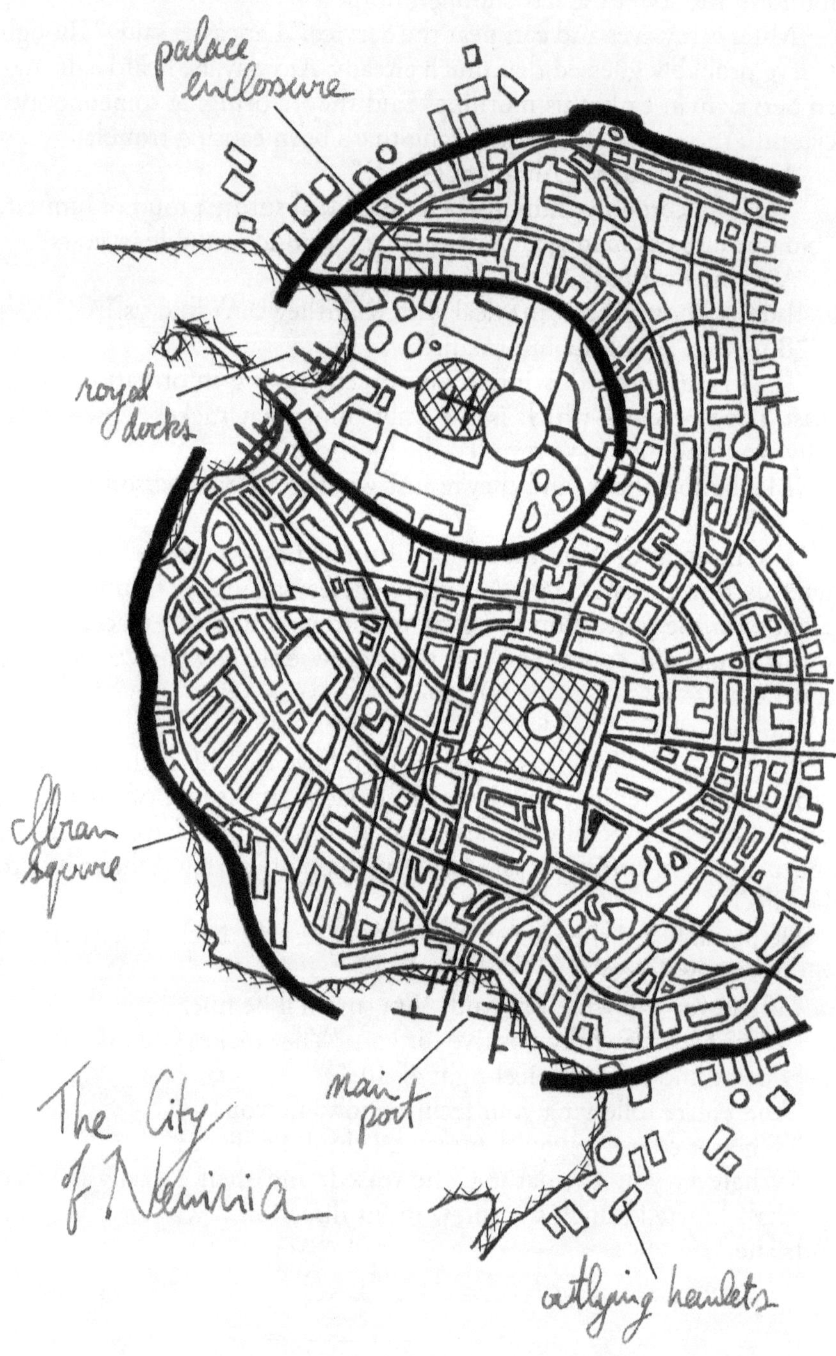

palace enclosure
royal docks
Urban Square
The City of Neuuia
main port
outlying hamlets

IO

THE SEERS

Fourteen Months Ago
Meara, in Westlake, Saint Brazen

Rise kicked at the bluish chains around his wrists as hard has he could, swearing when the pain in his hand increased. *It's no use,* he thought. *Shades! Shades, shadows, and darkness take them.*

"Shades take you all!" he screamed aloud, trying to find release for the pressure building inside him. His left hand throbbed painfully, and then a shock tore into him from the chains around his wrists. He sank to the floor, whimpering.

"Make it stop." They kept sending the shocks whenever the wound on his hand flared up, as if they thought he was doing it again. He didn't even know how he'd done it in the first place. He'd never meant to do it at all.

No natural light reached his cell, but torchlight flickered in through the small, barred opening in the door. It was a cell much like the one he'd rescued Daniel from a year earlier.

"Sweet, sweet irony," he muttered. "Now it's me."

After Daniel had gotten away, Rise had been called to see his commanding officer. He'd been ordered to recapture his brother. He'd expected it. He'd been prepared to do it too.

"Daniel was always to blame," Rise murmured, still crouching on the dirty floor. He laughed for a second, trying on a semblance of madness, then gave it up. The hollowness in his chest suited him much better.

I almost had the bastard. Caught up to him in Meara, then lay in wait for him. He would have caught Daniel if it weren't for one tiny little problem—he'd discovered he had magic of his own.

Rise could see the scene in his head, an abandoned city street at dusk, himself and his fellow Servicemembers cornering Daniel against a wall. There'd been no way for him to escape, but he hadn't pleaded or begged for mercy. He'd just looked at Rise.

Then the anger had come. Rise had been furious—furious at Daniel getting captured in the first place, at having to get him out, at having to recapture him. His anger had built up, and the heat of it had focused in his hand, burning him. He'd looked down in shock to see a blazing magical flame eating away at his flesh, lit up white and blue instead of a normal fiery orange.

His hand throbbed worse at the memory, and Rise squinted at it through the dim light. The burns would leave scars when they healed. *No infection yet, but this cell's so filthy it's bound to happen.* If he didn't get any medical attention soon, he could expect infection to rot his hand clean off.

"Something to look forward to."

The shock of seeing fire magic from their leader had distracted the other Servicemembers, and Daniel had escaped into the night. They hadn't even cared. They'd been too intent on beating Rise and then locking him in indobalt chains. A Serviceman, a member of the Protectorate, hiding magic? It was unheard of. Never mind the fact that Rise hadn't known about it himself.

"Bastards. Hypocrites." Rise roared louder with every word. "Shades take you for all I care! YOU HEAR ME?!" Even those he'd called his friends—Marie and Elizah and Calen—even Lena. They'd all turned on him in a heartbeat.

Rise heard a jangle of keys as someone unlocked his cell. *They gonna beat me again?* he thought, uncaring. They and their precious Service could rot. He'd done the right thing, he'd done everything for them, and they'd cast him aside without a care. *Daniel was right about them.*

The door swung open to reveal a tall silhouette framing the doorway. *Wait a minute. I'd know that self-righteous posture anywhere.*

"Daniel?" Rise whispered, suddenly breathless.

The figure threw a heavy indobalt key at him. "Yeah. Let's go."

⸻ ⊗ ⸻

Present Day

Tobin could see Neminia's walls rising in the distance. *Another couple of hours, and we'll be there*, he thought. He'd already sent out advance riders to announce their arrival. Tobin would be sorry to see Lady Kesma go, but the rest of that lot had done nothing but complain since Runie had left them, and Tobin had hardly felt qualified enough to tell them to shut it. He'd be glad to be rid of them and head back home.

"Is that Neminia?" Lady Kesma rode up behind him.

Tobin couldn't help but smile at her. "Yeah. We'll be there by noon."

"Are you staying there long?"

Tobin shook his head. "We'll be there tonight and then set out in the morning."

"I wonder if you would do me a favor," she said carefully, and Tobin turned to look at her again.

"Sure. What is it?"

"Would you tell me another one of your Tales?"

Tobin's eyebrows rose. *She must've enjoyed my tellings*, he thought. Perhaps he hadn't been going about things wrong after all, not where she was concerned.

"Of course, Lady Kesma." He tried to maintain an air of dignity. "Is there anything in particular you'd like me to tell a Tale about?"

"I'm curious about the tribe you call Seers. They seem the most unique of all these tribes you've been telling us about. And much less base than the dog-folk we have in Saint Brazen." She wrinkled her nose delicately.

Suppressing a wince, Tobin decided not to remind her of how insulting that term was in Ideon. "Okay, sure," he said. "I know loads of Tales about them. Let me see… Okay, I got one. This Tale is called 'The Curse of the Second Moon.'

"A long, long time ago, not long after the Camorin tribes first set eyes on the continent, there came a dark night on which some of the tribes glimpsed a second moon in the sky, so pale as to be translucent. At first, they wondered about this, and they consulted each other fearfully, for they thought it was a terrible omen. But the second moon did not appear again, and when no calamities came, all but the Seers soon forgot about the event.

"Unlike their sister tribes, who had begun putting on the likeness of all manner of beasts and animals, the Seers put on the likeness of spirit creatures in order to grow in wisdom. And as each Seer grew into their power, they saw again that second, ghostly moon in the sky.

"The Seers who saw a full second moon found their gazes turned to the past, where they could see events long forgotten unfold before their very eyes. Other Seers saw the second moon as a half moon, and they gained powers

of observation and recollection. Some Seers saw the second moon in its last quarter and became able to move through solid objects at will, having lost their grasp on the physical world, and still other Seers saw the second moon reduced to a mere crescent, and they found they could glimpse the future. The Seers accepted their powers, recognizing that the second moon they saw revealed the nature of their abilities.

"One particular Seer, whose power first showed itself under that second ghostly crescent moon, a Seer named Emilia after the light of the stars, saw farther into the future than any Seer before. She saw a Seer child born under complete darkness, under a new moon. Unlike other Seers, those who revealed their power under a full moon, a half moon, a quarter moon, or a crescent moon, this child first glimpsed the future on a second moonless night. The child saw something terrible there, though Emilia could not say what precisely it was. When she first revealed her vision to the tribe's elders, she would only say that the child had great power and a terrible fate—this child would predict the greatest catastrophe to ever face the continent, and it would have the power to prevent this catastrophe, at great cost to itself and its family.

"As the Seers realized the connection their power had to the moon, many tried to manipulate the magic to their own purposes, arranging favorable circumstances for their children to reveal their Seer powers when the moon was at a certain phase. However, after hearing Emilia's prophecy, they all whisked their children safely to bed at each new moon, fearing that their child should become the child of the prophecy.

"However, a girlchild was eventually born to Seer parents on a new moon, and at the age of four, her powers revealed themselves under a second new moon. When the girl's parents found out, they were frightened. Visions of fire and destruction plagued the child, and as she grew taller and stronger, she also grew more terrified.

"Afraid for the life of their child and the safety of their family, the parents confronted the Seer elders for a solution. The elders deliberated and finally sent the child's parents on a quest into the wilderness, to find the continent's guardian spirit.

"The parents searched day and night until, exhausted, they arrived at a small grove of willow trees where they fell asleep. They woke to find themselves surrounded by white and blue lights and a shapeless spirit who introduced itself as Rehu. They told the spirit their fears, and it revealed a way to sever the child from its fate.

"The parents were ecstatic and asked the spirit to perform this miracle, when Rehu revealed that a price had to be paid for the safety of their child.

If it severed the child's fate, a chance existed, however small, that the fate would befall someone else.

"After much deliberation, the parents decided the risk was worth it, and Rehu performed its magic before disappearing into the sky. The parents returned home to find the girl safe and unharmed, sleeping peacefully, no longer plagued by nightmares.

"Some say the child escaped its fate without consequence that day, since no other Seer child ever fit the prophecy. Other Seers, however, whisper of a great shadow hanging over the future. A shadow harbouring an unseen, afflicted child, who inherited the second moon's curse."

Lady Kesma was silent for so long, Tobin hoped she hadn't thought the story childish or boring.

"These tribes, as you call them," she finally said. "Their magic is not like other Ideian magic you've told me about."

"That's because it isn't magic at all," Tobin said, puzzled.

"But this Tale you've just told describes powers that cannot be attributed to any regular skills or abilities. We Republicans might dismiss your Tales as mere stories, but unless I'm mistaken, they are much more than stories to you Ideians."

Tobin floundered for a second. "Erm, well, yes. I mean, we believe the Tales come from true stories. There's still people descended from the tribes today, and they all carry the characteristics described in the stories, though in slightly less extreme forms. But the Seers died out years ago." *Well, 'were massacred by the Republic' is more accurate, but I'm trying to be tactful here,* Tobin thought. "We're not actually sure how much of their power was real and how much of it has been amplified by legend."

"So you maintain that it cannot be magic."

"Yes. I mean—" Tobin shut up for a second. He glanced at Lady Kesma, whose eyes were trained on his in a rare display of undivided attention. *Maybe I shouldn't say this… But what harm can it do?*

He pursed his lips, then made up his mind. "People descended from the tribes, the ones that are left anyway… they don't inherit magic. I've never met a Kane or Fellin who could wield magic, and even those who aren't full-bloods only rarely possess a magical gift. So even if the Seers had fantastical abilities, they couldn't be said to be magic in the same way a mage nowadays has magic."

"Your second-in-command is a mage."

"You mean Timothy? Yeah, but he's not a full-blood. His mother was a Kane, and his father a Descendant. That's what we call those who aren't part of the tribes."

"I see." Lady Kesma's expression soured. She excused herself and returned to the cluster of nobles she usually rode with.

Nice going, Tobin thought, mentally kicking himself. *Stop mentioning the tribes and Descendants mixing.* Then again, why should he? The Republicans were the ones who had it wrong, treating the tribes like animals. Still, it wasn't her fault. She was only supporting the ideals and values she'd grown up with. Tobin frowned. *I suppose I am, too.*

They reached Neminia later that day. The city's walls rose out from behind a solid curtain of forest, doing little to contain the sprawling districts which rose and dipped with the surrounding hills. A large lake lay to the south, and Tobin knew the lake's waters extended all the way into the city by means of large, barred gates. A few alabaster buildings shone out from the city's interior, mirroring the sparkle of the water.

The Ideon Nation was unique in many respects, and its system of government was no exception. Though Neminia was considered the Ideon Nation's capital, a second city, Heron, also bore that same title.

Heron was the peoples' city. Situated further west on the Ideon Coast, it contained the elected part of Ideon's government which was controlled by the middle, working, and lower classes.

Neminia, on the other hand, was the monarchs' city. Here the aristocracy—the lords and ladies of the various greater and lesser Houses—and the ruling family reigned supreme. Though the current monarch, King Torren vinn Opalesce, was a member of House Heron–Neminia and part of the longest-ruling family, the king or queen could come from any of the lesser Houses, provided they did not wield any magic. Neminia also housed foreign dignitaries in the royal palace built at the city's center, and it was to this palace that Tobin and his squad were bringing the Republicans.

The city seemed clean from afar, with brightly-painted colours and little turrets poking up over the wall, but the streets became more crowded and dirtier the closer they got. When they entered through the eastern gates amidst a gaggle of wagon-toting merchants, Tobin couldn't help but gape at the mix of smells and sights that greeted them. Though his parents had often gone to Neminia during the summer court season, he had never come with them, having left for Silas' Hill as soon as he had come of age. The city was just as they'd described: colourfully bedecked to the point of unreasonableness, bright, and gleaming with newly-made promises, yet-unrealized dreams, and whitewash.

Tobin gave his squad the order to split into columns and form a protective perimeter around the diplomats, then kneed Spiffy to the front. Though everything seemed bigger once the city swallowed them, with tall buildings shadowing their every move, he still knew where to go. The main roads were straight, and they all led towards the city's center, where the palace lay.

Lady Kesma had said nothing more to him since their discussion about Seers and magic, and she and her companions had taken turns in the wagons to change into suitable attire. The women were now bedecked in layered skirts and freshly pressed, embroidered blouses and the men in form-fitting coats with shiny, detailed buttons over dark pants and crisp, pale shirts. They rode silently amidst the Ideians, wearing their most indifferent faces, noses upturned to the masses.

It took a full hour to reach the palace. Following the directions of a palace guard, Tobin led the party to a small but beautifully kept courtyard to the north of the palace's main entrance. Short walls kept a good deal of the city's noise and dust away from the palace, and the courtyard gave an impression of tranquil serenity, with only a trickling fountain and the noise of their horses and wagons disturbing the quiet.

Liveried servants in grass green and navy waited by three sets of double doors. Additionally, a herald and a man bedecked in Republican finery stood by to welcome the diplomats. Tobin gaped at the man's clothing: dark trousers like the rest of the men, impeccably polished boots with fine, gold accents, a dark shirt that sparkled with inlaid sequins the colour of blood worn over a collared, cream undershirt, and one of those odd coats, buttons engraved with twisting, machinery-like symbols that denoted rank and family history. Tobin swallowed, knowing he must be the chief Republican ambassador, Lord Kile Briar himself. He was even more imposing than Tobin had expected. *Are all these Republicans stiff as hanged men and as serious to boot?* It wasn't his place to comment on their culture, but they did seem rather overbearing.

Tobin managed to get through the required introductions and farewells without making a fool of himself. The servants took charge of the diplomats, and hostlers came for their mounts. Relieved and resigned, Tobin went to find the guest barracks where his squad would stay.

Someone touched his shoulder, and he turned to see Lady Kesma standing regally before him.

"I'll be sad to see you go," he said, with his most formal bow. He only noticed how much she'd relaxed around him during their journey now that she was back to being imposing and sinister.

"Thank you for your service," she said, and his heart sank. He'd known, of course, that she was desperately—hilariously—beyond his stature, but he'd hoped nonetheless. *Hoped for what?* he admonished himself. *You were never more than a travelling guide to her.*

"It was my honour and pleasure," he said, then, impulsively grabbed her hand and kissed it. Was it his imagination, or did he see a hint of a smile form behind her mask of a face?

"Perhaps we will meet again," Lady Kesma said. "I will be hard-pressed to find a bard as well-spoken as you in this city."

With another bow, he let her go, though he watched her all the while she made her way up the steps and through the doors, back straight, every move bespeaking precision, poise, and that deadly beauty of hers. *Out of reach is right*, he thought dreamily. She did not look back.

Jenna flipped through the battered pages of *The Search for A Source*, squinting at the words. A clear, calm night was falling, but she still had light enough to read. Her mare clopped along behind Castor's Copper, relieving her of the need to pay attention to riding.

Was that forest guardian drawn to death the way my magic is? But spirit creatures generally avoid humans and their noisy, violent ways. Could it be the magic itself? It had said something was delicious. *But what could that be?*

Jenna found she kept coming back to 'The Tale of the Ghost-Fire Templar,' or at least the inaccurate version recorded in the book. She was sure that must be who it was referring to, even if it didn't name him. *Spirit creatures drawn to magic. Soul and aether. It's connected. I'm sure of it.*

"Dead man," Jenna murmured. "Magic calls to us. Is calling to us? Ugh, what was the precise wording it used?" She scribbled a note down on a scrap of parchment, trying to recall exactly what the forest guardian had said.

The 'us' implied it wasn't an isolated incident. Was there a category of creatures who were drawn to magic? Or to magic connected to death?

"Hey Jenna."

"Hmm?"

"This looks like a good spot."

Jenna looked up from the book. Castor had halted Copper and was unhooking the tent strapped to the back of his saddle. They were in a small clearing without too many rocks or roots cluttering the ground.

"Okay." She undid the saddle straps and dismounted. Her legs weren't even sore from riding all day.

Together she and Castor set up camp. They dug a small pit for a fire, erected the tent, and fed and brushed the horses. Dinner was a simple affair of bread and dried meat, but Jenna didn't mind. The day had been beautiful, the weather was still summery, and Castor was there with her. Best of all, there had been no more trouble or unexpected encounters. They'd passed through another village, and Castor had worked for a few hours, assisting with the pouring of a new bell for the village's tiny but well-built hall of statues.

Once they'd eaten, Jenna settled against Castor. They left the tent door open, admitting the cool night air.

"It's days like this I'm sure that everything will be okay," Jenna said.

"Me too. It's so peaceful."

"Yeah." She stretched and yawned. "Too bad they didn't have more work for you."

"Don't worry, we'll find something in the next town. Besides, I enjoy having more time to spend with you, love." Castor nuzzled her shoulder with his sloped nose.

Jenna found her eyes drooping shut. "Me too. But I'm ready to get back to normal." It was only a little further. The map marked a spot that looked to be a few hours east of Firrlway, the next town along the road.

Castor hesitated. "What if this is the new normal?"

"Sleeping outdoors? Researching while being restricted to as many books as my saddlebags can fit?"

Castor chuckled. "No. I mean your magic. I'm sure you'll be able to get it under control again, but it might not go back to being weak and unimpressive. You know, two months ago I'd never have thought we'd be hiding out in the woods chasing off after an impossible claim about some shrine. Now look at us. Look at—" he stopped himself.

"—what I've done," Jenna finished for him.

Her eyes were still closed, but she could feel him shrug.

"Does it bother you?"

He considered the question. "No, it doesn't bother me exactly. But I'm worried. You can't imagine how that felt, when I found you in that clearing, on the ground, with Servicemen near. I thought you were dead for a moment—before I noticed the man you killed."

She grabbed his hand, relishing the feeling of his fingers entwined with her own. "I worry too—for you. When I felt the energy, I feared they'd killed you."

"I guess we're both in over our heads."

"What are you talking about?" she joked. "I have everything under control."

"Sure you do." Castor stretched, then ducked outside to douse the fire. "All the same, I'll be glad to be back home."

"Me too," she said, drifting off to sleep. "Goodnight."

An hour past midnight, Jenna woke, cold. *Something's not right.*

The crickets had stopped chirping, and the night's silence was eerie. Nothing moved nor made a sound.

Carefully pulling back her blankets to avoid waking Castor, she crawled to the tent flap and undid the leather fastenings. She grabbed one of her crutches for support and slipped out into the darkness.

Jenna regarded the small clearing, but nothing seemed out of place. Still standing by the entrance to the tent, she cast out her magic and gathered the little energy she found. *Guess I'm just restless*, she thought. *We're so close to finding the shrine, so close to finding answers.*

Jenna turned to slip back into the tent, her bare feet curling around the prickly grass. A high-pitched whistle pierced the night: the sound of something being thrown. *What does that—*

Too late Jenna realized it was coming right at her. She twisted instinctively out of the way. *Crack.* The tip of a whip split the air where her shoulder had been a second ago.

"Castor!"

She heard him stir inside the tent, but before she could do anything more, her wrist exploded in pain. She dropped her crutch and fell to her knees, clutching at the whip that had curled around her arm.

clubbolt attachments

Service
whips

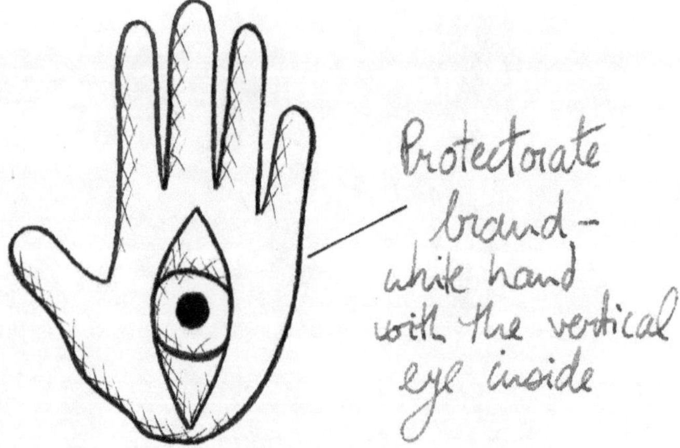
Protectorate
brand —
white hand
with the vertical
eye inside

II

STEP FIVE

One Month Ago
Teel, in Arahill, Saint Brazen

Imp and Nero ascended the steps to the tower's entrance, flanked by a Servicewoman and her two officers. All three sported the standard eye insignia, but with a white hand underneath. No doubt they'd have the accompanying brand of an eye burned into their flesh—they were all part of the Protectorate.

They entered the tower, passed through a semicircular atrium, and went through one of the many doors set into the black stone wall. Imp noted the door was almost a handspan thick and made of ironwood bound with steel bands. *Now that would be a real challenge to light.* Was it built to keep someone out or someone in? *Probably both.*

"What's this place used for anyways?"

The Servicewoman turned to look at him. A stubborn chin, recently broken nose, and broad shoulders were at odds with her otherwise delicate face and slender hips. The contrast made her seem both imperious and crooked; no one could find the combination beautiful exactly, but it was definitely imposing. Her commanding gaze and steely eyes made Imp certain she was someone of great importance. *Though she looks pretty young.*

"We use it for technological trials," she said. "And as a secure holding facility."

They descended into a maze of hallways. The Servicewoman led them to a small, plain room, where two rod-shaped containers lay on a simple wooden bench.

She took the first of these down and handed it to Imp. "This one's yours. Or it will be, once it's done. We need some more specifics on your fire-making preferences, but then we can build you a kit you can do wonders with."

"I have all the fuses and starters I need," Imp said.

"Well, yes," Nero butted in, "but like I told you earlier, the situation in Cain requires a bit more firepower than your usual missions. Your equipment will include certain Service-approved explosives and—" The lady shot him a look, and he fell silent.

"Cool." Imp's mind raced as he imagined the possibilities explosives would bring. "What's the other one for?"

"This…" The lady turned to the second container, handling it almost lovingly. "This is my brainchild. They'll be a standard-issue weapon soon, but we're giving your team prototypes to try out."

She opened the canister and pulled out a long, slender whip. Strange indobalt-blue attachments were fixed at both its tip and handle. She handed the weapon to Nero, who flicked it lazily, before returning it to the canister that formed its sheath.

"I've had them brought to your carriage," the Servicewoman said, sneering at Nero's handling of her invention.

"What so different about these?" Imp asked, bending to get a better look. The Service used whips all the time, since they were non-lethal weapons and easy to wield, but he'd never seen indobalt on them before.

"They're mage-stoppers. The connection formed by the indobalt pieces runs a shock through the whip. This interrupts the magic of any mage it's touching, provided the mage isn't touching someone else, thereby deflecting the shock."

Imp ooed appreciatively. It seemed the Service had finally managed to find an offensive use for indobalt's magic-nullifying properties. The metal had been used for shields and protective partitions ever since its discovery during the Indobalt Wars, but this was the first Imp had heard of it used on a weapon.

Although Imp didn't know much about the Service's history with magic, his most recent classes had educated him on the basics. Mages posed a threat because they were unpredictable. Anyone could be a mage, even a thief with no morals or a noble seeking to rebel. It was better for that threat to be neutralized or turned to the Service's—Saint Brazen's—advantage.

The indobalt whips were perfect, because they could grab on to a mage to deliver their shock. Their symbolism wasn't lost on Imp either: The Service was a convoluted descendant of the old royal guard, back from when Saint Brazen had been a monarchy, and the royal crest had incorporated a crossed pair of whips. *Power and symbolism. Just what the Service likes.*

The Servicewoman led them to another room, where a man asked Imp about a hundred different questions about his fire-starting methods. Everything from the length of his fuses to the amount of care he took in placing accelerators and starters. Nero left to oversee the transfer of the whips, and Imp was left alone among strangers, somehow glad for the woman's company. She seemed kinder than the others and didn't treat him like a child.

Imp had never fully revealed his methods to the Service, and though he was good, he'd never figured he was all that important. *Even if I am the best at setting fires.* With all the questions he was being asked, he guessed they wanted to train more people like him. He answered as best as he could, then left quietly when they were done, unsure of what he thought of it all. The lady walked back with him, and a few steps down the hall outside the equipment room, she broke the silence.

"Your name's Peter?" she asked.

"I'm Imp." Imp was curious to see if she, unlike the other Servicemembers, would allow the use of a nickname. She smiled as if she knew what he was thinking.

"Well, Imp, I'm Vine."

"Not your real name?"

She looked at him, eyes twinkling. "Kiera Vinnick. But if you get to use your nickname with me, I get to use mine with you."

Imp wondered at the liberties Vine was taking. *Not like most Servicewomen. She's gotta be one of the higher-ups. That, or she's not very bright.* Somehow, he didn't think it was the latter. There was steel hiding behind her gaze.

"Why did they ask me all those questions?" Imp said, deciding to try bluntness.

"The Service would like a few more fire-starters in its ranks, that's all. And we do need to know your skillset if we're to make you a new set of tools. Believe me, you'll need it in Cain." Her face turned grim, a frown tugging at her lips.

"That bad?"

"You don't know the half of it. A couple Servicemen were murdered under my command, and now they've decided to bring in Jesaisah to take over my work." Vine's frown deepened.

Imp's eyebrows twitched upwards. "Your work…?" he prodded.

She smiled again, and he knew she saw right through his clumsy attempts at information gathering. However, she stopped walking and leaned against the wall, evidently prepared to answer his questions.

"I'm in charge of, oh, let's say a certain area in the north. I'm here because of the mages. We have two confirmed in the area, and several others suspected—more than in the south or west. I handle mages quite well."

"Does it mean you're coming with us then?"

"No. Like I said, they've decided Jesaisah's baser talents are better for your fire-run." The way she spat the words out made it clear there was no love lost between her and the Gaunt. "I've been reassigned. All my attentions are directed towards new developments now."

"You said this place was not just for technological development though," Imp said. "You said it was a holding area."

She gave him an appraising look. "Did I?"

Vine stood straight again and put a hand on his shoulder, steering him gently onwards. Though she remained friendly, Imp sensed she would answer no more difficult questions.

She's given me enough to think on already, he thought. He recalled how she had uncurled the indobalt whip and shuddered. *All the fires I've set. All the buildings I've burned…* He loved his fires, loved the heat and the colour and the life, but in some moments, he knew the Service was wrong. He knew that his fires had cost others their lives. *But it's the Service's fault. They planned it that way.* He shook his head, trying to rid himself of the thoughts. He'd learned early on it was better not to think too much.

Imp and Nero spent the night at the tower, which was called Teel. Though the sleeping quarters were comfortable and the food delicious, Imp slept fitfully, dreams disturbing his sleep.

He dreamed of setting fires with beautiful colours in them only to return home to find the Chisel deserted and Uncle Bento gone. A Serviceman waited for him in his dreams, and delicate, lacy scraps of paper floated in front of his face. They all had the same writing on them, but Imp's dream-self couldn't read.

Then the dream shifted, and he was having an argument with Uncle Bento. Imp was going to join the Service—they'd promised him oiled hemp and dried tobacco leaves, all he needed to make his fuses and cigarettes—but somehow Uncle Bento didn't understand and was telling him to leave the city. Imp stalked from the room, disgusted, and slammed the door behind him, shattering the dream as he did so.

He jerked awake. It was barely light out, and the dream—too much like a memory—still clung to him. It wasn't his fault he'd gone; it was the Service's. *Uncle Bento should've come for me.* It had seemed like fate had brought them together after Uncle Bento had saved him from being caught for fire-setting, and those years spent with Uncle Bento had felt like having a family. *Why didn't he come for me?*

Imp didn't want to go back to sleep, so he made his way to the mess hall. He was surprised to find Vine there. She seemed tired and drawn. A half-emptied glass bottle stood stoically on the table before her; it looked like she was nursing her own demons.

Imp sat next to her and waited.

"Couldn't sleep much?" she asked after a minute. He could smell the alcohol on her breath.

Imp shook his head.

"Did you wonder why they brought you here? Why they let you in? They didn't need to, for all the excuse of showing you things." She took another drink from the bottle. "But they did it anyway. Because they need your abilities. They need your trust. You know, Imp, we're similar, you and me. Both valuable to the Service, both haunted by it, both taken in by it."

"I was never taken in by the Service," Imp said. To his great mortification, he found that his eyes burned.

"You remind me of myself, when I was your age." Vine leaned closer to him, and draped her arm around his shoulders, reassuring him the way he imagined his mother would've. He pushed his face into her side, smelling herbs and dust on her, with a hint of blood-smell underneath. It was comforting.

"They took *me* in, you know." Vine's speech slurred slightly. "I was three when my parents died, and the only family I've ever known is here. Joseph is like my older brother. Even when he became the Service's prime, he always had time for me. I'd do anything for him."

Imp flinched before allowing himself to relax against her once more. If she was on first name terms with Mr. Haze, the Service's leader, then she must be part of the Board. Way too high up to notice the likes of him. But she had said they were the same. Comfortable by her side, he allowed her words to wash over him. Her voice held something intriguing.

"Not all the Service is like that. Some just want to use you, right Imp?"

He nodded.

"I find myself doing things I think I'd hate if Joseph hadn't promised me they're needed. I believe him you know, but it's still hard sometimes. I know what I have to do and why, but it's hard." She sounded like she was trying to talk herself into doing something. *Maybe this has to do with her reassignment, with the Gaunt taking over her old position.*

"Whatever it is," Imp said, "I'm sure you can do it. It'll be okay." It felt funny, trying to make her feel better. Imp had never comforted anyone before, but he tried his best. "I know I can do my job, even when it gets hard. And I like it. Even though I destroy things, I like it. Nobody gets hurt, you know." The sentence slipped out before he fully realized what he was saying. Did he still believe that to be true?

She looked at him then, and he felt her pull away. "I truly hope you can believe that, Imp," she murmured, the booze gone from her voice. "For your own sake, always believe that you are doing right." She got up, squeezed his shoulder, and then left, heading back up to the dormitories. She didn't take the bottle.

Imp stayed sitting in the near-darkness for a long time, staring at it, contemplating her words. He tried to convince himself. *I do believe it. I do.* That must be how the world worked. *It must.*

He reached out his hand for the smooth glass bottle and tried a drink.

⊸⊸⊸

Present Day

Adriane sat on a soft cushion, leaning against broken wooden shutters, and drank in the evening's cool air, her eyes closed. Though Lancaster had not yet found a proper safe-house for her to stay in, he had given her a room in one of the buildings across the street, still on Abel Way, but in the most dilapidated and abandoned-looking section. It was safer than headquarters, he'd said. Adriane didn't mind much. The solitude gave her time to think.

The shutters creaked, protesting her weight, and she sat up again, rubbing her forehead where she had rested it on the dusty wood. Lancaster had said he would try to stop by with supper. If he didn't, Mia would bring it.

Adriane couldn't help but smile. Now that she was no longer confused about Lancaster, she didn't mind being cooped up. It was the uncertainty that had driven her mad, not the confinement. In truth, relaxing seemed to do her good. She'd never had much time for it before.

A soft knock sounded on the door.

"Come in." She turned from the window, facing the strange room that had been hers for the past week. It was a big room, but run-down, with broken ceiling tiles and old wooden floorboards that creaked. A pile of blankets on two thin mattresses made her bed, and soft cushions served as chairs around the wooden slab of a table, which looked to be made from an old piece of gilded hardwood door. A set of shelves held her clothing and the green pebble, her last reminder of home.

It's been months since I've seen Hannah and Max, Master Adner and the others, she thought. *I hope they're okay.*

The door squeaked open, admitting Lancaster. He wore a clean blue shirt and full black breeches tucked into calf-high boots. She couldn't help but notice how well the colour suited him.

"Breakfast," Lancaster trilled, "is served. Room service, as requested." He bore a covered tray from which delicious smells were emanating.

"I didn't request it actually."

"And yet I brought it all the same." He smirked, placing the tray down on the table and proffering his cheek as if expecting a kiss.

She scrunched her face at him and walked around him to the food.

"Alas, there 'tis again!" he exclaimed. "I've been replaced by the basest of all sustenance when I would offer to forever sustain you with my love…"

"Well I'm hungry, and the food's not getting any warmer."

"Fine," he grumbled, seating himself across from her. "I'll eat with you, and then you can indulge my romanticism."

He watched her as she sat down, and she blushed at the intensity in his gaze.

"Something the matter?"

He looked at her for another long moment before speaking. "Has anyone ever told you you're unfairly beautiful?"

"No. Can we eat now?"

He sighed dramatically and then pulled the cloth from the tray with a flourish, revealing bowls of steaming soup and a plate of fresh bread.

They ate in silence for a few minutes—Lancaster seemed as hungry as she despite his jokes—but they soon fell into the comfortable rhythm of conversation they had developed.

"Do much?" Lancaster asked through a bite of the thick bread.

Adriane shook her head. "I did read one of the books I found stashed under the floorboards." She tipped her head towards one of the room's corners where a stack of dusty volumes rested against an upended piece of flooring. "It was… interesting."

Lancaster grinned. "I had a feeling you might like my little collection of banned texts."

"Banned?"

"Yeah. You were reading *Shadows: Beasts of Spirit*?"

She nodded. "How'd you know?"

"It seemed the most likely to catch your eye. You've got a taste for the exotic you know. Maybe it's the whole magic thing."

She didn't bother making a face at him. Her neutral glare said it all. "Right."

They finished their dinner and then sat together on the cushions by the window. They talked of books and Lancaster's 'current investments,' as he called them. Lancaster's easy explanations and thoughtful questions made Adriane realize how much she'd come to depend on him. He kept her safe, and she, well, she loved him, but he was also her best friend. It was odd—she'd never felt so close to someone before. *Other than Hannah, of course, but that's different. I've known her all my life.*

Tearing herself away from her nostalgic thoughts, she focused on the present moment instead. Lancaster. His hand casually resting on her arm. The room, cozy despite, or perhaps because of, its state of disrepair. The beauty of existing together in whatever space they could find, the evening air cool on their faces, the scent of soap and paper with a hint of smoke comfortable in her lungs. It smelled like Lancaster, and, startled, she realized that meant it smelled like home. As if they'd known each other forever.

They sat together for an hour before Lancaster got up.

"I should go."

"Can I come?"

The corners of his mouth twitched downwards. "I don't know if it's safe, Adriane."

"It'll be fine. I've been in here for days; even I need some fresh air."

"There's always the window."

Adriane kicked at his shins, and he winced.

"Alright," he decided. "Fine. You can come. I won't take you out into the city, but Miles has a report waiting for me at headquarters. Mia will be there, and Jacob should be too, though I can't say he's been about as much as usual lately. I'm a bit worried, to be honest."

"What's with him?"

Lancaster shrugged. "You never can tell with thieves; most are good liars. But I think the thought of a leak is getting him worked up. He grew up with the Guild, knows everybody. The thought that one of your friends is working behind your back, betraying you?" He shook his head. "It's not a nice feeling."

They walked to the room's door and out into a narrow corridor that ran the length of the building. As she left the room, Adriane turned to see the last glimmer of the sun's rays disappear behind the looming city buildings. Dusk had fallen, and night was coming. She noted Lancaster's small smile and knew he had seen it too. It was time for the Guild to ply its unholy trade.

They walked down the corridor at a comfortable pace. The air was cool and dry yet tinged with the undertones of the city: slops and decaying meat, fruit and dust, and below it all, the rough scent of pungent wood-fire smoke. *Wait.*

"Smoke—" Adriane began, right as Lancaster's head snapped sideways, nostrils flaring.

"What in the shades?"

The smell had been there before, she was certain of it, but now it filled the air in thick pervasive layers. Lancaster accelerated to a trot, and she ran to keep up.

"Fire?" she asked, horror rising. A fire in the city spelled catastrophe. Though Cain's larger steam and water pipes had valves that could be opened to help contain fires, the Poors Quarter was hardly supplied well enough to gain much from the system.

"What are the chances," Lancaster muttered, halting mid-stride. "A fire, here of all places? I wouldn't put in past the Service."

She skidded to a stop, understanding. "They'd torch their own city to capture you?"

Lancaster faced her. "Adriane, I need you to stay here. Promise me."

"What? Not a chance."

"We don't know if this is the Service. It could be nothing." An explosion rocked the building, and they raced to the nearest window to watch the Abraham Guild's headquarters go up in a blaze of smoke. "Okay, it's definitely something," Lancaster amended. "But you're not risking capture. Stay and hide. Please." His eyes begged her to do as he said.

"And what are you going to do? What difference can you make?"

He gave her a roguish grin. "Probably none. But if it is the Service, the least I can do is buy some time for the others to escape. This is my guild, my family. Look, we don't have time to argue. I'll send Mia or Jacob—someone I trust—to find you."

She gritted her teeth. *It's my family too, now.* She'd run from Hannah and Max to protect them. Would she run to protect herself now while others were in danger?

He turned to go, and she caught his sleeve. "Don't you dare leave me alone," she whispered, suddenly fighting against her emotions. Her parents were dead; Hannah and Max were gone. "You're all the family I have left." Shadows flickered around her, calming when Lancaster leaned in for a quick kiss.

"Wouldn't dream of it," he said, then extricated himself and ran.

Refusing to allow herself to wallow in sadness, Adriane sprinted back to her room and grabbed her pack, filling it with her clothes, the green pebble, and a few of Lancaster's books. Lastly, she dug out the two hunting traps she'd brought with her from Kaeville, inspecting them for damage. She hadn't needed them since travelling to Cain, but perhaps she would find a use for them yet.

⸺∘∞∘⸺

"Jenna?" Castor shouted.

She fumbled for her magic, but a spark lit up the night. A shock jolted down the whip curled around her arm, biting into her.

She yelled as her body contorted in pain and all the energy she'd gathered rushed right out of her. "Castor!"

She heard the whisper of steel from behind her, then the sounds of a scuffle. Castor was struggling with someone.

Dark figures rushed out of the woods and towards her. She tried to get up, but another shock forced her back down. Gritting her teeth against the pain, she cast out for energy, but the current buzzed through her mind, somehow blocking her magic. *What's going on?*

The horses whinnied in fright. Two dark-clad men grabbed Silverphile and Copper and cut their hobbles.

"No!" She jerked forward as someone tugged at the whip. One of the men who'd grabbed her mare picked Jenna up as easily as if she was a child, slinging her over his shoulder.

"Jenna! No!"

She twisted backwards to see Castor struggling against a man wielding a sword. Her heart leaped into her throat as the man swung his weapon, but then she realized Castor had his hammer in hand. He knocked the strike away and buried the hammer in his opponent's shoulder with a massive crunch.

Jenna's vision flickered purple as the available energy built up around her. Invigorated, she tried to twist out of the man's grasp. Her hands found his face, and she clawed at his eyes. The man swore and flung her from him. Before she could get up, another whip curled around her ankle, and a shock raced through her, ripping the magic from her grasp.

Her eyesight flashed back to normal, and she gasped in pain. Her body fell limp, somehow unable to deal with the jarring sensation of losing that much energy. Just a second ago it had filled her, and now it was gone, a yawning emptiness in its stead.

She tried to turn her head to see Castor, but her vision blurred and darkness crept in. It took all her concentration to keep from blacking out. Someone grabbed her, and she was slung onto a horse. Castor's terrified face swung into view one last time—then he was gone.

Adriane paced the hallway, constantly checking the window, anxious beyond anything she had ever felt before. She feared for Lancaster's life more than she had for the lives of her parents, for Max, or even for Hannah. Perhaps that was simply due to waiting and being unable to do anything, but the intensity of her emotions still scared her.

Another explosion rocked the structure, and she raced to the window just in time to see a neighbouring storage barn succumb to flames. She itched to run—whether towards the fire and Lancaster or away from danger she wasn't sure—but whoever Lancaster sent wouldn't be able to find her if she moved.

She breathed a prayer to the shades, thanking them for the recent rainfall. The fire might have spread even faster without the lingering dampness. As it was, it had already claimed three buildings, including headquarters. A steady stream of people rushed from the afflicted structures, funneled into Abel Way. *Is no one escaping through the back? Did they block the exits?*

New cries sprung up, and she craned her neck to see. Dark figures sprang out of the shadows, towards the people fleeing the fire. Firelight glinted off shiny coats, and she realized she was seeing Servicemembers. She growled in frustration, unable to prevent the catastrophe unfolding beneath her. The Abraham Guild had been smoked out like rabbits, then caught in a snare.

Adriane cursed, the sound a little less clumsy on her lips after her time with the Guild. *What about Lancaster?* She searched the figures below but couldn't make out enough detail to identify anyone.

Someone skidded to a stop beside her, and Adriane whirled to find herself facing Mia.

"Adriane! Thank the shadows. You okay?"

"I'm fine. Where's Lancaster?"

Mia's face and hands were sooty, and her hair looked singed. She seemed unhurt, though she gasped for air. "Haven't seen him. Curse it's chaos down there. I was in the practice yard when the headquarters exploded, so I climbed the roof. Managed to get past the Servicemen. Jacob's out looking for Lancaster. I told him to meet us—" She dissolved into a coughing fit.

Adriane ducked away from the window, noticing a few Servicemen glancing upwards. The fire was getting closer too. Her hands balled into fists as her magic surrounded her, cutting off all sensation for a moment. Wisps of black shadow rolled off her skin, and then the magic was gone as quickly as it had come. She looked up to see that Mia had jumped two steps back.

"What?" Mia rasped at the look Adriane shot her. "It's creepy when you do that. So, what's the plan?"

Adriane tried to think, her calm demeanor betrayed by shaking hands. "The flames will reach us soon. We've got to get out of here either way, and I'm going to go find Lancaster. You coming?"

"Sure. We'll find him. Don't worry."

Adriane was glad for the reassurance, even though she knew it was unfounded. She grabbed her pack and turned down the hallway to a connecting door, Mia behind her. She opened the door and jumped back as a cloud of thick, choking smoke rolled in.

Coughing again, Mia handed Adriane a handkerchief soaked in something strong. Adriane tied it over nose and mouth before continuing. Though breathing was easier now, the smoke still stung her eyes, and she crept along half blind.

"We'd better take the lower exit," Mia said, voice muffled.

Adriane nodded and turned towards the stairs, where the air seemed marginally clearer.

Before they reached the first step, Adriane glimpsed a shadowy silhouette below them, climbing up the stairs. She signaled for Mia to wait, glancing back at the approaching waves of smoke.

"The Service wouldn't know you're here," Mia whispered.

"They may check the buildings just in case," Adriane said, trying not to panic.

They retreated into an alcove, unwilling to take chances. Tense seconds passed before a scrawny figure slunk past them.

"Jacob," Mia hissed.

The boy jumped in surprise before turning towards them, and Adriane gasped at the state of him. Jacob was streaked with bloodied soot from head to toe. His clothes, usually kept neat, if not clean, were bedraggled and hung on him as if he'd lost several pounds in a heartbeat. A shallow cut dripped bright red against the blackness of his face, and several chunks of his hair were sticking out or burnt clean off. The worst part was the blistered skin on his arms, rough and reptilian-looking in the dim, smoke-shrouded light. One arm hung loose and useless, bruised and cracked skin stretched taut across swollen flesh.

He coughed, the crackling sound dragged out of damaged lungs. He'd been breathing in the smoke.

Mia rushed to him and inspected his arms. She was crying, though that might have been from the smoke. Taking off the cloth covering her face, she handed it to the boy, who looked like he might fall over at the slightest breath of wind.

"Jacob, you should've just gotten out," Adriane said. She took a deep breath and removed her own handkerchief, handing it to Mia.

"But you need it—"

"I haven't been out in the smoke yet. You have, so take it." Mia accepted the proffered piece of dirty cloth and tied it over her face.

Adriane tried breathing, and a rush of foul air assaulted her nose. For a moment she couldn't breathe at all for the soot that clamored for entrance into her sinuses. She coughed then, not quite as deeply as her friends had, though it was a close thing. Recovering, she realized Jacob had just said something.

"What was that? Come on, let's get out of here." The smoke was getting thicker.

"It's Lancaster," Jacob said as they raced down the stairs.

Adriane froze. "What about him?"

A hollow sob broke through Jacob's lips. "They got him. The Service did. I saw it."

For a brief moment—an hour, a day—time stood still, balanced on a razor-sharp edge. In the space of a breath, Adriane had time to think. *Don't do it*, her mind said, and she knew it was right. *But there's a chance*, she thought. This was also right. *I can get him back. I have to.*

"Adriane. Adriane!" Mia shook her by the shoulders.

Adriane said nothing, merely stared at her.

"We need to get out. The fire."

She glanced back and saw flames roaring at the top of the stairs, advancing towards their landing. Mia gripped her hand and pulled her down, following Jacob who was already racing ahead, his stride awkward and bent.

They reached fresh air, though Adriane did not remember making it down the stairs and out the door. Flames shot up behind them, but the heat on Adriane's back merely fueled her rage and despair.

After the smoky hallway, everything seemed abnormally bright and clear around her. There were Servicemen in the distance, but far enough away that they shouldn't notice them. A few stragglers still ran from the fire, but most were able to escape into sewers and alleys, no doubt aware of the Service's threat by now.

Wagon wheels creaked in the distance. A hundred paces or so ahead a black-painted Service carriage jerked into the street, black-coated riders on tall horses flanking it. Two arms pulled at the carriage's door from the inside, two soot-blackened arms cloaked by blue sleeves which she could see through the barred windows. Adriane thought vaguely, hopefully, that she knew those arms.

"Lancaster!" she shouted, and the hands grew still for an instant before struggling all the harder with the door. A hand grabbed the scruff of her neck from behind and whipped her around, snaking to cover her mouth.

"Shut up," Mia hissed. "Do you want to give yourself away?" She grabbed Adriane's pack, shaking her.

"I don't care." Adriane ripped Mia's hand away from her mouth. "I'll get him. I'll get him back." Mia's next words were lost to her as she cloaked herself in shadow, the magic coming easily at the call of her emotions.

Rage was all she felt. Rage and then hopelessness and then nothing at all. Mia's hand—along with the pack—melted off her as shadows burst from her skin in waves of darkness and she entered the now-familiar embrace where time and distance did not seem to matter.

Adriane could still see the carriage. It was further away now, far enough that she could not reach it running; the horses had picked up their pace. She could hear voices shouting, see arms pointing like broken sticks in her direction. Black coats flashed in a wind whipped to a fury by the fan of the flames.

Her magic was all she needed. That and her legs. Drawing her massive knife from the sheath in her boot, Adriane sprinted with all her strength, her magic pulsing with each step she took. At first, she ran normally, and then, as if a coin had been flipped, a gear turned, a snare triggered, her magic took over, and she dashed through shadows instead of air, each step spanning many paces. She began to gain on them.

Adriane rushed along Abel Way, clad in shadows much darker than the night that surrounded her. The carriage jolted in and out of view as it turned through the streets, the Servicemen on horses keeping pace with it. That surprised her. She'd expected they would double back or try to catch her.

A man leaped from a building and onto the carriage, brandishing knives and whipping them at the riders—two went down. A whip flicked, and the man yelled in pain, lost his grip, fell off, and rolled out of the street and into a gutter, twitching. *So, I'm not the only one who'd risk my skin for him.* The Guild would come for him, even scattered as they were. *They must.*

With each massive shadow-step, Adriane got closer and closer to the carriage. She rushed through the darkness, barely visible, noting the fearful glance a Servicemen cast back at her. In three steps she'd be there. Silence closed in around her. *Two.* A hiss of steam, her breath escaping. *One.*

She rushed through the shadows and to the first rider, slipping her knife neatly in between his ribs like Jacob had taught her. It was almost as easy as it had been in practice. The night and her shadows cloaked the man's rough scream and the spurt of blood, the smell of it. All she felt was her grip loosen on her knife's hilt, now slippery with spilled life.

The first rider dispatched—not dead, but unhorsed and injured—Adriane strode through the shadows once again, dark wisps curling off her skin and clothes. The echo of her magic bouncing back brought her the first man's scream. She could feel his horse careening, could imagine his slumped figure falling from the mount.

The second rider had a moment to prepare, but it wasn't enough. She lamed his horse before he'd halfway drawn the dagger he reached for.

Surprised that the carriage was still plodding forward, Adriane turned to find the next rider, only to catch a flash of movement in her peripheral vision. Turning instinctively saved her life—the slash meant for her neck bit into her left arm instead. She barely felt it, stopping in her shadow-run to pivot on one foot as the horse rushed past, thrusting her knife out and into the rider's thigh. Another rider came at her right after the first, and she rushed through the shadows, avoiding his blow but also missing hers.

The two horses swerved, then came at her from different sides. Setting her feet and ignoring the heartbeat that throbbed in her arm, she waited until they were almost upon her, then used her magic to move three steps to the side in an instant. The horses collided in a mass of screams, tangled reins, and flailing hooves and went down on top of their riders. It was a dangerous dance she performed, but a dance nonetheless. Nothing was wrong. No one dead, not for certain anyway. She wasn't a killer. *They are the killers.*

Taking a moment to breathe—the echoes washing back over her were disorienting—Adriane let the pain of her wound drip away, sealing it up with all the other things she didn't want to think about. She cut a strip of cloth from her shirt and fashioned a makeshift bandage out of it, then looked ahead to where the carriage was plodding on, the remaining three riders at its sides. *I can still catch them.*

Falling back into a run, she flashed into the shadows just as the carriage turned onto Flames' Road, which led to the Service headquarters. She had to get to him now, before it was too late.

Feeling her burst of adrenaline slipping away, Adriane forced herself to keep moving. She shadow-ran forwards until she was almost to the carriage. She could see Lancaster clearly, his silhouette beating against the carriage door, trying to get out.

"Lancaster!" she shouted, and she saw his eyes searching the dark street.

"Go back." His shout sounded thin by the time it reached her ears. "Go back. Don't be stupid. They'll catch you!"

I don't care, she thought. *I'll make sure you're safe first.* Once he was in the Service's dungeons there'd be little chance of getting him out.

The three remaining riders sped up, racing ahead of her and leaving the carriage unprotected. Unsure of what was going on, she faltered but then caught her step. Even if it was a trap, she couldn't stop. She was so close.

A final step, her magic pushing her ahead, and Adriane stretched out her hands, latching onto the bars of the carriage. Lancaster's warm hand seized hers—she hadn't noticed how cold she was—and she relaxed slightly. Everything would be alright. She reached for the latch, fingers curling past the hilt of her knife and around the heavy metal.

Pain laced her wrist, making her drop the weapon. Whipping her head around, she caught sight of the end of a slender whip snaking back into the night.

"What the—"

Another whip caught her back, and a third snaked around her ankle, latching on like a suckered eel.

"No! Adriane—" Lancaster called, seeing her grip loosen. He lunged for her, tried to hold her there, but the carriage jolted around a bump in the road, and he lost his grip. A shock rolled down the whip on her leg and into her, and her magic slipped from her grasp. She tumbled from the careening carriage like a rag doll.

Time seemed to blink out for a moment, and Adriane found herself lying in the street, the whip still snaked around her ankle. She could hear the clop of horses' hooves and the creak of the cart wheels getting further away. Lacking the energy to stand, she reached for her magic instead. The rush of emotion surrounded her, replaced quickly by the emptiness, and her magic dragged her through the shadows and down the street, scraping her back against the rough cobbles. Adriane could feel a trickle of blood and cold stones through rips in her shirt.

Exhausted, she reached for the magic again—she needed to get out before the Service got to her—but another whip latched on to her, trapping her already-hurt arm. She reached for the magic a second time, a third, but the shock of electricity raced down the whip and into her erasing all thought and feeling in a jarring rush of pain.

Adriane convulsed on the ground. The shock rushed through her. It consumed her consciousness, and when it stopped she lay limp and exhausted, unable to move, barely able to drag a breath into her empty lungs.

Dark-cloaked figures surrounded her, conversing in low, urgent voices. Adriane couldn't do anything. Soft hands reached for her, and she stirred feebly, trying to push them away, but they held her down, then lifted her onto some sort of stretcher which was picked up and carried, the swaying motion making her feel ill. A blanket covered her head, and Adriane welcomed the darkness, succumbing to sleep which let her escape from the despair raging within her.

Tongue pierced
by an
arrow

The symbol on
Granny Melkin's
doorway is indicative
of a spy or
informant

12

Neminia

One Month Ago
Near Neminia, in House Heron–Neminia, Ideon

Rise had been following Daniel's trail of letters for too long now. *Carn't the bastard find a place to lay low until I carn catch up?* Rise was frustrated and worried—and annoyed at those emotions too.

He'd crossed the bridge from Elmsmount Island to the mainland several days ago and had travelled north ever since. He'd avoided the big cities so far, but if the map he'd picked up was right, he'd reach the Ideon Nation's capital, Neminia, soon. Farmsteads and villages were cropping up more and more often. He was on the right track.

A flash of movement caught his eye, and he squinted into the distance. *There.* A stooped old woman was tending a small garden by the wayside, hacking at weeds with a sickle much too large for her. A dilapidated building, half house and half barn, rose up behind the motely garden.

Is that what I think it is? Rise thought he could see faded lines carved into the house's doorway, forming a tongue pierced by an arrow. He smiled to himself. *Must be my lucky day.*

He approached the old lady and dismounted when he reached her property. "Excuse me, grandmother. I have some seeds I'd like to exchange." He was out of practice, but the code words still came easily.

She looked up from her work with a cackle. "Another suitor already? Everyone's in the business these days it seems. Come in dearie, come in. Let's hear what you have to sell, and Granny Melkin will tell you if she's buying." She gestured for Rise to walk to her house with her, then made him hold the door open so she could enter.

"What d'you mean 'everyone's in the business these days'?"

"Well, first that freckled young man came, an Eleszanin judging by his wrap-around cloak and the hummingbird pendant he was hiding. Then a whisper-man from our southern friends. It's been a busy month. Now, what are you selling?" She waved her hand at a dusty bench, the only piece of furniture in the narrow room.

Rise ducked at the gesture—she still had the massive sickle in her hand—and then sat. "I've got some news on the eyes."

"Sounds like an interesting tidbit. I assume you're here for the letter?"

Daniel. He must be the Eleszanin she was talking about. Rise had figured the Ideian cloak he'd been given was disguise enough. It sounded like Daniel had taken further measures.

"Yeah." Rise cleared his throat. "Word out is the eyes are cooking up something big in the east. No one knows exactly what, but I'm sure you've already heard of the increased border raids. What's new though is the goods they're after. Indobalt is being smuggled across. People too, some say. What's more is the eyes themselves are crossing, not just leaving the legwork up to bandits and the like."

Granny Melkin whistled through craggy teeth. "You don't say. That's some big news you're carrying. Too bad I can't repay the same."

"What do you mean? I thought you said you had a letter?"

"Well, I did, 'til that southern whisper-man took it off my hands for a nice price."

"What?! Shadows take me." Rise sprang to his feet. "What happened?"

"That Eleszanin dropped off a letter with a southern name scrawled on it, then headed up north. The whisper-man who picked it up followed him, to the city like as not. More than that I shouldn't say—better for the business to mind my own business, you know… but you did pay so nicely…" She muttered to herself for a minute before seeming to make up her mind. "I'll tell you one thing, that second fellow may have had a whisper-man's words, but Granny Melkin is sharper than your average pumpkin-headed farmer, and she saw what he was hiding."

Rise's heart filled with dread. *Carn't be what I think it is. Curse it carn't.* "Tell me."

The old lady leaned towards him conspiratorially. "A third eye is what. I saw him hiding it in his hand."

Rise clenched his fists. *Shade and flame, so there really is a Serviceman following Daniel. An elitist at that. One with connections to the under-*

ground. He could be sure the old woman's information was accurate; the news he'd given her was more than enough pay for an informant like her. *I hope she's a canary, even a fink, rather than a rat*, Rise thought. Canaries were informants who kept to their sides, but rats would sell to the highest bidder. Then again, she had given the letter to the first man to come looking for it.

That the Serviceman was part of the Protectorate made things more complicated. *Could it be...?* Rise drove the thought from his head. *Surely it can't be* him. *My luck is bad enough as is.*

⸎

Present Day

Long ago, said a voice, *this land—and I—did not exist. Earthquakes plagued the world and brought forth the continent from the ocean's depths. I awoke to this new land boiling around me, with magic tearing it apart and then putting it back together. In this frantic web of destruction and reconstruction, I saw something.*

I saw a possibility. The chance that here, life could grow and thrive. The chance that it could wither and die.

There was always a balance between the two. Plants and animals came to the land and so too did creatures of spirit, counterparts of the magic that flowed through the reservoirs of the earth. They were like me, in a way, but less defined. My shadows. I was—I am—the guardian of this land. A life to offset the magic's lifelessness. A pattern to organise its directionless flow. A soul to contrast the aether.

Humans came after. Eight tribes, exiled from the Isles of Jade, found this land after being blown off course by a mighty storm. Their lives were saved in finding it, and from then on, their lives were also tied to it.

Humans came a second time, this time as settlers instead of refugees, colonists who had lost their way. Once again, the great storms swept them towards the land and led them to its safety. They, too, were tied to the land from that time on.

For a while peace reigned. For a while things were good.

Jenna stirred in her sleep. *Ouch. What was that?*

You are waking, child, the voice said. *But there are still more things I must tell you. Rest assured that we will meet again. You must know the past if you are ever to prevent...* The words drifted off into nothingness.

Jenna woke to a strange rocking, swaying motion, like that of a hammock but up and down instead of sideways. *I must've fallen asleep.* Her eyes focused in a blur of greens and browns. Her head bumped into a horse's flank and a whinny bored into her ear.

Slung over a saddle. How dignified.

She tried to raise her head to see, but a sharp cuff forced it down again. She groaned. "Where am I?" *Yoel's heart, we were attacked. And then I heard a voice? Was I dreaming?* The memories of the fight came rushing back into her head, and all thoughts of the strange dream fled. "What happened? Who are you people?"

"Shut up."

Bouncing along like a sack of potatoes, Jenna tried to move each finger, then her hands and arms, feeling around the saddle to see if anything useful was within her reach. Her arm was sore where the whip had locked around it, but other than that and the headache starting to form, she seemed fine. She debated trying her magic but discarded the thought. *I don't want another taste of those whips, whatever they were. Maybe if I can figure out what lets them know I'm using my magic...*

A second blow hit the back of the neck, softer this time.

"Stop moving." A man's voice. "We're almost there."

Jenna lay still but found the saddle horn dug painfully into her stomach now that she'd shifted. Her arms ached, and her head kept bouncing against the horse's chest. Tack and buckles and straps dug into her shoulders, chest, and neck. Her legs—*I can't feel my legs,* she realized. *I can't feel them at all.*

Fear at being so incredibly helpless filled her, and her discomfort faded as she strove to focus her thoughts on something—anything—else. She concentrated on the ground, observing the patterns of roots and stones littering the small track they rode on. Then the ground changed to the deep brown and light green of churned-up mud in a grassy clearing. Without warning, the rider grabbed her by the shoulder and rolled her off the horse and into a pile of wet, dirty leaves.

She tried to take it all in, dark-clad soldiers, mail glinting from underneath dirty coats, sweat-stained horses, the bustle of a small camp being set up around a cluster of trees. Her mind zoned in on a single thought. *Republican soldiers.* Then, she recognized one of them—the Serviceman from Hemsford, now wearing the blue eye sigil openly. She looked to the others, seeing the mark mirrored on their coats. All Servicemen. Fear churned in her gut, and she fought to keep from being sick.

It took her a minute before she saw the Ideians. Seven men and women, crouching down in the dirt, eyes downcast, travel-stained, and weary. A giant of a man extracted himself from the bustle of soldiers—*Fifteen? Twenty in all?*—and made his way to the first of them, a young man with a scruffy beard. He took the man's right hand and tied it to his back with a length of sturdy rope, then tied the rope to one of the trees in the clearing's center. He did the same to the others. *Prisoners like me,* Jenna realized.

Having finished with the other seven, the man approached her.

"Picked you up last night, little murderer." He smiled humorlessly through filthy teeth. "Sergeant told us all about you. Don't expect too many comforts for your trouble."

He grabbed the front of her riding dress with a gloved hand and picked her up like she weighed nothing.

"Just a girl, are you?" he said, regarding her. "Tall for one." Jenna saw a glinting intellect hiding behind his rough demeanour. "Now, here are the rules. Do as you're told, and don't even think of trying to run away. Some of the men might not take too kindly to that, especially after you killed our comrade."

"I…" Jenna began, but the man's look silenced her.

"I say fair is fair, we kill some of yours, you kill some of ours." He held her closer, and she could smell his sour breath. "We protect our investments, same as anyone. But don't you go forgetting your place. Think you can do that, girl?"

She stared, dumbfounded, until he shook her, and she realized he wanted an answer. She licked her lips. "Yes." It came out as a squeak, and she cleared her throat. "Yes."

The man pushed her onto the ground, then yanked her right hand up behind her back. She tried to raise her head to spit out the mouthful of dirt and leaves she had gotten, but he lazily pushed it back with one gigantic foot.

"Stay down."

Having tied her hand tightly behind her back, the man returned to the other Servicemen who had been busy setting up tents and hobbling horses. Jenna caught a glimmer of grey among the brown and tan soldier's horses. Silverphile.

It hit her then. *Castor. Is he…?* She glanced around frantically, but there was no sign of him or of Copper. *Does that mean he escaped them? Or…* She didn't want to finish the thought but forced herself to consider it. *The Serviceman mentioned killing Ideians. If Castor's dead there's nothing I can do about it right now. And it would mean there's no help coming for me. I don't know for sure, so I'll have to rely on myself to get out of this mess.* She looked back at the Servicemen. *If I can.*

"Don't even think about it."

Jenna jumped, or rather, she would have if she'd been able to feel her legs.

"Sorry, I didn't mean to startle you." The speaker was a young woman, perhaps a few years older than Jenna and tied to the nearest tree. She had straight black hair, and the mud that bespattered her face did little to hide her beauty. A Republican might simply find her bright, yellowed eyes and sharp nose strange, but Jenna knew the features signified a partial Kane heritage.

"I'm Zenia." She gazed intensely at Jenna. "And don't even think about going anywhere or trying to get out. Just stay put."

"How'd you know that's what I was thinking?"

"Oh, I just know." Her eyes still twinkled even though she seemed just as bad off as Jenna.

Jenna raised an eyebrow. "You're not a mind reader, are you?"

"Not exactly." Her eyes jerked towards the Servicemen around them. "Trust me, it's best if you don't know. Suffice it to say I'm more perceptive than most."

Seems odd, Jenna thought, *but she's obviously been here longer than I have. Wait a minute.* "Zenia!"

"What?"

"You said that was your name, right? Zenia? Are you Michael Grassman's daughter?"

"Yes?" The woman's look of bewilderment managed to draw a chuckle out of Jenna. "Do I know you?"

"No, but I heard about you from some villagers when we…" Jenna trailed off, remembering. *When we found your father dead at the hands of Servicemen.* So, they'd taken the man's daughter and these other people. And her. "Do you… You weren't travelling with your father, were you?"

Zenia looked down, sadness written plainly across her face. "Yes," she said. "I was. The Servicemen killed him right in front of me."

Jenna crawled closer and reached out with her free hand. "I'm so sorry. I—that is, we—my husband and I, well, we found your father. The deathsayer in Stillbrook laid him to rest."

Tears formed in Zenia's eyes, but she blinked them away. "He was given a proper burial then. I suppose I couldn't ask for more. Thank you." She took a moment to compose herself. "Your husband. Is he...?"

Jenna shook her head. "I don't know. I don't think so. I remember him fighting back, and his horse isn't here. He might have gotten away." *If he did, help will be coming. But if he didn't—*

"Stop," Zenia intruded. "Don't even think about it. There's no way you can escape from here."

"How do you do that?" Jenna asked. "Know what I'm thinking? And I can't help it. I can't just sit here and expect to be rescued."

"Never mind how I know. Just—be careful. See that man over there, the one in the green cloak?" Zenia pointed at one of the other prisoners, a middle-aged man sitting with his back against a tree, seemingly sleeping. "He tried running for it two days ago. They beat him badly. He can barely stand now."

At least he can stand.

"You haven't told me your name."

"Right. I'm Jenna. Jenna Brightshade."

It was Zenia's turn to raise an eyebrow. "You're young to have earned a last name already."

"I didn't. Brightshade was my mother's name." Jenna smiled. "She once saved a caravan from some raiders. The elders ruled the namedeed great enough to allow her to pass her name down, and she chose to give it to me when I was born. She gave me my magic too, so I suppose it made sense."

Zenia tensed as soon as Jenna mentioned magic. "That's another thing," she said with a surreptitious glance back. "Don't talk about magic here."

"Why not?"

Zenia shook her head. "Just don't. Please, trust me on that. The Servicemen aren't used to it, and it gets them treating us even worse if they're reminded that we're mages. Not that they can't help but think of it every time they look at us. It'll be better for everyone if you keep your head down and do as they say."

The next morning, Tobin let the squad sleep in, though he himself woke up early and crept out of bed. His room—as the commanding officer he'd been assigned a room of his own—was already alight with sunlight streaming in through a good-sized window. It had real glass panes, and the floor was made of wood, polished to a shine.

Tobin left the room and got directions to the nobles' accommodations from a passing servant after identifying himself with his seal, crossed tonfa on a field of silver-rimmed blue. His parents had written they were staying at court until the month of Essill, and Tobin wanted to surprise them with a visit.

He wandered through palace courtyards and hallways and soon made it to his parents' apartments. He hesitated, then knocked. The door creaked open, and a shriek of excitement sounded. Tobin barely had time to brace himself before his three sisters threw themselves at him in delight.

"Tobin! What—how are you here?"

"How is training?"

"Are you staying for breakfast?"

Tobin grunted, trying to get them off him. When they finally released him, he gasped for air. "Fine. I'm fine. Breakfast?" They grinned and let him in.

He told his sisters all about his mission and the bandits his squad had encountered while they rang for breakfast and woke their parents. When his half-asleep mother and father found their way into the sitting room, Tobin had to start his story all over again after another affectionate round of greetings.

Nijam and Terra, twins a year older than him, kept interrupting with questions, and they were halfway through breakfast by the time he thought he'd done his journey justice. He had, however, omitted the parts containing Lady Kesma for fear they'd tease him.

"Meet any fine ladies out on the road?" Eva, the oldest, asked conspiratorially when he'd finished.

Tobin forced a laugh. "Nah, I don't have time for that sort of thing. I need to focus on my training, you know."

The sisters exchanged knowing glances at his answer, and he suppressed a grimace, but thankfully they switched to talking about their shenanigans court.

"Miso's been anxious for those new Republicans to come," Nijam remarked with a grin, naming one of their cousins. "She's been dying to try and catch them with our injured noble charade."

"What's the...?"

"It's simple. I pretend I've cut myself on a broken piece of jewelry or some other nonsense, call for help, the Republicans all freak out, and then Miso shows up like a hero and uses her magic to heal—"

"Nijam!" Tobin's father exclaimed, scandalized. "Don't tell me you've been participating in those unseemly pranks of your cousin's!"

"Just an idea we had," Nijam was quick to murmur, though she winked at Tobin while she said it.

"Papa thinks the pranks are Miso's idea," Terra whispered to Tobin, "but it's Nijam who comes up with them all."

"Girls," their mother scolded, "some of these Republicans are actually afraid of magic. It's hardly proper to terrorize them for it—they're not used to it."

"You're seventeen—two years into adulthood," their father snapped. "Act like it."

Eva sniffed as if the pranks of her younger siblings were far beneath her.

Terra prodded Tobin with an elbow. "Don't let Eva fool you," she whispered as their parents continued to berate Nijam. "She's in on it too."

Tobin let the familiar bickering of his sisters wash over him as he ate his fill.

"…and to use magic to heal for a prank," his mother was saying, "is a frightful waste of your cousin's abilities. Even if Miso is still a child, you three aren't, and I expect better of you than to reflect poorly on our House."

"Like we care," Nijam murmured happily under her breath, plastering on an innocent smile for the sake of their parents. Her magic let her both create fake scars and marks on her skin as well as get rid of existing ones, and she had used this ability in many ways their parents would think were inappropriate. *I would guess the injured noble charade depends on Nijam actually hurting herself and then covering up the evidence once Miso heals it,* Tobin thought with a smirk.

An hour later, after delaying as long as he could, Tobin said his farewells and left. Extracting himself from the last of his sisters' hugs, he sprinted back to the barracks and quickly repacked his saddlebags, adding a cloth satchel of sweets his parents had given him. They treated his sisters and him as if they were still children, but they weren't so bad. Tobin loved his family, though he knew he'd been right to train as a soldier in Silas' Hill. *It's my way of making a difference in the world.*

Several hours later, Tobin was once again riding through Neminia, this time heading back east. He'd caught up with his squad in the stables but told them to start without him. It was probably a terrible idea, but he wanted to stop by the diplomats' quarters before he left, in case he could get one last glimpse of the beautiful Lady Kesma.

After half an hour wasted on casually walking past the Republicans' quarters without so much as a glimpse of any of them, Tobin gave up and started back across the city. He was halfway to the gate when someone ran into his horse.

"Hey! Are you alright?"

The figure, a Republican aristocrat by the looks of him, stumbled backwards, glanced behind him, then took off down an alley. A second man crashed out from behind a fence and set off in pursuit. A glint of light bounced off something in his hand. *A dagger.*

"Hey!" Tobin called. "Stop!" He looked around, but there were no guards in sight. Thinking quickly, he wheeled Spiffy and took off in pursuit.

Any advantage gained by having a horse was lost by the sheer nimbleness afforded by running on foot. Tobin managed to keep the two men in sight as he rode, directing Spiffy carefully to keep from trampling anyone. He passed a stable and, in a flash of inspiration, slid from the saddle. He tossed Spiffy's reins and a coin to a waiting hostler, who didn't seem the least bit ruffled when Tobin immediately disappeared into the crowd. City folk were used to the hustle and bustle of city life.

Tobin had lost sight of the Republican man, but the one with the dagger clutched in his hand was still sprinting through the crowds, so Tobin continued to follow him. The streets they passed became more and more rundown until Tobin knew they must be approaching Neminia's Quarter District, where the city's only slum simmered in the late-summer heat. The dilapidated alleys they now ran through became increasingly deserted; it seemed the city dwellers knew to stay away from a chase.

Tobin's lungs burned, but still he pursued the man, keeping his dark, fluttering cloak in sight. They passed the gaping mouth of an alleyway, and the Republican leapt out from the shadows, catching hold of the armed man's cape.

The armed man exploded into action, swinging forward the hand with the dagger. The Republican dodged, hand racing to his opponent's throat. The man blocked but left himself open to the Republican's knee which caught him between the legs. He dropped with a hoarse cry, and the Republican whipped out a rope, wrapped it around the man's neck, and pulled his head back.

Realizing what was about to happen, Tobin reached for his tonfa, about to join the fight, but then realized he'd left them tied to Spiffy's saddle with the rest of his possessions. Hoping he wasn't about to get himself killed, he jumped at the Republican, pulling him off the other man.

The Republican punched at him, but Tobin saw the blows coming and steeled himself for the impact. He wasn't the best unarmed fighter, but he was strong, and he used that strength to hurl the Republican away from himself and the other man, who was still gasping for breath on the alley's crumbling cobblestones. The Republican made as if to re-enter the fight, then apparently thought better of it, turned, and disappeared back into the maze of streets.

Tobin made sure he was gone, then kneeled beside the other man, who barely looked older than him. He was tall and thin, with pale skin and a mop of dark brown hair. He clutched at this throat with hands covered by ladylike white gloves.

"Are you okay?"

"Get—off!" The man coughed, trying to scramble to his feet.

Tobin held him down. "I can't do that. My name is Tobin vinn Baorock, and I'm with Yoel's Atonement. I ought to bring you in to the city guards."

"You don't understand! That's him—I need to get—"

"What were you planning to do, kill that other guy? Who are you anyway?" The man's clothes looked normal enough, but he spoke with a slight accent, and he had bandages wrapped around his calves in a distinctly Republican style of dress.

"Please!" the man screamed.

The anguish in his voice made Tobin hesitate, and he let go, allowing the man to lurch to his feet. His head told him not to trust the man, but his gut said otherwise, and the pain in his eyes was real enough. *He can't hurt that Republican anymore. Besides, there's gotta be a reason he was chasing him.*

"Look, my name is Rise." The man's voice was hoarse, though that was probably due to being half-strangled. "I need to—just let me go after him. I'll explain later. I carn't lose the trail." Feverish with desperation, he turned, racing back into the street.

Confused, Tobin followed him. He didn't see how Rise stood a chance of finding the Republican, who had disappeared back into the city's bowels.

Rise dug a hand into a satchel hanging from his belt and brought out some sort of powder that shimmered when light hit it. He threw it into the air, and it fell like motes of dust through sunlight, spreading out and settling on the worn-out cobbles. Rise studied the patters it made, then stumbled forward.

Tobin caught his arm before he could go far. "What…?"

"Fireflee powder," Rise said by way of explanation, which meant nothing to Tobin. He yanked his arm away, then ran. In a split second, Tobin made his decision. He followed.

"I won't let you kill that Republican if that's what your plan is," Tobin said. He'd already decided not to stop the man from leaving, but he wouldn't allow him to commit a crime either. He didn't know this man's story, didn't know why he'd chased the Republican, but he did know the desperation in his voice had been all too real.

"Follow if you've got to," Rise shouted back over his shoulder with a curse that made Tobin's eyebrows shoot up. "Curse you think I'll kill him, but I won't until I find out the truth." He was muttering now, almost too quietly for Tobin to hear. "He has the letter. He's got to."

Rise kept on the Serviceman's trail with the last of the fireflee powder, an illegal substance he'd picked up in Neminia's black market. That young soldier, Tobin vinn Baorock, was still following him, though he hadn't made further attempts to stop him. That was all that mattered.

Rise was so bent on following the glowing trail left behind by the powder that he almost ran headlong into a wall. He swore under his breath. "Where is he?" he muttered, as the soldier skidded to a stop beside him. "C'mon."

"The roof," Tobin whispered, pointing at a thin beam protruding from the wall. Rise hadn't noticed it before. He gripped it in a gloved hand, pulling on it to make sure it would hold his weight, when a chill ran down his spine.

Rise looked up to see a thin, grey hand gripping one of his fingers. The hand, small as that of a child, was reaching right out from the building. It gripped harder, and a small body detached itself from inside the wall, lopsided, thin, and slate-grey, like stone. Tobin hadn't been pointing at the beam after all.

"You called?" the creature whispered eerily.

The hair on Rise's arms stood on end. "What the—"

"No called?"

Tobin's breath caught audibly behind Rise. "Stone sprite," he whispered, and Rise realized what the creature must be.

"Shades take me," he said awed, his troubles momentarily forgotten. "They *are* real. The shadows." They called them spirit creatures here, but they would always be the shades, or shadows, to him. Creatures of solitude and darkness, revered by some, cursed by others, disbelieved by most.

"Men disturb the night," the sprite hissed. It looked at him with huge, blank eyes. "Up there," it whispered. "Up there." It let go of his finger, slunk back to the wall, and vanished inside the stone. Rise sagged, let loose from its gripping gaze. He hadn't realized how much those eyes had transfixed him until they were gone.

A rustle came from above, followed by the squeak of shoe-leather on dry timber. *Did the shadow just… help me?*

Rise shook himself. "Got 'im," he murmured. He shimmied up the beam, goosebumps rising when he touched the cold stone. A brief glance downwards showed Tobin following, albeit at a much slower rate.

He made it to the roof's edge and pulled himself up, trying to keep as silent as possible. A flicker of motion caught his eye: The Serviceman rushed across the roof, skidding to a halt at its edge. A wide gap lay between the building they were on and the one next to it. The Serviceman swayed on his feet as if contemplating the leap.

"Hey," Rise shouted, and the figure turned reflexively to look at him.

The man's face glinted with sweat in the sunlight, and Rise froze. "Calen?" *No, no, no,* whispered a voice in his mind. *Anyone but him.*

A flash of recognition lit up Calen's face. "Rise." He swore, incredulity and anger mixing in his face. "Why are you here?"

"The letter." Rise ground his teeth. "Give it to me."

"The letter? That's—that's all you want?" Calen tried to cover the slip in his speech, but Rise knew there was something else he'd meant to say, something he wasn't telling him.

Rise strode forward. He'd lost his knife back in that alley, but Calen needn't know that. He looked his former friend straight in the eyes. "Something I should know, Calen?" he spat.

Calen had betrayed him. Together, they'd chased Daniel down after Rise had secretly helped his brother escape. Then, when Rise's magic had revealed itself… Rise flinched, remembering. He and Calen had been the best of friends. Until that day.

"What'll you do with the letter?" Calen asked.

"I'll find him before a Service bastard like you has a go at it. What else would I do?"

Calen glanced at the drop behind him. "You'll let me go if I give it to you? For old times' sake?"

"What's going on here?" Tobin had finally made it up the beam and was marching across the roof.

"He's got something of mine," Rise growled. "A letter." He turned back to Calen. "Show it to me. Do you have it, or are you just trying to save your own skin?" He took another threatening step forward, and Calen stepped back, his foot tipping downwards where it met the roof's edge.

"I have it. Here." Calen reached into his sweat-stained coat and took out a creased white envelope. He held it out to Rise. "Take it and let me go."

Rise reached for the letter and clutched it to his chest. As soon as he had it, Calen slipped around him, heading back towards the beam. Tobin just stood there, watching the exchange.

"Wait," Rise said. Calen hesitated, then turned back around. "Why didn't you try to kill me?"

Calen laughed without a trace of amusement. "What do you think I was trying to do in that alley?"

"Don't kid yourself. You were trying to stop a stranger from following you. You didn't even recognize me."

Calen's face shone pale and sickly. "Well I'm letting you live now. For old times' sake. Like you did, eh?" He turned his back on Rise. "Don't expect as much again, alright?" He cast a derisive glance at Tobin who still looked to be frozen in confusion. "Along with whoever else gets in my way."

"What about Daniel?"

"What *about* Daniel?"

Rise felt a hint of dread bubbling up inside him followed by hope. "Why aren't you shadowing him? Is he close by?"

"I'm done with Daniel," Calen said, his voice shaking. "I'm done with him."

"What did he do to you?"

"Enough," he hissed. "The bastard did enough."

"Don't you call him that. What happened? Tell me." Rise stepped towards him again, but Calen took off, sprinting across the roof and sliding down the beam with a curse.

"No!" Rise yelled, dread welling up inside him. "Tell me!" He hurtled past Tobin and raced after Calen again.

Barely thinking, Rise followed him through streets and into alleyways, crossing a bridge and heading into the Lake District. He was only vaguely aware of Tobin still following behind, consumed as he was by the effort of keeping the pace and pushing through the pain of burning lungs and aching feet. Calen had always been the better runner.

Rise soon realized Calen was heading towards the city's affluent center. *What the*, he thought, turning a corner. *What is he*—before he could complete the thought, a city guard came into view, holding Calen, who was arguing furiously, by the arm. Rise stumbled to a halt, seeing Calen point back at him.

"Hey, you!" the guard shouted. He'd let Calen go and was trotting in Rise's direction.

"Shades." Rise turned to run, but Tobin raced past him, stopping when he reached the guard.

"Stand back sir—" The guard stopped, evidently recognizing the insignia on Tobin's uniform.

"Why didn't you apprehend that man?" Tobin snapped. "Where was he heading?"

Rise hesitated. Would Tobin be able to get Calen after all?

"He said he was with the Republican delegation, so I let him go. Apologies, Squadleader." The guard snapped into a crisp salute.

"You didn't ask his name?"

Rise had heard enough. Calen had disappeared back into the city, and there was no hope of catching him now. Even if he'd had some fireflee powder left, the street was too crowded for that to work.

Tobin looked back at him. "A word if you will, Rise—"

Rise turned and bolted two steps, determined to make his own escape, when a second guard appeared out of nowhere, catching his arm in a vise-like grip.

Naturally. They let Calen go, but took the trouble to surround him. *Looks like I've got to talk my way out of this one.* Rise cursed under his breath.

light, lacy
paper
wax seal with
a stylized
eye and letter
"N"
Nero's
note

13

HE SCREAMS A LOT

Jenna ate the stale bread she was given without complaint, though it tasted like dirt and didn't fill her up. Zenia kept her company, and they talked of inconsequential things—anything to distract them from the reality of being held captive.

When they'd finished the meager meal, Jenna saw another one of the Servicemen make his way to the prisoners and tie their ropes tighter, so their backs were up against their tree's bark.

"Happens every night," Zenia said, noticing her gaze. "They tie us all up, and there's sentries posted to watch us. It'll be worse for you."

"What do you mean?"

"There aren't enough trees close to the campsite, and they won't tie two of us together."

The Serviceman finished with the last prisoner and turned to Zenia, yanking her closer to the tree and tying her in place, his motions quick and efficient. Zenia went along meekly.

He turned to Jenna. "Come here, girl."

Jenna went to get up before realizing that her legs were still as unresponsive as they'd been all day. *Talking to Zenia made me forget for a while.* "I—I can't," she said.

"What do you mean you can't?" The Serviceman scowled. "Don't play games with me."

"I have a degenerative muscle disease in my legs." Jenna shrank away from him. "I can't move."

The man strode towards her with a growl. Before she could react, he kicked her shoulder, and she fell backwards into a heap of churned-up grass and leaves. Picking her up, he dragged her to a spot of clear ground close to Zenia's tree, dropped her, grabbed a bundle of rope and two stakes that had lain there, and proceeded to tie her hands and feet together.

Jenna winced at his rough touch, but the sound only made him pull the ropes tighter.

"Think you can play games with us?" he spat. "Did you play games with Rickson before you slaughtered him with your magic? Didn't even think of him, did you? Better learn quickly: You mess with us, and you'll pay for it." He looped the ropes together until her arms and legs were twisted back, then tied them to the stakes. He drove the stakes into the ground and left with another disgusted mutter.

It took several minutes before the ache in her shoulder subsided. Jenna groaned. "Do they expect me to get any sleep tied this way?"

She'd spoken quietly, but Zenia still heard. "You shouldn't have talked back to him."

Jenna turned her head, so she could look at her new friend. "I didn't have much of a choice, did I? I wasn't kidding about not being able to move."

"What's wrong with your legs?"

Jenna scowled. "I contracted twitching sickness when I was a child. It killed several others my age, and it nearly killed me. I recovered for the most part, but my legs didn't. I was told I'd never walk again, but I was stubborn enough not to let that stop me, so with the healers' help, I learned to walk with crutches. Some days are worse than others, though. Getting knocked around and slung over a horse didn't exactly help."

"I see." Zenia paused, biting her lip, then continued. "What did he mean about—about playing games? He seemed... sad."

"Not the emotion I would've picked." Jenna's mouth twisted. "I killed a Serviceman a few days ago. More by accident than anything else." She looked Zenia in the eyes, seeing her own fear reflected there. "But I don't regret it. Not one bit."

Zenia's eyes widened, but she said nothing further.

As dusk fell, Jenna wriggled around, trying to get more comfortable and ease the cramps in her neck and back. She glanced back to where the horses were tied, hoping to get a glimpse of Silverphile. *If only I had my books with me to pass the time. But I unpacked them at the campsite. Who knows what happened to them.*

"Do you get bored at all?" she asked.

Zenia chuckled hoarsely. "You're held captive by a group of Servicemen intending who knows what, and you're worried about being bored?"

Jenna shrugged, then wished she hadn't when her arms twinged in protest. "I think if I let myself consider my circumstances too much I may die of fright." She could feel panic bubbling up inside her. "I just need to stay calm and not think about all this." Despite her words, fear and worry surged into her. She hadn't even realized how much she'd pushed them back during the day. She began to shake with the emotion, and sobs welled up in her throat.

"Hey, it's alright. It'll be okay."

"I dunno," Jenna said through chattering teeth. "I don't even know what's going on. I don't even know how I ended up here."

"None of us do, but it's not hopeless. You say you found my father and told some village elders about it. That means for sure there's someone who'll be looking for me. And if your Castor got away then that's someone else. Someone who's looking for you."

But what if he didn't? Jenna thought. *And why did they capture us in the first place? What do they want with me?* She shivered. *First my magic, then the university… how in Tabitha's name did I end up here?*

Wait a minute. Jenna froze. *My magic. It hasn't sparked at all. And the guardian hasn't been back.* She cast out for sources, testing her surroundings. There was energy present, but it was fueled by the destruction the Servicemen had caused in setting up their camp, as well as the bruises and scrapes of the prisoners. *I was knocked out for a while, but I would've felt it if someone died around me—and that means Castor must still be alive.* The thought filled her with a surge of joy.

"Jenna? What is it?"

"I figured something out. My magic—"

"I told you not to—"

"Hear me out, okay? My magic is fueled by energy drawn from death and destruction. I haven't felt anything—well, any death—which means Castor must still be alive."

The night was dark, but Jenna saw a smile flash across Zenia's face. "I told you there's hope yet."

"That you did."

"But you shouldn't have told me that."

"Why not? What has you so paranoid about magic? You're an Ideian, aren't you?"

"Of course I am. It's just—" Zenia lowered her voice. "All the people they've captured here are mages. Every few days they take one of us, question us about our magic. It hasn't been my turn yet, so I don't know exactly what happens, and the others won't talk about it. But they're shaken up afterwards. Bruised and battered as well—Tabitha's eyes, they beat one of them to death. I know there's something sinister going on. I can feel it through my own magic, okay? But I don't know what it is. All I know is it's better I don't know about you and you don't know about me. It'll be safer for the both of us."

Jenna took some time to digest this. "But… what do Republicans want with Ideian mages? They have mages of their own, don't they? Even if they're rare?"

"I wouldn't know. I'm a farmer's daughter, you know. Not educated like you are by the sound of things."

Jenna blushed. "Sorry, I didn't mean to—"

"No, it's okay. Never apologize for being smart." This time her smile was brimming with sadness. "My father always said that."

An impatient hand shook Imp awake, pulling him from his dreams. Nero's bulbous, clean-shaven face drifted into view—not the most pleasant sight to wake to—and Imp tumbled out of bed, rubbing his eyes.

Nero dragged Imp out the door before he was fully dressed, telling him there was a debrief to attend. *Not that they've ever needed me for fancy meetings before*, Imp thought, wishing he had gotten more sleep. It had been a long, long night.

Tromping down the stairs with his gear half-on, Imp was trying to listen to Nero's prattle while simultaneously getting his hand into the sleeve of his jacket.

"…and of course, the Standard Force didn't bother giving us the ground report, so I suppose I'll have to crack some heads and get a first-hand account of it. However, of the little we can confirm, other than the fact that both the gang leader and the mage were captured and that the prototypes were a stunning success, little is relevant, and so I told Michael he should—"

"Wait—" Imp stopped, turning to face his mentor. "What did you say?"

Nero scowled. "Well, the reports we received were quite badly put together, and as I was saying, Michael—"

"No, not about that. You said you captured the mage?"

"We did, Peter, and the new line of indobalt whips Ms. Vinnick developed really—"

"Let me see him."

"What?"

"I want to see the mage," Imp repeated, knowing it wasn't within his power to order Nero around but attempting to sound imperious all the same. The Service had always kept him away from those caught in his fires, but this was different. He'd never seen a mage before.

"I'm not certain it would be wise, Peter," Nero said in a superior tone of voice. "However, you've already been cleared for interviewing the criminal. Mr. Jesaisah apparently would like to see you take some initiative, and you've done that by asking."

"Can I see him now?"

"You can head down to the dungeons after the meeting." Nero was already scribbling the necessary authorization down on a piece of paper, adding a dab of soft wax taken from his writing case. He pressed the top button of his coat into it as a seal. "And please remember proper etiquette. The captive is female and not to be referred to by name. Understood, Peter?"

His mentor's tone didn't even faze him. "Yes, Nero." Imp grabbed the note with an innocent grin that didn't reach his eyes.

Two hours later, Imp perched by the edge of a trapdoor, staring down at the small figure of a young woman slumped motionless on the floor, her hands chained to the floorboards in front of her. Screams and shouts echoed from below, but he didn't really hear them; he was transfixed by the sight of her. The dim light left much of her appearance to his imagination, but he could see that her skin was pale beneath splotches of dirt and blood and that her hair was long and dark.

She twitched suddenly, violently, and he sprang back, startled, before slinking back to the opening. She was still asleep. One arm was bandaged, and her breaths were ragged but steady. That was good. Prisoners in poor condition were more trouble than they were worth. You had to take proper care of them, so you could do things slowly. *That's what Nero always says.* No one talked about what it was they did with prisoners, and at the beginning, Imp hadn't cared. But the screams gave him ideas enough, and he shivered.

Why am I here? The thought startled Imp—he usually tried not to think too deeply, to avoid being confronted with anything other than his fires and the Service itself. Technically, he wasn't even supposed to be here by himself. He should wait for one of the guards before viewing a prisoner.

He glanced at her again, frowning. He'd never shown much interest in the rabble crowding the Service dungeons, but something about the lady kept drawing his eyes. *Maybe because she's a mage*, Imp thought. *Or maybe because my fire caught her.*

In a rush, all the thoughts that had been simmering in his mind for months jumbled out of him. The Service had given him everything. It protected him. But it used him, like a part in a machine, a cog—at once essential and easily replaced. *They can't replace me. I'm too good.* The thought brought a sliver of comfort that dissipated as soon as he looked down at the mage again, reminded of his doubts.

A scream sounded from one of the adjoining rooms. He flinched. *I brought her here.* He knew now that he shouldn't have come down to look at her. Who knew what the Service intended to do with her? Imp's conscience reared its head, and he tried to beat it back. *Why should I care? What does this have to do with me?*

Memories surfaced. His mother, selflessly protecting him, even while they were surrounded by enemies. Uncle Bento, saving him from the consequences of his own fire. *They didn't ask why they should care*, Imp thought. *They just saw someone in need—and helped.*

The sound of booted feet approached, and Imp jumped, startled from his thoughts. He snapped the trapdoor shut, brushed the dust off his coat, and leaned back against the wall with an air of nonchalance. The same impish innocence he pretended when walking away from a fire just set.

"Peter." It was Golen, one of Jesaisah's men, accompanied by Kov, the jailer. "You here to see her?"

Imp nodded. "Sure." He stood straight and followed the two men to a door set into the wall. It banged as they thrust it open, the sound echoing through the underground. They went down a set of stairs and into a hallway flanked by iron doors on either side.

Golen went straight to the first door on the right and threw open a small metal cover, thrusting his lamp against it.

"Is she awake?" Kov asked.

Golen smiled.

Adriane awoke to darkness. Fear stabbed at her, and she tried to jerk up but was stopped by a rough pull on her wrists and the clank of chains. *This is it, then. This is what I get for trying to save him.* She forced his name out of her mind. She was alone now. It was up to her. It was always this way, just her and the world and the danger. *And the fear*, she added, shivering with it. *There's always the fear.*

Metal grated on metal, and a small, bright light blinded her.

"So," a sophisticated, oily sort of voice said. "This is the mage then."

Keys clanked in the door, and the light expanded as it opened, accompanied by the hollow sound of gears clicking and turning. Burying her face in her immobilized hands to escape the light, Adriane relied on her ears to measure the approaching footsteps, estimating the man's weight and stature by the way he walked, something Mia had taught her.

The steps stopped right in front of her face, and rough hands lifted her up by the shoulders. She froze.

"Let her up, Kov," the voice said, and the chains—*blue* chains, she noticed with a shudder—rattled, letting her lift her hands and scrabble onto her feet, jumping away from the man in front of her. Opening her eyes a slit, she could make out his tall stature and two others, mere silhouettes standing in the doorway behind him.

"Before you try your magic, girl," the man said disdainfully, "you should know this building is surrounded by Servicemen, and those chains can transmit shocks, same as the whips you became so well-acquainted with earlier. They interrupt any kind of spell you mages try to procure."

His use of the word 'spell' gave away the fact that he really knew nothing about magic, but his words stuck in her head. *Mages*, he'd said. That confirmed there were others—others like her. She hadn't been sure about it.

The guards unfastened the chains from the floor and brought her to a small room with a desk and three chairs in it. It was a normal room by all appearances, except for the heavy table that dominated the center, with two pairs of cuffs on it and red stains beneath. The smell hit her then, and she almost gagged. *Blood. Not just old, but fresh blood too.* The Servicemen saw her flinch and smiled.

The tall man who'd spoken to her, the one who stank of aristocracy, sat himself behind the desk. The second man—Kov, most likely—pushed her down in one of the other two chairs, then stood imposingly behind her. A boy walked in with an air of confident nonchalance and sat in the third chair. He had reddish streaks in his hair, an angular face, and the palest eyes she'd ever seen. *Can't be older than Jacob. What's a kid doing here?*

The first man cleared his throat, and she turned to face him. "Tell me your name and where you're from."

The simplicity of the question startled her; her mind raced for an effective way to avoid implicating her family—they would not be taken on her account—even while realizing she'd already taken too long to answer.

"I said," the man stipulated with exaggerated patience, "tell me your name and where you're from."

She paused before answering. "Adriane. I'm Adriane Stephensdaughter. From Wrovetown." It was the first suitable place that came to mind. Not so small that they could disprove her claim and not too far away.

"Wrovetown, eh?" The man grinned. Had she given herself away?

"Just so happens we have a local expert around." He nodded at the boy.

"What's the oldest building there nicknamed?" The boy's cheerfulness only further emphasized the gloom and terror of the dungeon.

"The—the Ruin." She knew it was wrong as soon as she said it, but the boy nodded, and the man's fingers tightened into a fist on the desk.

"Our intel says you're from one of the hamlets, mage," he spat. "And coincidentally, there were some inquiries made into a mage with your same description who cropped up in Kaeville not four months ago before being sighted in Cain."

Adriane's heart sprang into her throat. She felt like her face must be both bright red and deathly pale, but knew it was probably as blank as ever. *Hannah—Max—the Service might be on its way for you already.*

"You'll make this easier on everyone, including your friend next door, if you cooperate."

Lancaster. She had to.

"Okay." Her voice was thin but resolute.

"If you like, Adriane, we can make a deal." The oil in his voice as he spoke her name was a thin film of grime that in no way masked the blackness underneath. "You want to save your friend and your family? Well, you can."

She sensed the trap but saw no way to avoid it. "For what?"

He smiled mockingly. "For yourself. Your service." The pun was hollow in his mouth.

An eternity passed before she found herself nodding. *What choice do*

I have? "I'll tell you everything," she said, all too aware of the jailer's threatening presence behind her. "If you free Lancaster."

The man regarded her coolly. His Servicebadge stood out from the cuff of his shirt, contrasting the white hand depicted underneath. "In return for your full cooperation, we will, of course, keep your family and friends... safe."

"You'll let them *go*." Could she trust them to keep their word?

The man nodded. "Before I can release your friend, however, I need some answers. I understand you may not want to be fully honest with me, but rest assured that I will know if you're lying. And that would do your friend a great disservice."

Adriane tried not to shrink beneath his gaze, seeing an intense emotion behind his eyes. *Is it hate? Fear?* She didn't know.

"Now, this Lancaster—what is his full name?"

"Abraham Lancaster."

"Is he known to you by any other name?"

Could this be Lancaster's aristocratic past coming back to haunt him? Thankfully, he'd only mentioned his family's name to her once, and she couldn't remember it. She shook her head. "No."

"You're telling the truth." It was a statement, not a question.

"I am." She stole a glance to the side, but the boy simply sat there, watching.

"At the time of the fire, Lancaster was attempting to steal an object from the Service headquarters. I need to know what."

Adriane racked her brain but realized she was saved from deciding what to answer by the simple fact that she didn't know anything. She said as much, and the man frowned. He did not, however, accuse her of lying. *Maybe he really can tell.*

Back and forth he went with more questions, all of which she answered to the best of her ability. There wasn't much to divulge at any rate. Then he began asking about the other members of the Guild.

"We already know of a boy named Jacob, a man called Miles, and several knife fighters who are of no interest to us at this point in time." His eyes had a glassy shine to them. *What is it with him?* She wasn't good at reading people to begin with, but something told her she should recognize the look. "I need you to divulge the name of every member in Lancaster's gang you had contact with and provide details about their possible whereabouts."

"I didn't meet most of them," Adriane said evasively. *If you can't afford to lie,* Mia had once told her, *tell a half-truth.* "After all, I was trying to hide." *From the Service*, she wanted to say, but stopped herself. Instead, she began listing a few names, trying to name only those the Service would already know of, the brawlers, one of the pickpockets, the two knife fighters who always vied for Mia's attention.

"Very well," the man said when she was finished. He nodded to the jailer. "Return her to her cell."

"Wait." Adriane looked straight at him as she stood up. "Now that I've answered, you'll let Lancaster free?" She felt confident enough to voice it as half a statement, since the man had been neither cruel nor unreasonable with her.

He stopped and considered her, raising an eyebrow. "Do not presume to give orders when you are the one captive."

"But—"

His hand hit her cheekbone; her face snapped sideways. "Enough. Don't forget yourself, mage. You're still ours. We will let him go once we verify your facts. We will keep our word if you keep yours."

Adriane bit back a retort, swallowing the blood that dribbled into her mouth. Her jaw ached with the motion. *I have seen that expression before*, she realized. She'd first seen it when she'd entered Cain, on faces and gazes that slipped past her, choosing to ignore. *Indifference*. She suppressed a shudder. Somehow that was more frightening than if he'd shown rage or fear—passion of any kind was better than treating her like she was some object, unworthy of humanity. *Even if I am a mage.*

The jailer pushed her towards the door, and she stumbled out, resisting the urge to rub the bruise spreading across her face. The boy ducked past her, heading towards the stairs. A few steps away he turned, and for a split second, she thought she saw understanding etched across his innocent features.

After returning to the main floor with Golen and Kov, Imp backtracked and made his way down to the dungeon again, where he stood in front of the door to the lady's—Adriane's—cell. He debated back and forth, then determined that he'd go in. It wasn't strictly protocol, but then again, Nero had sort of given him permission. Sort of. He started to search his pockets for the note and then stopped. *If I'm going to break the rules, I might as well break the rules.* He doubted the note would get him out of trouble if he was found out.

Unsure of how to approach, Imp decided to knock. His fist clanged against the cell door with a hollow sound. When he didn't hear anything, he knocked again.

"Am I supposed to tell you to enter?" The mage's voice echoed sarcastically from inside the cell. Imp unbolted the door, opened it, and stepped inside.

"I dunno," he said. "I figured I'd try to be nice."

The light from the hallway lamps played off Adriane's face, and Imp studied her, interested and no longer as careful to appear casual as he had been with the other Servicemen around. The mage said nothing.

She was still chained to the floor but had been given enough room to stand and walk about a few steps. She was leaning against the wall now, her stance casually threatening, making her seem much taller than she was. Green eyes glared at him from an impassive face, conveying both resentment and disinterest. Only her twitching fingers belied her attempted calmness.

"I lied for you in there," Imp said after a while. She still said nothing, and so he continued. "I didn't have to, but I did." He wasn't sure, but he thought he sounded like he was pleading. Why was he pleading? "I don't know why I did." He looked to the floor. *Or maybe I do. It's what Uncle Bento would've done.*

"Maybe you're just a little boy caught up in their schemes." Adriane shifted her weight. "Or maybe you're a part of it. How should I know? What do you want from me?"

Imp felt shame well up in his chest. All his doubts, the things he tried not to think about, the reality of what the Service was and what it did bloomed in his mind.

"It's my fault," he said. "I put you in here. I haven't done that before—to anyone." *Not like this.* He was a kid again, a boy caught up, like she'd said, in the Service's schemes.

Adriane looked at the boy in front of her, and realized his eyes held tears that he didn't seem to notice. He just stood there, almost crying, and said nothing else.

She sighed. "It's not, really. My decisions, your decisions, they all played a part. If you want to blame someone, blame the Service." The words came automatically. She was used to trying to protect those more vulnerable than her.

"You're not mad at me?" The childish question hung suspended in the air between them, at odds with the layered walls and steel door, the severity, the pain tucked into the room's corners. Anger didn't matter here. But how would he understand that?

"I'm not," she finally said, and the boy sagged, relieved. A thought came to her then. "My—my friend, the one they took. Is he here?"

The boy nodded. "He's down the hall. In the—" he broke off, changing what he'd been about to say. "He's in another room."

She sensed he meant well, but that wasn't enough. "What are you not telling me?"

The boy shrugged. "You can't hear because of the walls, but he screams a lot."

She jerked back, a shudder lengthening her spine. *What an innocent way to phrase it*, she thought distantly. *He screams a lot.* Another shudder. Adriane didn't feel the magic until it was upon her, reaching out, embracing her thoughts. *No. It won't do any*—her thoughts were swallowed up, and the nightmare of shadows drew her in.

Suddenly a shock jerked into her. Once, twice—and then she was on the ground, bones aching, lights dancing in front of her eyes. The boy stood pressed against the door, surprise and fear etched into his already-sharp features.

She groaned. "So these chains really do work."

The boy slunk towards her, hesitated, then helped her up. "I could've told you that. They're indobalt."

Adriane shivered. She couldn't do anything, but there had to be a way to get to Lancaster, to stop whatever madness was going on. They had said she could strike a deal—she'd get him free. "Will they let him go? If I cooperate?"

"Who? Your friend?"

Who else? she wanted to shout, but all she did was nod.

"I don't know. It's the Service. You never know with the Service, but they'd likely want to keep their leverage."

"But what do they want with him? With me?" She was surprised the boy was still talking. This was treason for him, a deadly game.

He looked at her seriously then, the naiveté gone, only a thin veneer of innocence still shining in his eyes. They stared, oh, how they stared. Pale and broken. A little wild.

"Him they want to kill," the boy said in his simple way. "And you? I dunno again. But it's probably something worse." He paused, wavering. "I'm sorry," he blurted. "I don't think I can stay." He took hasty steps backwards until he was right in front of the door again. "I—I'll come back." He fled, swinging the door shut behind him. The bolt rasped into place, and there was silence.

Her momentary bravery fled with the boy, and in came the fear, accompanied by sadness. She pushed it back, lest it activate her magic again.

Lancaster. She hoped he was alright but knew he couldn't be. All she'd gotten so far were these mage-chains, and he… she tried not to think, but her mind filled in whatever gaps she was missing. The Service was tormenting him, punishing him for thinking he could uncover their faults and stand for something better.

Though silence reigned around her, she imagined she could hear his screams. They echoed off the walls, they ripped through the floor, they tore her heart apart. She was useless, and the screams she thought she heard imprinted her helplessness into her mind with white-hot iron thoughts. She sank back against the wall, feeling utterly alone.

The Service Uniform
embroidered Service insignia
shiny black coat
engraved brass buttons

14

BLUE

Rise licked his lips. "I'm a refugee. From the Saint Brazen Republic." He'd have preferred to pretend he was Eleszanin, since their political neutrality made them accepted by most, but Tobin struck him as smart enough to see the holes that claim would leave in his story. For now, telling the truth might keep him out of prison. *If that's the best I carn do, so be it*, he thought.

Tobin sat across from him, shifting uncomfortably on a high-backed wooden chair behind a plain desk. The planks above them were wood as well, as was the floor, though the walls, solid and impregnable, were stone. They were in one of Neminia's guard stations, and Tobin, young though he was, had told the city guards he'd question Rise himself. They'd accepted his authority too, probably because of his rank, or, more likely, because he was a noble. Rise could practically smell it on him. *I carn use that childishness of his too*, Rise mused, *as long as he believes my story.*

"What are you doing in Neminia? And who was that other Republican?"

Rise hesitated. "I came here to find my brother, Daniel. He came ahead of me, leaving letters for me to follow. The man I was following today stole one of the letters. We met on the road a few days ago, and he must've taken the letter from my things. I was just getting it back. I don't want any trouble." Best not talk about their involvement with the Service. That could lead to some awkward questions.

Tobin's shoulders twitched at the mention of letters, and adrenaline surged into Rise, though he still pretended to slouch in his chair. Had Tobin come across some of the letters? *Does he know where Daniel is?* It seemed improbable, impossible even, but after years of chasing down people for the Service, Rise was used to strange coincidences. *Shadows, our escape was strange as anything. Why not have this soldier find Daniel?*

I'd say it's about time for some good luck.

"What made you decide to leave the Republic? Is there any evidence that supports your story?"

Rise cleared his throat, stalling for a few precious seconds. He knew the Ideians wouldn't find his magic strange, and magic was the best proof he had of not being a spy for the Service. However, they might ask to see it, which would involve revealing his branded hand. *Too risky.*

"My brother has magic," he found himself saying. It wasn't as good a reason since he had no proof, but it would do. "The Service found out about it, and we were forced to leave the country. That, or risk getting killed. I don't have proof of my brother's magic or anything, but once I find him he can show you."

There it was again, that twitch in Tobin's shoulders. "What's your last name?"

The question took Rise off guard. "My last name? Does it matter?" He shook his head. "It's Rezah. Rise Rezah."

Tobin exhaled slowly, then looked him straight in the eye. "Look, Rise... my squad and I came here from the eastern training camps, escorting some Republican diplomats. We met some bandits along the way, and when we cleared their camp, well, there was a letter. With your name on it."

No. It carn't be. Not true. Curse it carn't. No, no, no!

"We found the remains of a Republican-style coat as well."

This wasn't supposed to happen. Why hadn't Daniel waited for him? Why had the Service chased him so far? *What's going on?*

"I believe your brother was likely killed by those bandits. I'm sorry." Tobin's voice was formal, but Rise could tell he was sincere. Did sincerity matter in a soldier? Did anything matter anymore?

"No," he whispered.

Everything clicked together. Daniel's letters, Calen's odd behaviour in the city. He'd seemed surprised when Rise only asked for the letter. He'd acted like Daniel had done something to him. *He killed him*, Rise thought, numb. *He killed Daniel, and that changed him.* Killing did that to people. Rise knew all too well, though not from personal experience. He'd seen it happen to others. Servicemen were promoted to the Protectorate, and then they changed. *He killed him.* His once-best friend had murdered his brother.

"Rise." Tobin had risen to place his arm on Rise's shoulder. "Are you alright?"

Rise felt his head clear. He felt calm. "I'm fine."

Revenge, a voice whispered in his head. *Calen's still in the city. You can find him. It's what you do.*

"The letter," Rise said. "Do you have it?"

"My superior took it with her. She'll be back at Silas' Hill by now." He hesitated for a moment as if thinking over something. "You can come with me, if you like. I'll clear you with the guards either way."

Revenge or answers? A year ago, Rise would've picked revenge, but now he was not so sure. Daniel had been right all along, and even though Rise had hated him for it, he'd come for him in the end.

"I'll come," he heard himself saying. "I need to read it." *I need to know.*

Imp returned to his room, troubled and pensive. He'd thought the aftermath of the fire would be like it had always been. He'd smoke a cigarette and watch the buildings burn. Festive. But it was different now, because of the mage. Adriane's presence made him think of all his other fires, made him think of how his fires affected people. People who existed not just in their own heads but who were real and present. They breathed and lived and laughed like he did. He didn't think they laughed much afterwards.

Was it wrong? Was it wrong if the Service said it was right? Was it wrong if he liked it? Was it wrong if others did not? Imp thought he was beginning to know the answers to those questions, but truth be told, he preferred not knowing. *I'm stupid,* he thought. *Stupid for going to see her, stupid for thinking of her as a human.* He'd learned early on it was smarter not to care.

But caring was okay, he remembered distantly. Uncle Bento had cared. Even Vine, in her own way, had cared. And if caring was okay… then that meant he had to do something, right? *But how am I supposed to know?* He felt like he knew nothing at all. All he had were his thoughts and his memories.

Ducking into his room, Imp shut the door behind him. The room was only his temporarily, but it was a small refuge nonetheless. He could hide from the world here, at least for a little while.

His eyes streaked over the large bed, the gold trim on the walls, and the crackling fire in the furnace. Hemp leaves and cigarette paper were laid out on a small desk. His few things—clothes, starters and fuses, books for his lessons, and writing utensils—were packed away in the spacious closet, adding to the room's hollow, borrowed feel.

He took a step forward, and the closet door sprang open, a dark blur crossing his vision. A hand clamped over his mouth, stifling the shout he'd been about to voice, and strong arms dragged his body forward. Scrabbling for a foothold, Imp tried to twist out of the grip, but the hands holding him were unyielding.

"Hush," a voice rasped into his ear. "Don't move and don't speak." It sounded familiar. "We're going to get you out, Imp."

Imp realized where he'd heard the voice before, why he knew it so well. He struggled past the hands and craned his neck around. A dark-cloaked figure came into view.

"Uncle Bento?" It was almost too good to be true.

"Yes, Imp. It's me."

Imp's insides turned to jelly. He would've fallen if Uncle Bento hadn't been holding him up. Tears of relief flooded his face, and he fought the urge to both laugh and cry at the same time.

They sat down on the bed, Imp keeping his eyes on Uncle Bento, hardly believing he was there. *Everything's okay now. Everything.* Uncle Bento had always been there, had always cautioned Imp and, when necessary, gotten him out of trouble. Always. *Except... except for when the Service came for me.* He stiffened at the thought, and his feelings of relief shattered. Tears stopped threatening to burst out of him, and he looked up to see that Uncle Bento was not alone.

A second cloaked figure—a lady by the shape of her; he could tell even with the cloak—emerged from the closet. Imp looked back and forth between the two intruders. Bento had removed his hood.

"What's going on?" He wiped the last of the tears away with a deliberate swipe, as if daring them to comment.

"We're here to get you out," Bento said. "If you want us to."

The lady twitched forward, as if she was about to interject something, but then stilled.

"You're here... to get me out." Imp didn't get it. "Why? Why now? Why are you here!?" His anger came even quicker than the tears. "You didn't get me before—you never tried to stop them!" He thrust an accusing finger at Old Man Bento. "There's no way you couldn't have found me; you'd know my fires anywhere!"

"Hush, boy," the lady snapped. "Do you want someone to barge in and find us?"

"It's alright, Kyra." Uncle Bento turned back to Imp. "I know you don't understand right now, but sometimes we have to let others make their own choices. I've made as many mistakes as anyone—probably more—but sometimes mistakes are important. Sometimes we can't just jump in to save someone. You made a decision, and I had to respect that. There's no freedom in being told what to do every step of the way."

"Then what's different now?"

The lady tapped an impatient foot on the floorboards. "Now you've gone and gotten someone else caught up in this mess."

"You don't mean… the mage?"

The lady nodded. "Adriane."

"Why? What makes her so special?"

The two exchanged a knowing glance. "I promise you, Imp," Uncle Bento rasped, "I'll explain everything I can. But right now we need to act quickly."

Imp blinked. "We're going right now?" Bento's nod sent him scurrying for his pack, gathering a change of clothes and a blanket-roll. After a second's hesitation, Imp tucked a few fuses and starters into his coat pockets. He left the rest of his things behind, even the hemp leaves and cigarette paper.

Is this really happening? Imp pinched himself to make sure he wasn't dreaming.

"Here." The lady handed him a heavy, cloth-wrapped package. "Some supplies you'll need." He stuffed it into his pack.

"All set?" Bento asked. Imp nodded, slinging the pack over his shoulder. He headed towards the door, but the lady stopped him.

"Not that way." She strode to the middle of the room where Old Man Bento was waiting.

At Imp's questioning look, Bento beckoned to him, holding out his hand.

"Did you ever wonder, Imp, why I did not speak much of my past?" he whispered. Imp shook his head. Somehow it had never seemed important. Bento smiled, as if he knew. "Well, right now you just need to know one thing."

"What's that?" The hush in the air made Imp lower his own voice.

Bento smiled again, a roguish grin. "I," he whispered, "have magic." He grasped Imp's hand with his left and the lady's with his right, and a bright light flashed around them.

A second later Imp found himself back in the upper level of the dungeon, still holding Bento's hand. He let go, stunned.

"You—you—you never said." Imp heaved air back into his lungs, which seemed to have deflated. Bento didn't seem to share the problem, but the lady at least coughed.

"To be fair," Bento countered, the smile still in his voice, though more tired now, "you never did ask." He turned and walked towards the stairs.

⚬⚬⚬

Tobin watched Rise uncertainly. They had left the city behind and were riding down the East Way, called 'the Snake' by Neminians for the way it twisted through the gently rolling hills in this part of the country. Rise had dropped his reins, letting his mare follow Spiffy, and was clutching a piece of dirty paper in his pristinely gloved hands—the letter he'd recovered from the thief in the city. Tobin had asked the city guards to keep an eye out for the man, but he doubted the thief would be caught. Stealing a letter wasn't exactly an offense worth pursuing. All the same, Rise had been wronged, and Tobin wanted to look out for him.

Rise hadn't said much of anything after they left, but he opened the letter as soon as they cleared the city's traffic, and he hadn't stopped staring at it since.

Finally, Tobin worked up the courage to clear his throat and speak. "What's the letter say?"

Rise looked up, no hint of emotion betraying his face. "Not much. Daniel meant to stop in Neminia, but he was unable to and kept going. If he made it halfway across the province before getting killed, he must've been riding like the shades themselves were on his heels. This tells me how to find him."

Tobin knew people handled grief in all sorts of different ways, but Rise's complete lack of a reaction was unnerving. *How can he be so calm about it?*

"I see." Tobin scanned the road ahead, looking for the wayfarer's house he'd told his squad to meet him by. Sure enough, he spotted an old stone chimney rising from the scattered trees. Spiffy whinnied, smelling the other horses, and distant whinnies answered from the stone building down the road.

"My squad's waiting for us," Tobin said unnecessarily.

They rode towards the smattering of horses and dismounted soldiers outside the wayfarer's house, which squatted where the Snake bisected a smaller road. Tobin's squadmates jumped up to greet him.

"About time," Timothy said, swinging back into his saddle. "What in Ibram's name took you so long?"

"And who's that behind you?" Felias chimed in.

Tobin turned back towards Rise. "Rise, meet my squad. This here's Timothy and there's Yemena—they're my officers—and then there's Felias, Amaldie, Miels, Phillip who goes by 'Horse,' and then Era, Mathas, and Rico. Squad Fourteen, this is Rise Rezah. He's going to be returning to Silas' Hill with us."

"Only a day in the city and you've already conscripted some of the population," Timothy joked. He turned to Rise "Are you from Neminia, Rise? How come you're coming with us?"

Tobin looked towards the west, where Neminia's walls and the outlying towns were still visible through the patches of trees. Had it really been a single day since he'd met Rise and chased him halfway across the city?

Rise didn't seem much inclined to answer Timothy's questions, so Tobin turned back to his squad. "It's a long story," he said. "Now mount up."

As they descended the stairs, Imp heard the shuffling sound of movement echoing from below.

"Guardsman," he mouthed at Bento, who nodded and turned to look at the lady. She smirked and walked ahead.

"Imp." Bento's rasping voice was barely a whisper. "There may be guards and Servicemen around. I need you to promise me something— if we get separated and you don't see either of us again, take Adriane into Ideon. You'll both be safe there. Head west into Ideon. Alright?"

"Alright." Imp said. *It'll hardly come to that.* But then again, who knew.

They followed the lady—had Bento called her Kyra?—down the stairs and crowded into the narrow hallway at the bottom. Things went wrong right away. Imp heard the click of a bolt sliding into place just as a man came into view, turning away from the door he had shut.

"Hey, what are ya—" before he could finish his sentence, the lady was there. A quick cut with her palm, sprawling limbs, a flash of movement, and the man was on his back, knocked out. She fought as if she was born to it.

Imp started forward, and a shout rang out; a push from Bento almost sent him sprawling.

"Go, Imp!"

The shouts intensified, and the lady raced ahead to cut them off. Apparently, she was the muscle of the operation. It was a half-hearted thought among the scramble of getting to the cell, throwing back the bolt, heaving open the door.

"You." Adriane hardly seemed surprised.

Imp grabbed keys from the fallen guard and scrabbled to her cuffs. "We're leaving. Both of us."

His shaking hands wasted precious seconds before he realized none of the keys fit. He turned, suddenly helpless again. "What do we do?"

She growled a curse. "My magic could get me out if it wasn't for the indobalt."

Imp hesitated, remembering something Vine had said about the whips she'd invented. *The shock created by the indobalt pieces blocks magic as long as the mage doesn't deflect it on someone else.* "Do you trust me?"

She raised an eyebrow. "No. What's the plan?"

He grabbed her hands and took a deep breath. "Try it now. If we're touching, the shock should go clean through you and into me." Imp squeezed his eyes shut.

Something flickered, and then pain exploded, forcing him to his knees. Ears ringing, Imp cracked an eye open. His hands weren't clutching hers anymore. *Did it work?*

He turned to see her standing behind him, rubbing her wrists, approval in her gaze. Imp stood shakily. "That was horrible."

A shout echoed from somewhere in the dungeon, and Imp remembered they had to hurry.

"Quick, let's go."

"We need to get Lancaster."

"What?"

"Lancaster. I'm not leaving without him."

The shouts approached down the hallway, accompanied by the metal clashes of a swordfight, then faded. The lady had drawn them further away. They couldn't waste any time, but one look at the mage's face told

Imp she wouldn't budge.

"Imp!" Uncle Bento's head slid into view from behind the cell door. "Remember what I said. I'll see you again, but for now, get out. We'll keep them off for you." He ducked away, his heavy steps heading towards the fight.

"Imp, is it," the mage murmured, and Imp's head snapped back towards her. She merely looked at him.

"Fine," he said. "Let's get your friend and get out of here. No telling how long we've got."

Nudging her fallen chains to the side, Adriane gestured for Imp to lead the way. The boy's fingers twitched nervously around the keys still in his hands, and he darted to the side and out of the room. She dashed out behind him.

Imp grabbed a lantern from the wall as he ran, and Adriane followed the happily blinking light, terribly at odds with the overall gloom of the dungeon. They turned a corner, and Imp slid to a stop, fumbling with the keys.

"Through here," he said, voice unsteady.

She grabbed the keys from his clammy fingers and pushed them, one after another, into the lock on the door. Finally, it clicked. The door sprang open.

Lancaster lay sprawled asleep on a bloodstained patch of stone floor.

"Lancaster!" Adriane rushed to him, knowing he'd have to wake quickly. *Darkness shield him, I hope he can walk*, she thought. *He must; I can't carry him.* She shook him, ignoring the frightened look in Imp's eyes. Why was there so much blood on the floor?

"Just give him a minute. He'll be up." She didn't realize it. She didn't see it then, didn't want to know. The blood was bright red. It leaked from him as if he were bloated with it.

Nothing happened. She shook him, and sound began to rush into her ears, sound like what she'd always imagined the waves of an ocean would sound like, cold and distant and relentless.

"Lancaster. Lancaster." He didn't move.

"Adriane—" It was Imp. His voice sounded sick. "Adriane, I think he's—"

"No!" She shook him again. "No. Lancaster. Lancaster—Abraham— can you hear me?" His skin was white, almost transparent in the lamplight. "Wake up. Shades, please, wake up! Wake up for me." His arms pressed into the floor, useless, and his vacant eyes stared from an expressionless face. *No.* "Lancaster—" her throat cut out before she could sob. Lancaster. Lancaster was—

"I think he's dead," Imp whispered into the silence—a silence filled with the absence of her cries, the emptiness of her unvoiced anguish. "He looks awful."

I think he's dead. The words stopped the ringing in her ears. He was dead.

Adriane grasped Lancaster's hand. His skin was cold, and his flesh was simple dead weight, without life or vigor or motion. His fingers didn't cup hers, just slipped loosely from her grasp. He was dead. She was alive. What new darkness was this?

She got up quickly, ashamed somehow. His hand fell and hit the floor without a noise. Impulsively, she bent and ripped a shred of fabric off his shirt. Blue. Of course. He'd worn the shirt the day of the fire. The fire. Imp.

Tucking the ragged fabric into her boot, she turned away, straight towards the ashen figure of the boy, seemingly frozen in the doorway. She'd figure out who to blame later. "We need to go," she said, the steel in her voice overwhelming. "Now."

Imp nodded tersely and turned again. "Better go out the lower level side,"

Adriane followed him out of the room, stepping over a mouthful of bile by the door. Imp glanced guiltily at her, but she didn't care. She hadn't even heard him being sick.

Without another word exchanged, they ran. Down the hallway, past a corner, towards freedom. It suddenly seemed so meaningless to her. She was free, but she was empty. Shade and flame; full of nothing.

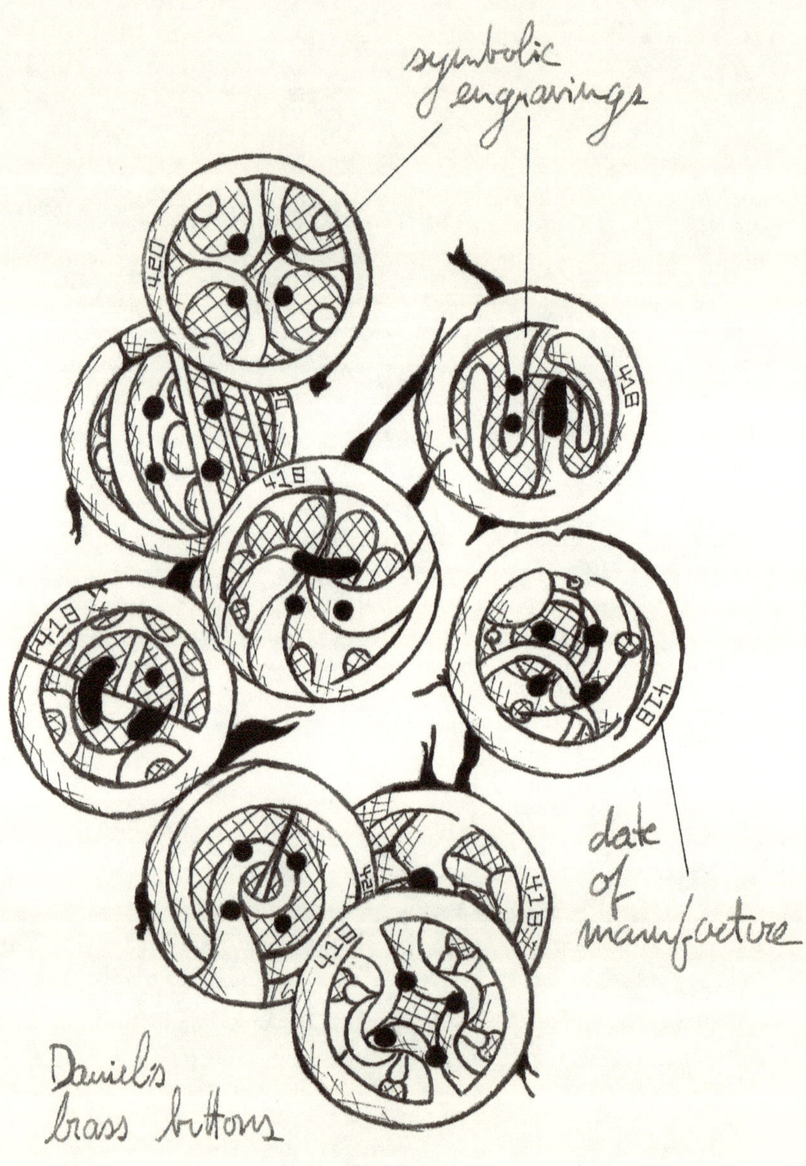

symbolic
engravings
date
of
manufacture
Daniels
brass buttons

15

THE FLAMES

After a mostly sleepless night, Jenna finally managed to doze off during the early hours of the morning. She dreamed of frightening men in shiny, black coats who kept trying to take Silverphile away from her. Every so often a strange, surreal voice would break in, saying something about the beginning of the world. The voice sounded eerily familiar, but all too soon it melded into the harsh voices of Servicemen breaking camp. She opened her eyes in time to see Zenia falling to her knees beside her, having been untied from her tree.

Zenia winced and stretched her legs. "If only they tried sleeping against a tree for a night, I doubt they'd tie us like that."

Jenna felt her bonds being loosened and turned her head to see the soldier who had tied her up walking away. She tried to move her joints, but she found she was stiff all over.

"Here." Zenia helped Jenna get her arms out of their cramped position, kneading feeling back into them with deft fingers. She turned to Jenna's legs, reaching out to straighten them.

Jenna groaned as pain flooded her cramped leg muscles. It felt like they were on fire. She gritted her teeth to prevent herself from crying out again.

"Easy there," Zenia said. "Sorry if that was a bit rough."

"No, this is good," Jenna spat through her gritted teeth. "I couldn't feel my legs at all yesterday, so I'd say this is an improvement."

"Well aren't you feeling positive today." Zenia helped her into a sitting position.

"Thanks."

"Get up, get up," a voice called. Another soldier was stomping around the first few prisoners, getting them up and moving. He was younger than most of the others, just a few years her senior. His black hair stuck up from his head in a spiky mess. "Let's go," he said, reaching

Zenia and Jenna.

Zenia got to her feet and reached for Jenna's hand to pull her up. Jenna took a deep breath and tried rising, but her legs collapsed underneath her.

"Come on, on your feet." The man pulled Jenna up by one arm, with Zenia supporting her other side. "What's wrong with you, girl?"

Pain shot through Jenna's legs, and she fought to keep from falling, balanced as she was between her two human crutches. "I'm a cripple," she said, cringing inwardly. She hated the word, but sometimes you had to make it obvious for people. "I can't walk well, and I can't walk at all what with being tied like that all night." She couldn't keep a hint of impertinence from her voice.

Zenia's eyes widened in fear, but the man threw back his head and laughed. "So one of you mages has a spine. Okay. How do I know you're telling the truth? Cause if you're lying to me..." He hefted the whip hanging by his side.

Jenna saw a flash of indobalt blue at the weapon's end and gulped. "I'm not. I had crutches with me when you attacked. And my horse has straps on the saddle. You can see for yourself." She pointed Silverphile out to the Serviceman, who seemed to accept her explanation.

His face softened. "How did you get like that?"

"Childhood disease."

"Twitching sickness?" he asked, and she nodded assent. "If you'd been born a Republican, we'd have gotten you proper medical care."

"Our healers got me back to walking, didn't they? That's more than they'd hoped for."

The man shrugged. "Same thing happened to my cousin when she was a kid. Spent years unable to walk. Then I joined the Service and got her access to the care she needed. Now she can run along with her friends. I don't know about your magic healers, but our apothecaries can cure that disease of yours."

Does that mean... there's a chance I could walk again some day?

"Now come on. We'll get you right to your horse." He hesitated, then nodded at her. "My name is Rhoy, by the way. I'll let the officers know you can't walk, but if the other Servicemembers give you trouble, they can take it up with me. Okay, mage?"

"My name's—"

The Serviceman—Rhoy—cut her off with jerk of his head. "I'm sorry," he said. "It's better if I don't know."

He indicated they should go, and Jenna gritted her teeth, supporting herself with his and Zenia's help. Together they walked towards Silverphile, as odd a sight as anything—a Serviceman, a farmer's daughter, and a crippled theorist working together in some twisted version of a three-legged-race.

⊶⊷

Rise had put away the letter once they'd met up with the rest of Tobin's soldiers, but the words stuck in his head for days, repeating over and over.

Dear Rise,

You're probably pissed by now, since you haven't caught up yet. It's for the best, though. I can't seem to shake the Serviceman tailing me, but he hasn't caught me yet, so I'm going to keep going until I figure out what to do. Truth be told, I'm getting worried. They've chased me hundreds of miles into enemy territory without easing off or turning back to catch you instead. I think they're after me for a reason other than escaping from them and freeing you.

I should tell you why. You see, I haven't been completely honest with you. To be fair, I didn't think it would matter if you knew, and I thought it'd be safer if I kept what I heard to myself. What I'm trying to say is… I overheard some things back when I was locked in the Service dungeons. I won't say what in this letter, in case the wrong person finds it, but suffice it to say that if the Service knew about what I heard, they would want me dead. I guess maybe they know already, since it looks like they're trying to kill me.

I'm telling you this by way of explanation, but I don't want you to worry too much. I'm not completely helpless, and I'm sure I'll find a way to lose my pursuer soon. Until then, I'm sorry for all the secrets. I'll be sure to tell you what I know once we meet up. Who knows, we might even be able to do something with my information. I'll bet these Ideians would pay us handsomely, but that's more your department than mine.

I'll stay in Neminia if I can, but if the Serviceman keeps on me, I'll head into the interior provinces. Follow the eastern highway. If I change directions, I'll try to find a discreet way of letting you know. Hopefully you're finding these letters. If not, well, I guess we'll see each other eventually.

Daniel.

More secrets. More answers to chase after. Rise muttered curses under his breath as the words kept repeating. He hadn't meant to memorize them, but he'd read the letter so often they stuck in his mind.

He hadn't even considered there might be another reason for the Serviceman tailing his brother. He'd been too caught up in escaping and then finding Daniel. He glanced ahead, towards the rising sun casting golden rays on the upwards-sloping land that led to the hills and western mountains.

The letter will tell me. The thought was almost a prayer. *Shadows cover me, it must. It must. It must.* His thoughts beat a new rhythm against the words repeating in his head. With an empty chuckle, Rise nudged his mare forward, urging her to catch up to Tobin who was in the lead. One way or another, he'd find his answers. He'd chosen right in not staying in the city to find Calen, but once he'd recovered his brother's last words, he would go after the traitor—after the Service itself.

Shades witness, he thought. You could use the shades to curse, but you could also use them to pray. He liked that about them. *I'll have my revenge if it kills me.*

Adriane had nothing to say, and so she merely ran. Somehow, they made it down Flames' Road and through the Left Quarter. She couldn't remember much of it afterward. They got out. The world didn't end. Lancaster was dead. Her thoughts churned out a heartbeat in time with her pounding feet.

Imp's friends had cleared the way, stirring up a ruckus that occupied the Service long enough for them to escape. With luck, their absence wouldn't be discovered for a few hours yet. Nevertheless, it was important to keep moving. In more ways than one.

Using a side door, they made it out onto the street. Then, Imp lost his way, so Adriane took over. The streets were as familiar to her as the palm of her hand. She didn't even need to think about it.

Now they were running west. It was strange to be running during the day, but they kept to the side streets. Dusk would fall shortly, and with any luck at all, no one would bother two dirty-faced street dwellers crossing the Poors Quarter. She'd made Imp take off his shiny coat and smear dirt over his clothes before they left the Service headquarters. She'd ripped the badges off too.

"How much longer," Imp puffed, "'til we're at the West Gate?"

"We're not going to the West Gate."

"But we've gotta get out of the city as soon as possible."

"There's other ways out."

"Right. 'Course. Where?"

Adriane smiled for the first time in what felt like years. It was a cold, grim sort of smile. Humourless. "The Death Gates."

Imp's steps faltered, but he caught himself and kept running. "You know there's bound to be Servicemen all over there?"

"There won't be."

"Why's that?"

"Because they'll either be off drinking like they always are or running to the commotion at headquarters. There's been a raid, so they've had grim work the past day—hanging people I know—and want to get their minds off it. Now can we stop wasting our breath and get on?"

Imp shut up, and Adriane sighed in relief. *Finally.*

They reached the far edge of the Poors Quarter, where buildings met the rugged wall that separated city from landscape. The Poors Quarter was situated where it was for a reason: It ran right along the stretch of wall that held the Death Gates—walls where criminals and thieves, traitors and murderers were hanged for their crimes and displayed like trophies of the Service's sick schemes. Some of them deserved it of course, but others did not. It was always like that with the Service.

The wall had another, similar use. The thief king and the guilds used it to display their own traitors, so-called finks who sold out to the Standard Force or Service and rats who gave information to whoever offered the most plaits. Those were always the worst to see.

The guards who stood watch there were prone to drunkenness and inattention. And why shouldn't they be? It was a grim duty to be assigned to, and besides, no one came here voluntarily. There wasn't much to guard.

Adriane turned along the wall, following echoes of gloom and the smell of rotting meat until they reached two low black gates. They were closed, of course, but like she'd predicted, no one was around. Today of all days was good for getting out. The walls would be full of trophies, and the guards would be drained and depleted. She steeled herself for what she knew lay ahead. There'd be guild members up on the wall. People the Service had captured and found no use for.

At least I won't find Lancaster here, she thought stoically. It would have been too much; it would have broken her.

Adriane headed towards the small gatehouse, Imp following behind her. She entered through the unlocked door, alert for any sign of movement, but as she'd predicted, the single room was unoccupied. A few papers cluttered a small desk, and a cabinet sulked in the back corner. She rifled through its drawers, digging out a coil of rope and a small knife.

"Not much else of use." She stuffed the knife into her boot and handed Imp the rope, heading outside. "We can't open the gate, but we'll climb over it. Stand on my shoulders and get up on the sill."

She leaned into the wall and gave him a boost with her hands. For a moment his weight pressed down on her shoulders, and then it lifted. She looked up to see him perched on the narrow wooden ledge that formed the top portion of the gate's frame.

He tied the rope to a peg in the wall, and she climbed up after him. Then they scaled the shorter distance from the ledge to the flat top of the wall, low as it was in this part of the city. She looked down the wall's other side and saw the bulges of hanging corpses standing out dimly in the twilight.

Swallowing her fear, Adriane tied the rope to one of the many pegs set into the wall—they were used for displaying the bodies—and motioned for Imp to climb down first.

"Don't look at them," she instructed, remembering his reaction in the dungeon. "Look at the wall in front of you." She'd chosen a spot that was clear straight to the ground. Climbing over a corpse was too much, even for her.

Imp nodded, the muscles in his jaw stretched taut, and turned his back to her, beginning to descend. She couldn't help but notice the bit of exposed skin at the nape of his neck, pale and vulnerable. Adriane's hand jerked to the knife in her boot for one horrible, instinctive moment. *He killed Lancaster*, her mind whispered. *Who knows how many others died in his fire? Why are you helping him now? He deserves to die.*

She hesitated, then clenched her fist. *Lancaster wouldn't have done it.* He killed to protect and to keep the Service from expanding their influence. Imp was just a pawn. *I won't stoop to the Service's level. I won't do their dirty work for them.*

The rope slackened. Shaking her head to clear the unwanted thoughts, Adriane crawled over the edge. Ignoring her own advice, she looked at the corpses she passed, noting their faces. *Someone ought to give them a death-tribute*, she thought. *Even if it's just me.* The first two she didn't recognize, for which she was grateful… but then came Miles… and Gera, the healer… and a man she recognized as a constant patron to the Guild's common room. He'd offered her a drink the first time she'd met the Abraham Guild. *Terrasin, I think.*

It was alright until she saw *him*. Jacob. A chill ran down her spine as she saw the spikes driven through his shoulder blades, holding him up, and the tar smeared across his body to preserve it. That wasn't the Service's way—the Service always hanged their victims. No, this killing had been performed by the guilds. *Which means that Jacob is—* she stopped the thought and looked at his face, lit by dim moonlight. Blood bruises beneath burns marred his complexion, and his head lolled grotesquely. A sign was tied to his neck, covered in crude letters painted from his own blood. She glanced at it, then jerked away. The words were imprinted onto her tightly shut eyelids.

Traitor. Traitor to those who died in the fire on Abel Way.

Jacob, she thought. *It was Jacob who sold us out.*

Adriane tore herself away from the sight—the sight of a once-exuberant boy who had called himself her friend, who had been more devoted to Lancaster than anyone. She climbed down the rope, lost in thought. *Of course.* It would come back to Lancaster. She thought she understood. Jacob had been taken in by Lancaster when he as a boy, had been brought up in the Guild. She wouldn't put it past the Service to have convinced him that he should turn in the Guild to secure Lancaster's safety. She wouldn't put it past the Service to lie, either. That's what they'd done to her.

Her feet reached solid ground before she knew it, but she still held on to the rope. She felt like falling. She had to believe the best of what Jacob had done. He must've thought it was the only way.

"Adriane?"

She almost sprang back before she realized the youthful voice belonged to Imp, not Jacob.

"You okay?"

She thought about it. "No. But we have to keep moving."

Adriane drew the small knife from her boot, flipped it so she was holding on to the tip, and then aimed it at the rope. She threw, and it sliced neatly through the knot she'd tied, dropping to the ground with the coils of rope that thudded into the dust. No reason to leave it and advertise where they'd gone.

Imp gathered the rope and tied it around his pack. Adriane picked up the knife.

They headed west at a steady trot, towards a thin stripe of garish orange light on the horizon, the last remnant of a sun now set. The ever-present shroud of coal and indobalt dust shielded them as they ran, obscuring the city of Cain and its mines behind them.

⚬⚬⚬

Imp had forgotten how quickly things could change. It had happened once before, back in Wrovetown, when the Service had gotten to him. But this was only the second time, so it still felt new.

Funny, how he'd been excited about capturing a mage. Funny, how his fire had gotten him out and away. Strange, how it had been so good for him and so bad for her. At least she was getting away too. A pang of guilt threatened to surface, but Imp shook it off. She'd been right. No one person was to blame for anything. The Service was made of countless people. It was a machine; all he'd been was a cog.

Still, he kept quiet as they went on. The ground beneath his feet became uneven after a short while, and soon it was all he could do to keep from tripping over roots and stones. His eyes were fixed on the backs of Adriane's feet, and he followed her lead without question. His steps became heavier and heavier, and when they finally slowed and stopped, all he could do was pant, sucking in heaving gulps of air. He looked back and was surprised when all he could see was a distant, misty bank of fog or maybe coal dust. The city had disappeared.

"We'll rest here for a couple of hours," Adriane said.

So much for me *taking* her *west*, Imp thought. But he wasn't bitter. He didn't like being in charge anyways.

Looking around, he could make out looming shadows ahead and beside them—trees, he realized—and the smaller shadows of bushes and bracken behind them. He slung his pack off his shoulders, wincing at the sore spots the straps had dug into his skin, and unfastened his bedroll from it. He offered it to Adriane.

"I can take first watch," he said, and she nodded.

She lay down on the hard ground and seemed to fall asleep instantly. The air grew cooler, so Imp pulled extra clothes from his pack, draping them around himself in layers.

Remembering the package Kyra had given him, Imp dug it out and peeled back the thick paper.

The first thing he saw was a massive knife in a boot sheath, sitting atop folded layers of cloth, with a green stone tucked underneath it. He set the knife aside and opened the package further. There was wrapped food and a water bag. Two metal contraptions were lodged at the bottom. *That explains the weight.* When he realized the rest of the package contained clothes—*girl clothes*—his face reddened, and he tied it shut again, putting it back inside his back. As he was about to pick up the knife, Adriane stirred and turned towards him.

"That's mine."

Imp's cheeks flushed again as he picked up the knife and handed it to her. "What do you use that for?" he whispered.

"Anything. Everything. Now good night." There was a hard edge to her voice.

Adriane took the small knife from her boot and handed it to him before she tucked the large hunting knife into the folds of the blanket and curled up.

Imp stared into the blackness of the night, tired, but determined to keep his watch. Though he stayed awake, his mind drifted, and he found it hard to focus his attention on the present. His mind's eye was busy watching flames. He could see them, see how they danced and weaved about, see how they jumped up before flickering low again. They were entrancing.

He almost didn't notice when Adriane's hand shook him roughly, and her voice told him to go to bed. He lay down in the bedroll she'd vacated and fell asleep. The flames remained with him, however, dancing through his dreams.

PART 2

clmp's
fire visions

The images form
inside a floating
white light

the smaller
the fire, the
clearer the
pictures

16

SUCH BEAUTIFUL EYES

Two Weeks Later
Somewhere in the western forest, in Arahill, Saint Brazen

Jenna awoke with a start. *Where am I? What—*

Words echoed in her head. *Long ago, I saw a possibility… Life could thrive here. The chance it could wither and die… die… die…*

The words seemed familiar. Had she dreamed about them? *There are still more things that I must tell you, if you are to prevent—*

That's right, Jenna thought. *I dreamed about the Tales or something, back when the Servicemen captured me. All the research must be getting to my head. I wish I still had my books.*

She shook her head, clearing sleep from her mind. It was barely light out; they wouldn't be moving for another hour at least. She stretched her arms and managed a smile. Her body was getting used to being tied to a tree every night, and her muscles weren't as sore as they'd been before. She couldn't feel her legs, true, but that was no surprise. For now, Jenna was content to settle for a few, small victories. *Being a prisoner has turned me into half an optimist,* she thought, chagrinned.

"What? No!"

The shout made her jerk around, and all the optimism flew from her mind.

"C'mon, girl, get moving." Two Servicemen dragged Zenia away from the clearing they were camped in and towards a clump of trees.

That's where they took the others, Jenna realized.

Zenia struggled wildly, fear etched into her features.

Jenna felt a burst of adrenaline. She staggered to her feet, clinging to a branch for support. "Don't be stupid, Zenia," she breathed. "Take your own advice." Zenia had cautioned her not to struggle against the Servicemen, lest they treat her any worse. "Zenia," she whispered.

Zenia must have felt something with whatever her magic did, because she looked straight at Jenna. Their eyes met. Jenna could see her friend's terror even at that distance.

She hesitated, trying to will herself to spring up and yell at the Servicemen, get them to take her instead, but she found she was frozen where she stood. All the other captives had been dragged into the patch of forest already, and all of them now huddled against the trees they were tied to, frightened. When they moved to get up in the morning, they did so docilely, and they walked as if in great pain. The only prisoner who hadn't been intimidated after they took him had been killed, his body thrown into the underbrush like an animal's carcass. Jenna shuddered at the memory, fingers tracing the bruises and welts on her arms. Her magic had sparked, and they'd beaten her. *They'll beat me again if I try to interfere now.*

One of the Servicemen must have seen the look Zenia shot her. "Don't worry, dearie," he drawled, eyeing Jenna. "Your turn'll come soon enough." He yanked Zenia out of sight, and Jenna's friend was gone.

Jenna sank back down onto the grass. *What were you going to do?* she scolded herself. *You're a theorist, not a soldier. You can't even walk properly, let alone control your magic.* She trembled, trying to forget. Three times her magic had betrayed her control, and three times she'd been beaten or shocked with their terrible whips.

Thankfully, the fear of knowing what would happen if she used her magic somehow enabled Jenna to control it better. After the last time, she'd managed to stop her magic from bursting out, even when a Serviceman archer shot a doe that passed by their camp.

Tabitha shield me. What if I accept the risk of being beaten and use my magic? But what would it bring? Her interference wouldn't stop them hurting Zenia. It would anger and scare the Servicemen—for Jenna was convinced that part of their inhumane treatment of the prisoners was simply due to their fear of magic—and that might cause them to lash out more.

Hating herself for it, Jenna forced herself to stay seated and do nothing. Her mind raced, trying to figure out what to do. She had never been good at keeping her head in a crisis, but she needed to find a way to escape. *If only the Republicans didn't have those whips,* she thought, *and if only I could walk.* With access to her magic and legs that worked as they were supposed to, escape would have been child's play.

Jenna had not discussed escaping with Zenia, who insisted they keep silent about matters of importance in case the Servicemen were listening. She knew the other girl would jump at the chance, however, and Jenna was determined to make that chance happen.

A scream split the silence, and Jenna shuddered, drawing her knees up to her chest as a burst of energy hit her, calling to her magic. She squeezed her eyes shut, blocking out the purple tones seeping into her vision. There was a moment of quiet, then a sob.

"Please," Zenia whimpered.

One of the remaining Servicemen looked up from the boots he was polishing. "Bet she doesn't last a minute."

The other Servicemen laughed as another scream rent the air.

Jenna's magic didn't burst from her, but with every passing minute the available energy built. She could feel the pressure inside her chest, tightening on her lungs, and her fingers stretched and contorted, scrabbling for release. She shivered and curled into a ball, trying to shut out the soldiers' coarse voices and Zenia's sobs echoing through the clearing. They had crossed over the border days ago; there was no hope of any potential rescuers hearing them. They were alone, stranded in enemy territory.

Jenna couldn't stand to listen any longer. She concentrated as hard as she could, even while her heart pounded away in her chest, trying to think of something—anything—else.

Magic. Soul and aether magic. Her books were gone, but she'd read some of her materials to the point of having them memorized. *One of the most practical aspects of soul and aether magic is its unique ability to be shaped into a myriad of forms,* she remembered. It was a passage from *A History of Elemental Magics.*

She heard the sound of blows connecting with soft tissue, followed by a cry.

What comes after that? Something about how soul and aether magic is different from the other elements? Another scream, then muted curses. Jenna made herself even smaller, trying to remember the passage as if her life depended on it. The screams grew more intense.

Soul and aether can be used to create almost anything, provided the object in question reflects some element of darkness or light. It is suggested soul and aether wielders practice using the creativity and flexibility inherent in their magic to their advantage. She could remember the words now. The excerpt dealt with magical taboos. Jenna had read it multiple times, trying to figure out if she'd done something to trigger her magic.

Several taboos govern the use of shaping objects. If broken, these can result in dire consequences. Foremost among these is the limit on copying exactly any living being known to the mage. The shouts continued, but Jenna managed to block them out for the most part. Remembering the words exactly required concentration. *Although it is, in most cases, easier to work from a mold well known to the wielder, creating a magical copy of an existing living being remains a most dangerous endeavour, since exact copies tend to gain some form of sentience which prevents the mage from controlling them.*

When she was young, she'd wanted to make little spirit creatures out of her magic. Her tutor had given her a scolding when he'd found out, quoting this exact passage. Another scream. *Focus, Jenna. The words. Focus on the words.*

The sentences flowed through her mind faster and faster, and Jenna's perception of everything else faded as she focused inwards on those precious, precious words. After what seemed like hours, she finally ceased her inner monologue, realizing that the screams had faded away. Relieved and utterly exhausted, Jenna shifted on the hard ground, eyes squeezed shut.

She would have fallen asleep if it weren't for the Servicemen. The ones who weren't on watch ambled over to the trees, chatting as if nothing were wrong, as if they were used to the terrified screams of their prisoners.

"—broke down easier than the others," a Servicewoman said.

"Once we get the last one, we'll finally set out," another said. "It's a pain, but Vinnick won't thank us if we bring her any unbroken mages. You know, I can't wait for my leave—can you believe my Lily's turning four years old?"

Jenna wanted to block out their voices but forced herself to listen. *Sounds like we're almost at our destination. And what was that about getting the last one?* She gulped, realizing what they must have meant. *They're done with Zenia. I'm next.*

⚬⚬⚬

Adriane didn't bother looking back to see if the boy was following. He'd done nothing but follow and stare ever since they'd begun their trek through the forest. She was no longer worried about losing him, even if he did stomp around like a true city dweller. The sound of cracking twigs accompanied his every step.

She felt comfortable in the forest. It was like hunting back home. Her knife rested safely in her boot, and the woods were familiar. Yet there were differences she could not escape. Nothing was the same. Not her clothes, not her mind, not her grief. Not even her magic. The forest was the same, but she had changed—instead of the hunter, she was the rabbit approaching the snare. It was all backwards.

Adriane rolled her shoulders, feeling the weight of the too-hot coat. It made a half-decent bedroll and would be good once winter arrived, but it was a burden in the late-summer heat. Imp had brought some of her old things in that pack of his, but he'd mostly brought her new clothes, including a pair of trousers, which she was thankful for. They were much more practical than the skirt she'd worn on the day of the fire… She culled the thought before she got caught up in it. *Don't think about it.*

Imp tripped on a root behind her, and she heard the muffled thump as he hit loamy earth and rolled a step. She turned, making sure he was okay. They were in this together, and she'd have to make sure they both made it to safety. He certainly wasn't in the frame of mind to do so.

"You okay, Imp?"

"Fine."

She imagined being able to hear him grit his teeth, imagined determination etched onto his drawn features. He didn't look determined, of course, just tired and dirty and hungry and young. But she was sure he was determined, because he never complained. Whenever he fell he scrambled up again and kept going, without needing her to urge him on.

She worried about Imp. She felt like she should hate him for what he'd done, but she couldn't help but see his naïve innocence and the conflicting thoughts that plagued him. It was hard to hate someone so hurt, yet so determined not to show it. Sometimes Imp appeared angry or sad, but the rest of the time he was stoically silent. She didn't know how long he'd been part of the Service, but choosing to leave them and free her couldn't have been easy. The constant running and little sleep probably weren't helping either.

They'd alternated running and walking through the forest all day. Now the trees were thinning. Adriane guessed they'd be clear of the dense woods in an hour or two, though she hoped there would continue to be cover. Adriane stopped Imp so she could climb a tree. She'd guessed right. The trees continued to thin up ahead, and there were low hills in the distance. Hills meant they were nearing the border.

Ideon. *We might actually make it there.* It was a land of magic and savagery, of course, but she had her share of both of those. She might even fit in. Adriane had decided they would pretend to be from Eleszan. Ideians might welcome Saint Brazen refugees, but she didn't want to be a refugee. She wanted—she *needed*—to learn to fight and use her magic. *I'll learn what I can and then I'll come back*, she thought. *I'll come back for Hannah and Max.* It wasn't much of a plan, but she could figure out the details later.

Imp stumbled again, and she glanced up at the sound. He stopped and wordlessly handed her the pack he'd been carrying. She took it; she'd meant to take it sooner.

That was another thing he'd learned, knowing when to take help and when to be tough. She was proud of him, in a way. He'd make a good thief.

Thief—the thought threatened to break her like it always did, reminding her of the Guild. *Nothing, nothing, nothing*, Adriane thought, trying to block out the memories. She knew grief wasn't nothing. It was something but something indefinite. Undefined. She knew she felt grief, but she didn't quite know what to do about it, and there was no sense in letting Imp see it either. So she grieved on the inside and kept her thoughts to herself.

"How much longer 'til we stop?" Imp wiped sweat from his brow.

She judged the position of the sun. "We can go another two hours. I doubt there'll be any more villages. Everything should be empty from now on." Empty of people. That was all they cared about.

The emptiness was inside of her again, and she fingered the green stone tied into her long braid like a talisman. The stone always seemed to help, though she didn't know why. It had been with the things Imp brought, the clothes for her, the trail food and water. Even her old hunting traps. She didn't know who'd packed, but they'd known what she and Imp would need, and they must have found the pack she'd discarded the day of the fire. When she'd asked the boy, he'd told her about the lady, Kyra, but she couldn't make sense of it. *I suppose it'll stay a mystery.*

As they walked, Adriane listened to the forest, straining her ears for any sound that might indicate another human presence. She heard nothing but knew that needn't mean anything. The Servicemen had been following them ever since they left the city. They'd almost caught them a day out from Cain, but Adriane's magic had saved them. She grimaced. *I guess I might as well use the tools I've got, however much I dislike them.*

Part of the problem with magic was it meant thinking about Lancaster again. She didn't want to, not really, but she let the grief well up anyway. She'd never see him again. He was gone.

Digging her hand into a pocket sewn into the lining of the coat, she felt for the scrap of blue fabric she'd torn from his shirt. At least that was still there. A reminder. The dagger and pebble too. A lot of reminders.

A twig snapped behind them, and Adriane froze mid-step, closing her eyes, letting the grief seep into her. Her magic gathered at the edges of her eyelids, and she sensed her way through the shadows, trying to hear and see through the echoes, to tell what was behind them. Branches stirred; the wind was whispering through the trees. Adriane shuddered, knowing the magic would activate at her command. *I'm getting good at this.*

"What is it?" Imp said, frozen behind her.

"Nothing, I thin—" The edge of a boot flitted into her vision, the echoes bouncing it back. It was a black boot, made of soft leather, not unusual for someone walking through the forest. But it was bright, oh so bright. Mia's words popped into her mind. *Like a Serviceman whose boots won't take a shine.*

"Imp." Adriane's voice was lower than a whisper. "Don't move now. Don't look around. But when I tell you to, run. Run, and I'll catch up with you."

He heard the fear in her flat voice and licked his lips. "Okay," he whispered. "Okay." He knew what it meant.

He looked on the point of speaking again but stopped himself. *Good.* She almost smiled.

The grief was under control, but she felt it inside her, tearing her to shreds. It had to. That was how grief worked. She hadn't recognized that as a child, grieving over her parents, or in the city, when she missed her brother and sister. But now she knew it well, now that Lancaster was dead.

Lancaster. His name gathered the magic to her, and she let it, intending to shift into the shadows. *Wait a second.* How had she seen that Serviceman's boot? The thought broke her concentration, and her magic escaped her grasp. The forest seemed suddenly silent, as if the sounds had been muted and her eyes obscured by a mist.

Is it the magic itself? Adriane focused on her grief again, calling the shadows to her. They bounced back through the landscape, and she realized she could see things around her, not with her eyes, but in her mind. She heard Imp's small intake of breath, heard another twig snap several paces beyond her sightline, felt the movement of a cloak in her mind.

I've done this before, she realized. She always felt more focused when she used her magic, alert and able to fully use her senses. She'd imagined it was just the rush of knowing danger lay nearby, but this clarity was too pronounced to ignore. She was using her magic—somehow—to sense the landscape around her. Trying to refocus, Adriane concentrated on what she could see and hear. If her magic helped with that, fine, she would use it—to escape and to protect. Nothing more mattered. All she needed to care about was Imp and safety and the booted person behind them.

Another twig snapped, and Adriane felt the echoes bounce off the motion. The boot stepped in their direction, followed by something else. Soft snuffling sounds reached her ears. *They brought dogs.*

Adriane motioned to Imp who set off at a run. She turned back, melting into the underbrush. A light breeze was blowing towards her. The dogs wouldn't smell her coming.

Mere seconds later, Adriane saw the beasts approaching, following the trail she and Imp had blazed through the bush. Their short coats rippled with muscle and spittle fell from their teeth, glinting in the dim light that filtered down from the canopy. Those dogs could tear her apart.

Three Servicemen followed, dressed for deep woods work in greens and browns. Too bad the bold brass buttons and the shiny boots gave them away. She'd be able to surprise them, but Adriane knew she couldn't be overconfident. She squinted at their belts, and sure enough, found coiled whips hanging there. They'd have daggers too, and maybe swords, though she couldn't see any under their coats. She'd try to incapacitate the men and kill the dogs. They wouldn't be able to track her without them.

Letting her grief come out once more, Adriane felt the icy chill that told her the magic was working. She glanced at her hands and saw wisps of shadow curling there. *Too easy.* Narrowing her sight on the dogs, she pulled out both knives and jumped forwards, dissolving into shadow.

"Did you see that?" One of the Servicemen gestured.

"See what?"

She appeared in front of one of the dogs, and the men shouted in astonishment. A quick jab with her knives and a dog leaped back, howling. She twisted to meet the other brute hurtling at her and stepped to the side lest its weight drive her downwards. She blocked a swipe of its claws with a blade and slashed with her free hand, wincing as the beast's other paw clipped her wrist. She stabbed it in the eye—it fell, whimpering—and then a whip cracked past her face. It stole the very air from her lungs. *So close.*

She cloaked herself in shadows once again, moved to the side, spanning several strides with one step. Where were the dogs? *There.* One of them had stumbled to its feet, and she shadow-rushed towards it, slicing through its throat and dodging away before the blood hit her.

Two more dogs jumped towards her. *Two?* She slashed and felt her knife connect with something. Teeth ripped into her leg. A weight knocked her over, but Adriane shadow-dashed again and stood up. She saw two Servicemen retreating with the remaining dog, heads turning as they searched for her.

Two lumps lay on the ground, the dead… *dogs?* No. There had been two dogs and three men. She took a careful step forward, then stared at the sight. A dead dog, blood still dripping from its throat, and the still figure of a man, his head at a sick angle. *I killed him*, she thought, shivering. She checked for a pulse to be sure; there was none.

Adriane dropped to her knees. The fight in the city hadn't been like this. She didn't even know if she'd killed someone then. *This is different.* She looked at the still form. His neck was broken, whether from falling or from her blows, she didn't know. *Does that matter? Either way, I did this. And I'll do it again if I have to.*

She hated her callousness but knew it was necessary. Adriane stood and let her magic surround her, let it drag her backwards, step by step, until she reached a fallen log on which she sat. She touched the stone in her hair again, and its cool, tactile surface kept her in the present, kept the memories under control. It kept her grounded somehow.

I'm too far from home. That was the only thing that made sense. She'd been content enough as a trapper's daughter. She'd never wanted magic, adventure, any of it.

Adriane jerked, remembering Imp. She tested her injured leg—the dog hadn't had the time to apply a full bite—and found she could walk without much difficulty. It took her some minutes to find his trail, but once found it was easy enough to follow, and she set off behind him at a jog.

We'll find water to cover our scent, she decided. *Once we reach the border they won't follow, not with dogs anyway.* She could see the land rising into hills up ahead, and the mountains on her right seemed closer than ever. *We'll make it. Tomorrow, maybe, or the day after that. And I'll do whatever it takes to get us to safety.*

⸙

Imp had the first shift. Adriane insisted they keep watch at night, even though they'd snuck past the Ideian border outpost without trouble. He was exhausted, and his mind drifted. He was running again. All they'd done was run and run for ages. He wished the running would stop. He wished all of it would stop.

It's not like the city, he thought drowsily. *No walls to scamper over, no crates to hide behind, no heaps of scrap and refuse to jump over. Just roots and bracken growing in unknowable patterns.* It was like running blind.

"Imp."

He jerked upright as a hand clamped down on his knee. *Adriane,* he realized. Now *she* knew how to run through the forest. She never tripped, not even once.

"Try to stay awake this time, okay?"

"Okay."

Adriane dampened the small fire until only a single, flickering flame remained among the embers. She curled into that heavy coat of hers, and her breathing changed as she fell asleep.

Imp felt the tension drain out of him as he looked at the fire. She hadn't let him light any fires while they were still in Saint Brazen. This was his first fire in *ages.* He'd never gone this long without one.

A small, white light formed in the flame, and Imp sat up straight, suddenly wide awake. He hadn't seen one of those lights in ages either, but he knew what it was. It was the only connection he had to a mother long gone. *That and the fire imps.*

The white lights only appeared in small, controlled fires, and they got fuzzy if the fire grew too big. This fire was perfect. Imp gazed into the light, waiting for the images to form.

A figure appeared in the light, a man in a dark, obscuring cloak. He was travelling somewhere, Imp guessed—the man carried a staff, and Imp thought he saw mountains looming behind him.

The man turned, and Imp gasped in surprise. *Uncle Bento!* Could it be? He looked younger, and he had more hair, but there was no mistaking it. He was seeing his mentor.

The image changed, flickering with the fire, and a second man, also cloaked, joined Uncle Bento. They walked up to a third person who was kneeling on the ground. A woman, judging by the long hair.

"The spirit said you'd come and find me." The woman's voice sounded vaguely familiar.

"Have you decided to join the Markois, then?" Bento rasped, his voice still as scratchy as always.

The woman looked up. "Yes."

The other man, whose face was still hidden, put his hand on the woman's shoulder, and suddenly images flickered across the white light in quick succession. An army forming up in a field. The woman, looking much younger, wearing light armour and leading a horse. A man with a little girl in his arms, climbing into a carriage. The child was sobbing, and Imp shifted, feeling uncomfortable. He never saw happy stories in the white light. Only stories like his own.

The images flickered faster, until Imp could hardly make out what was happening. When they slowed again, he could see a road scattered with pieces of wood and metal, a broken carriage wheel, ripped leather straps. Red stains covered the ground. *Someone must have died here.*

Imp had thought about death often as a kid. He wondered if his mother had died, but he wasn't sure. *She was special,* he remembered. Had she really been able to move through solid objects, or had he imagined that part?

He'd set a lot of fires when he was young, but he'd never gotten caught, not unless you counted Uncle Bento and then the time when the Service had found him. Adriane was like that too. She'd run from the Service, been caught, and then escaped. *With my help.*

In some ways they were similar, but Imp also knew Adriane was stronger than him. He could set fires and then run away, but she would kill to protect others. She hadn't told him about it, but he knew it anyways. *That night when she took care of the Servicemen following us… She was covered in blood.* He had pushed it out of his mind then, but now that they were safe he figured he'd better think about it. Did he mind the fact that she had killed someone? Even if they were Servicemen?

He recognized it now, recognized that the Service had done wrong. But what about Herald and Vine and others like them? He'd spent time with them. Liked them. What if Adriane had killed them?

Imp imagined Adriane fighting, shifting fluidly through the shadows, wielding her knife. He imagined Nero facing her, succumbing to a quick thrust to the heart. He'd thought the image might make him laugh—Nero was absurdly comical and a pain to boot, and Imp wouldn't miss him in the slightest—but instead, Imp shivered, suddenly cold.

Killing is right, he decided, *as long as she did it to protect someone.* His mind was quite good with these things. He could always find reasons to justify what needed to be done.

I wonder if she kills like the Service does. He didn't know why he should think about it. It didn't matter, really, it was just one of the things he'd overheard. The Service had a good way of killing people, even if they killed for the wrong reasons. The secret was the Service always took responsibility for their members' actions. Servicemen could kill as long as they said the right words afterwards to absolve themselves of guilt.

Imp tried to think, tried to remember those words. He should say them for Adriane, just in case. *In case she needs the Service to take the blame for her killing.* He shivered, then remembered.

It was easy. You served the Service, and they took the blame.

He licked his lips. "Service for service." He muttered the words, so as not to wake Adriane, and felt better immediately. He smiled.

It's okay, Adriane, he thought. *Even though you killed someone, it's okay.*

He shook his head and turned his attention back to the fire. His heart sank when he saw the little white light had flickered out.

A twig snapped, and Imp whirled around. *Nothing out there*, he told himself, scanning the underbrush. *Probably an animal.* He kept looking.

"Peter?" a voice whispered.

Imp jerked in fright. He reached for the small knife Adriane had given him, wishing he had a better weapon. The voice sounded familiar. He didn't wake Adriane. The two thoughts were connected in his head.

"Who's there?" He wouldn't be surprised to find his heart so high in his throat that he could spit it out. Had he imagined the voice?

Another rustle, and a dark figure detached itself from the forest and slunk towards the flickering glow of the single flame. Just one figure, and rather unintimidating if he didn't count the fact that it had startled him.

Wait a second. "Herald?"

A brief flash of white. The figure grinned. "The same, Peter."

How in the shadows had Herald gotten there? They wouldn't send

Servicemen over the border, would they? What if he wasn't with the Service? Could that be?

"They promote you after all?" It was the first safe topic Imp could think of.

That grin again. "Sure did. Mind if I sit?"

Imp hesitated, then nodded tersely, seating himself across from his comrade. His friend.

Herald extended his arm and held his palm out. Imp could see the meager light glinting off his scarred flesh. *Not scarred,* he corrected himself. *Burned.* He couldn't tell with the poor light, but he knew what the brand would look like. A simple Service insignia carved into Herald's skin forever.

"Why are you here, Herald?"

"What, can't I sit and chat with an old acquaintance?"

"You know what I mean."

"I know." Herald paused, and Imp found himself listening to the quiet nighttime noises while studying his friend. The forest appeared to be silent until you paid attention, until you noticed things. Herald was taller than him and thin, but he'd filled out some since he'd seen him. There were a few crickets chirping, and the wind made sounds against leaves and branches. Herald's smile was tighter than last time too. An owl hooted, and Imp almost jumped again.

"They sent me."

Imp could feel goosebumps rising on his skin. Was Herald bait for a trap?

"With a message." Herald shrugged. "I was stationed on the border anyway, so it could've been anyone."

Imp doubted it. He wouldn't have let most Servicemembers sit by his fire and talk. Only Herald. *And Vine.* "What's the message?"

"They wanted me to tell you that you can come back. No hard feelings; you're young and everybody makes mistakes." He hesitated. "We need you, Imp. You're the best fire-setter we've got, and we'll take you back no questions asked."

Imp noted the switch in pronouns. It felt important, somehow. "What's the alternative?"

"You know what it is. We hunt you down."

"Don't kid yourself. The Service wouldn't risk a war by setting foot in Ideon for a mage and a deserter."

"Yeah? And I suppose you know all there is, Imp?" Heat touched Herald's voice for the first time. "Know better than I do what the

Service will and won't do? Well I say they're gonna hunt you down, and shades take the Ideians. There's gonna be a war eventually anyway and—" Herald broke off.

Did he say too much? War? Does the Service want a war?

"And you're worse than dead either way." Herald tried to cover his slip. "The mage too," he sneered. "Think of how great she could be, helping the Service. You're heading to your death if you don't and taking her with y—"

Shock blossomed across Herald's face as a knife implanted itself in his shoulder.

Imp whirled around to see Adriane, hand still extended, eyes full of fire, sitting up in her blankets.

"What in the shadows' names are you doing Imp? Run!"

Run? *Run.* Imp scrambled to his feet and grabbed the pack that sat next to the blankets. He caught a glimpse of Adriane's boot scuffing earth over the coals and heard a groan from where Herald lay bleeding. *Wrong. It's all wrong.* A hand grabbed his arm—Adriane—and shoved him towards the trees.

"Go! Get out of here."

He ran. He looked back—Adriane, blankets on her shoulders, bloody knife in her hand—but he ran.

"What were you thinking?" She was behind him in a heartbeat, voice steady and quiet.

"I—I know him." Imp fought back sobs. *What happened back there?* "It couldn't hurt—he just wanted to talk. He… he said I could come back to them." Could he? Had Herald meant that? Was he telling the truth?

"Imp look out!"

Imp dodged the sword thrust just in time, jumping to the side and stumbling over a root, his momentum still pushing him forward. *Sword?* The clash of steel behind him meant Adriane had parried with her knife. He looked over his shoulder to see a man's silhouette slumping to the ground. Adriane flicked her knife to the side, then caught up to him.

"Keep your eyes open. There must be more than—"

A second silhouette darted out of the shadows before she could finish her sentence. Imp's mind froze with panic—it was all he could do to keep on running—but Adriane pivoted smoothly, flickering into shadow as she did so, appearing a fraction to the side of where she should have been, and planted her knife between the man's ribs.

It was so easy for her. *Herald.* Had it been easy for her with him? Was it all the same? Imp supposed killing must be like fire to her but didn't know what made him think so. *Is Herald dead?*

Crackling leaves behind them alerted him to more pursuers. Adriane nudged him to the side and onto a game trail. He hadn't seen it in the dark. No longer stumbling, Imp increased his speed. They were running again, Servicemen behind, but they'd been doing this for weeks. It felt normal. Except it was his fault this time. Just his.

Imp's stomach clenched as he thought about what he'd done. If Adriane hadn't woken up... *They'd have ambushed us for real. A few more seconds and we'd be dead—or worse.* At least he knew now, knew he couldn't go back. Things wouldn't be the same ever again.

By pure luck they stumbled into a village scant minutes later. They hadn't even seen it through the trees. Dogs barked, and Adriane hastily wiped her knife clean and hid it in her boot as a door opened.

"What's all the commotion about?" A middle-aged man stood shirtless in the doorway of a house, looking at them with an expression of bewilderment.

Imp glanced backwards. He thought he saw the Servicemen's silhouettes shifting among the trees, unwilling to reveal themselves.

He turned back to the man. Adriane was talking quickly. Imp didn't bother paying attention to the words. *She'll keep me safe*, he thought, relieved. She'd done it over and over again. He frowned at the thought of Herald still bleeding back in the forest. *Even though I keep messing it all up.*

Footsteps approached Jenna, and something heavy hit the ground beside her. She jerked up—it was Zenia.

Raucous laughter reached her ears as the Servicemen who had dropped Zenia walked away. One of them directed a kick at Jenna as he passed. "Your friend has such beautiful eyes." She thought she smelled alcohol on him. "Too bad we had to bruise them up a little."

Jenna waited until they had gone and then made to get up, but a massive surge of energy hit her. Her magic threatened to burst out of her again. Only the thought of the Servicemen and their indobalt weapons helped her keep it under control. She managed to sit up and then crawled towards Zenia, nudging her to see if she was conscious.

"Zenia. Zenia, are you okay?" Apart from a few bruises she looked unhurt, but her eyes remained shut.

"I'm… fine." Zenia's voice was hoarse. "Trying not to lose hope, but otherwise fine."

Jenna forced a chuckle. "Well thank the Patrons you've kept your optimism. Can you get up? What happened? They hurt you."

Zenia winced, then sat up with Jenna's help, eyes still closed. "I'm not hurt much. Just a few new bruises."

A splatter of liquid dropped from her eyes, and Jenna sucked in a breath, her magic bubbling up as a fresh surge of energy hit her. A single purple spark escaped from her fingertips, and she looked around, frightened, but the Serviceman guarding the prisoners was glancing in a different direction.

"Zenia," she said as calmly as she could. "Your eyes are bleeding."

"I know. You wouldn't have a handkerchief or anything, would you?"

Jenna grimaced. "Even if I did, it wouldn't be clean. Here." She ripped the cleanest corner of her shirt off and began wiping blood from Zenia's face.

Zenia carefully opened her eyes, which Jenna now saw were puffy and swollen, and a few more drops of blood flowed down like angry red tears.

Someone cleared their throat behind them, and Jenna turned her head to see Rhoy, the Serviceman who'd been kind to her after finding out she couldn't walk. He kept away from the prisoners mostly, but every so often he came by to make sure Jenna wasn't given trouble for being unable to keep up. It was ironic, since they were still treated terribly, but Jenna thanked Tabitha for every little bit of kindness. She'd come to depend on it.

He held up a clean square of cloth and a small vial of clear liquid. "Keep the wounds clean with this. I convinced my sergeant the higher-ups wouldn't thank him for letting his prisoners' wounds fester."

Jenna took them from him with her still-bound hands. "Thank you."

The man inclined his head awkwardly, then retreated.

She dripped some of the liquid onto the cloth, using it to wipe the blood off her friend's face. To her credit, Zenia didn't wince or move, though Jenna's hands were trembling, and she knew it must sting.

"That's it," Jenna whispered. "We need to get out of here."

"But—"

"I know you're scared. I'm terrified. But I'm even more terrified of staying. First the others, now you. Why would they do this—any of this?"

Zenia hesitated for a moment. "My magic," she finally whispered.

"What?"

"They were trying to find out what my magic was. They don't know about all types of magic, but they knew some draw energy from your body, so they gave me a beating to figure out where I drew my energy from."

Jenna winced. "I'm not an expert on body magic, but I'm going to guess your power comes from your eyes."

Zenia nodded. "I told them after the first few blows so they'd stop. I figured they'd find out eventually, but they kept going like they were enjoying it. And then they hit my eyes, to make sure I'd told the truth."

"I don't understand. Why would they care where your magic comes from? You can't use someone else's magic or siphon it off or anything."

"They could always threaten me with it." Zenia shrugged. "Drawing magic from your body comes with downsides, like any other magic. Whatever you draw energy from gets weakened and hurt easily. They barely had to touch my eyes to cause pain."

Jenna was still half-lost in thought. "That Serviceman has been kind to us. We could use that somehow. We could escape."

Zenia hesitated, but then nodded. "Maybe," she said. "Staying here is worse than anything else."

As the Servicemen packed up camp, Jenna and Zenia huddled together, compiling ideas. The situation was hardly ideal, but the thought of doing something gave Jenna both hope and purpose.

"If you make it without me," Zenia was saying, "promise me you'll keep going without turning back."

"Of course I won't! We're doing this together."

"You don't understand. My magic... I can see emotions, sometimes thoughts." She shrugged at Jenna's raised eyebrows. "You might as well know, if we really want to try escaping. From what I've observed about you, your magic is a whole lot stronger. I don't understand it, but I felt something strange after they'd hurt me. The Servicemen were feeling angry and scared and satisfied, and the prisoners were terrified as always. But you—you were feeling powerful."

"I don't underst—"

"It's hard to explain. I don't read minds, but I could tell something was fueling your magic after I got hurt, magnifying it. If we can magnify your magic like that again, maybe you could get out, even if I can't."

"I wouldn't dream of leaving you behind—"

"That's not what I mean. You need to bring word back to Ideon. I have a brother back in Silas' Hill—Timothy. He's in a small squad in Yoel's Redemption. He'd get the combat groups to send a rescue party. At any rate, they need to know what the Republic is doing. Stealing mages, testing their power? It can't be good."

Jenna hesitated, but Zenia's logic was sound. "Fine," she said. "If I escape and you don't, I'll take word to Silas' Hill. But I promise I'll get you out of here one way or another."

Zenia smiled, though Jenna could tell it was forced. "I know you will."

Jenna thought for a minute. "I've told you my magic runs off death and destruction… but I don't understand why it felt stronger before. There are too many variables."

"Maybe we could test it out," Zenia said. "What was different that time?"

The merest hint of enthusiasm lighting up Zenia's features reminded Jenna that she had been heading to Kalaaman Tower to begin work as a theorist.

"I'd just woken up, but I doubt that was it. Could it… Could it be the fact that I was drawing energy from the pain of another mage? Or someone I care about rather than a stranger?"

"Either of those conditions would be met if I was the one getting hurt," Zenia said. "Assuming I'm not just another sack of meat to you."

It took Jenna a second to follow her train of thought. "Are you saying…?"

"I could let myself get hurt badly enough that you can use your magic to escape. If you have enough energy available, you could ward off their weapons, right?"

"Slow down," Jenna said, "I won't let you get harmed for a tiny chance at escape."

Zenia shook her head. "No. This could work. I have an idea."

Jenna remained skeptical but listened as Zenia suggested her plan. *Did she come up with all this even while telling me to keep quiet and forget about escaping?* Jenna had admittedly taken Zenia as a coward at first, but now she realized that was wrong. *She's terrified and she's cautious, but now that there's a real chance of getting out she's willing to risk everything, even if I'm the only one who escapes.*

The thought made Jenna all the more determined to see both of them return home safely.

The sun was close to setting by the time Imp and Adriane reached the city called Silas' Hill. A merchant caravan had picked them up on the road two days ago, and they'd ridden on the backs of wagons, running errands in exchange for food. Even with the respite from walking, Adriane was sore and tired, her leg wound still aching, and she knew Imp must be exhausted as well. At least they'd been able to travel on roads once they'd passed the border—not game trails and root-riddled forest paths. Imp kept up a better pace with hard dirt beneath his feet.

The city was not cramped and fenced-in like Cain, but it was just as big, sprawling over two large hills. Adriane supposed Imp might find the man-made constructions beautiful, but it was the pastures, fenced yards, and stands of trees that caught her eye. The city felt connected to nature, bursting with life.

From a distance, she thought the city had no walls to shield it, but when they got closer, Adriane could see a squadron of guards by a low, stone wall. There were no proper gates, just wide openings set between stone plinths raising up statues twice the size of regular people.

The caravan got them past the guards at the gate. Once they had passed into the city proper, Adriane and Imp took their leave, following the merchants' suggestion to walk up the northern hilltop where an Ideian military outpost controlled the soldiers stationed in and around Silas' Hill. The city was known for its military camps; the merchants said they might find work among the soldiers.

Adriane passed clusters of shops intermingled with larger buildings and yards, keeping a careful eye out for pickpockets. Imp followed her without saying a word. There should have been people out even this late, but the streets were quiet for the most part, though Adriane could hear the precise shouts of someone calling drills in the distance. Light shone out from friendly cracks in doors and windows, but it all seemed off somehow. They walked for half an hour, the cityscape melting from shop district to some sort of military or residential area, before Adriane realized what it was. *There's no nightfolk about. No gangs hiding in alleys. Shades, there aren't even any proper alleys for gangs to hide in.*

"Am I gonna have to work?"

Adriane almost jumped before remembering Imp. "I'd guess so." She fingered the knife at her side, thinking back to their days of wandering through Arahill's woods. "The military's as good as anything else." She didn't know what she was going to do, but she wanted to learn to control her magic. Mastering it was the only thing that would allow her to return to her family.

"I don't want to fight."

"You won't have to. I don't know if they'd even let you. Even if we say we're travellers from Eleszan they might turn us away." They'd have to find somewhere else to stay if that was the case.

"Guess we'll find out."

They had been passing strange barrack-like structures for a while now, but they thinned out up ahead. The hillside was cut into wide terraces, and a set of stairs led to the topmost level which they were now approaching. It was all bare grass and trees except for a small collection of old stone buildings. They had lamps burning at the door, so someone must still be awake.

Several hours later, Adriane lay on a soft mattress, waiting for sleep to come. She wasn't entirely sure what she'd gotten herself into, but it involved a bed to sleep in, free meals, and plenty of straw targets to throw her knife at. For now, that was enough, even though she was worried.

It almost seems too easy. One of the city's elders, a man named Iram, had met with them and offered them work. Imp could run messages for city officials, and Adriane had been offered a choice.

"We can find regular work for you if that's all you want," Iram had said kindly. "But if you want to train your magic you must do so within the structure of the combat groups. Since you're not a native Ideian, we could only accept you as a hummingbird."

Her face must have shown her confusion, because the man was quick to explain. "Ideon and Eleszan have a treaty that allows for Eleszanin mages to train in Ideon's combat groups. The Elesson Agreement, participants of which are nicknamed 'hummingbirds' for the Eleszanin crest. You must agree to a probation period and a commitment of at least five years, and for that time you will be considered an Ideian citizen as far as the army is concerned."

Iram explained the terms of the agreement, which involved a lot of rules and responsibilities. In some ways, that was familiar. Cain's nightfolk had been organized into a strict hierarchy, and Adriane had learned to navigate their sometimes-confusing customs from Mia and Lancaster himself.

She felt a pang of sadness at the thought of Lancaster, but she beat it back. *I can do this,* she thought. *I'll learn to control my magic. I've already begun.*

As she lay in bed, listening to Imp's regular breaths, Adriane contemplated the choice she'd made. *Five years away from Hannah. Five years away from Max. Five years sworn to a foreign nation's army.* She could always go back on her word. After all, she wasn't from Eleszan like they thought. Would they think her a spy if she ran off, if it all proved too much? *I don't know if I could risk it,* she decided. *I need this.*

After Adriane had agreed to Iram's terms, the elder had made her sign an official-looking sheaf of papers. She didn't own a seal or anything, but she'd used the green pebble, picked from the street outside her home. The impression it had left in the wax was smooth except for a small crack running through the middle. It felt appropriate somehow, but it also felt like a promise.

Shades alone know what's coming, Adriane thought, *but I'll stay and learn what I can.* She had lied about where she was from, but that didn't matter. What mattered was finding her way back home. That and taking care of Imp. She supposed he was her responsibility now.

Adriane tried to calm her thoughts, knowing she'd better get some sleep. Morning would bring new adjustments. She would report to a mage who would place her into one of the army's combat groups and assign someone to watch over her. Iram had promised to be there, which strangely brought her some comfort.

At least there will be one familiar face, she thought, before falling asleep.

BRIGHT MIDNIGHT
Flags are
tall and
narrow
YOEL'S ATONEMENT
THEOLD'S MOUNTAINS
BENDEKAN'S BASTIONS
Aldeon's combat
group insignias

17

BRIGHT MIDNIGHT

Rise couldn't help but gape at the buildings, his grief forgotten for the moment. Ideians were casual and sometimes needlessly flamboyant, but this city of Tobin's was a whole new level of absurd, even when compared to the bright colours and shiny walls of Neminia.

Tobin had called Silas' Hill a collection of training camps, and Rise had visualized neat rows of barracks interrupted by practice yards, fields, stables, and perhaps a market area with shop-riddled streets. Something akin to Saint Brazen's military bases or perhaps the Service's training grounds. The reality couldn't be further from what he'd imagined.

A thick stone wall, shorter than a man standing, encircled a vast array of buildings, arranged in rough circles on and around two hills that had been partially cut into level terraces. More of a city than a camp, Silas' Hill extended far into the distance, buildings melding into a stretch of plains that extended for a few miles before turning back into forest. Though a definite sense of planned order lay about the place, it was still messier than any military post Rise had seen.

Three weathered statues stood on tall plinths with two entrances tucked into the wall between them. The first depicted a beautiful woman, the middle statue a slender old man with a walking staff, and the third an elderly matron holding a broken arrow. *More Patrons from these Ideian Tales*, Rise figured.

They rode past the wall, Tobin exchanging brief words with the soldiers guarding the entrance. The road shifted from dirt to well-used cobbles surrounded by grass, low buildings, and fenced practice yards. There were small gates in the wall near buildings Rise would guess were stables, and plenty of pastures beyond. As the land rose towards the hills it became increasingly cluttered, with buildings rising higher and higher and streets becoming specialized, devoted to either shops or common housing surrounded by gardens and courtyards or warehouses, stables, and other industry.

Rico and Yemena took charge of the horses after they entered the city, and Tobin explained that mounts were only allowed in the outermost sections of Silas' Hill. The company turned down a different street that led to a broad, busy road up towards the hills. The higher they climbed, the more the buildings changed. Large compound-like structures dominated the terraced parts of both hills, with each compound boasting a collection of outbuildings and yards clustered around a pole flying a tall, narrow flag.

Each compound was unique. One held buildings made of a dark type of wood, stained in patterns that echoed the emblem on its flag. Another was twice as large as the average, boasting buildings set on stone foundations with minimalist gardens surrounding a central courtyard and a flag showing a snow-capped mountain. After passing several terraces, Tobin's squad approached a medium-sized compound whose flag depicted a grey dagger, broken in two and entwined by a serpent.

Tobin turned to Rise. "This is Yoel's Atonement, or Yoel's Redemption as some call it." He shrugged. "It's not much to look at, but the people are good, and the food is even better."

Over their days of travel Tobin had explained about Ideon's combat groups, as well as other strange parts of Ideon's culture, such as their use of healers instead of apothecaries and their horribly inconvenient political system. This had only cemented Rise's opinion that Tobin talked too much and thought too little—like most Ideians. However, Rise also found himself drawn to the young squadleader.

They reached a barracks designated '13–16,' and Tobin dismissed his squad. He indicated Rise should follow him, and the two of them backtracked to the main road and climbed towards the hill's peak. Instead of ramps, stairs connected the higher terraces, and the uppermost level held only a few, low buildings; the rest of it was covered with grass.

Tobin explained the sights as they went, pointing out different combat groups and their banners and remarking on the camp's command structure. Like most Ideian cities, Silas' Hill was governed by an assembly of elders. Military operations, however, were largely in the hands of an appointed council who relied on the elders and other aides to run day-to-day affairs. Rise memorized as much as he could; he'd learned early on with the Service that information was always valuable.

"Combat groups seem like an odd way to organize an army," Rise remarked once Tobin's stream of chatter ended.

The squadleader shrugged. "I thought so too at first. But each group has a special set of skills; it makes a lot of sense once you learn them all. Bendekan's Bastions are the border guards, for instance, or Bright Midnight—their second is the one who has your letter—they deal with espionage and stealth missions."

Rise massaged his left hand with his right, suddenly nervous. "Will I get my brother's letter back today?"

"Yeah. I just need to report back to Elder Iram. He'll sort out what's going to happen with you." Tobin's smile was easygoing. "Don't worry, Rise. They won't kick you out or anything. It's easy enough to get refugee status as family to a magic-wielder. It happens more often than you'd think."

Rise nodded, feeling numb. He hadn't really thought of what he wanted to do next. *There's no going back to Saint Brazen*, he thought. *Curse I carn always go back to Neminia to hunt Calen down.* The prospect should have strengthened his resolve, but Rise just felt hollow.

Once they reached the command center, Tobin sought out the elders' offices, Rise following. Several of the rooms were occupied, their doors—each bearing a stylized letter—cracked open. Tobin immediately steered Rise to a small room labeled with an 'I' made to look like a dragon. He instructed him to wait outside, then entered with a knock on the doorpost, closing the door behind him.

A few minutes later, Tobin opened the door and beckoned to Rise.

The room was small, but it boasted several comfortable-looking seats and a cluttered desk behind which sat a thin, old man. He was unremarkable except for his intense gaze and the fact that his face shone with a youthful vigor. His eyes twinkled amid crow's feet, and his white beard was braided down to his chest.

"And you must be Rise," he said as Rise entered. "Have a seat, if you please. I am Elder Iram of Silas' Hill, originally from House Coleslake. Welcome."

Rise shook the proffered hand and sat on one of the chairs. Tobin remained standing, though he looked comfortable, without the stiffness of a soldier standing at attention before his superior. *Though I suppose that would look different here.*

"I understand you're a refugee from the Saint Brazen Republic," Elder Iram said.

"That's right." Rise looked at Tobin, unsure if he should say more.

"I told Elder Iram about your situation," Tobin said. "We'll head to Bright Midnight tonight to recover your letter, and Elder Iram has agreed to arrange a hearing to review your case."

"A hearing?" Rise frowned. Tobin had said nothing about a hearing before.

The squadleader shrugged. "Well, I didn't know the exact protocol."

"Don't worry," Elder Iram said. "The hearing is simply a formality to establish your legal right to stay here. They may want to read your letters as proof, but I expect they will approve your request. In the meantime, you can stay in the barracks with Tobin's Squad. Officially, they will keep an eye on you, but you'll have the freedom to go about the city as you like."

A chill went down Rise's spine. *The letters. I just had to get involved with the military instead of staying out of the way like a sensible bastard,* he thought. *If they read Daniel's letters, they might ask questions I carn't answer.* As a Republican in Ideon he was already bound to arouse some routine suspicion. *If they'd thought I was from Eleszan, I wouldn't have that problem.* Ideon and Saint Brazen had been warring for years, and the recent peace could not undo years of mistrust and violence. He'd have to make them believe he really was a refugee, and he couldn't do that if they knew of his involvement with the Service.

"Of course," was all he said. *Should I run for it?* But no, that would surely lead them to believe he had something to hide.

Resigning himself to an uncertain future—*no more than I've had since now*—Rise thanked Elder Iram before following Tobin out. Together, they made their way down a few terraces, across a bridge, and to the second hill, where they approached an unassuming grey compound designated by a flag showing a sliver of moon and three stars in an indigo sky.

"Here we are," Tobin said. "You ready?"

Once again, Rise fingered the half-healed burns on his gloved left hand. *Don't be dead,* a voice in his mind whispered. *Don't be dead, Daniel.* He almost cursed aloud but then stopped himself. *If you* are *dead,* he amended his thought, *then at least tell me something. Tell me why this happened. Tell me what to do.*

"I'm ready."

Jenna took a deep breath. Silverphile's muscles flexed beneath her as if the mare could feel her tension, echoing it. *I'm ready*, Jenna thought. Was it going to work?

The Servicemen wanted to move faster, so they let her ride. They still watched the prisoners day and night, but they assumed they were all beaten. They were wrong.

A commotion broke out behind her, horses whinnying and Servicemen shouting. *Zenia's doing.* She hadn't specified what she would do to arouse the Servicemen's anger, but she'd promised it would cause enough destruction to provide fuel for Jenna's magic. Besides, these Servicemen were eager to lord over their magic-wielding captives whom they hated and feared and occasionally envied—according to Zenia's magic, at least.

The burst of energy was almost more than Jenna could handle. Instead of trying to shape the magic into anything specific, she simply let it take on whatever form it wanted. Tendrils of aether burst from her hands, shooting out all around her. Before the remaining guards could react, she had wheeled Silverphile around and urged her into a gallop. A whip split the air behind her, but Jenna was too fast. Her magic burst out of her in fits and spurts, cutting through the ropes tying her to Silverphile, flickering towards the Servicemen in eager streaks of purple lightning.

The Servicemen reeled in their saddles as the magic hit them, twitching and jerking as if they had gotten a taste of their own shock-inducing whips.

Interesting, Jenna thought, her scholarly side taking control for a moment. *My magic is arranging itself to befit the situation, targeting the Servicemen. Is that due to their proximity? Or because they're my enemies? And why does aether come more naturally than soul?* She shook her head, knowing she needed to focus, and urged Silverphile off the small road they'd been following and into the woods.

Shouts sounded behind her, and horses whinnied as the Servicemen set off in pursuit. Jenna's magic dissipated as quickly as it had burst out, the purple tinge fading from her vision, and she slumped against her saddle, exhausted yet elated.

I'm free, she thought. *I'm finally free.* Now all she had to do was make it back to Ideon.

Tobin stood by anxiously, having fallen into parade rest by default. Rise was bent over the dirtied sheaf of paper that presumably held his brother's last words, and Runie was leaning against the barrack's outer wall, watching both of them.

He hadn't seen her since returning to camp, and she'd told him about the rest of her squad's bandit hunt before giving Rise his letter. Most of the bandits had escaped for good, but they'd caught another four, and their confessions had confirmed an indobalt supplier in the Republic. Three of them had been hanged for their crimes, with the fourth serving a mitigated sentence; his family had come forward and pleaded for him.

Tobin desperately wanted to breach the subject of her squad's next mission but had found no opportunity to do so before Rise started reading. *She said my squad could come along.* Did that promise still stand? Did she even have the authority for it?

As Bright Midnight's second, Runie was responsible for the group's day-to-day running as well as leading a squad of ten. Overseeing missions was technically the sole's responsibility. *She'd have to get her superior to agree, and even then, the council would have to approve it.*

Rise finally put down the letter, his face as stoic as always.

"What did it say?" Tobin asked after a few seconds of respectful silence.

Rise shrugged. "Part of it's pretty torn up, but it explains a few things." He looked at Runie. "I suppose you've read it."

She nodded. "I got the gist of it. But I don't quite understand why the Service would send an assassin deep into Ideon for a single deserter, whether he's a mage or not."

Rise shifted uncomfortably. "Have you given the letter to anyone else to read?"

Runie's eyes narrowed at the evasion. "No. I didn't think it stated much beyond the obvious: We've another refugee hiding out in our woods."

"The last letter I got from him, Daniel wrote he had something important to tell me, something he didn't want to write down. He—he spent several weeks in the Service prisons below the headquarters in Brane. Apparently, he overheard something he shouldn't have, and the Service realized it." He looked at the paper, sadness clouding his face.

"He knew he was about to die. And I think I know what he was trying to tell me."

Tobin had followed their conversation mutely, but now joined in. "You mean he wrote it here in some sort of code?" He curbed his excitement, lest he came across as insensitive.

"Something like that." Rise read aloud from the battered pages:

"'I must trust you found my previous letter, since without it, I don't know if my last words will make much sense. I don't think I will escape the Serviceman behind me, but don't despair, Rise. We never know what the future holds. Besides, there are others we must think of. I can't be the only refugee to have suffered at the Service's hands, and shadows know, neither are you.

"'It's funny how it all seems to come back to Saint Brazen, even though we're so far from home now. I wonder if these crazy Ideians even have a clue. Really, they're not so different from us though. Shades, some are too similar for my liking, and I hope they don't suffer a similar fate.

"'Perhaps you'll fit in with them. I suppose that's what you'll have to do, though you'd better tell them you're Eleszanin. Shadows know—maybe you could go north and become Eleszanin for real. Build a life for yourself. If you try to fight against the Service, you'll just end up dead.'"

Rise stopped, folding the papers back into a neat little stack and, after a questioning glance at Runie, stuffed them into his belt.

"What about the rest of it?" Tobin asked.

"The rest isn't coded," Rise said, "but this first part had markings on it to let me know of another meaning to his words. He said there are others to think of—Ideians too similar to us who might suffer a similar fate." He waited as if expecting the words to sink in.

Tobin glanced at Runie, who didn't seem to get it either.

Rise hesitated. "Look," he said slowly, "there's no going back for me."

"You've already been offered refugee status, if you're worried about us sending you back," Tobin assured him.

"It's not that. What the letter said about resisting the Service—Daniel's wrong. I want to fight. If I'm here, in Ideon, I don't want to sit by under guard, having you think I might be a spy."

Tobin exchanged a careful look with Runie. He didn't think Rise was a spy, not after the chase and the letters and the death of Daniel, who really did seem to be Rise's brother. But Ideon still had laws and restrictions set for refugees, and besides, they couldn't be sure.

As if he guessed their thoughts, Rise held up his hands, still gloved in white, all innocence and pleading. "I know you have to keep a close watch on me. But if I tell you what's in this letter, if it's good enough to count for me—I want to do something. I want to end those bastards." Something in his expression shifted, became dark and menacing, and Tobin inadvertently took a step back.

Runie merely raised an eyebrow. "Tell us what the letter means, and I'll see what I can do."

"Ideians too similar to us—that's mages," Rise said. "He's saying Saint Brazen isn't just after their own mages—they're looking to capture Ideian mages too."

Tobin nearly snorted at the absurdity of the statement before he caught himself, seeing the intensity displayed on Rise's face. "You're serious?"

"Dead serious. Shades haunt me if I lie, but that's what Daniel overheard from the Service themselves. That's why they hunted him down for so long."

But how would they hold them? Tobin wanted to protest, though he knew the answer well enough. *Indobalt chains. Bendekan knows those could hold even the strongest mage.*

Runie nodded with a decisive finality. "I believe you, Rise. But it wouldn't do for anyone else to hear this. Keep your suspicions to yourself for the moment, and I'll see what I can do to help your case. Dismissed."

Rise saluted in his own way, left palm covering his eye, then departed for his appointment with the Yoel's Atonement quartermaster—he desperately needed a change of clothes. Besides, being attached to Tobin's squad meant he required an identifying stripe in their colours: grey and white.

Runie beckoned Tobin to her study, a comfortable room set into the smallest of Bright Midnight's slate-gray buildings.

Soles and seconds received privileges far beyond those of ordinary squadleaders, and Tobin marveled at the space Runie had for books, maps, and various logistic supplies. Bright Midnight wasn't a large group, since their specialization was nightwork and espionage, and this showed in the size of their compound. However, the smaller the group, the more elite. This meant Bright Midnight—along with Ibram's Tombs, Neri's Hawks, and Whitelight—was one of Silas' Hill's most respected.

Tobin's eyes were drawn to the heavy volumes of histories and recorded Tales on Runie's shelves, and in his appreciation of them, he failed to realize there was someone else already in the room.

"Adriane," Runie said. The slight young woman snapped into a hasty salute. "I'd forgotten you were in here. Wait outside for a moment. I've a quick matter to discuss with Squadleader Tobin, and then I'll see to your lesson."

Tobin smiled at the soldier as she left, but she kept her gaze down, moving with the balanced precision of someone expecting to encounter combat at any moment.

Runie must have noticed his curiosity. "She's our hummingbird. A recruit under the Elesson Agreement. Skilled in combat, and she's got impressive teleportation magic, though she's obviously self-taught." She shook her head. "I'm not sure if I want to know what she's been through to make her so jumpy, but you can bet it wasn't good."

They didn't get many Eleszanin training with them, but Tobin knew the ones who did always had their reasons for journeying to Ideon, even if they wouldn't share them, used as they were to Eleszan's cautious and aloof culture. The mages especially were… different. Tobin supposed it must be hard learning magic in a country that didn't openly discourage magic but didn't provide centers of magical learning either.

"Now, I wanted to have a word with you about a certain promise I made when we fought those bandits," Runie said.

Tobin could feel a grin stealing across his face. "You'll take us with you? We'll get a real—I mean," he cleared his throat, "is my squad able to accompany yours on their next mission?"

"I cleared it with Sole Kathreen, and the council approved the initiative taken by a senior squad to assist in the development of a junior team. I'll warn you right now though, we don't know when or where we'll be called to. Bright Midnight deploys with three hours' notice, sometimes less, so get your squad to pack light and have their things ready."

"You think you'll be called up again so soon?" Squads tended to work in rough rotations, so Runie's group shouldn't be deployed again for a few weeks, especially considering Bright Midnight's niche role.

"I don't know. We wouldn't usually, but if what Rise said is true… Well, there'll be a whole lot of work for Bright Midnight before everything is said and done."

Imp exulted in the cool wind hitting his face as he sprinted past shoppers clogging the stalls of Silas' Hill's high market. He didn't mind running, provided it wasn't in the forest. He was good at city running, mostly because of his Service training, though he liked to think running from his fires had taught him as well as they had.

He slowed to a jog as he hit a busier thoroughfare, dodging a few clusters of guards. There were soldiers everywhere here, but Imp couldn't make sense of the way things were organized, with colourful banners and stripes depicting groups and rank but no way of determining what each group actually did. He supposed he would learn in time.

When Imp reached the armourer's shop, he strode to the counter and handed the woman there a neatly folded note with a blue wax seal on it. *Ideians are crazy*, he thought for the umpteenth time. *Sending runners when they could build up message tubes.* But Ideians didn't like technology, and so they wasted their resources on runners. Not that Imp minded. Running was a job that felt right, and besides, after days of trudging through Arahill's border forests, the city bustle was a welcome relief.

Imp fingered the copper coins—kernels, they called them here—jingling in a satchel tied to his belt and smiled. *Enough for some cigarettes*, he mused. *If I can find someone who sells.* He left the armoury, job completed for the moment, and adjusted the yellow half-cape that marked him as a messenger. Glancing at the shops around him, Imp meandered down the street, letting his breathing return to normal.

Imp browsed through a few market streets without any luck. *Do they think cigarettes are technology too?* He frowned. He didn't need a cigarette, not really, but the thought of having that little fire in his hands comforted him. He hadn't set a fire in days—nothing larger than lighting some candles anyway—and he itched for it. It was like hunger but in his hands, gnawing and tense and nervous.

Eventually, Imp returned to the broad street that wound up to the first few terraces, eyes gravitating to the slate-grey buildings of Adriane's new home. While Imp had been quartered in one of the halls at the top of the northern hill and ran messages for Elder Iram and the other city officials, Adriane had delved into lessons on fighting and magic and soldierly things with an intensity that left little time for him. At least she had promised to see him tomorrow. Imp wished she had more time to see him, but he also understood her fervour. *It's like my fires*, he thought. *She has to do something.*

He walked the hill and meandered towards Bright Midnight's compound, hoping to catch a glimpse of her all the same. He didn't want to admit it—he'd never needed *anybody*—but Adriane made him feel safe. *Besides, she's the only one here who knows, who understands everything.* Vine and Uncle Bento were the only others like that.

He'd left behind the shoppers and townspeople, and the road was empty except for a few combat squads. A tall, lanky traveller suddenly caught Imp's eye, and he ducked behind a cluster of soldiers, heart racing. The traveller hadn't noticed him, but his pale skin was unusual here, so he stood out. That alone shouldn't have Imp worried, but the man had bandages wrapped in a criss-cross pattern around his calves, and he didn't wear the colours of any combat group.

Imp glanced reflexively at the traveller's cloak and hands, searching for the telltale eye pin or brand, then stopped himself. *He wouldn't have it in plain sight if he were a Serviceman,* Imp chided himself. *Besides, he could be a refugee. Or maybe he just likes the Saint Brazen dress styles.*

Still, Imp's heart beat even faster at the sight of the thin fabric obscuring the man's palms. *Gloves in summer? Why would he have those except to cover something up?* Imp tried to think of reasons, but all he could picture was the blue-painted iris of a Service eye, covered up by the soft cloth of a glove.

Imp's fingers itched to do something, to find out. Making his decision, he turned around and walked back the way he'd come, following the man at a distance. As soon as the high market's crowds closed in, he snuck closer, a mere pace behind the traveller. Imp reached out for the once-white glove of his left hand, catching it by a torn corner.

Imp whipped the stranger's glove off as quickly as he could. Startled, the man cried out and automatically curled his hand into a fist, but not before Imp had seen the man's palm.

A Servicebrand! Imp ducked, melting into the crowd as the man whipped around, barely-concealed terror playing across his face.

Shades they're here. Flames, they're everywhere. The Servicebrand hadn't been the only mark on the man's skin. There were burns there too and a tattoo marking him out as a Scroll Brotherhood member. *Which one? Serviceman or thief?* Either way, it didn't bode well.

As soon as Imp reached the first terrace, he raced back to his quarters, though his eyes were fixed on the narrow flag that marked Bright Midnight's compound. Had the man noticed him? Had he been quick enough? His head pounded with fear, but one thought shone through clearly: He'd keep a low profile until tomorrow, and then he would tell her. *Adriane will know what to do.* She always did.

Early land distribution
ca. 304 in the
Peace Legend

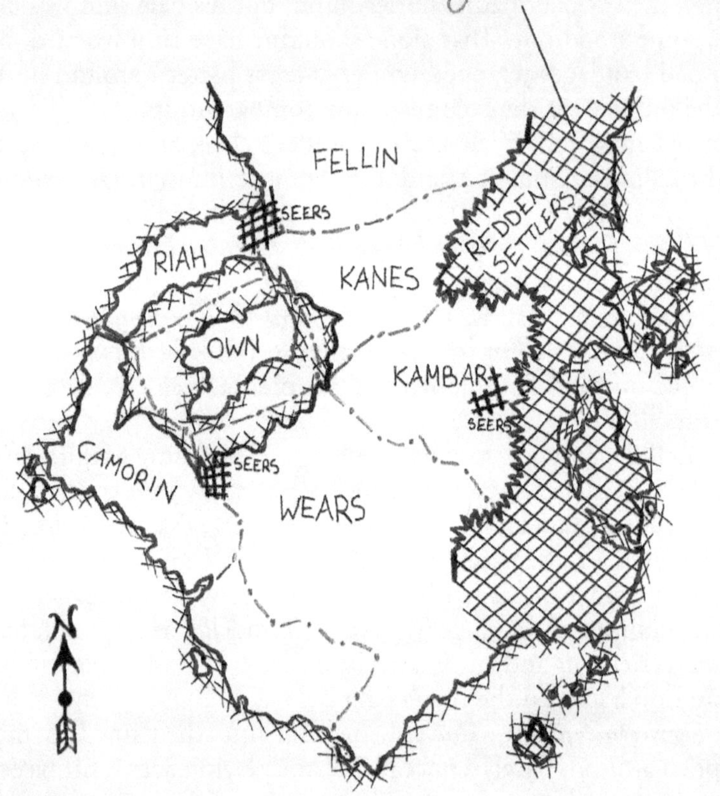

Redden settlers
are the precursors
to the Eldeon Nation
and the Saint-Brazen
Republic

18

SILVERPHILE

Silverphile raced through the trees, dodging branches and roots and jumping the occasional fallen log. Jenna spotted a rough mark carved into the bark on a pine tree, the unfamiliar trailhead reminding her that she was in Republican territory. *Can it be this easy?* Jenna wondered, elated at the lack of restraints and the wind in her face. Perhaps the Servicemen had been too stunned to pursue her. *Did I really—*

Things went sideways before she'd completed the thought. Two mounted Servicemen burst through the bushes behind her, one cracking a whip, the other hefting a spear.

Jenna cast out for sources of energy to fuel her magic. She let Silverphile choose her own path through the trees and concentrated on her surroundings.

"Yoel's heart," she cursed. *There's plenty of sources when I don't need my magic, and now there's nothing.* Glancing behind her, she saw the two Servicemen joined by a third. The spearman hefted his weapon, but the distance and the trees between them prevented him from using it just yet.

There. A flare of energy burst to life ahead of her, and she seized it, letting it turn to aether beneath her skin. She concentrated the pressure in her hand, purple and black tendrils spiderwebbing across her skin, then sent it flying towards the soldiers.

A trunk exploded, and a falling branch caught one of the men. He tumbled from his horse.

"Faster, girl," Jenna urged Silverphile, before grabbing at another source of energy. Her vision flickered into shades of purple, and she focused on the pressure building underneath her skin, struggling to form it. When it seemed under control, she glanced back: The Servicemen loomed mere paces behind her. Silverphile dodged a tree; the spear wielder rode around the other way, preparing to throw his weapon.

Ducking under a branch, Jenna twisted in her saddle to face him. The Serviceman's shoulder twitched as he prepared his throw, but before he could release the spear, Jenna sent a pulse of aether hurtling towards him. A flash of purple-black fire lit up the man's face—and then Silverphile's legs give way. Jenna flew from the saddle, the heat from the blast hitting her back.

Stunned, she tried to roll with the fall, hitting dirt and roots as she went. She tumbled over several times, hearing the remaining Servicemen's horses whinny as they wheeled to avoid trampling her. She thumped into something soft and warm and wet.

She groaned and opened her eyes; a large grey mass streaked with red swam into view.

"Silverphile?"

She braced herself against Silverphile's back, trying to stand, but between the fall and her shock, her legs might as well have been made of lead.

"Silverphile," she whispered again, gazing in horror at her fallen horse. The mare was wheezing for breath in great horrible gasps. The Serviceman's spear protruded from her flank, and there were burns along her back from Jenna's last blast of aether.

"I'm sorry," Jenna whispered through tears. *I did this.* She felt numb and weak, but the remaining Serviceman wheeled his horse around and rode towards her, whip flickering at his side. She had to do something.

Glancing between the approaching soldier and her horse, Jenna felt the energy released from Silverphile's wounds surge into her. She hesitated. *Silverphile or the enemy?* The decision took a split second, but it felt like forever. *Tabitha knows how much we've done together.* Silverphile had given her the freedom of movement. They'd been companions for years. Her decision made, Jenna prepared her last burst of magic.

She had practically grown up riding, and she had learned enough of horse-handling to recognize Silverphile's wounds as fatal. *Soul and aether can be used to create almost anything, provided the object in question reflects some element of darkness or light.* The memorized words popped into her mind, and she welcomed the distance they afforded her. *It is suggested soul and aether wielders practice using the creativity and flexibility inherent in their magic to their advantage.* Jenna concentrated and forced the energy to turn to both soul and aether, intuitively combining the two, all thoughts of ineptitude cast aside by shock. Her skin began to glow purple and white, and she rested her head on Silverphile's flank. *Several taboos govern the use of shaping objects. If broken, these can result in dire consequences. Foremost among these is the limit on copying exactly any living being known to the mage.*

"Sleep," Jenna whispered, letting the magic seep from her skin into her horse. She was vaguely aware of the Serviceman dismounting, gazing at her glowing skin with something akin to awe or terror. *Although it is, in most cases, easier to work from a mold well known to the wielder, creating a magical copy of an existing living being remains a most dangerous endeavour, since exact copies tend to gain some form of sentience which prevents the mage from controlling them.* The words flowed on inside her head, and Jenna gently poured soul and aether into Silverphile. The mare's breathing eased, and she lay her head down with a soft whinny.

Tears trickling down her face, Jenna waited there—the Serviceman standing like a guard above her, reverent, frozen in shock or fear—until Silverphile's breathing stopped. *The least I could give her is a peaceful death.*

The glow faded from her skin, and the Serviceman seemed to decide it was safe to touch her. He pulled her up, then heaved her into his saddle and walked his horse back towards the camp. Jenna lay limp, exhausted from the complex magic she'd performed. Defeated.

Her escape had failed.

⁂

"*History begins with eight tribes of a nation once called Camori. From them we take our name. From them we take our wisdom. From them we take our shame. For we failed them long ago, and we are ever paying the price.*"

Unable to sleep, Adriane sat by the crackling fire, listening to the Ideian soldiers tell their stories. They'd started at the beginning of one of their cycles for her, explaining that one Tale flowed into the next like a stream into a river.

"*Each tribe exemplified an ideal, and this ideal manifested itself in their bodies. The Kane tribe was loyal. The Kambar tribe, brave. The Fellin tribe, independent. The Riah, ambitious. The Own, knowledgeable. The Wears, creative. The Camorin, responsible. And the Seers, they were wise.*"

In Saint Brazen, Adriane had only heard rumors about the dog-folk, but here they walked about plain as day. Some even fought for the

Ideians, along with frightening cat-like creatures they called Fellin. But most of the other tribes had died out, and the Ideians blamed Saint Brazen for their deaths.

"When Redden ships first arrived on the Camorin continent, they found a magical land, lush and fruitful. They found a thriving society of creatures strange to them, melding human characteristics with those of beasts. However, the tribes did not feel apprehension towards the Redden settlers, and they welcomed them, sharing their land and resources, while the Redden shared their technology. The land's magic, which had transformed the tribes' physical features, flowed through these new settlers and they learned to direct it into the objects they crafted, creating powerful magical artifacts."

The story was a myth, of course, but Adriane found herself connecting it to the few fragments of history she knew. Though Saint Brazen didn't educate its masses in history and politics—after all, what need had a farmer to know of past battles and treaties?—Ma and Pa had taught her the little they knew, before they'd died. Lancaster had furthered that knowledge, and he'd occasionally mentioned the other countries, Ideon and Eleszan, as well as distant wars that, according to him, still influenced events in the city.

"It's the wars and the discovery of indobalt that shaped the Service into what it is now," he'd told her once.

Adriane fought the grief welling up inside her at the memory. She listened to the story to distract herself.

"These magical artifacts became objects of contention between the two peoples. Though they strove to live in peace, their cultures differed, as did their appreciation of the continent's riches. While the tribes preferred to live in harmony with one another and their surroundings, the settlers preferred to domesticate nature, and they used the technologies and magical objects they created to subdue the land, growing in power and prosperity."

The tribes represent Ideians, Adriane decided, *and the settlers represent Saint Brazeners.* She knew the countries had once been united, and the storyteller described a treaty drawn up between tribes and settlers, allowing them to live in harmony once more. *It's subtle, but the story favors the Ideians,* she thought. *Do they believe the wars were all Saint Brazen's fault?*

A hand gripped her shoulder, and Adriane spun, reaching for the hunting knife sheathed in her boot. The storyteller broke off, wide-eyed, and a few of the soldiers reached for their weapons at her reaction, before realizing the disruption was simply caused by a messenger.

"Sorry." Adriane returned her knife and faced the yellow-caped youth who'd interrupted her thoughts. He was about Imp's age, though taller and with more muscle on him, and the dark skin and hair of a southern Ideian.

"Pardon me," he panted, trembling with exertion and surprise at her reaction. "I bring word from Second Runie of Bright Midnight. You're to report for duty right away."

He snapped into a salute, which Adriane returned, mouth twitching into a frown. Runie had warned her they might be called up for a mission soon. Adriane hardly felt like she'd learned anything yet, but they would expect her to pull her weight—use her magic to scout and spy for them. *At least Imp won't be there. I won't need to take care of both him and myself.*

Adriane threw on her cloak and sprinted up the few terraces to Bright Midnight's base, pushing thoughts of Imp out of her mind as she tried to curb her nervousness. Her magic flickered at the edge of her vision, and she fingered the green stone still looped into her braid, letting her sense of touch ground her, and the magic dissipated. Runie had taught her that object magic gone volatile could sometimes be controlled by focusing on tactile things, basically by distracting herself. *It's strange, to have a category of magic I belong to.*

Silas' Hill was largely silent and dark, but Bright Midnight's court-yard was bustling with activity. When Adriane arrived, Runie was just leaving her study, an imposing sight in full military dress, with rippled armour plates covering her right leg and left arm. Slinging saddlebags over her shoulders, Runie called for Adriane to grab her things and arm herself.

Bright Midnight travelled light and was prepared for quick depar-tures, so all Adriane had to do was change into a fresh uniform—mottled grey and green to blend in with the night, with a grey hummingbird pin identifying her as an Eleszanin mage—grab her own saddle-bags from under her bed, and pick up a standard-issue dagger, armguard, and greave from Bright Midnight's small armoury. She completed the tasks silently, counting people as she went.

At least two, maybe three squads heading out. Some of the soldiers wore the white and grey of Yoel's Atonement, a small combat group that always seemed to be the subject of jibes, for reasons Adriane did not understand, though she knew it had to do with those Tales of theirs.

"Need any help?" Squadleader Birch, a thick, dark-skinned dog-folk held out a hand for Adriane's packs.

She hesitated but then handed them to him; he slung them over his back with two other sets of saddlebags as if they weighed nothing.

"We're mustering by Commiste's Stables in ten minutes," he informed her. "Squads Three and Five, with Fourteen from Yoel's Redemption." He used the combat group's alternate name, Redemption instead of Atonement, like many of the dog-folk—Kanes—and Fellin did.

Shaking herself from her thoughts, Adriane saluted Squadleader Birch, then sprinted off towards the East Way, which led through the city and to the outermost practice yards and stables, following the last of the soldiers.

She arrived amid the quiet bustle of hostlers efficiently pairing saddlebags with horses, and then horses with soldiers. Adriane herself couldn't ride well, but one of the hostlers led a small, dark horse with an ambling gait to her. Squadleader Birch appeared behind her with the saddlebags, which the hostler helped her affix. Adriane mounted, noting that her horse didn't have its own reins, but was attached to a lead.

Another rider approached her, Benja, from Runie's squad. "I'll be leading Serenity," he said, pointing at Adriane's horse. "We've got to ride quickly, but he's used to following, so that should make it easier for you."

Resigning herself to the embarrassment of being dependent, Adriane nodded.

"Form ranks," came a call from somewhere ahead of them, and the soldiers maneuvered their horses until each squad stood together in three columns of three, with their leader ahead. Adriane's horse had clopped behind Benja, who had positioned his horse behind the last row of Squad Three's horses.

Imp, she realized suddenly. *He won't know I'm gone until the morning.*

"A Republican raiding party was sighted in House Silas' Hill's east, near Firrlway." Runie sat astride facing the other soldiers, her face drawn and serious. "They captured an Ideian mage by the name of Jenna Brightshade and are suspected in the disappearance of at least two others. We'll be as close behind as we can, but this mission may take us into Republican territory. This is a rescue mission, not an invasion, but if it comes to a fight, Kyra prevail, we'll take it."

Adriane's heart jumped into her throat, and the shadows flickered in her peripheral vision. *So soon.* She hadn't expected to set foot in Saint Brazen again for months.

"Squad Five of Bright Midnight and Squad Fourteen of Yoel's Atonement, you are riding under my command, within the charge of your own squadleaders. Squadleader Birch, set pace."

Runie wheeled her horse around and set off at a trot. Birch galloped ahead of her, then fell into a quick canter, which Runie imitated. The squads moved one at a time, forming ranks behind them, with two other riders—Squadleader Tobin, fresh faced as a Standard Force watchling, and a tall, lanky fellow Adriane didn't recognize—taking up the column's tail.

When Imp awoke, his soft blankets and mattress and the warm sunlight flashing across his face almost made him forget. He ran his hands across the sanded wood of his bedframe, one of ten identical frames in a long, wood-paneled room, tracing patters across the soft grain. Then he remembered.

Servicebrand. Imp sat up with a jolt. *What time is it?* Most of the other boys were already out, but when he poked his head out of the window set above his pillow, the sun was barely above the horizon. If he hurried, he could catch Adriane at breakfast, before she went out to train with her new squad.

Imp had tried to find her last night, deciding the matter of a Serviceman in Silas' Hill took precedence, but she'd been away, training with her magic, and then he'd had a slew of messages to run, which kept him occupied until after most of the soldiers had gone to bed. He threw on his new clothes—tunic and thick cloth belt over a shirt and loose breeches in the Ideian style covered by his yellow cape—and left the quarters.

Imp checked the message board as he was heading out. Message boys (and girls) worked in rough shifts, with instructions communicated via the message board or in person by elders and officials. No new instructions were chalked onto the square marked with his name, so Imp took off down the hill, descending the first set of steps that would lead him to the bridge connecting the city's two hills.

"Imp! Wait a minute."

Face falling, Imp slowed, caught his breath, then turned around. Elder Iram was the equivalent of Nero here, and that meant he had to listen to him.

"What is it Elder Iram? Can the message wait? I was going to go see Adriane."

"Ah, that is precisely what I wished to discuss with you." Elder Iram might have the equivalent authority over Imp as Nero, but the elderly man fit the position, unlike Nero who'd always carried himself with the dignity of a peacock unknowingly bereft of his feathers.

"What do you mean?" Imp stiffened. Did Iram know about the Saint Brazener in the city? Did he think Imp had something to do with him?

Iram seemed to take his reaction for something else. "Have you heard already? Adriane's squad was called up late last night. They left at an hour's notice."

"Wait, what?"

"I'm sorry, lad, I'm sure she meant to tell you, but they had to make what haste they could."

"Where are they going?" Imp could feel a lump rising in his throat, and he fought to keep his voice from cracking.

Iram looked at him with his deep, soul-searching green eyes, and Imp shrank under his gaze. "I'm afraid I cannot tell you. That information is sensitive."

"Will she come back?" Imp's brain felt fevered, and he couldn't stop the naïve words before they tumbled from his mouth.

Iram set his mouth in a flat line. "Why don't you come up to my study. We'll have some nice hot tea—and some breakfast," he amended, correctly interpreting Imp's most recent disappointed facial expression.

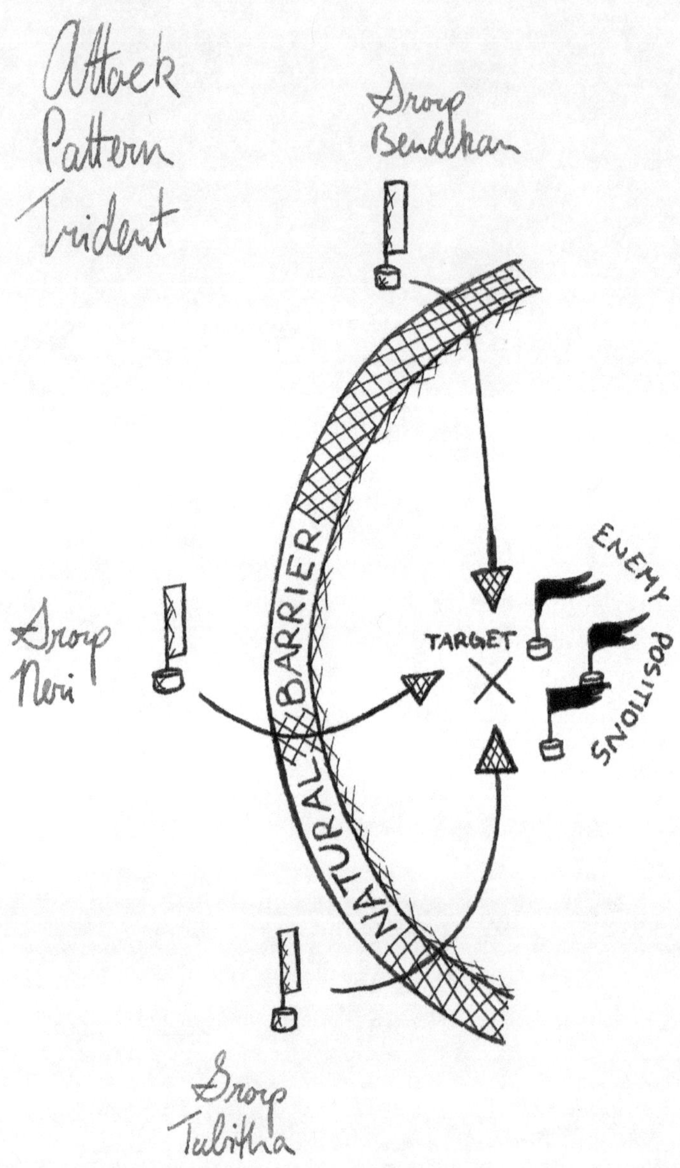
Attack Pattern Trident
Group Bendekan
Group Nevi
Group Tabitha
NATURAL BARRIER
TARGET
ENEMY POSITIONS

19

NECESSARY WOUNDS

Rise had never ridden so hard in his life. Having left the main highway, the company thundered along narrow goat tracks in double file, led by Squadleader Birch, who seemed to know the countryside like the back of his hand. The horses maintained a steady trot, which seemed faster in the confines of the forest, and every so often the soldiers would dismount and run, leading their horses by the reins.

Reminds me of the Service's forced marches, Rise thought, gloved left hand meandering to the short sword now hung at his waist. He'd 'borrowed' it from Tobin's armoury. *Good thing these Ideians can't work me any harder than the Service did.*

Eventually, the pace became cathartic, one hour blurring into the next. Only the changing light marked the passage of time. Even Tobin, who had kept up a steady stream of chatter at the beginning, fell silent, and all the others' faces were grim and set, focused only on the path in front of them.

It seemed like days passed before Second Runie called a halt, and the exhausted soldiers pitched camp in a grassy clearing. Tobin made his way to the front, where Squadleader Birch and Second Runie were waiting. Rise followed, lack of sleep failing to rob him of curiosity.

"How far did we travel?" he asked Tobin.

"We're at the border."

Rise glanced around, eyebrows rising, but nothing seemed all that different. "How do you know?"

"See that?" Tobin pointed at a mark carved onto a craggy boulder half-hidden by a fallen log. "That not only tells us we're at the border, but it also lets us know we've ended up just off the northern shore of Cole's Lake. The ambush site is close to here, according to the Kane who raised the warning. I presume we'll have some scouts check it over tonight."

They reached the other two leaders, and Rise did a double-take. A young woman was with them, hovering behind the second, her horse on a lead rein. *Shades take me, isn't she a sight.* Rise couldn't help the thought. She was short and slender. Her shoulders were stiff with tension, but her large eyes glinted beautifully from a delicate face. Her long, dark hair was braided over her shoulder, revealing pale skin, much lighter than that of most Ideians.

Tobin's elbow caught him in the ribs, and Rise dragged his gaze away from the girl.

"That's Adriane," Tobin said. "An Eleszanin mage attached to Runie's group. Don't stare like that."

Rise smirked, chagrinned. *Curse it's been some time since a girl's got me staring.*

Runie commanded them to set up camp while she and Adriane went to check the ambush site and chart their path for the next day. Tobin beckoned Rise to a corner unclaimed by blanketed soldiers, though Rise couldn't help but glance back at Adriane as she and Runie rode away.

Tobin fell asleep within seconds, but Rise lay awake for what seemed like hours, mind turning from thoughts of pretty girls, to Eleszan, to the Republic, and finally settling on Daniel. *He's gone. And he's not coming back. It's all Calen's fault. If I can find him... end him. I can make things right.* He caught himself, grimacing at his idealism. *Who am I kidding? I carn't make anything right, not by killing the evil villain. This is reality, not one of Tobin's shades-forsaken Tales.* Rise had begun to think of Tobin if not as a friend, then at least an ally to his cause, but shades be true, the boy was still ignorant of the way the world really worked. *But what I carn do is even the score.* Calen was untouchable for the moment, but the rest of the Service—*I can make a few of 'em bleed for their crimes.*

Rise woke the next morning without having remembered falling asleep. He joined the fray of saddle-bag-packing soldiers with quiet determination. Tobin pulled him to the front as soon as they had stowed their blankets and grabbed some buttered rolls and salted beef for breakfast. They walked into what appeared to be an argument between Squadleader Birch, Adriane, and the second.

"Their trail leads south-east, but they won't keep that direction," Adriane said. "The nearest city, Cain, lies east of us. The mountains around the Eleszanin border aren't widely populated, and the nearest

Service headquarters to the south is much further than Cain."

"If we go directly east on a whim, we might miss them," Squadleader Birch said. "We can't afford to lose their trail. We have to stick to it, even if it slows us down."

"Or we could catch up to them," Adriane argued, "by following the direction they're most likely to go."

"Enough." Runie's voice remained calm, but her shoulders tensed. "We cannot afford to lose track of them. Your suggestion is valid, Adriane, but you don't understand tracking the Service like we do. I trust Squadleader Birch's judgement in this."

Adriane opened her mouth, hesitated, then pursed her lips and stepped back with a salute. Rise stifled a smirk. *Looks like she's got some backbone… but not enough to get herself listened to*, he thought, amused. He couldn't help but eye her as they dispersed to their horses. Her stance was still slight and diminutive, and she kept her head down, but the fire never left her eyes.

She's seen the shades, Rise decided, *and made it out the other side. And how in the shadows does she know about Cain and the Service Headquarters there? If they don't know it in Ideon, would they know it in Eleszan?*

"Rise." Tobin gestured to Rise's horse. "Let's go."

"Right."

Rise mounted, trying to suppress another bout of chagrin. *Hope I didn't stare after Adriane like some dog-folk again.* He glanced ahead to where Squadleader Birch was wheeling his horse around, canine nose twitching, perhaps with some trace scent. *On second thought, not like a halfwit dog-folk. I carn't say things like that around here.*

They rode south until they spotted the Servicemen's tracks. The trail didn't look like much to Rise, but the Bright Midnight scouts were excellent trackers and moved ahead and to the sides to guide their way. They kept up that same, strenuous pace throughout the day and into the night, and after another short rest were on their way again. *If they'd nationalized their horses like Saint Brazen does, they wouldn't have to worry about resting them so often,* Rise thought with a shake of his head.

The hours spent following the vague imprints of hooves on the forest floor blended together in Rise's head. He'd left Daniel's letters behind in Silas' Hill, but he'd memorised the words and kept repeating them in his head like some demented mantra.

I finally know what to do, he thought. He only hoped they'd catch the bastards fast enough for him to have his revenge. Perhaps the girl, Adriane, had been on to something and they could've cut them off. Then again, if they kept following the trail, they would catch the Servicemen sooner or later. Rise hoped it would be enough.

Rhoy, the Serviceman whom Jenna had once thought of as kind, cursed vilely.

She shifted her face against the hardwood post she was tied to, held up by loops of rope around her wrists, mind hazy with pain. They'd brought her here after her failed escape. At first, the place had smelled like an old barn, but now all she could smell was her own sweat and the blood that dripped from her back. They'd whipped her.

"You had to run off," the Serviceman snarled, pacing with a bloodied whip in hand.

He's angry. Jenna blinked away tears, feeling helpless. *So angry.*

"You just had to play the hero, get us to waste time chasing you down. You've yourself to blame for this. If you'd have followed orders, we would've treated you well."

What in Tabitha's name does he think amounts to being treated well?

"Now I've got no choice." His mouth was twisted, ugly. "I don't like this part, you know. I never joined the Service to hurt people. But you're not giving me a choice."

"Please," Jenna whispered, trying to focus. "Where are the others?"

"They went ahead, to Teel. But what do you care?" He grimaced and hefted his whip—the regular kind, not the magic-nullifying type. "You left them all behind, didn't you?"

He lashed out again, and Jenna whimpered as the whip hit her, too exhausted to scream. She couldn't see his face as the blow fell, but she imagined she could, his spiky hair drooping with sweat, features distorted in anger. Blood trickled down from a cut on her cheek. *I thought he was different,* her mind whispered. *I thought he might be good.* She was beginning to realize that absolutes like good and evil had no place in the Service. Perhaps not anywhere.

"You left everyone else to rot and tried to save yourself." He spat on the ground beside her.

She jerked as another blow hit her back. *I suppose I did, in a way,* she realized. *Zenia's gone.* The thought focused her mind, and she scrabbled for a handhold on the post, trying to get her legs to support her weight, to relieve the pressure on her wrists.

"You should be glad they didn't tell me to kill you for riding off like that," the Serviceman muttered, then cursed again. "Shades take the lot of you. *Mages.*" The word still sounded unfamiliar to him. "They're right, you know. You deserve what's coming to you if all you care is to desert your own."

"Did you think I had a choice?" Jenna croaked, her throat hoarse. Had she been screaming? She couldn't quite remember.

The Serviceman paused. "Everyone has a choice," he said carefully. She imagined him looking from his blood-stained whip to the welts on her back, imagined a hint of pity clouding the anger.

"Zenia had a choice." She didn't know why she said it, and Rhoy— the Serviceman, she amended, refusing to humanize him—didn't seem to hear. *What was Zenia's choice?* Jenna couldn't feel the pain anymore, but her body still jerked at the next blow. *Something's different. Something important.* She couldn't seem to focus on the thought.

The blows ceased, and the Serviceman left Jenna to her muddy thoughts. Her back began to throb, and then it erupted in agony. She shivered with it, jerking against her restraints, before falling still. *Something's different.* Jenna cracked her eyes open to see purple flecks dancing in her vision. Pain cleared her mind, and realization bloomed in her thoughts. *Energy. Everywhere.*

Zenia had caused a commotion so Jenna would have energy to fuel her magic. Now the Service had inadvertently given Jenna a second chance to escape. She managed a smile as she let the energy flow into her, rippling through her, building up pressure beneath her skin. It seemed her magic could feed off her own destruction as well as that of others.

She could hardly believe how much energy a simple whipping had created. *Then again,* she thought, *Zenia's theory that the energy is strong when fueled by the destruction of someone I care about holds true for myself as well. Either that, or I'm more hurt than I know.* She didn't think her wounds were severe. They wouldn't have been captured if the Service didn't need them for something. The fact that she was conscious after a whipping only proved they didn't mean to hurt her too much.

Taking a deep breath, Jenna let a small flare of magic escape. Burning aether flames tore through the bonds tying her to the post, and she slumped to the ground. The pressure surged, the remaining energy clamoring for release, and Jenna twitched as tendrils of soul and aether formed beneath her skin, crawling up her arms.

She struggled to keep the magic under control as her vision changed further, the purples becoming more vibrant, every other colour extinguished by that of her magic. Violet. Amethyst. Charcoal. Lilac. Iris. Obsidian. She'd never been so aware of the different shades composing the tendrils of aether.

A spark shot out from her hands, and a shout went up from outside the building. *Someone must have seen.*

More shouts sounded, and Jenna could hear metal clashing. Footsteps thumped on wood, nearing, and she knew she had to act quickly. Wriggling so she faced a wall with a window, Jenna focused, allowing the magic to manifest. A blast ripped through the wooden framing. Aether sparks caught on thatch, and flames began to lick at the roof.

"Hey! Stop!"

The Serviceman barreled back into the room, and Jenna pushed herself off the ground, using the post to hold herself upright. She faced him. Rhoy.

The blast had barely touched the reserves of energy available to her, and her magic filled her to the brim, causing her skin to glow visibly. He skidded to a stop several paces away from her, face alight with fear, the glow of her magic reflected in his terror-stricken eyes.

She wanted to say something clever and spiteful, but her mind froze, and she merely looked at him. They stayed like that for a few strange seconds. Then the rest of Jenna's magic burst out of her, sending her flying several paces through the opening she'd created and into a grassy field.

Day and night blended into each other as the tiny invasion force rode through the western Republic, skirting the few villages nestled into the woods. Not long after they'd crossed the border, however, the forest's shadows thinned. The trail became clearer. Even the weather seemed to resist their intrusion into Republican lands, the sun bright and revealing, with no mist or rain to shield them from view. Tobin felt with unshakeable certainty that they must be closing in on their prey. Either that, or they would lose them when the land opened, and their cover disappeared.

The sun had begun to set when Tobin turned in his saddle. "I think we might catch them by nightfall," he said to Rise, who scowled in reply. The farther they rode, hooves churning dirt into mud, horses as silent and focused as their riders, the moodier Rise seemed, retreating into whatever dark thoughts occupied his mind. The pace was wearing on them all, but the adrenaline of knowing a battle was coming kept them alert. That, and the knowledge that they were in enemy territory. If something went awry, no help would come.

The trail they now followed was a few hours old and obvious even to the most unskilled tracker. The other soldiers knew what was coming. As dusk deepened, some grew tense and irritable, some talked too much and too loudly, and some, like Rise, cloaked themselves in silence.

The clop of hooves seemed to muffle their conversation, and the first few stars shone through the ever-widening gaps between the trees. The constellations, at least, were familiar, and Tobin's heart rose as he recognized the cluster of stars marking Bendekan's Ash right ahead of them.

"Don't worry, Felias. It'll be fine." Timothy's voice caught Tobin's ear.

He turned to see Felias blushing.

"I know," Felias said. "It just—it's not like chasing bandits, is it?"

Timothy shot Tobin a brief look of helplessness—after all, none of them had fielded any battles other than their skirmish with the bandits—before turning back to the younger man. "Probably not. But we'll do our job, and we'll do it well."

Felias nodded resolutely, and Rico and Yemena, riding behind them, murmured assent.

"If we die, we die," Yemena said, voice trembling. "At least our deaths will have meaning."

Though the words sent a chill up his spine, Tobin couldn't help but feel excited. *It'll be different from those bandits alright*, he thought, nudging his horse closer to the head of the column. *We're fighting a real enemy this time, a trained force of fighters.*

He reached the front, where Rise rode behind the other two squadleaders and Adriane, whom Second Runie kept by her side—though no longer attached by a lead rein. *I'm still not sure what's different about her*, Tobin mused, thoughts shifting. *I guess I shouldn't have expected an Eleszanin to be the same as us.* He looked beyond them to the moonlit trees and bracken—*Republican* trees and bracken—and amended the thought. *Then again, I somehow expected the Republic to look a whole lot different.* Perhaps the differences lay in less observable matters, the collective mindset of each nation, the way its people thought and spoke and learned and behaved.

Lost in his thoughts, with the forest's colours blended monotonously together in front of his eyes, a curtain of dark shadows backlit in silver, Tobin almost missed the shrouded figure riding towards them. It was Niecka, Squad Three's forward scout.

She approached Runie, and they exchanged whispers. *Probably another report*, Tobin thought, before Runie wheeled her horse around to face him and Squadleader Birch.

"There's a small village ahead that's playing host to the Republican raiding party. We'll attack before dawn, so prepare your squads. Pattern trident, with Squad Fourteen taking the south, Squad Three the middle, and Squad Five the north."

Tobin's thoughts disintegrated. *This is it. This is really it.* He felt hot and clammy, and his face flushed as he snapped into a quick salute before sending a few hand signals to Timothy and Yemena who'd prepare the squad and call in the scouts. He turned his horse then remembered Rise, who had been so quiet and unresponsive that Tobin had given up trying to talk to him and had subsequently nearly forgotten his presence.

"What about Rise?"

Rise turned to look at the second, a frightening intensity to his gaze.

Runie spoke to him directly. "You have a choice, Republican." Tobin wondered why she emphasized that title. "You may stand down, or you may fight with us. I'm sure I needn't tell you what we'll do if you warn the enemy of our approach." Her gaze was icy; the warmth Tobin had previously glimpsed eclipsed by her commander's presence.

I wish I could be that strong someday, Tobin thought, before looking to Rise for his answer.

Rise cocked his head. "Right." He saluted in that strange way of his, left palm up, nearly covering his eye. "I think I'll fight." He hefted the short sword sheathed at his side, and Tobin wondered again where he'd acquired it. *I certainly didn't issue it, but he does need a weapon.* He'd have to confront Rise about it later. The thought of that future responsibility stifled his thrill at the upcoming fight.

Rise, meanwhile, grinned with an iciness matching Runie's expression. "I have a score to settle."

Tobin and his squad turned south, with Second Runie heading straight ahead, and Squadleader Birch angling north. Scouts had sketched charcoal maps, and Runie had decided on their actions within minutes. Though Tobin had Silas' Hill's attack patterns and procedures memorized, he could still hardly believe what was happening. He'd imagined it would be… slower somehow. More methodical.

"It's late enough that there likely won't be an alert watch," Rise muttered, his accent strong. Perhaps he was nervous too. "Curse we could wait to attack, but every hour matters if they try for an early start."

"How'd you know I was wondering?"

Rise smirked. "It's the sort of thing I'd be asking if I was a noble-born innocent like you."

"Well at least you've found your sense of humor again." Tobin hoped the darkness hid his reddened face. He signaled for silence as they rode on, then flashed hand signs that sent Horse and Mathas, his two archer scouts, out front.

Following the scouts, they neared the village. The land was rippled with soft hills, which provided easy cover; Tobin suspected Second Runie had given him the easiest approach. They dismounted and settled behind a rise to await Runie's signal. Tobin fingered the smooth wood of his tonfa with shaking hands, pausing when he felt the rough grooves of the carving he'd been given only weeks ago. A crossed pair of daggers for surviving his first battle, just like Runie had said.

The next few hours were torture. They took turns trying to sleep, uncomfortably rolled in their cloaks. *Did I think this was too fast?* Tobin thought, feeling queasy. *Better to just get it over with.*

Sometime later, a hand jolted Tobin from his uneasy sleep. Horse's smooth-cheeked face blurred into view. "Second Runie just gave the command to form up."

Tobin untangled himself from his cloak and passed on the instruction. Era with her greatshield and Yemena and Amaldie with their spears, positioned themselves at the vanguard, with Tobin, Rise, Timothy, Miels, and Rico behind them. Horse joined young Felias at the rear; only Mathas remained outside formation, having ridden northward to receive the final signal.

Slowing his breath, Tobin closed his eyes for a moment. *In, out. In, out.* Excitement was gone, replaced by a curious mix of fear and… nothing. A deadly sort of calm.

Soft hoofbeats approached, and Tobin opened his eyes. Mathas, announcing the attack.

"This is it," Tobin murmured to his squadmates, signaling them forward. The girls broke into a trot, with the rest of them following. *I imagined I'd say more*, he thought. *Be brave and inspiring.* They accelerated to a canter. *But it's quiet.* They crested the last barely-forested rise to see a village nestled between open stretches of tree-rimmed farmland beneath them. *They're all sleeping, safe and unsuspecting in their homes.* A dog barked, and a horse whinnied, prompting a return whinny from Miels' frisky steed. The game was up. *Not so unsuspecting anymore. I wonder if they know we're coming? I wonder who will make it out of this?*

They thundered down the hill, no longer concerned with stealth. Tobin's thoughts extinguished, snuffed out by concentration. He could make out figures in the streets below, not commoners, but soldiers with shiny black coats and polished swords.

"Shadows," Rise hissed. "They're ready for us."

A black-cloaked figure rose out of a hollow in the ground. Tobin barely had time to blink before someone broke rank, slashing a sword. The figure crumpled with a gurgling sound. He looked to see Rise's grim face reflected eerily in the bloodstained steel of his blade.

A sudden hiss from above distracted him. His head snapped back as he tried to place it. *I know that sound. What—* Someone cried out in pain behind him, and Tobin whirled, tonfa ready. He was unprepared for the sight that met him, an empty saddle, a prone figure lying back on the ridge, an arrow sticking out of its chest.

No time, he thought. *We're under fire.* Several more shafts hit the ground in front of him, and some of the horses pranced nervously. Their riders looked to Tobin, waiting for orders, and he urged Spiffy forward with a chilling clarity, a sense of control amidst chaos, a mind sharp as the blade of a sword. Everything was on edge.

"Scatter," Tobin commanded, and his squad obeyed. Era rose in her saddle, hefting her greatshield to shelter Tobin, Horse, and Rico from the drizzle of arrows that came their way. The others urged their horses to the side. None of the remaining projectiles hit their mark; that first arrow, having struck down a nameless soldier left behind in the mud, a lonesome stroke of luck.

The arrows ceased, and a great commotion sounded from their left: Squad Three engaged the Servicemen. Shouts and screams rent the air. Light flashed and the ground trembled. Runie's elemental mages were doing their work. Out of the corner of his eye, Tobin saw a heap of stones fuse together to form a boulder that rolled towards a group of Servicemen. The wind grew stronger at his back, and thunder rumbled overhead.

Tobin and his soldiers reached the village's first few houses. Yemena ran a soldier clean through at a gallop, and Rise left formation to strike out at another. They thundered past the first few buildings.

A Servicewoman darted in towards Tobin, and instinct took over. He whacked her with a quick flick of the wrist and followed with a backhanded blow to the head. More soldiers gathered in the narrow street ahead of them, and Tobin's charge slowed as Squad Fourteen prepared to engage.

Amaldie and Rise were nowhere to be seen. Horse and Mathas had fallen back, wielding their bows from a distance. Era's horse collapsed at a Serviceman's sword thrust, and she rolled off it, barely avoiding getting caught beneath the creature's dead mass. Blocking another attack, she rammed the spike at the front of her shield into the man's arm; he lurched back with a cry of pain and Yemena buried her spear in his unprotected side.

Tobin met sword thrusts and cuts with his tonfa, as easily as if he were practicing, occasionally glancing around to check on his squadmates. Rico, also on foot, fought at his right, protecting Spiffy's flank, and Timothy was steadfast at his left.

A sword slashed through the air beside his face, and Tobin kneed Spiffy to the side, blocking the next strike. The Serviceman's face was shrouded by the night, which made killing easier. This wasn't like fighting the bandits; this was the calm clack of practice weapons and the knowledge that death and destruction, if metered out by his tonfa, was just.

The thought almost cost him his life. Distracted, he blocked a thrust, then felt pain bloom in his thigh. Tobin glanced down—*knife!*—and quickly returned his focus to the Serviceman in front of him. He blocked, then landed a blow to the man's face. Rico darted in from the side, cutting into the man's sword arm, and the soldier tumbled backwards. A spurt of blood sprayed Tobin's chest, obscuring his insignia. *Bendekan!*

Another threat loomed from the side—the knife wielder—but Rise was there, sword flashing, and the woman dropped.

Tobin whirled around, but there were no more enemies to face.

"Squadleader Tobin." Runie stood before him, astride her horse, a broken arrow sticking out of her right arm. Adriane stood half-hidden behind her. "Any sign of the mages?"

Right. The mages. Tobin glanced around, realizing he'd forgotten. "No, Second."

"The majority of civilians stayed inside, and the remaining Servicemen retreated to the town hall on the east side."

"Would the mages be kept there?" Tobin asked.

Runie looked at Adriane who shook her head. "I don't think so. They'd likely be—"

"In an outlying building," Rise said. "A barn maybe, away from the townsfolk."

Runie glanced between the two, and Tobin felt like he'd missed something. "Squadleader Birch is directing the attack on the hall. Squadleader Tobin, take your soldiers to the outskirts and find those mages."

Tobin hesitated for a breath—*sending us out when the fighting's not even done?*—before ordering his squad out in twos. Yoel's Atonement really did get the worst assignments.

Runie favored Tobin with a knowing look. "You've done well, but Birch is good at this sort of thing. He's keeping those cursed Servicemen busy, so we can get out of here. Find those mages and gather our wounded. Leave the dead."

She turned and trotted east as Tobin saluted. He could hear the battle—well, more of a skirmish now—still raging, but he and Rise rode back into the darkness, turning their backs on the noise and the grey false-light creeping across the sky.

Leave the dead. Suddenly, Tobin remembered the still silhouette of a soldier thrown from his horse, arrow buried in his gut. He spurred Spiffy to a gallop, Rise right behind him. They reached the hill they'd charged down, and Tobin slowed and leaped from the saddle.

A twisted figure in Yoel's Atonement white and grey lay on the ground, dim light reflecting off the arrow sunk in his chest. Tobin approached, knelt, and turned the soldier's head.

It was Felias.

Tobin's heart sank. He replayed the moment in his mind's eye, heard the hiss of arrows and saw the body tumbling from his horse with a cry. Felias was the youngest. Dead at fifteen years, and without a grave to hold his small body. Without a stone to commemorate his freckled face full of laughter, his quick wit, and his love for stories of battle and adventure, where the heroes always won, and the enemy was left on the war-churned ground, unburied.

A tear traced down Tobin's cheek. He was dimly aware of Rise standing at a respectful distance behind him, of the sounds of battle in the village where Squadleader Birch continued the assault. Life would go on without Felias, he realized. And Tobin couldn't afford to grieve him properly right now, not when there was work to do.

With a heavy heart, Tobin stood up and turned to Rise, who shrugged, a half-smirk on his face. A look of understanding passed between them.

"We have our orders," Rise said.

Tobin nodded. "Let's go."

Jenna lay on damp grass, gasping for air, but otherwise unable to move. Her right arm was bent at an angle beneath her, and her back was on fire, but she felt peaceful in a numb sort of way. *I must be going into shock.*

Part of her registered that the Serviceman hadn't come after her. The blast from her magic must have killed him, or at least knocked him out. He wouldn't hurt her again.

She shivered. It was dark outside, but the night was clear, and it reminded her of home. The Wheaton Estates, where she'd grown up, had plenty of grassy fields akin to the meadow, and she and Castor had often stayed up late or woken early to observe sunsets, sunrises, and stars. The circumstances were different, of course, but the cold air, the grass, and the familiar constellations—Artha's Boar, Still Water, Arrow North, The Small Runner—were the same.

Jenna let the memories wash over her, sweet and bitter and melancholy. Things had been simpler when she had been a child.

After a few moments, she forced herself back to the present, knowing she had to get further away from the Servicemen or risk getting recaptured. *Move,* she commanded her arms and legs, and slowly, painfully, she managed to sit up.

She could still hear a commotion coming from behind the barn she'd been kept in and realized the shouts and clash of metal must mean a battle. It could be the Ideians, come to recover their mages, or it could be bandits, thieves, or one of the Republic's other armed forces. Her mind was too unfocused to recall the current political situation between the different Republican factions.

Battle meant destruction and death, however, and she could feel energy building at the edges of her magical range—which was rather limited, considering her injuries and state of mind. *Focus Jenna,* she thought angrily. *Stop being a scholar for a second.*

Reaching for the energy, she visualized it as white and black strands wrapping around her good hand. The magic obliged, and soon her fingers were shrouded in a twisted bunch of energy vines. *I need to get away.* The thought seemed to resonate with her magic, and she forced the tendrils out of her hand, shaping them into Y-shaped rods, like crutches.

After several minutes of rubbing feeling back into her legs, Jenna managed to get up, leaning against the magical crutches. She tried taking a step, but her legs refused to hold her weight and her broken arm couldn't grip the crutch. She fell with a cry, and the crutches dissipated.

"Right," she muttered. "I need a horse." *Which is probably impossible.*

The interesting thing about fabrication was that it was easiest to create an exact replica of an existing object. However, aether and soul copies of sentient things often gained independence and could act against the mage's direction. The obvious dangers this posed had led to the Grand Council of Mages outlawing sentient fabrication after the Second Mage War. The only loophole that had been theorized to this rule was that of creating a generic sentient item—in her case, trying to create a random horse instead of replicating a specific one.

Gathering in the remaining energy, Jenna attempted to shape it into something sufficiently resembling a horse. This would allow her to ride it without breaking the taboo. Concentrating, she pictured what she wanted in her mind—muscled legs, a wide back, wisps of mane and tail, milky eyes, and the vigour of life. Her magic rushed out of her fingertips and onto the grass, as if pouring into a mold. Four distorted hooves began to form and grow into vaguely horse-like legs.

At first, it seemed to work. But as the magic was pouring out, Jenna felt fatigue descend. Sweat beaded on her skin, and she faltered, her back afire with renewed agony. The magic was pouring out of her too quickly. She tried to pull back, but the energy rushed through her and a thick stream of black, white, and purple tendrils pulled out of her skin, attaching to the half-formed legs in a chaotic mass as her concentration wavered.

Jenna's vision began to fade from purple to gray. *I have to stop before I faint,* she thought desperately.

She tried to stem the tide of magic. For a few terrifying seconds, nothing happened. Then, something inside of her snapped, and the magic rushed back under her skin, the shadow-horse dissolving back into her fingertips.

"Idiot," Jenna gasped, panting. *Just because you know the theory doesn't mean you can do it on a whim.* Better mages than her had killed themselves by overextending their abilities.

A particularly loud clash of swords brought Jenna's mind back to the present and renewed her sense of urgency. With no knowledge of who was winning—or fighting—she had to assume the Servicemen would come for her once more.

I won't go back. The thought of being captive again made her want to panic; she could feel her heart racing. Her breaths came in shallow gulps. *I can't face that again. Castor. I need Castor. I can't do this without him.* Choked sobs welled up in her throat.

For a few minutes, Jenna kneeled in the damp grass, trying to slow her breathing. Her thoughts alternated between devising elaborate plans that were sure to fail, dissolving into panic, and returning to the one forbidden course of action that might succeed in helping her escape.

"Tabitha guide me," Jenna prayed. "Yoel, steady my hand." Heart pounding, she gathered the energy once more and began the process of breaking a sacred magical taboo.

First, she pictured Silverphile in as much detail as she could. She'd grown up with the mare, so it didn't take nearly as much effort as trying to sustain a mental image of a vaguely horse-like being. She could see her beloved horse in her mind, and as she concentrated on that image, the magical energy around her flowed into the mental picture, so it shimmered and moved.

It was as if the picture lived and breathed of its own volition and she simply gave it the magic needed for it to assume a physical form. Aether and soul tendrils formed around her arms once more and poured out of her with a controlled slowness. Jenna knew this time there would be no stopping the magic if something went wrong. She could feel it.

Instead of filling a shape like a mold, the tendrils dispersed into a shimmering mist that expanded, becoming the familiar form of Silverphile. As the last bit of energy left her fingertips, Jenna slumped to her knees, panting with exhaustion.

Something's wrong. A horse now stood next to Jenna, whose bearing and shape was that of Silverphile—but it was different too. Its eyes glowed with the pure, soft light of soul magic, and its skin glittered with purplish-black tendrils that seemed to shift over each other like wriggling worms. The horse's mane and tail swished in a non-existent wind.

"Silverphile?" Jenna whispered, extending her hand towards it.

The horse stepped forward, regarding her with eyes that glittered intelligently. The muscles around its maw worked, as if it were trying to spit something out. Then, against all logic, against every law of magic she had ever studied, it opened its mouth and spoke.

"My name," it said, equestrian mouth working to form unfamiliar words, "is Yoel."

Imp's breath came in quick gasps, in time with his running feet, then faster and faster, until he thought he might pass out from the strain.

She left me.

Of course, Adriane hadn't meant to leave him, not entirely. Not on purpose.

She never liked me at first. Just like Uncle Bento, taking in a stray.

Imp supposed it wasn't strictly true, but he knew truth was what you made of it. Even if Adriane hadn't meant to disappear, she'd still left him alone in an unfamiliar city, with no one to watch over him.

I didn't need anyone, back with the Service. The thought gave him pause, and he almost tripped, catching himself before he accelerated too much on the hill's final slope. *Adriane came after, and Uncle Bento before.* And dimly, as if through a fog, he remembered one other guardian—his mother.

Imp found himself crying as he reached the hill's base and ran on towards the eastern city gate. The fenced yards, the gardens and pastures, the warehouses and maze of alleys he had begun to memorize blurred together into a tunnel, and the sunlight rising over the distant hills became the light at its end. A bright flash in his peripheral vision temporarily blinded him as sunlight bounced off a discarded buckle lying in the dirt, its edge shiny with use. The morning seemed as bright as a fire, and the silver mist curling around the hills was its smoke.

Elder Iram had needed to attend to reports soon after breakfast, and the early hour meant there were few people out to see Imp run. Farmers had long before gone to their fields, merchants and labourers were at their work, but the streets were not yet bustling, and only an occasional group of soldiers occupied the outer yards. They paid him little attention, seeing his fluttering yellow cloak and missing entirely the tears streaming from his eyes. For that, Imp was grateful.

He didn't think of his mother often, except when he lit fires. *How long has it been since I've seen her? Where am I going anyways?* Half-coherent, his mind answered his own questions. *Too long. And I'll know it when I get there.*

Imp ran for ages. *My mother was the only one who didn't go willingly.* He'd suspected for a while now that the Service had taken her from him, and he wondered once again if she had been killed that night, long ago, when she had first showed Imp the wonders of fire.

How long has it been? Imp tried to shake the thought off, though he felt in his pocket for a starter—no matches of course, not here, but flint and steel, or a striker, or a string.

How long? A tangle of trees loomed up ahead of him, and Imp stumbled to a stop. He felt as if he'd run a few minutes at most, but a quick glance back told him he'd left the city far behind.

String. That had been his last thought. Imp had no steel or flint, but the length of string in his pocket would do. He ducked into the undergrowth to find two sticks, as well as pine needles to act as kindling. He automatically turned his back to the wind to protect his creation, then bent down, wrapped and tied the string, set the makeshift bow in motion. Once he formed an ember, he set the pine needles ablaze, fed them with twigs dried in the late summer heat, watched the fire grow.

A white light appeared near the first of the flames, and Imp bent to observe the pictures moving within it: People were running, and the faint echoes of screams reached his ears. A man's silhouette—armed with daggers—flickered into the white light. He moved with graceful lunges and sidesteps, and Imp thought he was dancing, until he realized the man was fighting, though he could not see the man's adversary.

Suddenly, something bright and white obscured everything else inside the picture, and Imp jumped back with a strangled yelp. The white pulsed and glowed brighter, and the picture became blurrier.

The fire. Imp had ignored it, fixating on the images instead. Now he looked up with wide eyes and saw the flames rising higher, having caught on the trees. His mind urged caution, but his feet were frozen where they stood; the bright white light captured his gaze once more.

The pictures got blurrier the bigger the fire, so there was little left to see. A dark splotch—perhaps the man—and a bright light were dancing back and forth, fighting, Imp supposed. The two grew more frantic by the second, pulsing, weaving in between other coloured splotches, when the white light exploded outwards, settling onto the dark splotch, mingling with it until all that was left of the picture was a messy gray blob, now and then flickering black or white.

The fire! With a regret he didn't fully understand, Imp tore his eyes away from the fading white light and its pictures. *It's gone too big.* The flames weren't coming towards him, but the wind, fickle as it was and egged on by the flames, began to swirl around him, driving the fire with it. Whole trees were engulfed before his eyes, and the bracken covering the ground had caught. Imp stood at the center of it all, terrified. He'd never been quite this close before.

Imp backed up one step and then another. The fire began to rage in full, spreading faster and faster, so he stumbled back further, then turned and ran, lungs still burning from his earlier sprint.

Adriane left me, he insisted. A good enough excuse as any to set another fire.

Imp ran south before returning to Silas' Hill. By that time, alarm bells were ringing, and the townsfolk had formed a line, passing buckets down to fire, while soldiers used axes and sickles to clear away brush in danger of catching, forcing the fire to rage eastward.

Imp found it hard to care much about the trouble he'd caused them. As he made his way back towards the messengers' quarters, he nearly stumbled from exhaustion, and found he had little energy left for pity either.

Adriane's somewhere out there. He stopped in his tracks, contemplating the thought. Turning east, Imp watched smoke and flames rise into the air. *Somewhere. North, south, and west are fine.* He inclined his head towards the mingling lights of morning sun and flame. East. *Shadows send she didn't go that way.*

Coat of Arms
for each of
the five heroes

Yoel's coat of
arms was
changed after
his betrayal

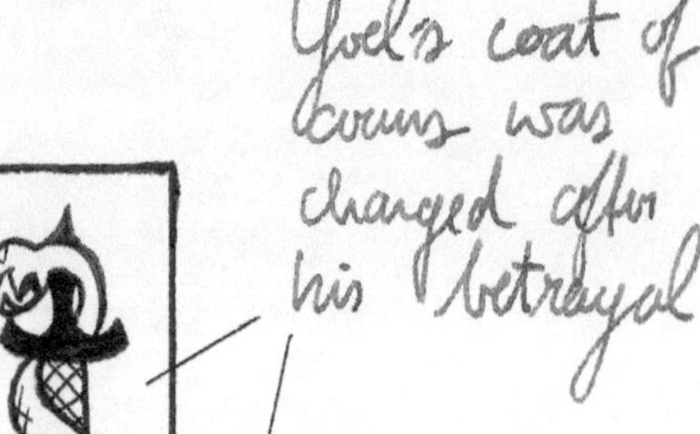

BENDEKAN

YOEL (NEW)

IBRAM

YOEL (OLD)

TABITHA

NERI

20

ATONEMENT

The battle was over, but they hadn't won, not by any measure that counted. The remaining Servicemen fled, the villagers barricaded their homes, and the mages were nowhere to be found.

"Took them to the city by night," a wounded Serviceman had said, without needing to be asked. His eyes had been bright with pain and glee. "They're far beyond your reach." He'd died with a mocking smile on his face.

Adriane found the image stuck in her mind. She had killed four men now, but these latest few had been different, kills completed in the open, under the glare of village torches, without the shadows to hide her. She'd used her magic, but even that was different. It came easier with each day.

"They were ready for us," Runie muttered. She'd been furious to discover the mages weren't even there. "We lost good soldiers—for nothing."

Adriane glanced back, where the others rode, heads bowed, frowns or stoic faces all around, six rider-less horses mingling among them. The younger soldiers especially had taken things badly. *And they don't know this is just the beginning. They've only caught a glimpse of it.* She knew the full realization of what it meant to have lost someone only came after the initial shock, that first numbing blow to the soul, wore off.

"I still think we could've pursued them further," Squadleader Birch insisted yet again. He'd lost four soldiers, almost half his squad.

Runie shook her head. "They know we're here, and they'll send out a larger force. Besides, they must have known we were coming for a day at least to assemble all those Servicemen."

"I'm still not sure I trust the Republican."

Rise. Adriane glanced back at him and found his eyes on her. She jerked back, goosebumps rising on her arms. *Does he know I'm a Saint*

Brazener? She'd said too much, been a little too good at tracking the Servicemen. She'd told herself it would be worth it to save lives, to balance out the deaths of the people she'd had to kill. *But we didn't save anyone. And now he suspects me.*

"—could have easily been a hunter or trapper," Runie was saying. "It happens."

If they knew, Adriane thought, *they'd suspect me even more than Rise for not telling them.* She'd be sent back or imprisoned, like as not, and Imp with her. Her fingers inched to the hunting knife in her boot. Her magic was her weapon now, but the knife made her feel safe. She'd killed with it, and she would have to again. That much was certain.

They were back in the thick of the forest, trotting their horses to maintain a steady pace. Morning dawned behind them, but what little sky was visible above the trees before them was dark and cloudy, as if daylight would never come.

Wait a second. Something glimmered up ahead, and Adriane clumsily spurred her borrowed horse forward.

"Adriane, wait." Runie was right behind her.

"Hush," Adriane said, without realizing she was ordering her superior. "There's someone there." She dismounted and stepped through the underbrush, hardly making a sound.

"How do you know?" Runie asked, following on her horse.

"I—" Adriane hesitated. She hadn't seen someone, not really. "I don't know. But there's someone there."

"Magic?"

Right, Adriane realized. "Yes." Concentrating on the lingering grief which was always close enough to access, she flickered forward through the shadows, letting the magic's echoes bounce around her, letting her see the forest, or at least parts of it, in her mind. Trees and foliage. Scattered rocks. *There.* A crumpled figure. "Twelve paces northward."

Runie signaled for her to wait, then dismounted and snuck forward, cudgel in hand. Adriane felt a renewed respect for the second as she watched her move—it was as if the grass and underbrush parted before her steps; she walked through the leaf-strewn forest without a sound. *Even Lancaster and Mia couldn't move like that.*

That sense of silent, even reverent awe shattered when Runie's breath caught audibly.

"Adriane, help me," she ordered, and Adriane rushed forward.

A girl lay on a bed of damp leaves in a hollow between two trees and a rock. Pained breaths dragged her chest up and down. Her eyes were closed, and her face looked peaceful enough, but the rest of her was dirty and blood-streaked, clothes torn and singed, legs bent at awkward angles, and one arm obviously broken.

Runie called for a medic's pack, then knelt by the girl's side—the young woman's side, Adriane realized, approaching. She was rather thin, and her legs seemed too small and crooked for her body, but she was older than Adriane had first thought.

"What's wrong with her?"

Runie examined the young woman's wounds, speaking softly to her before turning to Adriane. "She's unconscious. I don't know what's wrong with her legs, and that arm looks bad—but the worst is her back. She's been whipped."

Looking down, Adriane realized the damp leaves beneath the woman's body were soaked with blood, not water. "Tell me what to do."

A soldier arrived with the medic's pack, and Runie had Adriane help her flip the young woman onto her stomach. The cuts on her back were deep but leaves and pine needles had staunched the flow of blood. They pressed a thick blanket against her back, then wrapped bandages around it to keep it in place. As they tied off the bandages, the girl began to shake, calling out unintelligibly.

Runie's frown deepened. "We have to get her out of here. I don't have time to treat her wounds properly."

She turned, calling for the squadleaders, while Adriane wrapped another blanket around the girl, murmuring in what she hoped was a reassuring way. *Hannah was always better at this sort of thing. She would've known what to do.*

"Squadleader Birch," Runie ordered, "set the scouts and then take your squad and ride ahead for a healer." He saluted, and she turned to Tobin, instructing his men to build a stretcher. Next, she set the woman's broken arm, pointing out the chafe marks on her wrist.

"We may have missed the rest of them," Runie said, "but we've found one of our mages at least. From the looks of her, she might be the one who got the warning raised. The Kane's description was dark skin, dreadlocks, and crippled legs, which looks right enough."

Adriane knelt down to help load the unconscious woman onto the rough stretcher, now strung between two horses. "Will she live?"

Runie nodded with a sure-fire callousness. "She'll live, Kyra willing."

"Shadows send it," Adriane replied, then cringed. Ideians didn't swear to the shades.

Runie said nothing, though Adriane saw her cast a quick, curious look in her direction before turning onto the well-trodden path ahead of them.

Rise was almost certain, now that he'd had a while to observe her. Adriane tracked the Service with more skill than any regular hunter, and she guessed at their intentions with an accuracy too great for coincidence. *She's Saint Brazen, little doubt. And no one knows.*

Adriane had also been the first to notice the horse—just as she'd been the first to notice the girl they were now carrying, unmoving, between two horses.

It wasn't a regular horse, near as they could tell. It had started following them after they'd picked up the girl, staying in the underbrush as if trying to hide from them. Its efforts hadn't been enough to conceal it from the scouts, but whenever someone rode towards it, the horse galloped away, and they didn't have the time to pursue it.

"Glowing white eyes," Mathas, who'd caught a glimpse of it, had described. "And skin like little black worms made of jelly, all quivery."

"It might be a familiar," Tobin had theorized. "Or some other magic she used to escape and hadn't yet finished."

"But any magic should have dissipated while she slept," Timothy argued. He'd had some magical education, since he and his sister were both mages. "There's no reason it should stick around that long or have that degree of sentience."

"Well, maybe it's not sentient but just fixated onto its mage."

Their discussion went on in circles, but in the end, they simply let the horse follow them and rode as hard as they could, stopping only to sleep. After all, they said, a magical creature could hardly be Republican. They had bigger problems to worry about.

Rise disagreed, though he realized his skepticism of magic was as biased as their inbred acceptance of it. "You carn't be sure it's harmless if it's magic," he muttered.

"True enough," Tobin said, overhearing, "but at least we have an idea of *what* it is."

A Bright Midnight soldier turned in her saddle with a superior smirk. "Sure we do. Familiar as Yoel's heart, isn't it?"

Tobin scowled at his saddle, while Runie promised the soldier a week's worth of latrine duty for showing disrespect to a commanding officer.

The whole business shouldn't have been remarkable, but Rise found a laugh bubbling up in his throat. A couple of the nearby soldiers chuckled at the woman's quick apology to Tobin, and the tension of the last few days seemed to fall away from them, the lost mages and the dead forgotten for now.

"Why's everyone hate Yoel anyway?" Rise asked, thinking of all the vulgarities he'd heard the soldiers utter in Yoel's name, then immediately wished he hadn't. The nervous energy, that sense of defeat and failure, was palpable once more.

"It's to do with our Tales." Tobin shifted in his saddle, then winced and touched the bandage around his thigh. "Yoel was one of the first mages, but he betrayed his friends, and they died because of him."

"He was arrogant and power-hungry." Yemena's cat-like tail swished past Rise's shoulder, and he almost dropped his reins.

"Although some of the Tale's versions say he was simply trying to save his wife and unborn child," Timothy said.

"So what?" Rise asked, curious. "He died, and those stories of yours moved on."

Tobin hesitated, and it was Runie who finally answered. "Some variations of the Tales say Yoel left his spirit behind. He betrayed his friends, and as punishment, he was denied rest in the afterlife, cursed to wander the wilderness forever until his descendants atoned for his betrayal."

"So Yoel's Atonement—you guys are all supposed to pay for what this one man in a myth did ages and ages ago?"

"Not exactly," Tobin said. "Technically, his descendants are those of House Weathslayer's Grave. Yoel's Atonement is just the combat group named after him. All the major heroes have a group affiliated with them. But it's true in part. We're known as specialized fighters, but we go on a lot of missions that are either boring or dangerous, or worse: both."

The soldiers all chuckled at this, no doubt finding a sick sort of humor in their present circumstances.

"At least it hasn't been boring," one of Runie's soldiers called.

"Nobody actually expects every person affiliated with Yoel to have to atone for what he did," Runie said, returning to the subject, "but there's still an inclination to avoid things associated with him. House Weathslayer's Grave has it especially bad, because they're the ones who get blamed for what happened."

"What happened though? Some people died, and he got blamed for it? People die all the time."

Another small silence, and then Runie replied. Rise noted she took on the hard questions, though he wasn't sure if that was due to her knowledge or her seniority.

"Tell the story, Tobin," she said, and a nervous hush fell like magic on the soldiers. "'The Tale of the Five Heroes.'"

Tobin sighed, then cleared his throat.

"*Tabitha. Ibram. Bendekan. Neri. Yoel. These first wielders of magic kept peace in the realms of Camorin for many years, and the people of the land prospered under the wisdom of their rule. Tabitha took Bendekan as her husband, and they had two children, while Yoel wooed Neri, and Ibram alone stayed unwed.*

"*As the years bled into each other, the prophecy concerning the great evil they would face lay heavy on their minds, and they wondered when it would come to pass. Yoel beseeched the continent's guardian spirit for help, asking the creature to show them the way. One day, the creature appeared to Yoel, granting him a vision of the future—a further glimpse into this prophecy, this danger they would face. The spirit told Yoel to wait with patience and humility, for it had foreseen a choice he would have to make: a choice that would either ensure peace or cause that great evil to rise.*

"*Yoel vowed to wait with patience and humility for all of time if he must. However, not two years after he had made this vow, Neri, who was now expecting their second child, grew deathly ill. Healers and wise women attended her, but nothing helped, and she grew worse each day until she lay on the brink of death.*

"*Yoel grew desperate and called on the spirit once again, begging and pleading for help.*

"'*If you would give me more magic,' he said, 'I will be able to save my love. Allow me to drink from the chalice of magic once more.'*

"*The guardian spirit despaired at his words, for they were prideful and selfish, and it regretted allowing Yoel to taste the temptations of magic in the first place. The spirit refused and forbade him from ever returning to the magical stream.*

"*Yoel agreed and apologized to the creature. However, that night Yoel went to his friends among the spirit creatures and asked them for help in retrieving more magic from the stream. Most of the creatures refused to go against the guardian's wishes, but the smallest of them all, a stunted little light worm agreed to help Yoel with his quest for power.*

"*The two ascended the mountain. The light worm guided Yoel to the forbidden stream, but they were unable to find the chalice that diluted the magic to make it safe. Determined to succeed at all costs, Yoel drank the water as it was, and in his desperation, didn't see the small light worm bend to drink as well.*

"The magic threatened to consume Yoel, and he was overcome by a fit of madness. To the light worm, however, the magic was intoxicating; it was filled with an even greater thirst for power. Driven ravenous by the need to feed, it left Yoel, racing back to the kingdom.

"By the time Yoel regained his senses and, full of a power he could barely control, went back to save his wife, the light worm had infiltrated the kingdom and claimed its first victim. Yoel returned to find his wife and unborn son dead—dead at the hands of that small light worm, now grown into a monstrous creature filled with magic and a thirst for human flesh.

"Enraged, Yoel tried to engage the creature, but it fled out of sight, and continued to search out victims to fill its insatiable appetite for humans— human souls who could balance out the magic tempest within it.

"Yoel roused his remaining three friends, and, full of grief and rage, described what had happened. The four took up their weapons and went in search of the light worm, now revealed to be the terrible evil threatening their people and their rule.

"Their battle raged for three days and three nights. Tabitha directed their attacks, Bendekan and Yoel faced the creature head on, and Ibram darted in from all sides. The light worm was now the size of a mountain, having grown with each soul it consumed, and on the third day, it felled Bendekan with a devastating strike after he crushed its eyes with his truncheons.

"Tabitha, in a spurt of enraged power, engaged the creature with a re-lentless fury, managing to sever its flailing tail before she, too, fell, never to rise again.

"With their last vestiges of strength, Yoel and Ibram attacked as one, cutting through the beast's body and into its heart. As the spirit creature perished, it burst open with a great roar that released the souls it had con-sumed.

"All should have been well, but the souls of those killed by the beast could not rest. They had been betrayed by one of their own, and in their wrath, they descended on Yoel, who succumbed to their terror and fear and faded away into madness—a madness brought on by his own actions, the magic he so desperately desired, and the people who paid for it with their lives."

There was silence.

"Yoel's act of treason became entwined with his identity," Runie said. "The Wifeslayer, the Gravemaker, he was called. That name gave rise to

House Weathslayer's Grave. Even his symbol, a grey dagger stuck into the earth, was changed to reflect his treachery." She nodded at Tobin's blood-spattered tunic, which bore his combat group's symbol, a broken dagger held together by what Rise had thought was a serpent, but now realized must be a so-called light worm.

Rise let the silence stretch respectfully before raising the argument once more. "That's horrible and all, but it's still no reason to look down on a bunch of people for what their ancestor did."

Runie answered yet again. "It's more than that. Many Ideians blame Yoel's betrayal and the events thereafter for the conflict between the two nations. If Yoel hadn't made the choices he had, peace would have prevailed. His example not only set the standard for both the misuse of magic and the injustice of powerful mages, it also caused a rift in relations between the tribes' and settlers' descendants. It is said the tension between the two races started after Yoel's betrayal, because many of those killed by the beast were Kanes or Fellin or of the other tribes. Things were smoothed over, but little cracks remained. These cracks grew during the golden age and finally exploded during the First War, where soon-to-be Republicans first slaughtered settlers and tribespeople alike."

Rise was about to protest the insinuation that Republicans did all the slaughtering in the First War—he didn't know much of history, but everyone knew that a war required two sides—when Runie snapped up straight in her saddle, motioning for quiet. Niecka, their forward scout, was approaching.

Niecka's horse pranced nervously, and for the first time, Rise noticed an acrid smell in the air. *Is that... smoke?*

"Second," Niecka said, "We have a problem." She pointed towards the dense cloud cover ahead of them.

Shades keep us, Rise thought, *not clouds*. A spear of red pierced the sky, and Niecka's horse pranced again.

"Fire," she said. "There's a blaze blocking our way home."

⸺◦∞◦⸺

Tobin remembered little of the bustle that ensued. Runie took command, and he couldn't help but feel a little insignificant. He knew he shouldn't, since she always took his opinions into account and respected his authority, but his sense of inadequacy was compounded by the fact that the situation seemed far beyond his control.

The scouts had all ridden out, trying to find out how far the fire extended. Runie, Tobin, Rise, and the others had increased their pace to a canter; ruining their horses was, at this point, better than getting caught in enemy territory by a wildfire.

The smoke stung their lungs, and they soaked handkerchiefs in water, tying them over their faces—Runie was sure to do so for the mage, still fitfully unconscious in the makeshift hammock. The mage cried out occasionally, but she didn't wake.

Niecka burst through a dark patch of underbrush, horse sweat-bedecked, soot-stained and terrified. "I've found us a gap. But hurry—it was two hundred paces of clear ground a few minutes ago and closing quickly."

"Call in the scouts," Runie barked. "Squadleader Tobin, send your squad ahead with the wounded."

Wait, that's me. Tobin snapped into a salute, then turned to Timothy, who nodded and called for Squad Fourteen to form up and gallop. Most of them had sustained minor scratches, and Rico and Yemena had proper wounds that needed looking after, but they could still ride. In a flurry of beaten leaves and kicked-up dust, they galloped ahead with Runie's wounded, led by Niecka's nervous mare.

"What about us?" Tobin asked.

Runie nodded toward the mage, who was strung up between two of the horses who'd lost their riders. "We can't gallop with her. And we need to wait for the scouts."

The stretcher jolted, as its occupant stirred. Adriane, still riding by Runie's side, was there in an instant, with Tobin and Runie close behind.

The girl's eyes cracked open, and she inhaled sharply. "What—" She stretched out her good hand, confusion and exhaustion shining in her eyes. Her shoulders worked, as if she was about to try get up, but Adriane stopped her.

"I'm Second Runie of Bright Midnight," Runie said, her commander's voice tempered by compassion. "Everything's fine. You're safe now, and we're heading back to Ideon."

"Ideon," the girl mumbled.

"What's your name?" Adriane asked.

"Jenna. Jenna Brightshade."

Runie flashed a relieved smile. "There's someone waiting back home for you, Jenna. A young Kane who was very concerned about you."

"Castor."

"Now all we need to do is get out of this fire, and we'll be home safe and sound," Rise drawled.

The scouts rode in, and Runie left to confer with them. She returned, looking stoic as ever, though her mouth curved in a slight frown. *She looks different*, Tobin thought.

"Tobin, a word please."

He dismounted, wincing when the knife-graze on his leg twinged in pain, and followed her out of the others' earshot. "What is it?" She'd declined to use his title, though he didn't know if that was intentional or not.

Runie looked back at Jenna, whom Adriane was helping with a water skin. "I'm sending the scouts and the rest of the soldiers ahead. You and Rise as well. Get the soldiers through that gap before it closes, and ride like Fate's Hand himself back to Silas' Hill."

"Wait, what about you?"

She glanced back again, this time to Adriane. "Jenna won't make that gallop, and neither will the horses, carrying a stretcher like that. I'll get them through. Adriane's magic lets her dash through shadows, so we'll have a better chance with her."

Understanding hit Tobin like a blow to the temples, that strange, disjointed clarity he'd felt during the battle taking over his mind once more. "But—you'll die. If Niecka's assessment was accurate—"

"The gap might not be there anymore by the time we arrive. I know. We may be able to find a burned-out section to conceal us until things clear up."

Tobin shook his head. "By that time, the Republicans might have caught up. We already know they won't respect the border. If you don't die by fire, you'll die at their hands."

Runie simply looked at him, and Tobin saw that same clarity reflected in her eyes. *She knows*, he realized, awestruck. *She knows, and she's doing it anyway. She's the reserve commander for one of the most important combat groups—a skilled warrior we can't afford to lose, and she's willing to risk death. For what?* He thought about it for a second, unsure. *Honour or duty? Saving that girl's life?*

"What if we leave her?" Tobin suggested, then immediately hated himself for voicing the thought. "I mean—"

"It's alright, Squadleader," Runie said. "A commander must think through all the options. But leaving Jenna behind isn't right. This mission would be a failure without her, and I couldn't live with myself if I left her behind to die alone. Some things are worse than death." She shrugged.

"I don't understand."

"Maybe you will someday. But we're wasting time. Take your soldiers and go. We'll see each other again. And if we don't, Adriane at least will make it back, Kyra willing."

This is what it means, Tobin realized, seeing the resolve in Runie's eyes. He'd had these hazy ideas of heroism—going on a mission, facing bandits, wooing Lady Kesma, even rescuing Rise—but this, Runie's quiet resolve, was the real thing. A second flash of realization came to him then, and he grabbed Runie's hand before she could leave.

"I'll do it. I'll stay."

"What?"

He let go and saluted, not because he was supposed to, but because it felt right. "You can't risk yourself here—your combat group needs you, and the rest of the army. But me, I'm—well, I know I'm green as grass. I have the same odds of getting out as you do, but it won't be as bad if I die." He swallowed, stomach heaving at the words. "Relatively speaking," he finished weakly.

Runie gazed at him for a moment. She nodded. "Then we'll see each other back in Silas' Hill."

She turned to leave, but Tobin stayed for a moment, collecting his thoughts. *Did she just… manipulate me?* Runie had repeatedly shown her ability to guess at his thoughts. Had she planned for him to stay instead of her? Did she want him to do this?

He had no doubt she would have stayed, would have given her life, if he had not offered. *All the same*, Tobin thought, *she knew what to say to me—to make me understand. She believes in me*, he realized. *She believes I can do this, and she trusts me to do it well. Maybe this is my chance to prove her right. My chance to be a hero.* Squaring his shoulders, he turned back to where the scouts were forming up, Runie mounted at their head.

She trotted to him, clasped his forearm, nodded. *Everything's moving so fast.* Then she was gone.

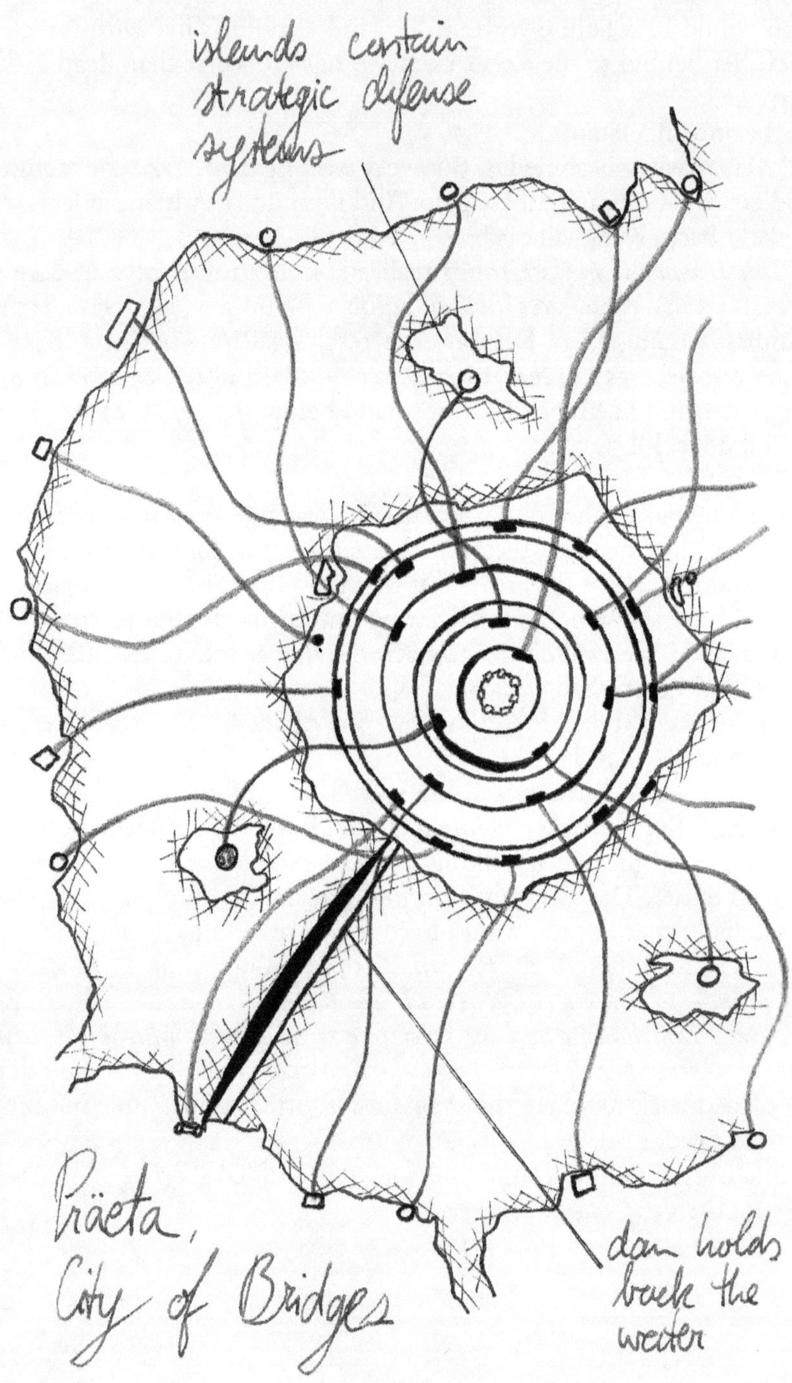

islands contain
strategic defense
systems

Präeta,
City of Bridges

dam holds
back the
water

21

ABOUT CHOICES

Although Adriane had spent a good deal of time thinking about fire and its consequences ever since taking Imp under her wing, she'd never imagined the terrifying cacophony of sound a forest fire produced. Branches and trees tore apart with ear-splitting cracks as they spurred their horses straight towards the blaze. Smoke stung her lungs, and Tobin, a mere silhouette obscured by the haze, coughed loudly.

It's happening again, Adriane's mind whispered. She recoiled inwardly but forced herself to appear calm on the outside. Jenna shifted, crying out in pain, and Adriane reached for her hand, offering the only comfort she could. *She's like me*, she thought, trying to distract herself. *I could have ended up like her, had the tables been turned—had I been born a few hundred miles to the west. A mage.*

"We've got to pick up the pace." Squadleader Tobin had to yell to be heard. "I know it'll hurt her, but the quicker we get back, the quicker we can find a healer."

Adriane didn't even flinch at the mention of healers but nodded in agreement. She urged her horse to go faster. Suddenly, it reared. Adriane lost her grip and shifted into shadows. The magic carried her out of harm's way as the horse turned and galloped away. A muted curse rang out behind her and a second set of hooves; Rise's horse had followed suit.

Tobin dismounted. "Help me with Jenna."

Adriane drew her knife and slashed the stretcher's bindings as the horses shifted nervously. Rise and Tobin took the weight, and the horses, freed from their burden, fled. Tobin's pony followed behind them.

Adriane squinted into the red haze ahead of them. The fire seemed distant still, but the increasing roar told her it was advancing steadily.

"Is that thing still following us?" Rise said.

Adriane glanced at him, eyes narrowing. She and Tobin were following orders, but Rise could have ridden ahead with the others. *Why did he stay? Because he suspects me?* She used her fear and anxiety to activate her magic, feeling the echoes bounce around her.

The flames were insubstantial wisps ahead, spread out before them in a great semicircle. Trees and bracken lay on all sides, deserted of animal life. *There.* Like a vacuum pulling at her magic, a great yawning emptiness. The strange, magic horse following them felt completely alien when her senses touched it.

"Still behind us," she said to the others, whose senses were hampered by the ever-thickening smoke.

Tobin coughed again. "Adriane, scout ahead and find that gap. We'll be right behind you. Rise, take Jenna."

Adriane nodded. She called her emotions back from that cold, empty place she tried to keep them in, shivering as they hit her.

Fear. She flashed forward, towards the fire, each step taking her through the shadows and teleporting her further ahead. Heat rolled over her skin in a terrifying wave, and she ducked, gulping for fresh air. The echoes brought back nothing but smoke and fire, so she stepped again, thoughts flickering with her magic.

I ran to save Hannah and Max. Then Lancaster. Now I'm risking everything just to save someone I've never even met? Runie had given her orders, sure, but Adriane would've disobeyed if she hadn't wanted to stay. She cast a quick glance back to where Tobin and Rise were grappling with the stretcher. Tobin seemed the type to play the hero, but still… he hadn't considered running either.

Adriane shadow-dashed forwards. The roar of the fire neared with each step—then engulfed her. *Gap, where's the gap?* A branch cracked and broke above her, and she dissolved into shadows, flickering a few paces to the left. A piece of falling wood caught her head, tearing through her braid and singeing her hair. *The stone!* She felt for the smooth green pebble she kept in her braid, the one she'd picked up outside the hut on the day she'd left home. *It's gone.*

Heat rolled over Adriane's skin as the flames whipped to a frenzy around her. She dashed back and forth, unable to see through the sparks and smoke, relying purely on instinct and magic. A flame sprang up to her left—she ducked right, but the ground seemed to drop away beneath her, and she nearly tumbled. Dashing again, she evaded further bursts of flame, bent low to avoid the worst of the smoke. Her magic's echoes revealed a break ahead of her and she dove for it, splashing into knee-deep water. She sucked air into her smoke-filled lungs, coughing, trying to get her bearings.

Suddenly, a voice sounded directly behind her. "I…"

She whirled around at the whisper, but no one was there. *Shades keep me.*

"I… am," the voice murmured again, this time echoing through the trees.

She thought she saw a silhouette duck behind a blackened, flame-wreathed trunk, but there was too much steam from the water to be sure. *Right, magic.* She flickered into shadows, following the water's slight current, letting the returning echoes act as her eyes and ears.

"Who am I?"

The voice was clearer now, but the burning forest was still devoid of life. The flames surrounded her on three sides, but there was a small path yet untouched by fire. Perhaps they could escape that way. *Wait. There.* A crouched figure, then another and another bloomed in her magical sight, and she dashed to them, her magic allowing her to evade the flames.

"Aiiiieee—oh. It's you," the first figure said, voice cracking, and she realized it was Tobin. Red firelight hid his blush.

"Anything?" Rise's voice was tight, perhaps with anger or exhaustion. He cradled Jenna like a child in his arms.

"Stream," Adriane croaked, throat parched. She felt sweat trickle down her back, a moment's cool comfort against the heat.

They fought their way forward, Adriane pointing out the clearest path. She dashed forwards and back again, chafing at Tobin and Rise's pace, slowed to a mere crawl.

"Look out!" Rise threw himself aside as a tree burst into flame. Tobin raced forward, momentarily reckless. He grabbed Jenna from Rise, who was panting with exertion and using choice words that would've made even Mia blush.

"I am… am… am," came another echo, barely audible over the fire's roar. Adriane froze.

A large splash told her Tobin had found the stream, a second that Rise wasn't far behind.

She joined them, relishing the relative coolness of the water. "I think there's something else out there. Some sort of shadow—spirit creature you'd call it."

"I suppose there's bound to be fire imps around," Tobin said, jerking Jenna's head up above the water; she didn't even stir at his rough treatment.

"I'll take her." Rise slung her over his shoulder with a gentleness Adriane hadn't expected.

"What matters right now is getting out of here," Tobin said. "The gap—"

"There is no gap," Adriane said.

"Runie said there was." Rise's voice was hoarse with smoke. "Check again."

"It may well have been there minutes ago, but it's not there now. Our best chance is to stay here and lie low."

"You can't be serious," Rise said, following up with a curse. "Suicide, more like. Curse you'd think you have it all figured out, you—"

Tobin elbowed him, making him wince. "Stop that. It's no good arguing."

Rise opened his mouth, looked at the steam-filled red light surrounding them, then grimaced. "We should retreat. Find somewhere safe to wait this out. This water won't last."

He was right. The steam gushed around them, burning their skin as fire fought water.

Tobin hesitated, then sank back into a crouch. "We'll keep moving. Servicemen are sure to be waiting for us if we go back."

"Then let's do ourselves a favour and take some of them with us when we die," Rise said. Still, he turned and followed Tobin, keeping Jenna clear of the water and flames surrounding them.

They inched forward, battling the heat. Adriane dashed ahead, directing them to the stream's deepest sections. The wind grew, whipping the fire to a greater frenzy. Desperate to find them shelter, Adriane dashed forward one step, two—and felt her hands land on burning soil.

She jerked back with a cry, instinctively shadow-dashing back into the water. A flame shot out where she'd been moments before; she could smell the skin on her hands burning. Tobin bumped into her a second later and almost tripped. Rise stopped more carefully behind them.

"The water's gone," she said. "There's only fire ahead."

Rise lay Jenna down across his knees and tried to wipe the soot from her face, leaving large black smears. "Is this it, then?"

They sat in silence for a moment, the fire raging around them. Adriane found she no longer felt the heat. Her mind flashed back to Abel Way for a second—the flames licking down the staircase, Mia and Jacob taking her to safety, Lancaster's hands clutching the bars of a cage, an explosion tearing through a nearby building. *There was a way out then, so why not now?*

It seemed like the world was ending, but in slow motion, as if every second spanned minutes. Red and orange explosions engulfed trees, and huge flames spit into the air, crackling as they consumed dry wood encrusted with sap. A branch burst ahead of them, and flaming splinters rained down, but Tobin's tonfa, quick as a breath, intercepted and batted away the largest falling pieces. They splashed what little remained of the stream over the rest, though the stink of burned flesh was growing stronger.

Rise cursed extensively under his breath. "I didn't stay with you fools to die here."

"Why did you stay anyway?" Tobin asked.

Rise shrugged. "I figured you wouldn't make it far without me. Already saved your noble hide once, didn't I?"

The water was growing hot; Adriane could feel the last of their protection melting away.

"You might have to save it again," Tobin said. "We could die here."

"Curse we carn." Muscles straining, Rise draped Jenna over his shoulders again, then rose from his crouch. "Reckon we can make it to that stump?" He gestured towards a large, flame-wreathed mass distinguishable ahead of them. "I've come too far to die in some shades-forsaken fire."

Tobin looked at Rise, seeing a new determination in his eyes. He rose unsteadily to his feet, feeling a brief dash of heroic pride before dissolving into a gut-wrenching coughing fit. He gasped once his lungs allowed him to gulp in some air again. The water's depth was down to a handspan. "Any other ways to go, Adriane?"

She shook her head, then sat up straight, eyes looking at something behind him, beyond the smoke.

"What is it?"

"That horse-thing. It's coming."

Tobin turned to look. He heard no sound as it approached, but soon enough he could see a black and white horse approaching through the flames. He racked his brains trying to remember the magic lore he knew from his sisters. "Second Runie said she had soul and aether magic, right?"

He realized he could no longer feel the wetness of the water. Just steam and heat.

"Quick. This way." Adriane dashed forwards.

Rise followed with Jenna, casting a frightened glance back at the horse, hand lowering to his short sword. "Are we gonna let that thing get this close?"

Tobin ran in a half-crouch, trying to avoid the flames. "How are we doing this?" he muttered to himself. They were in the thick of the fire now, but the flames weren't coming towards them. Tobin felt an icy breath on his neck and jerked around to see the horse right behind him. *The horse. If it's her magic it'll naturally seek to protect her.*

"Wait," he called to Adriane and Rise. "Stop!"

To his relief, they both froze, looking back at him, perched in a burnt-out patch momentarily devoid of flame. The horse reached the three of them and approached Rise, who leaned back apprehensively.

"Let it," Tobin said.

It bent its slimy black maw to Jenna's head and nuzzled her dreadlocked hair. Then, against all reason, its mouth worked up and down, and it spoke.

"Mine," it said.

Flabbergasted, Tobin tried to speak, but took precious seconds to get his dry mouth working again. "Yours?"

"Give me," the horse said. "Mine."

"You've got to be kidding me," Rise said as the horse fixed him with its eerie white stare. "It wants the mage."

Adriane said nothing, her gaze flickering from the horse, to the fire, to Tobin.

I guess I get to make the decisions now. Tobin grimaced. *I thought leadership would be more fun.* He squinted at the fiery cyclone around them, his eyes tearing up from smoke and ash. *Then again, I doubt it usually gets this bad.*

"Try putting Jenna on the horse."

"She'll fall off," Adriane countered.

"Yeah, that's a brilliant idea," Rise drawled, before coughing heavily.

"It's made of her magic, so it'll try to preserve the source of its life. It could help get her out of here at least. Besides, haven't you felt it? The fire stopped getting closer the moment this—thing showed up."

Rise didn't look convinced, but he lifted Jenna and placed her on the horse's slimy back. White tendrils shot out from the horse's sides. Rise ducked with a yell, but the tendrils merely wrapped around Jenna's legs, fixing them in place.

"Now what?" Adriane asked. "The most it can do is take her back to where the Service is waiting for us."

Tobin just stood, watching the beast. Its nostrils, made of wriggling tentacles like the rest of it, quivered delicately, and it turned to face the fire. The nearest flames were a few scant paces away, and a gust drove a bank of fire straight towards Tobin. He ducked, yelling in fright, and felt the fire singe his arms.

"Come on." Adriane gripped his arm and pulled him forwards into the clear spot where Rise was hunched, sweating and covered in dirt and angry burns.

"Look," Rise said.

Tobin followed his gaze to Jenna's magic horse, which advanced towards the flames.

"Don't—" Adriane began, but it was too late.

The beast lumbered into the fire and the flames shot up, consuming both the horse and the broken mage it carried.

Tobin froze. *Did she just…? Did I…?*

"Shade and flame," Rise cursed, crawling forwards on elbows and knees. "No way."

Adriane gasped.

Tobin made himself look, steeling himself for the sight of Jenna's burned form, when he realized the fire ahead was receding as well.

"Come on." Rise urged him forward. "Get out of the way."

It took Tobin a moment to notice the fire licking at his heels. He jumped forward, startled, then followed Rise. A flash of shadows, and Adriane joined them.

He looked ahead again, unable to believe his eyes. The lumbering shadow of a spectral horse and rider was barely discernible through the curtain of smoke and flame. In the horse's wake, however, the fire receded fractionally, just enough for the three of them to scramble along behind the beast.

"How in Bendekan's name is it doing that?"

"Shades if I care how," Rise said. "Let's just follow it out of here."

⸙

Imp hadn't left his perch in hours. He'd looked for the highest place he could reach and had settled on Silas' Hill's Patron Hall, a grand, circular building with a needle of a tower. The place reminded him of the Chisel. Though it differed in upkeep and location, it had that same slightly abandoned feel to it.

Where are they?

A black wall of smoke shot through with flames faced the city. A group of soldiers had come through already, but Adriane hadn't been among them.

Soft footfalls sounded below him, and Imp thought he knew who was coming up. Sure enough—

"Good afternoon, Imp," Elder Iram said.

Imp said nothing. He couldn't well disrespect the man who'd been kind to him, but all the same, he preferred his silence. It was like the waiting after a fire—a regular fire—but filled with fear instead of wonder. *Adriane's still out there. She left me, and I… am I going to kill her?* It wouldn't be killing her, not really, but all the same, Imp felt a shiver of fear.

It seemed like hours before Elder Iram spoke again. "Did you know it's Tales' Night tonight?"

Imp shrugged.

"I'll tell a story while we wait if you like."

Imp shrugged again, still focused on the view.

"My favorite stories were always about the tribes," the elder continued. "Now they had a *purpose*. Each tribe was focused on their values, their mission." He chuckled. "Sometimes I wish I could inspire that much devotion in my soldiers. Tabitha's eyes, sometimes I think we Ideians aren't very good at believing in things."

Imp turned to look at Elder Iram, surprised he would swear.

The elder simply gazed out into the smoke, hand stroking the worn stone of the tower. "The Patrons may have failed us, but sure as Neri's aim, we failed them too."

Imp recognized sadness in the old man's eyes and sought to distract him from it. "You were gonna tell a story?" *Just like with Vine*, he thought to himself. *I can be helpful.*

"A story. Yes. Let me tell you 'The Ghost People:'

"*Listen carefully, lest you hear and forget, lest you hear and not remember, lest the sound of this story dies in your ears. Listen to the ghost people, made of memory and light, walking through the shadows, running past the sunrise, searching for their home.*

"*Great cities once stood where the ghost people met. Their taverns and meeting places became palaces; their handshakes and whispers became the word of law. They were sought out for their wisdom and the guidance they could bring. They were sought out for the futures they could see and the warnings they could give."*

Imp listened despite trying to concentrate on the smoke-shrouded view. *I've never heard any of the other Ideians tell Tales like this,* he thought. Elder Iram wove an image of a grand city together with his words, a city perched on the cusp on a plateau, surrounded by lonely, winding roads frequented by travellers. *All the other tellers say what's happening. He's just describing things—but somehow making them real.* Imp looked back towards the east.

"The ghost people lived in their great city for hundreds of years as the very mountains changed beneath their feet. The forests moved, the lakes and rivers writhed where they lay, but the city always remained.

"War, however, brought change. It started in the east, like a wildfire consuming the land. Beasts fled before the violence of man, and those who refused to flee were slaughtered in their homes. The bears in their eastern forests died first. The snakes and birds, the creeping things, the packs of wolves; all were slain. Lizards retreated to their mountain caves, and water dwellers escaped to the depths where they found safety. Before long, the great flames of war reached the ghost people in their cities of stone.

"Listen carefully, lest you hear and forget, lest you hear and not remember, lest the sound of this story dies in your ears. The great city was torn apart as if by a great wind. Its walls crumbled to ashes, and its people fell like wood beneath the stroke of an axe—a great bonfire to sate the wrath of humankind.

"With their walls and lives fell their memories and prophecies. Now, all that remains is a whisper. All that remains is to tell the story of the ghost people. All that remains is to hear them wandering in the wilderness, calling for home."

They sat in silence for a moment, before Elder Iram spoke. "Do you know why I'm telling you this story, Imp?"

The fires. The lights. "I know," he said. His voice was breaking, and he couldn't seem to stop it. "Uncle Bento told me, back in—back home." He'd stopped himself in time. *Adriane said I have to be careful. No one can know we're from Saint Brazen.* "I'm not human." He hadn't thought about that part much. It hadn't mattered. "Like those ghost people. I'm a Seer."

The elder was silent for a while. "Well," he said finally, "you're as human as anyone else. The opposite of a Seer isn't a human—it's a Descendant. Being human isn't about your ancestors; it's about choices. Choosing good or bad, right or wrong. Choosing ignorance, or choosing to *see*, really see what's going on in front of you. That choice, Imp—*that* is why I told you this story."

"My uncle said something like that. About choices." Imp found he welcomed the distraction from the fire. "He said I can see things— things that happened, or are happening, or will happen. I suppose it's normal here."

"It's true enough, many Seers can. Others can walk through walls or memorize stores of information. Some can even turn invisible. But I wasn't referring to that sort of seeing, Imp. I was talking about realizing the consequences of your actions."

Imp turned to look at Elder Iram, but the man simply stared out towards the distant flames, expression unfathomable.

Does he suspect I set the fire? Imp didn't know how that could be. He'd been upset, perhaps, but his fire-setting was honed to perfection; he was always careful. The Service had drummed it into him. *Besides,* he thought, *why would they think someone set the fire at all? Late summer blazes can't be too rare here.*

A hint of movement caught his eye, and he turned back to the view. The garrison by the eastern gate was mobilizing.

"Perhaps luck is on our side," Elder Iram murmured, rising to his feet.

Imp scrambled up, trying to see what was going on. Soldiers were running out past the wall, towards two dark blobs materializing in the haze of smoke. *People,* he realized. Blackened from soot, walking all bent and weary. They stumbled towards the city gate with an escort of guardsmen, and Imp studied the small figures. One was tall and thin, cradling something in its arms, and the other was shorter and broad-shouldered. His heart fell.

Then a flash of black caught his eye. Another small figure materialized as if from the shadows. *Adriane,* he thought, grin rising on his face. *No one else can appear like that.*

"They're back," he shouted, a little too loud, and raced past Elder Iram who was already turning towards the stairs.

Imp hurtled down the uneven steps and ran out the building and down the cobbled street. He only stumbled to a halt when a drop of water hit his cheek, looking up to see where it had come from. *It's raining,* he realized as more droplets fell around him. *It's raining for the first time in weeks.*

Months
and seasons

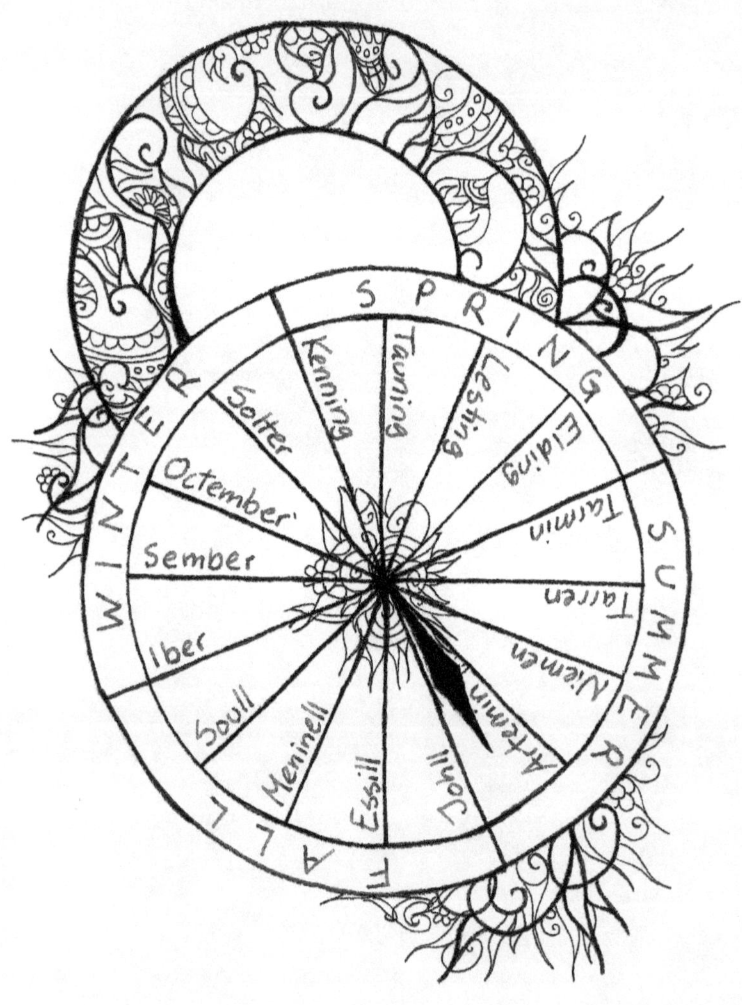
SPRING
SUMMER
FALL
WINTER
Solter
Kenning
Tauning
Lesting
Eilding
Tarmin
Tarren
Niemen
Artemin
Johl
Essill
Meninell
Soull
Iber
Sember
Octember

22

SOME SORT OF SENSE

Jenna started awake. Her eyes protested their exposure to bright daylight, so she closed them again and explored her surroundings with her remaining senses.

She lay on a comfortable mattress, her back covered by layers of bandages under a soft blanket. The gentle scents of fresh air and medicinal herbs filled the room, and everything was quiet except for the rhythmic breathing of someone asleep.

Jenna cracked her eyes open again, more carefully, and a small room slid into view, with lacquered wood walls slit open to let in light and a simple curtain for a door. It was furnished with the bed she lay on and a wicker chair that held an all-too familiar sleeping figure.

"Castor," Jenna said, and his eyes blinked open. Realizing she was awake, he jumped up and knelt at her bedside, reaching for her hand. Jenna made to get up but was forced to lie still when pain laced her back.

"Easy there." Castor smiled, though his eyes shone. "You're still pretty beat up."

Jenna made a face. "My back feels like a furnace. And everything aches."

Castor leaned forward and nuzzled her shoulder with his nose. "The healers did what they could, but they said you'll need to heal normally the rest of the way." She looked at him, and he nodded. "You'll have scars," he said. "But you should get back to normal."

"I missed you so much," she whispered after his lips found hers for a few precious seconds. "I thought you were dead."

"I thought *you* were," he countered. "When I—when I took down that Republican only to realize you were gone already… I didn't know what to do. I'm no warrior." He shrugged. "I ran for help. Can you forgive me?"

"There's nothing to forgive." Jenna wriggled closer to him, ignoring the pain. "I'm just so glad you're here. I'm so glad I made it back."

Castor stiffened. "Do you… remember anything? I mean, about the rescue?"

Jenna frowned. "Everything's hazy. I was badly hurt, but I got out somehow. Then there was a girl who took care of me. I—I remember knowing you were safe, that you had gotten a rescue party sent out. And there was a fire. At least, I remember this heat and smoke, I think. Is that crazy?"

"Well, there really was a fire, and you made it out just in time. But that's not exactly what I meant.

"What is it then?"

He sighed. "I know this isn't a good time, but—"

Before he could finish his sentence, a slimy, black, equestrian head poked through one of the window slits. The horse stubbornly pushed its neck through the narrow opening until it could lip at Jenna's blanket. Its skin was still a wriggling mass of black tendrils, and its eyes were still filmed in milky white intelligence, but at least it didn't try to talk again.

"Speak of misfortune," Castor breathed. "That… thing hasn't left your side. It won't let anyone touch it, it doesn't seem to eat or drink, and it certainly won't allow itself to be stabled.

Jenna reached out hesitantly to pat the horse's nose.

"It's still here?" she wondered, amazement filling her voice. "But… any active magic should've dissipated while I was sleeping."

"Apparently that doesn't apply to this… whatever it is." Castor made a vague gesture in the horse's direction. "But that's not the problem. The horse—thing—well, it… it spoke to me."

Jenna raised an eyebrow, remembering. "It told you its name?"

Castor nodded, a muscle twitching in his cheek. He looked around as if afraid they would be overheard. "I don't think anyone else heard it, but if anyone finds out it thinks it's—you know who—we'll be in serious trouble with the elders, not to mention the Council of Mages."

Absorbed as she had been in trying to escape, Jenna hadn't fully appreciated the ramifications of her new horse's claim to be named after a dead—and traitorous—Patron until that moment. It was worse, considering her House.

"I suppose we would be," she murmured. Part of her yearned merely to study her creation—how did it sustain itself without outside sources of energy? Was it tied to her in some manner despite being an independent creature?—but she forced herself to focus on the matter at hand.

"I broke a magical taboo in creating it," she confided to Castor, "but I'm not certain other mages could recognize that by simply looking at it. The name presents a problem—and several questions—but if it hasn't spoken to others and won't let them touch it, I can assume it's still bound to me in some way."

He nodded, content to let her take charge in magical matters. "What will you tell the council?"

She shrugged. "I conjured the creature in self-defence. That'll satisfy the council as long as they don't learn it can talk." *Though I'm not sure if its speech or its name is the bigger problem here*, she thought.

Castor huffed in relief, and the horse copied him with comic panache, eyes still glinting cleverly.

"That doesn't seem so bad then," he said. "I just wanted to make sure we talked about it before anyone else got here. The healers should be coming any moment now."

Sure enough, footsteps clattered in the hallway adjoining her room a moment later. Castor managed to wrestle the horse's head back out the window—it protested with another huff—and Jenna smoothed the blankets over before two healers entered bearing packets of medicine and fresh bandages.

With Jenna's assent, Castor took his leave to catch up on sleep—he'd waited hours for her to wake, apparently—and Jenna resigned herself to the healers' ministrations.

⁓∞⁓

"Shades, I'm glad you're okay," Imp said.

Adriane didn't feel like smiling. "We almost weren't thanks to that fire you set." Imp flinched. "I know it was you."

"I had to." Imp bent to pluck at the courtyard's brittle grass, still wet from the rain.

Adriane knelt to face him and took his hands in her own, bandaged hands. She was mending quickly thanks to Silas' Hill's healers.

"Look Imp, this is serious." His eyes met hers reluctantly. "You can't go setting fires whenever you feel like. I don't understand—why? Why do you do it?"

He was silent, but she noticed tears pooling in his eyes.

"Imp?"

"I dunno why. My Mama showed me how, showed me I can—" he broke off, glancing away. "You look like her," he muttered, "but it's not the same. I need the fires." His eyes met hers again, defiant this time. "You don't understand. I *need* them. I have to set fires. My hands make me."

My hands make me. He screams a lot. Adriane shook herself away from the memory of Imp's naïve words. "If you keep setting your fires, we'll get found out," she said. Her hand went to her braid, before she remembered the green stone was gone, lost in the fire he'd set. *I guess the fires are like that stone for him,* she thought. *A reminder of home.*

"No one suspects anything," Imp said. "Well, maybe Elder Iram. But there's no proof I did anything."

"This time. But there cannot be a next time." She understood the need to remember, but it wasn't worth the risk. "Can you promise me that? Promise you won't set another fire?"

His eyes flickered downwards before meeting hers again. "Fine. I promise."

Adriane hoped he meant it. "It's not just us anymore, you know," she said, gazing at the empty courtyard. Most of the soldiers had drills, but she and the others had, of course, been excused. She'd slept for almost a day after they'd made it back, but it still didn't quite feel real. Everything was different.

"What do you mean?" Imp stared at her accusingly.

"I met some people on the mission. We're returning the mage's belongings later today, so you can come meet them if you're free."

"Why do you want to bother with others?"

She'd known he would take it badly. Imp wasn't the jealous type, not exactly, but like her, he preferred to keep to himself. *I can understand that.*

"It's not so bad, having friends," she replied quietly. She thought of Lancaster and Mia—and Jacob who, in some ways, was not unlike Imp. "But if you set another fire, it doesn't affect just us. You're putting everybody here at risk."

"I'm good at what I do. I promise I'll be careful, okay? If I do set a fire, I won't let you get caught in it again. I promise."

Adriane sighed. *Is that's all I'll get from him?*

"You said you had something you wanted to tell me?" she asked, changing the subject.

Imp's eyes narrowed. "Yeah. I saw a Serviceman."

Fear flared up, and shadows flickered around her, but Adriane managed to keep the magic at bay. "Are you sure? Where? Who was he?"

Imp shook his head. "I don't know him. It was the day before you left. He was tall, with dark hair, and he wore white gloves to cover his brand. He was hiding out, I think. Pretending he was normal."

Adriane thought for a moment. "I don't see what we can do about it right now. I doubt they'd send a member of the Protectorate into Ideon just to find us."

Imp arched his eyebrows in a clear display of skepticism.

"Just—tell me if you see him again, Imp. I'll keep my eyes out as well. Shades send it won't come to anything."

Tobin tried not to strain under the weight of the box in his arms, but Rise must've noticed, because he took it from him after the first few terraces. Adriane, who followed mutely behind them, didn't blink an eye at the exchange, but Tobin noticed Rise eyeing her whenever he turned a corner. Imp, the boy following Adriane around—*is he her brother…?*—caught Rise looking and glared.

Tobin sighed to himself. Runie had asked him and Adriane to return Jenna's few recovered belongings, and it seemed Rise and Imp were part of two separate package deals. The looks worried him. He might not be a brilliant fighter, but his social instincts were sharp, honed from growing up among the nobility; he could practically smell the tension between his three companions. *Bendekan knows I must've weathered worse situations what with having three sisters.*

He'd have to keep an eye on them all. *On them, and the squad, and Jenna,* Tobin thought. Timothy had been devastated to hear of his father's death and his sister's—Zenia's—capture. There was still no sign of her or the other mages.

The rest of the squad had taken the whole mission badly as well. Then there was Felias' death. Tobin swallowed, allowing sadness to well up in his chest without letting himself to succumb to it. *I've got my work cut out for me if I'm supposed to lead them.*

They reached Jenna's temporary accommodations, which lay in the

Enmoor compound. Enmoor was one of the combat groups focused on healing and medicine, and they had several small huts and apartments scattered around the main buildings to allow long-term patients some privacy. Tobin led the way to one of these huts, marked with a brass number eleven.

Something akin to a massive heap of black worms lay next to the door. *Looks like that conjured horse still hasn't disappeared*, Tobin thought with interest. The tendrils that formed its skin weren't moving as quickly as they had the first time he'd seen it, but it was still a strange sight, even for someone used to magic.

The horse got up as they approached, tossing its black mane. Rise and Imp both jumped, but Adriane didn't flinch. Her face remained impassive as always.

"What in the shad—what is that thing?" Imp tripped over his words.

"A horse," Adriane said. Tobin would've believed she wasn't the least bit afraid of it had he not noticed her steel herself before walking past it. "I told you about it, remember?"

Imp nodded, then licked his lips before following her to the door.

Tobin knocked. "It's nothing to worry about," he said to Imp, trying to seem both friendly and tough. "The horse is bound to Jenna Brightshade, so you needn't fear it. It saved our hides, actually."

A voice called from inside, and they entered to find Jenna sitting by a table in the small living room, stacks of books, scrolls, and pyramid-shaped ions littering the limited space around her.

"I'm sorry, I'd forgotten you were coming." She looked so much better than when he'd last seen her, but she held herself stiffly, as if she was still in pain, and her arm was in a splint. "I'd get up to greet you, but I'm afraid I can't." Her smile held the merest touch of fragility.

It was Adriane who made the first move. She took the box from Rise, her entire body taut as if poised to fight or flee as she did so and set it on the table. "Don't worry about it." She relaxed as she approached Jenna.

While the two women unpacked, Tobin, Imp, and Rise stood by awkwardly, sizing up the room and each other.

"I can't believe it," Jenna said in an awed voice as she lifted a battered little book from the box. "I thought I'd lost it," she whispered.

"You're a scholar?" Adriane asked.

"I am. I've spent several years researching the various wars and their effects on the three nations and the tribes. I've also developed a side study into magic more recently."

"Elder Iram mentioned you're one of the foremost authorities on the early Magewars," Tobin said.

"I suppose so. Most of the elders and theorists don't like it, but I focused a large part of my studies on Ideon's relations with the Saint Brazen Republic."

Tobin frowned. "Was that part of why the Service wanted you then?" Adriane glared at him, and Rise elbowed him hard. "I mean," Tobin suppressed a wince, "if you don't mind me asking about the, um…"

Jenna raised a hand. "It's alright. But to be honest, I have no idea why those Servicemen followed and captured me. The only thing I know is it had something to do with my magic. I—I would prefer not to relive those memories, but if you've read the elders' statement, you'll know what they did to us. And all the other captives were mages too."

Tobin's mouth curled. "I did wonder why the council authorized a rescue operation that extreme," he said, thinking back to the conversation about magic and technology he'd had with Lady Kesma. *Magic really is for the elite.* "They wouldn't have done that under normal circumstances—if regular people had been captured."

Jenna nodded. "Maybe not. But either way, it's troubling that the Republican Service would dare kidnap Ideians at all. The fact that we were all mages doesn't explain anything."

"Actually," a low, nervous voice said, "perhaps it does." Rise stepped forward, hands shaking the slightest bit. "Remember the letter, Tobin?"

Jenna raised an eyebrow, and Rise explained about his Republican background and his brother's letters.

"What about the letter?" Tobin asked impatiently. "You were right about them capturing Ideian mages. But it still doesn't explain why."

"Well, I've been thinking about it… and I think maybe I know."

Rise's right hand flickered towards his left, massaging the clumsily healed burn concealed beneath his white glove. *I shouldn't be nervous,* he thought with an inward laugh. *Not after all I've gone through.*

"You sure the kid here can hear this?" he asked Adriane with a shrug towards Imp, who bristled at the designation.

Adriane merely nodded. She was on edge today—both her, and the boy. *Do they know I'm onto them?*

"I think the Republic's trying to mess with magic," Rise said.

Jenna inhaled sharply. "Mess with magic? What do you mean? How would they do that? How does it explain anything about the capture of Ideian mages?"

Rise shot her a look.

"Sorry," she said. "I'm just asking questions here."

"Fair enough." Rise gathered his thoughts. "For one thing, those whips they have already mess with magic, so I think it's fair to assume they're working on bigger things." He suppressed a laugh. "They're always working on bigger things. As for the mages, why else would they want Ideian ones? They're already hunting down Republican mages. They couldn't have mages on their side of course, not openly, so that means they need them for something else. If there's one thing I know about the Service, it's they like to try new things, and sure, some of them are horrible, but they always have a reason. I've—I've seen some of the things they do. What you said about your friend, Zenia, well it sounds like another one of their experiments to me." He swallowed nervously. *Have I ever talked this much before? To Ideians?*

Jenna looked at him. "I guess that begs the question, Rise: How do you know those things?"

He could feel his hands shaking. "I'm from the Republic. I grew up around the Service. Everybody knows." He managed a grin. "Most aren't smart enough to make sense of the facts."

He could see his words sink in, could see Jenna and Tobin accept what he said. Rise expelled the breath he hadn't realized he was holding. *They believe me. Thank the shades.*

Then Adriane's quiet, hard voice interrupted his relieved thoughts. "Liar." She turned to face him, eyes alight with anger, shadows flickering around her as she activated her magic.

Of course it was him. All the progress Adriane had made threatened to disappear as her seething anger called the magic to her. She flickered into shadows, but quickly reappeared again, managing to retain some control. Imp had pointed Rise out to her after they left for the Enmoor compound.

"You didn't suspect me," she whispered. "You *knew*. You knew all along, because you're one of them. You're a Serviceman."

The accusation hung in the room like a shadow. Tobin's mouth hung open, Imp's face was alight with fear, and Rise looked like a rabbit caught in a snare.

Jenna alone remained calm. She looked at Adriane, her gaze calculating. "I guess this means we have two Republicans here."

"Three," Imp said quickly, moving to stand beside Adriane. She wasn't sure whether she wanted to throttle or thank him for that. *I suppose I can do both*, she thought, *if I can get us out of this mess.*

"Do you have proof of your accusation?" Jenna asked.

Adriane took a deep breath and, with great effort, managed to push both the magic and the anger out of her head. *Lancaster could've talked himself out of this*, she thought. *Say what he would say.* She looked around the room, taking a moment to study the other four.

Rise still looked apprehensive, but more in control now that the suspicion had rebounded on her. Imp was afraid, but trying not to show it, as stubborn as he'd been every step of their long journey to reach Ideon. Squadleader Tobin's face was set, but also curious, and Jenna, pale and drawn though she looked, was calm and collected.

Adriane realized she could see a bit of Lancaster in each of them. Rise had his hard, criminal nature, his guild sponsor side, the side that would kill to protect those he loved. Imp's remarkable innocence, on the other hand, was not unlike Lancaster's own. He'd truly believed the best of each member of the Abraham Guild, Adriane included. Tobin had his curiosity. She could see it in his open face—the desire to know what was going on before he passed judgement. And Jenna—Jenna had that same smooth intelligence, the quiet questions, the calm feeling of safety.

"I'm from Saint Brazen, not Eleszan," Adriane began, "but Imp and I had good reason to hide our identities. The Service was after us both because I'm a… mage. It was safer this way." She turned to Rise. "I don't know what in the shades your story is, but you'd better tell it quickly. There's no way you'd know any of that unless you'd been high up in the Service or known someone who was. I only know because of my—friend. He left the Service after what he learned about mages there. He died helping me escape." It was true enough. "As for proof, Imp's seen what's under those gloves. A Serviceman's brand."

"Fine." Rise raised his left hand and carefully pulled the white glove off with his right. "It's true."

The hand he revealed was badly burned and scarred, with a tattoo and brand covering the middle of his palm. Adriane stiffened as the glove slipped off, revealing the eye burned right into his flesh. She glanced at Imp, who stood frozen like the others. A brief look of satisfaction flashed across his face.

"I used to be a Serviceman, okay?" Rise turned his hand to look at his palm. "Until they found out I have magic of my own. I was hunting down my brother at the time—I helped him escape from the Service dungeons—and I was so angry at him it triggered my magic for the first time. I had blue fire dripping from my hand in broad daylight, so they locked me up and forgot all about Daniel. That fire's what gave me the scar. Then Daniel managed to get me out, and we fled to Ideon. But the rest of what I said is all true. Just—please." His voice had an edge to it. "Don't tell anyone about this. They'd lock me up, like as not. I wouldn't be safe here either." He turned to Adriane, eyes glinting with a murderous intensity. "I'll kill myself before I get caged again."

Jenna cleared her throat, and they all looked at her. "We'll tell no one for now," she said decisively, then cast a questioning glance at Tobin, who hesitated, then nodded. "But with all that out, I'd say we have a much better chance at guessing why the Republican Service is doing all of this. I don't want to forget what happened to me. To forget the others. I want to know why it happened, and I want to do something about it."

Adriane took a deep breath, trying to focus back on the problem. "The captives were all taken due east, towards Cain."

Rise smirked. "I'm assuming that's where you're from? I did wonder how you found it so easy to track them and guess where they'd go."

Adriane suppressed a glare, electing to ignore Rise instead, and focus on Jenna. "From what I saw of Cain's dungeon, though, it wouldn't be practical to hold a large group of mages there."

"Teel," Imp said suddenly, certainty lighting up his face. "They're taking them to Teel."

Now that he'd spoken and everyone's eyes were on him, Imp felt a million times smaller. *The Service gave you everything,* a voice in his head whispered. *They didn't have to do that. Are you really gonna betray all their secrets now? They're the only ones who didn't walk out on you.* It was true. Imp was the one who had walked out on them.

He looked at Adriane. She'd left him, as had Uncle Bento, as had his own mother. But he—Imp—had left the Service. It had been his choice. *What about Vine? She didn't leave you either. You're betraying her too.*

"Imp," Adriane said. "If you've got something to say…"

Imp hesitated, swallowed past the lump in his throat, and decided. "There's a tower, a facility for the Service southwest of Cain. Some Servicemembers took me there once." There'd be time enough to think of a way to explain his complicated history with the Service later. "Vine— the Servicewoman in charge of it—she mentioned it was used for technological trials and as a holding facility. I figure that sounds like what you were saying." He couldn't bring himself to say the Serviceman's name, so he merely nodded towards him, Rise.

I'm sorry, Vine, Imp thought. *Maybe I'll be the one who comes back. But not yet. Adriane came back for me, so I need to stay with her. Besides, Uncle Bento said he'd see me again. Maybe he'll come back too.* He knew the thoughts were childish, but he clung to them anyway.

As the others continued talking, Imp retreated, then slipped out the door. He made his way to the stables. He borrowed Adriane's new military-issued horse and rode towards the remains of his fire. He needed to think. Or, even better, not to think at all.

The land was blackened and sooty where it bordered on the city, but further south a few flaming trees still burned like massive torches. The forest adjoining the nearby farms and pastures had been cleared, and it seemed they'd let the rest of the fire burn out naturally.

Imp approached the burning section, relishing the wood-burnt air, the eager stride of the horse beneath him, and the glorious red and yellow of the distant flames.

A movement caught his eye, and he spotted a figure in the midst of the flaming trees. *Oh no!* Had his fire trapped another victim? Horrified, Imp spurred the horse forwards, racing towards the figure. Something was wrong, he realized, as the figure became clearer. It ambled through a burning swatch of forest, seemingly unconcerned by the flames and smoke.

"Hey," Imp yelled. "You alright?"

His horse snorted, hesitant to approach the fire further, but Imp urged it just a little closer. He could make out the figure's—the man's—face now, his slack expression and closed eyes. Was he sick from the smoke maybe?

"Can you hear me?" Goosebumps rose on Imp's arms. This didn't feel right. The man felt wrong, somehow. He shouldn't be able to walk through the fire, breathe in the smoke, survive like that.

The man's mouth worked, and he began to whisper something. Then, his eyes snapped open.

Imp took one look at the space where the man's eyes should have been, then jerked the horse back with a yell. Was this one of those spirit creatures the Ideians kept mentioning? Somehow, Imp doubted it.

The man's murmurs grew louder as he repeated a single sentence over and over.

Shivering, Imp wheeled the horse around and galloped away, back towards the city. Would Adriane know what to do this time? He gulped, remembering his thoughts of spirit creatures. *I should tell an Ideian*, he thought. Elder Iram might know what the figure was. Or if he didn't, he'd know who to ask. If there was one thing the Service had taught Imp, it was to follow the chain of command.

Map showing
the shrine
of the Short-Fire Templar

23

MY NAME IS YOEL

Jenna guided Shadowphile through a shallow stream, then back onto the forested bank. Water splashed behind her as Castor and the soldiers followed, and she studied the trees to find their next trailhead, glancing at the clear autumn sky to get her bearings.

Once she was certain of her direction, Jenna let Shadowphile choose his own way through the leaf-strewn forest, focusing back on the sheaf of notes pinned to her leather saddle horn. She'd recorded Rise's warnings about the Servicemen, as well as notes on Adriane, Squadleader Tobin, and Imp. She'd spent much of their week-long journey contemplating their words.

They didn't trust each other—none of them did—but they'd reached a truce of sorts, deciding to keep each others' secrets for the sake of pursuing their own goals. Rise, Jenna guessed, wanted revenge, Tobin wanted adventure, and Adriane was trying to tame her unruly magic. *Not unlike me*, she thought, gripping her reins tighter. She was uncertain about Imp. He followed Adriane and did what she told him to, but his motives were unclear. *I hope he can keep a secret.*

Jenna's horse twitched, a movement she was getting used to. The tendrils forming his skin no longer writhed like they'd done when she had created him, but they still crawled over each other, and every so often a tendril would flare from aether black to the pale silver of soul magic like flickering candlelight.

She'd named him Shadowphile to allay any questions regarding his name—and she'd had to explain this to the horse, lest he continue going around calling himself Yoel. He'd pouted for an hour or so—something he seemed to have picked up from Tobin—and then resigned himself to the change.

Shadowphile raised his head, and his lips worked like they did when he was about to speak. "We—there yet?" he asked.

Jenna patted his neck. *He's forming more complex sentences, delving into the realm of questions and abstract ideas such as destination and time. He seems to learn from observing and imitating humans, though I'd guess his intelligence level is no higher than that of a child.* "Not yet, I think. I'll know it when I see it."

Castor had encouraged her to stay in Silas' Hill, even after she'd healed sufficiently to move on, but Jenna wanted—needed—to see her journey to its end. *The Search for a Source* was onto something. It had to be.

She turned to observe the dozen riders trailing in her wake. Castor, right behind her, gave her a smile, and the Kane squadleader riding after sat up a slight bit straighter at her gaze. Elder Iram had been kind enough to assign them an escort for their journey. Despite the lack of privacy that afforded, Jenna was grateful. The last thing she wanted was another encounter with the Republicans.

Jenna pulled out her map again, calculating the distances. *We should be within a few miles of it now.* Assuming, of course, that the Ghost-Fire Templar's missing shrine even existed and that the book hadn't just led her on a weeks-long quest of meaningless horrors. *Those are a lot of assumptions to act on. Aren't you supposed to be a scholar?*

A squawk sounded from a nearby tree. A mossy green spirit creature resembling something between a bird and a bat detached itself from the trunk, flapping towards her on misshapen wings.

Another greenwing, Jenna noted. *And significantly larger than the last few we encountered.* It was unusual—extraordinary, even—how many spirit creatures they'd seen during the past few days. Mostly greenwings and a few forest sprites, but that morning, Jenna had also caught a glimpse of the egg-yolk eyes and bark-like face of the local forest guardian.

Shadowphile saw the creature and whinnied in alarm, tossing his mane and sidestepping. Jenna couldn't figure out why, but the horse seemed to hate, or perhaps fear, spirit creatures. She'd tried asking him about it, but his only response had been to repeatedly cry 'Neri,' until she'd shushed him for fear of having more people know about both his ability to talk and his propensity for using the names of Ideian heroes remembered for their tragedy.

The greenwing flew right at her face, twitching its snout—Shadowphile trembled, but kept walking forward—and then it turned around with a friendly chirp. On impulse, Jenna followed it, leaving the small track they had been riding on.

It seemed to want her to follow, turning every few seconds to jabber at her, before resuming its flight. Most spirit creatures didn't know human speech, of course, but they were all more intelligent than beasts, and some scholars even argued that, given the opportunity, all spirit creatures had the potential to learn human methods of communication.

Shadowphile hesitantly trailed the greenwing, heading roughly northeast. The forest surrounding them thinned, then fell away, revealing charred stumps and blackened earth. They'd reached the swath of ground devastated by the fire.

A burst of energy hit Jenna, and sparks of purplish-white flame shot out from her face. Shadowphile didn't seem to mind, being made of the same magic, but Jenna jerked back in her saddle to avoid hitting him anyway. She cried out as aether and soul magic built up pressure, growing hot under her skin, trying to escape. Eyes screwed shut in concentration, she forced the magic out of her body and into the empty expanse ahead of her. She opened her eyes again in time to see the blast of purple flame.

Some of the soldiers cried out in surprise, and Castor rushed to her side. "Jenna! Are you alright?"

"Fine. I'm fine." Jenna glanced around her, eyes narrowing. There had been a burst of energy, but now it was gone. *Where did it come from?*

"That was the first in a while. Did something die nearby to set it off?"

Jenna frowned. *Yoel knows the only blessed thing that came from those Republicans was a certain control of my magic.* Being threatened with beatings and those horrid whips had allowed her to develop much more control than she'd had before. *But something made it go wild again.*

"I don't know," she said. "I only felt it right before it hit me."

The squadleader—Birch of Bright Midnight—rode up to ensure she was alright and, at her suggestion, ordered his men to fan out and comb the area.

Jenna composed herself, then followed the soldiers. She was looking for something, though she didn't know what exactly. She was used to listening to facts and reason, not feelings, but some instinct told her she must be close to the shrine. Perhaps it had something to do with her magic bursting out.

After several minutes of riding through the charred landscape, Jenna spotted a large stone, half-covered by ash and a few burnt logs. At her word, the soldiers joined her, then dismounted and cleared away the debris, stirring up clouds of ash as they did so. With Castor's help, she dismounted and knelt to examine the pockmarked rock.

Jenna's heart beat faster as she identified faint markings on the stone that might once have been letters and words.

"It's here," she breathed. The words had all but faded away, but here and there were legible pieces hidden under crusts of burnt moss and dirt. "It's really here."

"How do you know it's the right one?" Castor knelt beside her.

"I don't for sure, but it's definitely a shrine, and it's in the right place." She brushed more soot away to get a better sense of the words. *Five—came to—mountains—and he swore he would—consumed—magic in him.* The shrine was worn and weathered, but she could recognize pieces of the Tale. She guessed it told either of the five heroes or of the Ghost-Fire Templar's quest for magic.

"Castor, can you get everyone to move further away, please?"

"You think the magic will still work with the stone in this shape?"

She shrugged.

"I suppose it's always worth a shot." Castor called for the soldiers to move down to a clearing they'd passed earlier and set up camp there. She made them move the horses too, just in case. Shadowphile, refused to leave until Jenna personally explained why she wanted him gone.

A few moments later, Jenna sat alone with the remnants of an ancient shrine in the middle of a heap of rubble. *I hope the magic hasn't faded aw—*

Before Jenna could finish the thought, crunching footsteps sounded from behind her. She turned to ask Castor what was wrong, but the figure that met her eyes was far from Castor's tall, broad frame. It was a haggard, weather-worn man dressed in hunter's garb. His skin held a tinge of blue, which was strange enough, but it was his eyes that transfixed her. They were bright with an intensity that bordered on madness.

Jenna's hands went for her crutches before she realized she'd left them on Shadowphile's saddle. *Yoel protect me*, she thought, casting out for sources of energy. She scrambled to her feet, using the rock for support. The man didn't look dangerous, but after her encounter with the Servicemen... *I won't take any chances.*

The man chuckled hoarsely at her reaction. "You alright there, lass?" Unlike his eyes, his voice was calm and measured.

Jenna forced herself to take a deep breath. "I'm—I'm fine." *Castor*, she realized. *I didn't even think of calling for help.*

"Didn't mean to startle you."

"It's fine. I wasn't, I mean… who are you, if I may ask?" Jenna realized her hands were shaking, still caught up in the adrenaline.

His eyes twinkled. "A man, for the most part." He said it like a joke. "I saw your magic from the treeline." He gestured vaguely. "Impressive, if you don't count your lack of control."

"Are you a mage as well?" She couldn't help but think how much harder holding him off would be if he had magic of his own.

"That I am." He muttered something to himself, before approaching her. "I didn't want to do this," he murmured, and Jenna backed up against the rock. There was nothing threatening about his stance, but something felt wrong all the same. "Rehu made me," he whined. "It said this was important."

"Important?" The word came out as a squeak, and Jenna had to try again. "What are you talking about? You said—Rehu?"

"It's funny, meeting you here of all places. Went looking for the lost shrine, did you?" He chuckled again.

Jenna was about to call for help, when she felt the stone move beneath her fingers. She jerked around, lost her balance, and fell to her knees. The crumbled letters on the old stone were rearranging themselves, snapping into recognizable words. She read the single sentence, eyes widening, heart beating heavily. *You seek that which lies directly in front of you.* Confused, she looked ahead, the stone filling her view. A few more words formed, and she looked back down to read them. *A little to the left.*

Jenna turned her head, and the old man's face came into view, eyes meeting hers with a frightening intensity.

"You're him," she whispered. "You're the Ghost-Fire Templar."

"The fire wasn't dangerous anymore." Imp tried not to fidget in his chair, but his feet twitched of their own volition. He didn't like talking to adults, not since Uncle Bento, but this had scared him. "It was still smoking something fine though, so I wanted to see it closer. It—" He hesitated. *It's the first fire I've set properly since the Service.* "It's the first time I've seen a fire that close."

"And this figure—you saw him inside the flames?" Elder Iram took notes, his fingers nimble with the pen despite their gnarls and knots.

Imp thought he was taking it rather well, considering this only gave him more reason to suspect Imp's involvement with the fire. "Yeah. The fire was walled up against the land those Theold's Mountains soldiers cleared. I thought I'd—I thought he'd been hurt in the fire. The man, I mean. He was standing there inside it, not coughing or anything though, so I thought maybe he was just disoriented from the smoke."

The draw of the fire and the need to think, to be alone, hadn't been his only reasons for coming. After Iram had spoken of the Seers, Imp had wanted to see the pictures again, to find some lasting link, some proof of his mother's legacy. Smaller fires worked better, of course, but Adriane leaving had pushed him too far. Maybe if Vine had been there—Vine and her bottle of drink—maybe then he'd have a different outlet. *Or maybe it's just another excuse.* Imp's thoughts were as disjointed as his memories of the fire. *The fire.*

"I called to the man—well, I wasn't even sure if it was a man or a woman—but he just stood there, swaying like." Imp suppressed a hiccup. The weird part came next—the part that had made him run to tell Elder Iram. *The elder's not like Adriane, but he was here at least.* Besides, he was in charge, so he'd know what to do and be able to do it. "The man walked like he was drunk, and then, when he got closer—and I could tell it was a *he*—he opened his eyes." Imp shuddered.

"Imp?" Elder Iram said gently. "Take your time now. Just tell me what you saw."

"Fire," Imp whispered. "He didn't have any eyes, just black fire, and then white fire, and then black again."

"What about the rest of him? What did he look like?"

"His clothes were old. Not like, *old*, but old-fashioned, like something outta those stories the soldiers tell. And his skin was black in places, like burns, though the fire wasn't catchin' on him. It didn't look like it was hurting him at all."

Elder Iram was silent for a long while, and Imp sat fidgeting in his chair. "Like something outta those stories," he whispered again. "And there's something else. He was mumbling something over and over. I didn't catch it 'til—well, 'til I got closer. I was curious, see."

"Go on."

"He kept saying 'My name is Yoel, my name is Yoel,' over and over, like he was gonna forget it or something."

Elder Iram twitched, as if his impulse was to jump out of his chair. "Yoel—are you sure that's what he said? He called himself Yoel?"

"As near as I can tell." Imp shrugged. "That's one of the names from those Tales, isn't it?"

Elder Iram nodded, his face as carefully expressionless as that of a Serviceman. "It is."

⟶ ⟨⟨⟨∞⟩⟩⟩ ⟵

The man patted the stone like an old friend. "Rehu's got a sense of humor sometimes," he said, chuckling. His expression hardened. "I'd hoped I wouldn't be needed. I didn't want you to know. But yes, I'm Jesa, the one you call the Ghost-Fire Templar."

"Why—I mean, how are you alive? Where have you been all these years? What's going on?" A thousand questions surged through Jenna's mind, and she bit her tongue lest they all come flooding out.

"It doesn't matter," the man—Jesa—said. "You know too much already, if you ask me. Things never go well when Rehu tries to meddle with fate."

"Fate?"

He spat onto the stone, prompting Jenna to raise an eyebrow. "Destiny. Fate. Choice. Whatever you call it. You've got a whole lot of it coming your way." He shook his head. "Look at the whole mess that started this magic. Look at my own story for that matter."

It was like he was having a whole different conversation. *Is he truly mad?* "I don't understand," she said.

"You ever head of the Markois, lass?"

"Some of the Tales mention them. Guardian spirits who watch over Ideon and even walk unseen among its people. Some scholars argue they must be humans from the Tales, or Patrons, but others think they're more like spirit creatures."

"Close enough. There's more of us than you'd think. Long life isn't all it's cut out to be, you know. If I could die… but that's not why I'm here. I'm here to help you."

It was more than Jenna had hoped for, but something bothered her. "Why?"

He hesitated, eyes still shining bright and clear. They seemed *too* lucid. "A long time ago, Rehu told me there is a reason some are given magic and others aren't."

"Rehu? The guardian spirit mentioned in the Tales?"

"They still tell mine, you know. More to warn than anything else. I asked Rehu—had I been given magic, or had I not been given magic? After all, I took it for myself. Do you know what it told me? It said it was neither. I hadn't been given magic, nor had I not been given magic. I'm an outlier." He turned to gaze into her eyes again. "And so are you."

"I don't—"

"Rehu didn't plan for what happened with me. It's my fault your magic is like that." He barked a laugh, then continued, somehow terribly amused. "My only solace is Rehu promised one day I will die. I can rejoin my wife and daughters once my work here is done." He nodded in satisfaction, as if that had explained everything.

"So, let me get this straight." Jenna's mind was a whirlwind. "You're the Ghost-Fire Templar, and a spirit creature from the Tales wants you to teach me about magic... because it's your fault my magic is... difficult?"

"Rehu's not just some spirit. And I'm not going to teach you anything."

"But you said—"

"I'm going to *tell* you something. Something you might not believe if that rock wrote it plain as day." His bearing turned serious. "I was, as you've guessed, the Ghost-Fire Templar. But that was long ago. I'm not really a mage at all anymore. I stopped using my magic; the cost was too high."

"The cost?"

He ignored her question. "Why don't you show me some of your magic, lass?"

Jenna nodded and cast out for sources of energy, but he interrupted her.

"Walk with me while you do." He helped her stand and let her lean on him as she forced her feet forwards. Her legs still hadn't recovered from her ordeal.

Jenna renewed her concentration. Years ago, she had discovered that whatever destruction she caused with her magic did not leave behind energy for her to collect. This meant the aether flame she had released earlier left no energy for her to use, so she cast her senses further. She found nothing but the remains of a dead shrew, with enough energy left for her to create a single splinter, if that. Just her luck.

Jenna's vision went purple as she visualized strands of aether flowing out of her and into the air. Soon, a miniature blade hovered in front of her face, its smooth triangular facets formed by twisting purple aether strands.

"I don't have the energy for anything bigger," she said. "And it's harder to do while talking and walking."

"Your magic should be like breathing. There's no point to magic unless you can control it."

"Then why don't you use yours?"

He stopped and faced her. "Listen to me, lass." The light in his eyes was gone; they looked bleak and empty. "Rehu has a habit of collecting people. Like the heroes in the stories. Every so often, there's a crossroads—a time when the future is uncertain, a time when regular people can influence the whole realm with the simplest of actions."

"What are you saying?"

"Don't let Rehu have you. Don't become one of its pawns." Jesa laughed without a trace of humor. "It has its eyes on you already; it meant to send me to you before you got caught up with those Servicemen and learned how to control your magic all by yourself. It *meddles*. What's worse, it does not—cannot—learn from past mistakes. By some higher law, the more it tries to fix affairs to its benefit, the more they go awry."

Jenna nearly tripped over a stone but caught herself on his arm. She glanced at the ground, where a neat green pebble sat in the dirt, perfect except for a small chip cracked out of it. Curious, she knelt, letting go of Jesa's support in the process.

"Rehu's death," Jesa swore, noticing the pebble. "Even now, he's bringing you together."

She looked up, intending to demand he clarify what in Tabitha's name was going on—but he was gone. A chill ran up Jenna's spine, and she whirled around, thinking he must have stepped to the side.

There's no one here. Fear crept into her mind. *Am I the one who's mad? Was this even real?*

A shout came from the trees ahead of her. Castor ran into view.

"Jenna! The shrine—I forgot to give you your crutches—and when I came back—you were gone." Castor's words came in a thick torrent, almost incoherent.

He rushed to her and helped her stand; as she did so, she scooped up the green pebble, dusting it off. Jesa, if he had been real, had reacted to it. *It must mean something.*

"I'm fine," she said, pocketing the stone. "I think." He gave her a look, and she shook her head. "You wouldn't believe what just happened."

They spent a night in a clearing near the shrine, which had returned to its previous, dilapidated state and refused to change further. After studying it thoroughly without discovering anything new, Jenna and Castor reluctantly decided to return home to Kalaaman, though they would stop in Silas' Hill first. Their escorts needed to return there, and besides, Tobin, Rise, or Adriane might have thought of some new insight into the Service's behaviour. *If not, I'll continue my research and find answers that way. They'll have to let me back now that my magic's under control. Tabitha send they do.*

A thought suddenly hit her. *Patrons.* The Fate's Hand shrine… what had it said? She rummaged in her pack, digging out *The Search for a Source* and prying a sheaf of notes she had written weeks ago from its pages.

> A scholar more the fight becomes
> A soldier more the Tales of peace
> A farmer thieves, a thief recants
> The firebrand unites them all
>
> One blind, one lost
> One doomed to fall
> One leads, one loves
>
> This guidance grants
> An insight given once
> And never again

She'd thought the words referred to the five heroes in the Tales, but Jesa had talked about people. People chosen, people able to effect change, able to affect their very circumstances.

I'm the scholar. Tobin's the soldier. Is Adriane the thief? Or is it Rise? She didn't know how it all fit together, but five persons were mentioned, and five of them had met in most unusual circumstances back in Silas' Hill.

However, that theory didn't explain the second part—'One blind, one lost, one doomed to fall.' Here, her initial assumption made more sense. Perhaps this really was about the Heroes from the Tales. *It's just like Elder Breck said: I can find guidance in the stories passed down to me.*

They took their time in returning home, and soon leaves littered the forest paths in soft, carpeted layers. Autumn had firmly established its grip on the land, and the smell of it was everywhere, the smell of green things withering away, the smell of comfort and thick, black winter soil.

They avoided the larger towns, but spent nights in small, sturdy villages, relishing the comfort of sleeping in inns. One of these villages, a place aptly named Forest's Edge, boasted a bath house, which Jenna was all too eager to take advantage of. Soaking her aching legs in the warm water, she became aware of a heated conversation held by a group of women, both townspeople and travelling merchants.

"—and he hasn't shown his face since," a farmer said.

"Yiemen's always chasing girls," another added. "I've told his mother time and again one day she'll find him run off with one."

"What a shame." An elderly merchant shook her head. "I heard he had promising magic, that boy. The elders mentioned him with glowing praise every time I came through these parts."

"But what can you do," the first woman said. "Young love does what it will."

Jenna's heart beat faster as she realized what they were talking about. *Another mage missing. What if he was one of those taken by the Service?* There had been two young men among the captives, and all of them had been mages of respectable ability.

"Yoel send it isn't so," Jenna murmured, causing the women to look at her with astonishment. She blushed, realizing how her words could be misinterpreted.

"If you're going to swear to the Patrons, why not to Thalia or Denia?" the merchant said. "I doubt you have trouble attracting men with those looks of yours, but I do hear Jaim the barber's son was looking a right eye at you when you rode into town, with the soldiers behind you and all. He's Kane-born, and you can tell." The two younger women dissolved into giggles.

"Some like it rugged you know," one of them whispered.

Jenna blushed even deeper. She made excuses after that, gathered her things, and headed back to the inn, leaning heavily on her crutches. She thought she heard the women whisper in sympathy as she left.

They must mean well, and I suppose I should take their assumptions about my Patron as a compliment, Jenna thought, *but there's no way I want a soft home life when things are so wrong.* Did the townspeople here even know about the threat the Servicemen were posing? Did they realize there might be war again soon?

As Jenna crawled into bed next to Castor that night, she lay awake for a while, thinking. *With my magic reasonably under control, I could return to the library and continue my work as a theorist. But should I?* The question scared her; she'd always known what she wanted from life. She'd known she was called to be a scholar, to use her mind for the betterment of Ideon ever since her first few years studying under Tutor Rhia, who'd named her a prodigy.

"Castor?" she whispered.

"Hm?" He stirred, drawing her closer to him.

"Do you want to go back to Kalaaman? Do you think it's for the best?"

"I don't know." He yawned. "I thought you wanted to keep on with your research."

I do, she wanted to say. *But what if that's not what I'm supposed to do?* Her magic was strong, stronger than she'd ever dreamed it would be. Her escape from the Republicans was proof of that.

"What if we move to Silas' Hill? I'm sure they'd have need of another founder, and besides, you haven't completed your work as a journeyman."

"But what about you, love?"

Jenna hesitated. "I think I want to stay there for a while, to train my magic further." They wouldn't be able to teach her everything, but Silas' Hill was the place to go for combat magic. "If I'm able to fight—even if it's with my mind and not my magic—and if there's a war brewing, then I think I should do my part."

Jenna sighed. She did feel duty-bound to aid her country, but there was more to it. "I'll never be helpless again," she whispered, remembering the pain of the Servicemen's whips, and the fear of being captive and alone. The memories flashed before her eyes, until her mind settled on the image of a young woman, dirtied and bruised, with blood dripping from her eyes. "Not just that. I have a promise to keep. Zenia's still out there."

She wasn't sure if Castor heard that last part, since he muttered sleepily before nuzzling her hair with his nose.

"Goodnight," she whispered, rolling her eyes in amusement. She'd discuss things with him further in the morning.

I can learn more. Perhaps even learn to fight. Jenna had never expected to use her magic for anything so violent, but then again, she'd never thought her magic would be strong enough to kill someone or create a sentient being. *Power is important,* she thought, drifting off. She shifted her legs to a more comfortable position, groaning with the effort it took. *After all, what difference can I make if I'm weak?*

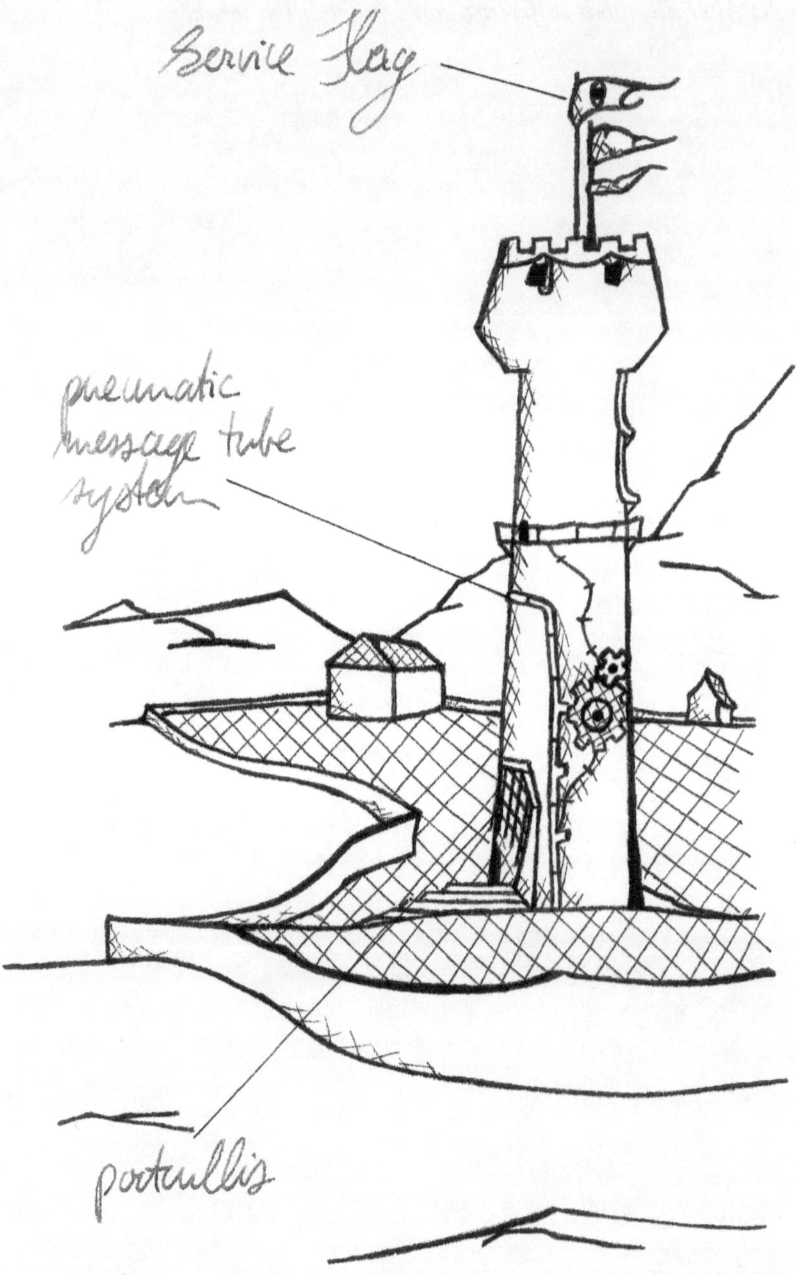

Service Flag
pneumatic message tube system
portcullis

EPILOGUE

Neminia, in House Heron–Neminia, Ideon

Lady Kesma sat in the ambassadors' gardens underneath the pale light of a full moon and smiled. The stories—Tales, they called them here—had confirmed her suspicions and shown her what she must do. Yet she still did not know everything. Why, for instance, had her mother chosen to have a child? *A resourceful woman like her could have feigned barrenness, even ended the pregnancy.* It would have been simpler. *Perhaps better.*

Lady Kesma stared absentmindedly at her forearm, as she often did when contemplating her unique position. Faint grey-and-brown lines formed angular patterns against the twisting blotches of scar tissue on her arm.

The scars had been her mother's idea. They gave her an excuse to cover her arm with bracelets or a bracer, and they kept people from asking about those strange patterns. Kesma had been forced to make the scars herself, as a pledge to follow the way of self-sacrifice. Few Republicans still followed those old traditions, of course, but they commanded respect nonetheless. The cuts had been painful. Precise. And they were only half as painful as they were ironic.

"Path of self-sacrifice indeed," Kesma muttered to herself with an amused chuckle. "If only they knew."

She pulled the decorative leather bracer back over her arm and turned to gaze up at the moon, a perfect circle in a perfectly bleak sky. She focused on the light, letting it draw her mind in, pushing all errant thoughts away.

The Tales spoke of a child who would have terrible power and an even more terrible fate. A child who would save the world yet sacrifice everything for it. A Seer.

Born under a new moon. Kesma had consulted her father's astronomers, who had confirmed her suspicions. *Coming into her power under a new moon.* She could remember that first, moonless night all too well. Her mother had been elated at the pictures Kesma saw inside the lights.

Had her mother known, even then? Had she asked for this fate to befall her child? Had she brought this wonderful, horrible destiny to Kesma on purpose?

The child will have great power. Kesma had tasted power such as she'd never thought could exist. It didn't come from her mother, that power. No, it came from a small, artificially dug shaft that Kesma had stumbled upon a year ago. Perhaps it had been destiny. *She will sacrifice everything and everyone she loves.* Kesma had lost so many people already. Her mother was gone. Her father, absent. Friends, left behind, cheated, exploited for the power she needed to save the world.

That thought—saving the world—didn't faze her, not anymore. Hardly anything did.

She looked down at one of the garden's many fountains, this one a simple pool set into the ground. She could see herself reflected in the water. Colour was hard to distinguish in the moon's cold light, but her imagination filled in the gaps for her. An imposing, cruelly beautiful face. Black hair with a few red strands. Extraordinarily pale blue eyes.

"Mother always said I was special," she whispered with a sardonic smile.

"Are you alright, my lady?"

Lady Kesma whirled around, but it was only Yhara. *Dear, sweet Yhara.*

"I'm fine, just fine," she said, keeping her voice steady.

"You look pale. Should I get you some mulled wine? Or cider?"

Lady Kesma sighed, though not in annoyance. "You can always tell, can't you."

Yhara approached, then kneeled in front of her mistress, taking Kesma's hands in her own. "Always," she said. "Whatever you need, my lady."

Kesma turned away. "I'm afraid all I need tonight is some solitude."

Yhara rose, head bowed. "Of course, my lady. I'll leave you be."

Nobody knew she was different—special, as her mother had put it. No one except Yhara, who had kept her secrets for years.

Lady Kesma turned her gaze back towards the sky and *blinked.* Her eyesight shifted, and the sky shattered in two. It was like seeing double, except one image was solid and real, and the second was translucent and ghostly. The full moon still shone down at her. And then a second, transparent moon hung in the sky, one only she, with her unique power, could see.

The Tales had been wrong about this part. The second moon didn't show Seers what kind of power they had. It was a warning. The second moon was the horrible vision that the first Seer—the one who had spoken the prophecy about a cursed child—had seen. It was a terrible danger threatening the continent. A pull so strong it would make the waters surge over the land, destroying it. A pull that would yank at that terrible, awesome power flowing beneath the ground—the power that had created magic itself.

There was one way to stop it. First, Lady Kesma would have to destroy magic to prevent the second moon from affecting it. Then, she would unite the continent, and united they would withstand the catastrophe. She would die in the end, but that didn't matter. Her quest had already consumed her. She would be the saviour of the world.

Lady Kesma looked up once more but didn't shift her vision. The sky was back to normal, with only a single full moon looking down on her. She smiled again. She couldn't help it.

⎯⎯⎯∞∞∞⎯⎯⎯

Silas' Hill, in House Silas' Hill, Ideon

Antonias, better known as Fate's Hand, who called himself Bento these days, put a comforting hand on Iram's shoulder. Iram couldn't stop the tears trickling down his face and into his braided white beard.

"After the boy came to me, I went to see for myself," Iram said. "I caught a glimpse of *him* in the flames—before he disappeared. He looked out of control, like he'd succumbed to the fire. Not a shred of humanity left in him."

Bento grunted in reply.

"And the boy!" Iram continued. "Imp." He shook his head dejectedly. "So much potential and so much anger and waste. The girl too. If she wasn't half-mad with grief, she'd have wondered how she got into the camp so easily. Never mind the fact that it's all I can do for her. She's wasting those skills of hers."

"And we must sit by and do nothing to help," Bento rasped bitterly.

Iram knew his friend felt like a father towards the boy. *It must be awful*, he thought, *to let a child of yours face the world alone.* Then again, Iram had done the same—to his friends and family, to countless young people he'd mentored over the years. Always there came a time when he had to step back and do nothing. Let them succeed—or fail—on their own.

"We must," he said, then sighed. "If only Rehu could see the whole future instead of singular moments and choices. Perhaps it would have us take a more active role."

"As it is, whenever we try to help, we make things worse," Bento said. "I sometimes think it would be better to end my service to the creature and die properly. Perhaps I could do some actual good in whatever afterlife awaits me." He turned towards Iram's writing desk and picked up the topmost report. "Have you heard from any of the others?"

Iram got up to look at the documents himself. "Sarah Brewer—you know, that old Republican who got you the girl's pack—she wrote a while ago to say the spare has been captured. The brother too, though she mentioned it as an afterthought more than anything."

As much as he hated himself for it, Iram found it was easier if he didn't use names for the people who had unwittingly become Rehu's pawns. Rehu's purpose, which Iram had devoted himself to, was essential, but all too often pawns died and had to be replaced. Even now, Rehu was pursuing several youngsters, hoping a few might rise to the occasion and help restore peace to the broken continent. Perhaps they might even prevent the disaster that loomed over them all.

"How long ago?"

"A few days?" Iram dug at the pile of reports on his table before he found the right one. He bent closer to study the date. "Three weeks," he exclaimed, shaking his head. "The longer this goes on, the harder it is to keep track of time. Wait until you reach my age."

"How long has it been now?"

Iram squinted, trying to remember. "Well over two hundred years."

"About the spare," Bento said, returning to the subject of reports. "Has Rehu tasked anyone with releasing her?"

"Kyra is on her way there now. Rehu asked her personally. I hope she doesn't lose her head and interfere too much."

"She'll do fine. She has a practical mind."

"She's young," Iram said crossly. "Compared to the rest of us anyway. Inexperienced. And she's sentimental when it comes to children, which is a poor trait in any Markois. We're at a crossroads, for Rehu's sake. If we don't stand back and let the youngsters fight it out, we risk destroying everything." There were too few of them left now.

Bento smiled grimly. "You always did have a dramatic way of framing these things, *Ibram*."

"Stop that," Iram said. The name brought back old and painful memories. "No one calls me that anymore."

⸻ ∞ ⸻

Teel, in Arahill, Saint Brazen

Zenia stirred, then winced as pain—white hot, like needles—pierced her eyes. *What have they done to me?* The pain had hardly stopped ever since they'd found out that her eyes were the source of her magic.

Zenia kept her eyes shut, but she could tell they must have arrived at their destination. The wagon she and the other captives shared no longer bumped along an uneven track but rolled smoothly along what was surely a paved road.

She siphoned some life from her eyes, breathing sharply in as the pain intensified, then used it to activate her magic. Flickering bundles of emotions ignited around her. It wasn't like seeing, but it was close. Emotions felt like colours, and she could sometimes tell what people were thinking. Blue. Black. Dark grey shot through with a garish orange. The captives were hurt and desperate. And they were scared, though they tried to hide it.

The wagon stopped, and hinges squeaked as the door was opened. Light streamed in, but still Zenia kept her eyes closed, concentrating on the Servicemembers outside. Perfect, steady off-white. A hint of aquamarine, pale pink, and that same garish orange. The brighter colours would intensify for a second and then flicker back to off-white. *They're so calm*, she thought, confused. They had impeccable control over the excitement, nervousness, and fear they felt. She'd never met a group so disciplined.

Orange blossomed around her own chest as her fear intensified. She let go of her magic, sighing with relief as the pain returned to a dull throb, easy enough to ignore. A Servicewoman barked at them to get up, and Zenia eased her eyes open. She winced at the bright light before following the other prisoners out of the wagon.

Thankfully, the Servicemembers felt no need to push them around. *Perhaps they feel more in control now they're in the Republic?* She took a closer look at their captors. *These aren't the same men and women who took us*, she realized. They stood straighter, and they seemed more... soldierly somehow. *That explains their difference in emotions.* She hadn't spent enough time around the ones who had caught her to be able to identify them by their emotions alone, but overall, they'd been far less controlled.

She shivered as she followed the others towards a black tower standing solidly on a field of browned grass speckled with outbuildings. The tower made her think of an evil chess queen surveying her pawns, and her magic tugged at her eyes, as if wanting her to activate it. Something was wrong here. Very, very, wrong.

As they climbed the steps to the tower's base and entered through a small door set in the side, Zenia siphoned some more life from her eyes to trigger her magic once more. Emotions flickered to life around her, and she gasped at the sight. A wall of bright, pure, shining white lay ahead of her, so thick she couldn't perceive anything else through it. Zenia dropped the magic as fast as she could, rubbing her eyes with shaking fingers. It *hurt*. She'd never seen anything like it. *What emotion is this?* she thought, terrified.

They descended a set of steps carved into the same black stone the tower was made of. Zenia shivered again as she noticed a steady noise coming from below. The sound undulated with a strange whirring, like a piece of fabric flapping in the wind, but metallic and menacing. Then the screaming began.

TO BE CONTINUED...

Thank you for reading *Brightshade*.

If you enjoyed this book, it would mean the Camorin Continent to me if you left a review on Amazon or Goodreads. I'd love to hear what you thought about it!

Cheers,
Miriam R. Dumitra

A NOTE ON THE CAMORIN CALENDAR

All dates are given in the Camorin style. This system has a 388-day year split into four quarters that coincide with the seasons (spring, summer, autumn, winter). Each quarter is further split into four 24- or 25-day months. This means there are a total of 16 months in each year.

ACKNOWLEDGMENTS

I can't seem to think of a clever way to start out these acknowledgments, so I'm just going to come out and say it: It takes a ton of highly-skilled people to publish a book.

First and foremost, I would like to thank all those folks who aren't mentioned by name. You know who you are (at least, I hope you do), and your support means the world to me even if I have unintentionally slighted you by not including you in these credits.

Secondly, I must thank my amazing sister, editor, and best frond, Emma Dumitra. Without you, Jenna and I would be lost in the woods, several degrees more boring, and infinitely less grammatically correct.

To Uncle James, the best content editor I could ask for: Thanks for everything. Our long discussions about everything from Republican swearwords to whether it's possible to kick someone from horseback paid off, and I'm so grateful for your attention to detail and love of hardcore fantasy.

To Kristina from Fictionary and all the fine folks at Friesenpress who got me started, I am so grateful you made this publishing journey possible for me. And to the fabulous Amalia Chitulescu who designed the cover: Just—wow. I'm impressed beyond words.

To my beta readers (whether you read the whole book or just a few snippets): Kaylee, Mal, Timna, and Jonathan. Thanks for your support, feedback, and encouragement. And a special mention to Andrew: you didn't read much of the book, but you were always willing to hear about it, give suggestions, and act as a sounding board. My heartfelt thanks to all of you!

My crazy, weird Janzitra family; thanks for always supporting me, providing nutritious meals (Mindy), celebratory champagne (Omi), and ideas for chapter and book titles (Jake, Zack, Timna, and Johnnyboy. If I ever create a spinoff it will definitely be called *Rise and Shrine*).

You guys inspire me, and your encouragement keeps me writing.

My friends—Canadian, Austrian, German, and Otherwise—you deserve a mention here as well. Perhaps you'll see glimpses of yourselves in some of these characters. I can only say that I was inspired by (the best parts of) you. You've contributed to Castor's steadfastness, Adriane's vulnerability, Jenna's love of knowledge, Rise's sass, Tobin's good heart, and Imp's innocence more than you know.

And lastly, to the creators of that one, random TV show I once watched, where a young man set a fire using a slow-burning cigarette. The Saint Brazen Republic has you to thank for several dozen cases of Service-approved arson.

About the Author

When she isn't writing, Miriam R. Dumitra can be found drawing, blacksmithing, contributing to theatre productions, or (currently) sitting in front of her laptop, attempting to write an author bio. Originally from Austria and Romania (and with a five-year stint spent in the Philippines), she has put her cultural and linguistic experience into practice by writing poetry, penning flash memoirs, and helping translate a German musical into English.

She is currently based in Victoria, Canada, where she studies theatre and creative writing during the day and—predictably—sleeps at night. *Brightshade* is her debut novel.

More of her work (and an in-depth look at the Camorin Continent) can be found on her website https://miriamrdumitra.com/